There is a cinematic quality to [King's Blood] that paints some wonderful action scenes, and the pacing of the novel's plot overall turns an epic journey into a fast-paced ride where readers are sure to keep begging for just one more chapter.

- K.C. Finn, Readers Favorite.

Dan's combat experience bleeds onto each page of King's Blood.

- Ken Rotcop, former Hollywood studio executive.

Biblical stories are often informative, educational, or convicting, but rarely are they experiential. That's what King's Blood brings to the table. You taste, smell, see, feel, hear along with the Man After God's Own Heart. Experience David with a fresh and engaging new perspective: right along side him, on the battlefield and on his ascent to the throne.

-Vincent B. Davis II, bestselling author of *"The Sertorius Scrolls"*

[King's Blood] quickly establishes its bona fides as an epic.

- The Black List.

KING'S BLOOD

RAISED A SHEPHERD
BORN A KING

Daniel J. Geisel

Legendmark Publishing

King's Blood
Copyright © 2020 by Daniel J. Geisel

The cataloging-in-publication data is on file with the Library of Congress.
Fiction_Historical   Fiction_War and Military

ISBN 978-0-578-63438-8

ACKNOWLEDGMENTS

The Marines that walked by my side through our own valley of the shadow of death, to those wounded for this great nation, and to the warriors that never came home. May we honor their sacrifice by living our lives full of passion with no regrets. It was in the darkest hours that I witnessed true loyalty, trust, and courage. You are the inspiration behind the legends of this book.

My mother, who is forever encouraging and listens to countless hours of me storyboarding, researching… and dreaming. My father, who never doubts and has the strongest spirit and drive I've ever witnessed. My brother and his wife Meire, the most generous and faithful man and woman I know. To my second parents, Frank and Cheryl, thank you for entrusting me with your most precious gift and being the greatest parents a "son-in-law" could ask for.

My children, Uraiah, Rielle, and Avielle, you are the most humbling gift a father could ever receive. It wasn't until you were born that I understood God's unconditional love. Your strength, passion, and love are a reminder of how I want to live.

Lastly, my wife, Stacey, who endures countless hours, endless nights, and unrewarding years as I sit alone, attempting to piece together and resurrect history. Your fearlessness drives me to be a better man and strive to live a life worthy of the calling. You are my Abigail.

NOTE TO THE READER

This novel is based on the many writings that detail the life and events of the ancient Biblical character David and his rise to the throne, but my intention was to write more than just a historical retelling. By history we can understand events, but I believe that only through story can we understand the mindset and motivations of individuals who caused those events.

Although I spent considerable time researching to maintain accurate timelines, events, individual names, and locations, there is always an element of the unknown. In these moments I relied on our understanding of human nature, the condition and pressures of the culture at the time, and the emotions that war often brings.

Some characters and dialogue have been added to help build the story line, but I believe you will find this to be an accurate and in-depth portrayal of the Scriptures. Any artistic imagination is designed to support the historical and Biblical accounts. This novel also contains mature themes, including sexual temptation and violence, which may not be appropriate for younger readers. Please use discretion.

My hope is that this book will bring clarity to situations that are often misunderstood, situations such as why a king would allow a boy to represent the entire nation against a giant, or how the relationship between David and King Saul would have affected David's decisions.

For more in-depth answers regarding my decisions and reasoning, please visit DanielJGeisel.com.

David was not superhuman. He lived a life full of humility, uncertainty, and at many times fear. He was much like any of us – unsure of his gift, certain he held purpose, and longed to fulfill both.

I am for peace; but when I speak, they are for war.

Psalms 120:7

1

YEAR 1011 B.C.
AGE 30

The seasoned commander shivers in the cold as the thin mountain air whips against his flesh. The rare appearance of snow materializes above as it falls gracefully from the sky. A single pure white flake catches his attention as it dances with gravity, slipping alongside the tall swaying pines. For now the horror preparing to unleash before him is forgotten. His mind embraces a moment of peace as he follows the flake until it lands and is immediately embraced by the mounting snow on a soldier's fur vest, a sliver of warmth that outlines his otherwise frigid breastplate.

Nervous rustling, clanging armor, and stamping horses fill the silence, drawing him back into reality, back into the imminent death that stands before him.

All around him, an army – his army – aligns, preparing swords and shields. The snow crunches beneath their heavy feet, weighed down by iron and bronze. His commands have spread, now nothing more than muffled orders shouted from afar. He glances across his three thousand men, highly trained men that he has hand-selected and marched here for this very moment. Their eyes, however, hold uncertainty, scanning the landscape.

His focus shifts. In the distance, only a few hundred stand against him, ready for battle. The opposing army's numbers are small, but the growing legends of their feats have clearly struck terror into the eyes of his men. The enemy stands firm, as if the perceptions are true. They are violent yet calculated. They have nothing to lose and yet they fight with experienced precision.

The commander watches as one man moves to the front of their ranks. All eyes are on him. Even across the vast expanse of the field he is unmistakable. He is the sole reason that thousands have marched here today. One man, this man, has become the focus of more than just a general. He has become the focus of an entire kingdom.

On the opposing hilltop, the warrior who just stepped to the front of his ranks now calmly surveys the three thousand soldiers preparing to attack his position. He studies their order, leadership, and body language. They are trained, but only because they have to be. They are dressed for warmth, not bloodshed. They are fidgeting, because they know their fate. He stands at the head of his men, knowing that the eyes of a few thousand soldiers are watching his every move. An entire army has assembled for one reason, to kill him.

His shoulders are bare but his chest is protected by armor. He doesn't shiver, not even a blink from his eyes which are iced with conviction, a conviction that appears to become more vibrant with each steam-filled breath. His frame is lean and chiseled. He stands tall, like a statue, fearless.

Glancing back over his shoulder, an army a fraction of the size he opposes stands behind him. Disciplined, his men stand firm. There is no rustling or nervousness. Their eyes, seared from years of bloodshed, are focused. Each realizes that in their number alone they do not stand a chance. For some reason they are not concerned.

He turns back, his attention narrows. The time has come. His hand grips the sword, veins pumping, ice-blue eyes staring…

...Brown eyes staring. A young, unassuming boy, David, stands still, his face stern. A lion slowly prowls thirty paces away, its head lowered, eyes focused... snarling.

Every fiber, every strand of muscle screams to run, but he can't. He won't. Light prickles crawl up his body as if his skin were trying to shed. But inside, a rising tide of courage saturates his doubts as he no longer worries for his own life. He is prepared to die, but something deep inside whispers to him that he won't. This overwhelming feeling has come once before. And he is convinced that it is not for his own protection.

David breaks the stare-down by glancing over his shoulder. Sheep muster behind, unaware, completely vulnerable. He glances back. The lion's neck cranes forward, each shoulder rising above its thick mane as it stalks closer. Its eyes glare through thick brows as it slows to a halt with a single raised paw hovering above grass.

David knows that he stands in the gap between the predator and the prey, the violent and the helpless. He will give anything to protect the weak. In this moment he feels like the impenetrable city walls of Gibeah.

He begins to think more clearly than ever before. Time slows and his nerves steady. David studies the lion's mannerisms. He knows it has no fear of death, and yet David still feels that he has the edge. He has something behind him, something to protect.

With one negative thought the fear could come racing back, but he doesn't let it. There is no place for it. Instead, he prepares to do the impossible. He tightens his grip on his staff as he steps forward, claiming his ground.

The lion gently places its paw to the warm soil as it continues to study David. It appears to have made its decision. It doesn't move. It becomes hauntingly still. The large cedar trees sway, rustling leaves together like waves calmly crashing to the shore. The sheep have since gone silent when the lion decides to take one last step forward, its muscles contracting.

Without warning, a ray of sunlight pierces down through an open canopy in the trees. The lion disappears as the bright golden hue, a majestic yet forbidding curtain, materializes. He tightens the grip on his staff, all but certain that the lion will be in midair when it crests through the glowing drape of sunlight. A thundering roar quakes the earth and quivers up through his feet, rattling his ribs as the foreboding warning escapes from somewhere deep behind the light. In an instant the ray is gone, and for a time, so is the lion.

2

A mattock swings into the dirt. Beads of sweat drip from David's face, his small frame already feeling the brunt of manual labor under the scorching sun. Only a short-day's travel to the Great Sea and yet the breeze is nowhere to be found. The numerous ridgelines to the west seem to block even the slightest wind. He lifts his head, hoping to survey the remaining work still to be done, but only for an instant. Anything longer will surely attract unwanted attention from any one or all of his seven older brothers. He knows that the more time his brothers spend focusing on him and not on their chores means there will be even more work left for him once they get called for dinner.

There isn't a job that gets done without his involvement, as he's the youngest in the family. When his brothers are off to war in the spring, it's David who keeps the fields tended, the animals fed, and the family's water replenished. It is exhausting being the youngest in a Hebrew family. The culture is such that the youngest is more of a slave to the family than a son. There is a very strict hierarchy and David is below the bottom. He is a servant with no authority, no freedom, and no voice. But there is one place where all of that changes.

David glances over the rolling hills to where the narrow dirt path disappears into the horizon, his gateway to freedom. His mind slips back to the trail where he is no longer the youngest. On that path, the world goes silent and his thoughts become clear. He is the leader, the authority, the protector, the shepherd.

A firm hand grabs his shoulder and a deep adolescent voice startles him from his thoughts. "Why were you late this morning?"

David lowers his head and continues working, already having explained why he was late. There is no need to be ridiculed again.

Eliab does not budge. In his early twenties, he is the firstborn and most stoic of the brothers, and his firm grip quickly reminds David of that fact.

"David, look at me." Eliab's voice is strong, but tender like a father. "I know what I heard. I just want to hear it from you."

David continues striking the ground with the mattock, ignoring his brother. He can only hope they will move on and leave him alone, but he knows better.

"The lion just decided to turn and run without you doing anything? Why would it do that?"

Like I'm supposed to know, David thinks, considering for the first time that the sunray that blocked his view may have also temporarily blinded the lion, causing it to abandon its attack.

"He has magic eyes, didn't you hear!" a brother's voice mockingly calls out from the field. "The king is going to outlaw him for the sorcery of those eyes."

Before David can finish the swing of his mattock laughter erupts.

"David!" another voice yells from behind.

David looks. Shimea and Abinadab, two of his older brothers, are staring at him, holding back laughter. Shimea approaches David like a cat stalking its prey and then without warning stands and shoves him off balance.

"Those eyes didn't stop *me*. I guess it only works with *real* lions," Shimea says before bursting into laughter.

David now regrets saying anything about the stare-down with the lion. Instead of earning respect for his bravery, he has handed his brothers more ideas for verbal punishment. It's a punishment for which they never seem to have a lack of enthusiasm.

Abinadab walks over and rubs David's head. "Relax, we're only teasing."

"Abinadab!" Shimea yells.

Abinadab turns. Shimea stares intently at him, again mocking David. Abinadab falls over as if in severe pain. His screaming turns into laughter. "Stop. Stop. Stop looking at me!"

Laughter erupts across the brothers, but David is not amused. He continues working as if he doesn't hear a thing.

Eliab hasn't moved. He is still standing next to him, watching his unwavering expression. "Why do you let them do that to you?"

Before David can respond, the sound of a horn blows from the small dwelling at the end of the field.

"Finally," Eliab says with an exhale. He drops his tools and places his hand on David's head. "Finish the rest and get out of this heat."

From a distance, David watches the door close behind his brothers. Once again he has seven times the work ahead of him, but at least he is alone. Any silence is always welcome with such a large family. And for David it is in the silence that he finds his peace, and in the peace that he finds his strength. He lifts the mattock and swings. The iron striking dirt and rock is now the only sound he hears. Even the birds have taken to shade.

He grips the wooden handle worn smooth from callused hands. The mattock is heavy, unbalanced, and dull, ideal for a test of accuracy.

Focusing, he aims, rolls his shoulders, and drives the tip deep between two stones, a perfect strike. Again and again, he continues perfecting the motion, training his body for precision, even in the most insignificant task. He must always be ready. His profession, although not a warrior, still requires proficiency. The shepherds that do not learn this early either lose sheep or die young. His brothers do not see it that way. He knows how they look at him. He knows what they think. But it doesn't matter. Not to David. He only has one opinion on his mind. The rest will find out his strength in time.

3

Just north of the capital city of Gibeah, the scent of death hangs heavy across the hilltops of Geba, Israel. The Peleshet, Philistines, or Sea People as they are known, come often from the coastline in hopes of acquiring easy treasure and able bodies to sell in the Egyptian slave trade. However, there will be no easy spoils for the taking here today.

The messenger has departed toward the king's camp, and the scavengers have already begun their descent on the slain human flesh littered across the landscape. To many it is nothing more than the stench of battle carnage, but to Aaron it is the smell of a victorious siege over an enemy outpost.

Aaron carefully chooses each step as he ascends the hill, avoiding jagged rocks, weapons, and body parts along the way. He knows that he must keep moving. In the midst of warfare his mind is desensitized, violent, and more aggressive than most, but in the calm, after the heat of battle has cooled, he is like any other. Worse even. His stomach quickly becomes squeamish.

It is not the sight of death that bothers him, although there are times in the thick of battle when a man becomes so eviscerated that it causes even the most hardened minds to pause. Nor is it the smell that bothers him. The pungent odor of decay burned his nostrils numb years ago. But rather it is the sounds. The breaking, snapping, and spilling of the slippery insides of a human has yet to become the standard for Aaron.

Suddenly, like a demon reaching up from Sheol, a hand grips his ankle, jerking him back. A soldier partially buried in the dirt moans as if waking from the dead. His grip on Aaron tightens with every painful groan. Each breath taken by the soldier whistles through his chest as the air is forced through an unlikely opening. Aaron can't pull his eyes from the gaping hole in the enemy's sternum as it closes before opening once again like the mouth of a hooked fish gasping for life.

The soldier's eyes widen just before a shadow overtakes his face. Without warning a shiny glint of light flashes from the shade and Aaron braces for impact. Seeing the soldier's white eyes bulging, he turns just before the man's ribs shatter as an iron blade plunges through his heart. As if a boulder is smashing down on a pile of sticks, the sound is almost too much for Aaron to handle. Gargling instantly replaces the soldier's whistle, and with a hard twist of the iron inside, the struggle abruptly ends.

Aaron fears the worst as his weak stomach rebels. The sensation of liquid rising from his gut enters his throat but somehow he is able to stop the embarrassment before he spews his rations once again. With a single dry heave Aaron has dodged an all too familiar scene, one that has become a means of humiliation.

Jonathan sheathes his bloody sword. "Ensure the rest receive the same treatment."

Every soldier within earshot, including Aaron, responds, "As you wish, commander," and immediately begins scouring the hillside for any living creature that remains amongst the dead.

Jonathan grabs Aaron's arm before he departs. "Aaron, you served me well today, brother. I need you to sound the horn. Let them know what has been done here today." A slight grin overtakes his face. "And I think the others would prefer if your vomit weren't covering the mouthpiece when you finish." Jonathan laughs.

Aaron's stern face cracks a smile. He nods, acknowledging the silent command.

Get away from the carnage with your stomach intact.

Jonathan noticed Aaron's loose stomach after his very first battle. Aaron had fought braver than any other in his line, and by the climax of the battle he was side by side with Jonathan, having moved through four ranks to defend his leader, who was soon to be overwhelmed. Jonathan was fending off the enemy single-handedly, having just lost his armor-bearer who now lies lifeless at his feet. With the enemy salivating over removing the heir to the kingdom in Jonathan, Aaron's move to his guard was all but suicide. That's when Jonathan knew that he had found his new armor-bearer.

The moment, however, was short-lived. After earning the attention of the king's son for his valor and receiving his new position as Jonathan's personal guard, Aaron's stomach turned upside down at the overwhelming sensory overload that war often brings. Immediately after Jonathan told him of his promotion, Aaron stepped on the remains of human organs and spewed all over the poor corpse sprawled across the ground before him. Thankfully, Jonathan just laughed and explained that he would get used to it. But he hasn't yet and he probably wouldn't.

Being the guard, the armor-bearer, for the heir of the kingdom is quite an honor. But there is nothing better than to be the armor-bearer to Jonathan. Aaron is convinced that Jonathan is the finest leader that has ever lived. He will be remembered with the likes of Moses, Joshua, and Caleb. He is brutal, even vicious, in battle, but when the war subsides he is tender, even humorous. His words carry more weight from respect than his position could ever deliver. Aaron would not just die for Jonathan. He would gladly die for Jonathan.

4

Dusk is quickly turning into nightfall as David crosses the field toward the single-room family dwelling. The air cools quickly in the shallow valley, and David welcomes the breeze that now wisps against the sweat still beading from his pores. The sky dips from the day's final golden hue to a darkening cast of sapphire as the moon now overcomes the hilltops. The faint firelight glimmering in the second floor window reflects the shadows moving inside.

David knows that there is only one reason the family would no longer be sitting together on the floor.

Dinner is over.

The dwelling before him is anything but inviting. Made almost entirely of stone with the inside supported by beams of timber that stand both vertically and horizontally, protruding from the partially whitewashed exterior walls. The structure stands two levels high, with the lower level open to the outside and often full of livestock.

Known mostly for living in tents after fleeing slavery in Egypt, Hebrews now bear the name tent-dwellers. But this wasn't solely from living in tents and being continually on the move. David learned early the reasoning behind the name. The belief, he remembers being told more than once, is that this life is only temporary and not the final destination, that they are only pilgrims passing through to the other side. The name Hebrew itself means "to cross over." This is the reason that their dwellings are nothing more than shelters. And why the word *home* isn't even in their vocabulary like it is in many of the other languages.

David climbs the stairs to the second floor living quarters. Through the door he can hear his family's muffled voices, enjoying the time of peace for a nation often at war.

David presses open the door and enters completely unnoticed. Other than the empty clay pan still resting on the coals to his right, the living quarters is nothing more than an open room with three oil lamps hanging like sconces against the wall and sleeping mats spread across the floor. His brothers are circled around the outer edge of the room. Pairing by twos they step forward and begin their customary test of strength.

David's father stands close by, watching with his arms crossed and a proud grin. His mother on the other hand gathers the bowls from dinner and pretends not to notice. She knows how violent it can get even amongst brothers, but it doesn't compare to the violence that the oldest three will again face following the next winter.

David would love to try his hand at the brotherly testing of strength, will, and fortitude, but he is never even acknowledged. He watches, sometimes pretending that he is just like the others. He knows each one of their tendencies, weaknesses, and strengths, of course. It is something that comes natural to him, the understanding of body movement and weight manipulation. Studying animals in the wild for hours as they stalk and kill their prey teaches in the simplest of ways. Yet he still craves to learn more.

Speaking of craving.

David is reminded of his hunger at the smell of the charred goat meat wafting throughout the room.

He moves to the stovetop where his leftovers are often waiting, cold. This time, however, there isn't even a crumb of bread. David feels the last pinch of energy seeping from his gut at the sight of the empty table.

"David."

The deep tone of his father's voice billows in the cramped space. It startles him enough that his arm jerks back from the plate. David turns quickly, ensuring a show of reverence to his firm-handed father. After all, he is not often the recipient of his father's attention when the family is gathered.

"They must eat like warriors. You will understand one day when they protect you. You are a shepherd, nothing more."

David forces a nod, as if he understands, but he doesn't. He knows the long history of the Hebraic culture, and yet the attitude from his father and brothers leads him to believe that he is considered even less than blood. It goes far beyond the birth order and sibling responsibility, far beyond rivalries. It appears he is not only a servant to his family but a repulsed servant, rejected by all but his mother.

The worst of it all is that he will never be given the chance to protect his family against the onslaught of enemies that attack each spring. After all, who would take care of the fields and livestock if every child were fit for warfare?

His father turns back to him. "Which reminds me, the sheep are overdue for grazing."

David lifts his gaze to meet his father's but David's focus is diverted. Over his father's shoulder, Shimea stands watching. His lips are curled into a mocking grin which is quickly mirrored by Abinadab. They love to torment, but David knows better than to give them a reaction. He leaves the room and heads back downstairs, acting as if he never saw them.

In the open-air stable below the living quarters, David arranges his satchel. He packs it with a handcrafted knife, a sling, and his harp, commonly called a lyre. He throws the satchel across his back, grabs his staff, and heads out into the night. Tonight he will have to find his own dinner.

5

Sprinting through the ravine, the messenger Henick begins to feel the effects of exhaustion, but it is his fear that keeps his body in motion. After running through the cover of darkness since nightfall, his safety, the concealment in the blackness, is quickly slipping away. He scans the top of the canyon walls as he races to report the victory to the king. There is no time to rest. On this journey he is alone and very aware that the enemy will do anything in its power to block the delivery of this triumph in fear that the Hebrew morale will be raised everywhere that the message is spread.

Understanding that if he is caught the Philistines will make a spectacle of his lifeless body, as they have done many times before to others, Henick keeps his eyes focused. He watches for any movement along the ridgelines. He has expected this journey to be filled with activity, however, so far it has been eerily quiet. There has been no movement, no indication of scouts watching from a distance. From his experience, this silence is often a sign of something building, something preparing.

He makes the last ascent on the stressful journey and finally the welcome sight of friendly forces materializes as he nears the top of the hill, giving him the final boost he needs to reach the peak.

East of the carnage caused by Jonathan's raid in Geba, a much larger camp surrounds not the heir, but the king himself. A man that stands head and shoulders above any other in the land, and possibly more handsome than any man since Adam, King Saul is an imposing presence of a human being. Henick feels intimidation begin crawling into his mind like a spider weaving a web of uncertainty between his ears, thicker and thicker with each step.

He senses the eyes of the king's guards drawing down upon him and immediately his stomach tightens. The dread that comes with approaching the king and his entourage never gets easier. The king, with the large tent behind him and his guards standing to his side, embodies everything his men would expect in a king as he sits at the peak of the hilltop of Gilgal overlooking the awakening troops. Henick prepares his words, unraveling them in his mind before speaking so they don't fumble from his mouth. He keeps his eyes down and continues up the hill.

Saul strokes his dark beard as he watches the two thousand hand-picked soldiers wake under the morning sun. Having already sent over ten thousand soldiers back to their families, his personal force has now dwindled into the small fraction before him. His division is small but lean, and with the season of bloodshed behind him, his only concern is the small skirmishes that are sure to arise while he guards the surrounding passes and trade routes that lead toward the capital.

For now there is no immediate threat, the morning is still cool, and most importantly it is quiet. It is Saul's favorite time of day. The stress of being king can at times become unbearable. Getting up first gives him time to clear his mind and prepare for the day while his men are still slowly rising to their feet. It helps him think through most situations clearly, often before they become surprises.

Suddenly, a soldier moving quickly through the ranks catches his eye. The soldier wastes no time ascending toward his tent which is avoided by anyone but commanders. As he approaches it is clear that he has traveled quite a distance. He is exhausted, dirty, and on a mission. It quickly becomes apparent that he is not just any soldier, but a messenger.

Saul's first reaction is fear, a concern not as a king but as a father, for his son Jonathan.

Is my son alive? Saul wonders. *Has he been overrun?*

As the messenger's distance closes faster now, Saul considers every circumstance possible. Then he notices the empty hands, and a messenger with empty hands can only mean one thing.

Before the boy can reach the king's tent he is approached by Saul's most trusted officer, General Abner. Not only does Abner serve as the highest-ranking member of the army as commander-in-captain, but also, being a blood cousin to Saul, he also serves as the ears and mouthpiece of the king. There is nothing that happens in the kingdom that does not go through General Abner first, and a messenger will be no exception.

The messenger slows his pace as he nears the hilltop. He ensures to avoid eye contact with any of the men surrounding Saul's tent, especially the general. It is his job to deliver the message, but Saul knows he and his men can be quite intimidating even for the most seasoned messenger. He watches as Abner snaps a few commands at the young soldier to make sure the boy knows who is in charge, as if he didn't already know.

The message is passed and Abner turns, preparing to deliver it, but Saul holds up his hand, stopping him. Having completed his task, the messenger is already making his way down the hill, distancing himself from the tent, but Saul isn't satisfied.

"Soldier," Saul says with a booming voice.

The boy, almost accomplishing his escape from Abner stops midstride and turns back hesitantly, his eyes never leaving the dirt. Saul knows that empty hands mean that his son is still alive. It is customary for a messenger to bring the sword or a ring of the slain warrior as a physical confirmation of death, and knowing Jonathan the way he does, Saul knows his son is either victorious or he is dead.

"Jonathan was victorious?" Saul asks.

The messenger drops to his knees, his quivering hands reach for the ground to steady him, visibly overwhelmed that he is being directly spoken to by the king of the nation. "My king, your hand has defeated the Philistines at Geba," the messenger says. "May you live forever."

"And your commander?"

"My Lord, your heir is preparing the..."

The messenger's words drift into a mumbled blur as Saul's attention is diverted to a rising dust trail in the distance. Across the ridgeline a small horse detachment races north of Geba. Saul calculates their direction as he contemplates their purpose.

"They're heading north of Michmash," General Abner says, eyeing the same commotion. "Possibly north of our troops in Bethel by the looks of the route they have taken."

"But why?" Saul asks, now standing at the crest of the hill, having moved past the messenger for a better view.

Deep in his gut he knows that something is wrong. It seems the wretched Philistine king, Achish, has already issued an order to inform the outposts of the defeat. The outposts are always last to find out, but it seems this time something much different is brewing.

"Sound the horns," Saul says.

The morning's peace has evaporated, leaving his mind to wander, to wind itself tightly into a knot of stress that now grips his head as it has done so many times before. It appears to have been a mistake to send a portion of his fighting force back to their dwellings. The cool spring air is long gone, but the season of war seems to be just beginning.

The horses vanish and the dust settles, but his eyes remain focused on the distant ridge. "Let all of Israel know that today I have been victorious."

Tomorrow, he thinks, *it may be too late.*

6

North of Bethlehem on the edge of a green oasis David leads his flock out of the scorching sun and into the shade. Surrounded by dense forest on all three sides, the landscape is complemented by a stream that trickles poetically between the two fields, perfectly shaded under large sycamores that have taken root along its banks. It beckons his parched tongue and he knows his sheep must be feeling the same desire. With a quick slap of his staff the sheep begin heading toward the clear water.

Once David is certain that every last sheep has taken a drink he lowers his knee into the moist soil, fully intending to cool his mouth. Before the water touches his lips, a flutter of movement catches his eye in the reflection of the stream. His mind races with excitement. And with a slow, deliberate movement he pulls his hand from the water, his fist clenched tight.

Above him, the branches sway, each of them moving to their own melody, each of them waving with shifting leaves and dancing limbs. He steps back into the field, focused, his eyes searching. He inspects each branch to the tip until he spots the cause of his attention. Nestled right in the midst of the tree branches, a perfectly camouflaged quail sits idle.

David glides his hand down and along the inside walls of his satchel made of soft animal hide. Finding a worn rope, he pulls it from the bag. In his clenched fist is the answer to his hunger. He releases the dripping wet stone into the sling's worn leather pouch. The light breeze blows against his face as he estimates the distance and elevation, all while building momentum, whipping the sling above his head. With one quick snap the stone hurls through the air. He watches it curve unexpectedly, shattering only his hopes as it does.

It's a miss, slightly to the right.

A tree branch snaps and falls to the ground. The stone tumbles to the other side of the stream and lands in the grass. David takes a deep breath, calming his doubts. He is hungry, parched, and growing impatient. There is no time for mistakes, but even more so there is no time to rush. Impatience leads to mistakes, which leads to more hunger. So, he calms, closes his eyes, and takes another deep breath, feeling the water drip from the stones in his left hand.

The water on the stone caused it to curve, David thinks as he drops all but one stone.

He rubs it with his thumb, drying it, palming its weight. He is proficient in the sling, but this time he remembers to lean on more than his own strength.

David begins whipping the sling, faster, faster.

Lord, I deliver my life into your hands.

He opens his eyes just as the stone releases. Feathers fly into the air, but the quail never falls. Instead, it flutters off through the trees and vanishes into the distance.

David sighs. His hunger is all but consuming him. He looks to the clear blue sky and allows the compounding thoughts of neglect and insignificance to build until they burst from his mouth as he cries out in a fit of hunger-induced anger.

Realizing that he's breathing heavily, alone in a field, yelling to the sky, he composes himself and heads back to his sheep mustering near the brook.

Although his anger caused by the lingering hunger has subsided, his thoughts still wonder about what just happened.

I trusted and yet still failed.

He cups his hands and raises the water to his mouth. It is still ice-cold from the mountaintop as it touches his lips and the chill causes an instant grin. He scoops another cup and pours it over the back of his neck. It is more refreshing than any water he has ever felt and the pure bliss of it draws his gaze back to the blue heavens above.

"Forgive me," David says, realizing how easy it is to overlook the subtle things.

The location is beautiful. The grass is lush and green. The water is cold and his sheep are nourished. David no longer feels alone. He is hungry still, but refreshed. Placing his sling back into the pouch, he grabs the only weapon he knows better than a sling. It is not a weapon for violence, but a weapon that is effective against his thoughts, his fears.

Sitting on the bank, David leans his back against a tree and props his feet up on a small boulder in the middle of the stream. The sheep sense the day's end and settle into the shade, giving David the time he needs to relax.

He rests the lyre on his lap and leans his head back. When his fingers stroke the strings, everything that was once on his mind fades to oblivion. He is transported into another world, one where fear, hunger, and anxiety no longer exist. There are times when he will play for an entire evening and it feels like he has only begun. He senses that tonight will be one of those nights.

The soft melody carries him away until he is unaware of anything but peace. His fingers glide up and down the strings, taking him directly before his God, before the comforting Presence of Yahweh. As David's spirit is replenished, his flesh suddenly reminds him of his location and the sheer danger that the wilderness can bring to those who do not respect it. An unnatural noise pulls him from his tranquility.

David stops playing and opens his eyes. He has lost track of time and can't believe that other than a glint of moonlight he is surrounded by darkness.

Was that sound in my head or in the tree line, he wonders.

He looks to the sheep for confirmation. Every one of them is perfectly still. He listens, but the blood thumping next to his ears is deafening in the silence.

He's leaning on the fact that maybe he was just falling asleep… it happens again. The all too familiar sound of a stick breaking rips the last bit of security from him. The sharp snap resonates in his ears like a tree splintering as it collapses to the ground. His mind races to the size of what may be approaching. Whatever it is, it's not his imagination. He slowly replaces the arched wood handle of the lyre for that of his staff and crouches forward, peering into the darkness.

He can see a dark shadow along the creek bed. Suddenly, it jumps from one side to the other, now placing it on David's bank, pinning his sheep in between them. David creeps forward along the water when he gets a better view of the shadowy figure. Surprised, he dips behind a tree and waits for it to approach.

7

A vibration pulses across the ground, startling Saul from his sleep. The sound of whispering voices grows louder as the unmistakable sounds of footsteps draw closer. Saul opens his eyes, but his fear has stricken him immobile as he listens to an advancing horde of soldiers nearing his tent. They are speaking a very familiar dialect, one he recognizes instantly.

Philistines.

Their once-soft tones erupt with blatant disregard for stealth. It's as if they want Saul to hear them coming. They begin laughing, mocking his inadequacies from only a pace or so outside the thin goat-hair walls. It's like they know his every thought. They have no fear of him or his army. The laughing grows louder as the tent flap is lifted and they enter with blades drawn.

Saul gasps as he awakes from the nightmare. He scans the darkness inside the tent, holding his breath, listening for any movement, but it's silent.

It was nothing more than a dream, he realizes.

Relieved, he exhales and lays his head back down. His heart, pounding in his chest only moments ago, has slowly settled as his body relaxes. But in an instant the nightmare returns, only this time Saul knows that he is awake. He remains still, his body stiffening as he strains to listen.

His bronze armor beside him rattles.

A low, booming rumble overwhelms the hillside, but he doesn't hear it as much as he feels it in his chest. His tent walls sway back and forth, tugging on the ropes that anchor them.

Please, Yahweh, let this be an earthquake.

He leaves the tent and immediately realizes that his greatest nightmare is coming true.

It seems the giants have been awakened from their slumber.

The sound of heavy feet, weighed down by armor, is marching across the rocky terrain and thundering through the valleys. Since he has been king, he has never witnessed such a quick response. Chariots, horses, and divisions of fully equipped men are all heading in one direction, toward Jonathan.

There must be tens of thousands, Saul thinks, staring in awe.

It seems he was right. Each outpost that held control points through the north was pulled from their duty in order to take control of the most important pass of them all. The deep canyons and steep ridgelines make movement south almost impassible except for one location, an area so broad even passage by an entire army is possible. It is the gateway to his capital.

"They're heading for the pass," a voice says from behind.

"Michmash," Saul responds, confirming.

General Abner steps forward. "It's too late for war. They know this."

"They know how weak we are right now." Saul lets out a deep sigh, watching his enemy prepare to position themselves just north of the capital. They are fast, well trained, better equipped, and more numerous than Saul could have imagined.

How do they breed such loyalty? Saul wonders.

The onetime heroic king now stands watching in utter horror at the night sky filled with dust that slowly rises, blotting out the moonlight. They ride with no fear of being attacked. They have been provoked and are preparing for a slaughter.

"Jonathan, what have you done?"

8

Along the creek bank a figure walks closer to where he first heard the music. The sound was soft, most likely a small stringed instrument, but the valley walls carried its notes as far as a ram's horn from the mountaintop. The only problem has been pinpointing the location where it was played. The notes continued far longer than he could have imagined which helped him close the distance to where it was originating. But now night has fallen and the music has come to an abrupt halt.

Something feels out of place. Ahead, under the moonlight the hillside is speckled with black dots. He approaches closer, cautiously. He has drifted from his own land and would hate to stumble upon a detachment of mercenaries preparing an ambush. He unsheathes his straight sword just to be safe.

Pausing to inspect the shadows, he notices that they are not human at all.

They're sheep.

His tension releases as he exhales the tightness in his chest that he didn't realize was present, and approaches the flock.

✦══╬══✦

David, concealed behind a tree, crouches with his staff tightly gripped, watching the figure move through his flock. The moonlight shimmers, reflecting off something dark, something held close to his side.

A sword?

David knows that not many Israelites carry swords. Especially swords made of iron. The Philistines have mastered the forging process, and Israelites know the repercussions of being caught by the enemy while carrying their weapons. Most Hebrews carry a simple farm tool and can blend back into society without worry of being labeled as warriors.

It's now or never. David decides to strike before this opportunity closes and he loses the element of surprise. With the figure's back turned toward him, David stealthily approaches. As he nears, he notices that the figure is not nearly the size he had first appeared. And now, standing this close, it's obvious that he couldn't be much older than David. Still, he can't take any chances.

David swings his staff, striking just above the hand, causing the warrior to drop his sword. He draws back and strikes a blow toward the head when the figure reacts, dropping under his swing. Before David can realize what just happened he feels a powerful crack against his chest and instantly he is on his back looking at the dark silhouette now standing over him. And it's a boy just as he thought, not but a few years older than himself. But he's not an Amorite mercenary or even a Moabite, and he's definitely not a Philistine. He *is* an Israelite. .

The boy sticks out his hand to pull David to his feet, but David hesitates, still unsure how the boy acquired an iron sword.

"Take it. I'm not a threat," the boy says.

David decides that he's in no position to disagree with what is and is not a threat. He takes the hand.

"The name is Benaiah."

David stands with help from the firm hand of Benaiah. He eyes the sword, still confused.

"It's a family heirloom," Benaiah says. "What's your name?

"David, son of Jesse."

"Well, David, son of Jesse, you have quite a strike for a shepherd." He raises the back of his hand inspecting the swollen lump.

"I'll be surprised if it isn't broken. But your hand-to-hand fighting could use some work." Benaiah smiles and hits David on the shoulder.

David tenses for the hit, but it still knocks him off balance. Benaiah could only be eleven or twelve years, but has training far beyond anything David has ever witnessed.

"Where did you learn to move like that? I have brothers older than you that don't move that fast."

"The palace," Benaiah says as he moves past David. "I came because I heard the music. Was that you playing?"

"It was," David says, his skepticism revealed in his tone.

The palace? David suspects he may be lying, but how can he explain the sword? David turns, following Benaiah who now nears his satchel and lyre that lean against a tree.

Benaiah bends down to look at the lyre, but notices worn braided twine partially sticking out of the satchel. "You have a sling?" he says, pulling it out and turning it as if inspecting it.

"I do."

"Are you proficient?"

David notices that Benaiah's speech is refined, his hand-to-hand fighting is well above the standard, and he is carrying an iron sword as an Israelite.

David decides to trust him. "I'll teach you to hit a sparrow at forty paces if you teach me that move of yours."

Benaiah stands. "You can hit a sparrow at forty paces?"

David grins. "No, sixty, but you're going to have to teach me a lot more than one move to learn that."

Benaiah stands with his hand presented. "It's settled." He then lowers to the dirt, gets comfortable against a tree, and closes his eyes. "Now let's get some rest. We'll journey my way in the morning. Something tells me you could use a nice meal."

9

Slowly approaching the city walls of Gibeah, the aging prophet Samuel realizes that his body is no longer what it used to be. His thin silver hair and sun-leathered skin are now the least of his concerns as he feels the wear on his bones that accompanies old age. The final climb up the hill, of which Samuel does not need reminding, is so steep the capital city was named after it. Gibeah literally means the "hill" and Samuel is about to feel every step of it.

It has been twelve days since he last saw the king which is sadly far too long considering Saul's insecurities and rash decision-making. It was obvious that the handsome, strong, and powerfully built Saul was a perfect image of what a king should look like, and that appearance was everything the masses could have ever requested to have in their king. Samuel watched as the newly crowned Saul hid from the assembly, forcing Samuel to practically drag him before the crowd so that a formal introduction could be made. One in which he would bind Saul to the regulations of kingship set forth by Moses.

Swearing by the covenant, Saul became the figurehead of the people. His modest approach and disdain for public appearance in the early years caused many to scoff at the notion of an unpretentious king, but Samuel was there to guide him every step of the way.

Breathing heavily, he continues the ascent, but being deep in thought he becomes careless. His foot slips on the rocky terrain, lunging him forward. Samuel gets his hands up just in time to catch himself before his face collides against the side of the hill. Staring, with the sand and rocks at his face, he wonders what went wrong.

I tried to warn them, Samuel thinks.

He recovers and quickly dusts himself off, pausing only for a glance at the beautiful panoramic view afforded at this height. He has journeyed deep into the night and with the moonlight soon to be blotted out by drifting clouds he knows there is no time to waste.

It is hard enough to climb this burdensome landscape in the light.

The higher he climbs the harder it becomes to forget that Saul personally chose this city as the capital. To lessen the sting of each step, Samuel reminds himself that it was chosen as a strategic stronghold, more so than because it was simply the birthplace of Saul. And it was here at the top of this hill that Saul also received the third confirmation of Samuel's prediction after he had anointed him. Seeing the evidence that Yahweh had truly chosen him, Saul had drawn closer to him, but now, having such miraculous happenings so far behind him, it seems that he is once again straying from the way.

Now, Samuel fears that the nation itself is drifting yet again. The last few days of rest in his hometown of Ramah were needed, but now he must return as promised to Saul.

At the crest of the hill he can see that the main gates have long been closed for the night. Entering through the small doorway to the side he arrives just as the drifting shadows settle over the ridges, turning the hazy blue landscape black. Inside, the city roars with laughter and overindulgence. Soldiers obnoxiously vie for the attention of women. Crowds of unruly and staggering citizens shout at one another. Almost the entire city is alive when it should be at rest.

It is obvious they did not expect Samuel's presence. As he passes through, a wave of silence follows in his wake. It seems that his arrival has drawn every eye as the crowds now disperse, provoking whispers to ensue. He makes his way toward the shrine, noticing more soldiers than he is accustomed to. It is not unusual for warriors to be sent back to the city, or even to their birthplaces, after the war season. Many of the lines will be replaced and replenished during the spring months, but that has already taken place. Saul has already released his reinforcements.

It is obvious that this is different. This is not the typical resupply and rest. These men are not acting like they are planning a return to the line. It seems more of a decompression, a night to release the built-up tension that stress can often bring, but still there should be no soldiers returning from the camps that guard the passes right now.

What is Saul doing?

Samuel turns toward the shrine, hoping to settle in for the night and make travel arrangements for the morning. A small group of farmers, dressed in their mismatched armor and wool tunics, having been called to war from their fields, are huddled right outside the shrine, laughing and shouting. Evidently, the news of Samuel has not yet reached them. The one in the group facing him notices first. He whispers. Then, the rest go quiet. They seem to all have made it a point to not make eye contact, as if they're ashamed of something.

"Can I help any of you gentlemen tonight?" Samuel asks, waving his hand toward the shrine door, as if to say they are welcome inside. "Perhaps a meal?"

They stand in silence, looking to each other in silent discussion of who will speak first. Finally, one of them answers. "Thank you, great prophet, but we will have to decline."

Their look is not comforting. They know something that they are not sharing, so Samuel probes deeper. "Well, perhaps I may ask a favor of you. Would it be too much to ask to travel with your band to the king's camp in the morning?" he says, eyeing their battle garb.

Again their bodies shift uncomfortably. The same man speaks after an awkward pause. "Great prophet, no disrespect, but no one is heading toward camp. The army is…" he pauses. "The army is disbanding."

Disbanding?

"I heard the trumpets sound. Victory was pronounced across the hilltops," Samuel says.

"Yes and it seems to have provoked the Philistines. They have since been moving their forces toward the pass at Michmash, thousands of them. And there is no end in sight."

He's losing trust, Samuel realizes.

The prophecy races back to Samuel. Years ago at Saul's coronation Samuel warned of the day that Saul would be forced to Gilgal and be in need of an answer from Yahweh. In that day, Samuel said, wait seven days and I will come offer up a sacrifice and show you what you are to do. It seems that very time may be approaching.

"Thank you for your trust," Samuel says. "I will meet with the king in Geba by morning. Go your way now and know that God will direct our nation's steps."

"Great prophet, excuse my correction, but the king is not in Geba with Jonathan, he is to the east in Gilgal.

The word Gilgal drops like the walls of Jericho, echoing through Samuel's mind. He presses a smile to the surface. "Then Gilgal it is."

Samuel pats each one of the men on the shoulder and thanks them for their service to the nation. While speaking to them he perceived that there was no plan or direction given by Saul, and with supplies running low, their withdrawal from the battlefield is anything except desertion. They are young in faith, having little knowledge of the nation's past. This is what happens, he fears, when a generation no longer teaches its youth the rich history of Yahweh's divine intervention.

"By the way, how long has the king been in Gilgal?"

"Tonight starts the seventh day, great prophet."

"Thank you, you have been a great help." Samuel presses another reassuring smile to the surface.

He enters the building, shuts the large wooden door, and collapses to his hands and knees. It is not merely physical exhaustion, although he is physically exhausted, but more so mental fatigue that brings him before Yahweh so quickly. After all, it was his own corrupt children that provoked the people to request a king. Once Samuel had placed them in power as Judges over Israel, they quickly perverted their power over justice for personal gain. Samuel has since felt the weight of the decision pressing on his shoulders, and with each mistake Saul makes the pressure builds.

Tomorrow, Samuel will travel to the king's camp in Gilgal as promised two years ago. With a large portion of the army now leaving the encampment, he knows his return couldn't come at a better time.

Saul is desperate for my arrival. The nation... is desperate for my arrival.

Still, his body needs rest. His aging muscles buckle, lowering him to the floor. He slumps against the corner walls of the shrine and fades with only one thing on his mind, the fate of his nation, his people.

Israel.

10

David's stomach growls, reminding him of the nice meal that Benaiah had promised. He rubs the sleep from his eyes and stands, realizing only now just how early it is. The sun has yet to shine upon the land, but soon its golden hue will creep across the hills. David has no intention of waiting. He walks through the center of slumbering sheep, making noise, hoping to wake them, hoping more so to wake Benaiah.

As the sheep slowly rise, David guides them to the water, as he always does, for the day of travel ahead. This time, however, he is unsure of the distance.

He couldn't have traveled too far, David considers, realizing that he has no idea where Benaiah actually lives.

"No one ever beats me to my feet in the morning," Benaiah says as he stands. "You must really take what you do seriously or be hungrier than I thought."

A little bit of both, David thinks.

"I just wanted to get a good start on the day. I realize that my flock will slow you down, and I'm not sure how much of a day's journey we have ahead of us."

A smile flashes across Benaiah's face. "I wouldn't worry too much. You can practically see my dwelling from here."

"You live in Bethany?"

Having headed northeast David knew that Bethany was the closest city, but a rather small city for the way Benaiah carried himself. He seemed a bit more refined or polished than many of the small village farmers such as himself.

"You seem surprised." Benaiah laughs. "I live just outside along the ridge. "You'll understand when you get there. Just be glad I don't still live in Kabzeel."

Benaiah jumps across the creek and doesn't look back. "Come on."

The flock huddles together, crossing the creek with ease. With Benaiah unknowingly leading them from the front, David is able to effortlessly control them from the side. They cross into the open field and Benaiah unexpectedly turns and runs in the opposite direction. The sheep instinctively follow behind.

What is he doing?

Benaiah doesn't strike David as reckless, but his actions make absolutely no sense right now. "What are you…?"

Benaiah bends down and pulls a dead bird from the grass. "It's still warm!" He removes a wrap from his sheath strap, ties it around the bird, and throws it over his shoulder.

The sheep, which were once bundled together, are now slowly separating. David runs, corralling them back into an order he can control.

He notices the bird that Benaiah is holding. It's a quail and it has a familiar hole in its side.

"My mother loves quail. Just wait until you taste the way she cooks it," Benaiah says, taking the lead of the flock again.

As they travel around the ridge, David lets the reality sink in. What seemed only last night to be a failure in the darkness has been revealed as provision in the light. Now, not only will he have food, but it will be prepared for him. His answer lay just on the other side of the water in the darkness, waiting for the timing of the morning light. David has learned a valuable lesson, patience. He decides to name the area "manna," or "answer," for Yahweh not only answered his desire for a beautiful escape with fresh water, but also his desire to eat.

Traversing down the back side of the ridge, David can see the small village of Bethany in the distance. Against the hills to the east, a single dwelling is positioned in a large open field. It's beautiful. Benaiah navigates down the final dirt path that leads into the grass and turns toward the secluded farmhouse.

That's his dwelling? David thinks, surprised.

They cross the grassy field and approach a cattle fence that surrounds the entire property. "Your flock will be safe in here while you stay," Benaiah says, opening the gate.

Inside, the dwelling is not a typical farmhouse. There is a wood-crafted table and iron sconces elegantly holding candles along the walls. Many of the furnishings are accented with iron which draws David's curiosity back to Benaiah's iron sword and his hand-to-hand training. He can't help but ask.

"Who could possess such a dwelling?"

A woman enters the room. "Benaiah, I was beginning to worry. Your sister made it home safely but I see that your attention was apparently diverted." She glances to David.

"Mother, this is David, son of Jesse of Bethlehem. He is well trained and has agreed to exchange proficiencies." Benaiah lowers the quail from his shoulder. "He also came bearing gifts."

She takes the quail in her hand. "I see you have good taste." She squeezes the bird firmly, blood spills into her palm followed by a stone. "If you are going to teach my son how to kill with a stone, please also teach him how to remove the stone before you eat it," she says with a grin, handing the stone back to David.

He grips the bloody stone in his hand but the last of her words fell on deaf ears. David's attention was focused on who just entered the room. A young girl stands in front of him appearing to be as surprised as he is. David can't help but notice her smile, her eyes, and the way her hair flows. He has never laid eyes on anything so gorgeous. She is perfect.

"David," Benaiah says, bumping his arm in an attempt to break his stare. "This is my sister, Ezsri, the reason I was out searching all last night."

David stands silent, still staring. He can't help it. He has never seen a girl so beautiful. He just can't believe how close he has been all these years.

I should have come to Bethany a long time ago.

11

Just north of the capital city, Aaron sits under the shade of a lone ficus tree with Jonathan's most trusted military minds. The trees are sparsely scattered across the hilltop, each one sheltering soldiers that hide from more than just the sun. Across the deep ravine and above the cliff of Michmash, Philistine warriors encamp. The size of their army outnumbers the stars in the night sky. Aaron can only imagine that from their point of view it must appear that the Israeli encampment of Geba has been deserted.

We look like a bunch of gutless jerboas scattering from vipers, he thinks.

Aaron knows that Jonathan won't take this for long. He would rather be slaughtered at the hand of action than live under the weight of regret. The twelve tribes of Israel have been under the hand of bondage for long enough. They are free and yet they are surrounded, constantly harassed by their neighbors, and no more than by the Aegean Sea People. For two hundred years they have tormented the lands of Abraham. Aaron knows that if there is anyone among them to lead the nation, it is Jonathan.

Aaron watches Jonathan as he stands in the open grass staring at the encampment of Philistine warriors, who from this distance look like nothing more than a dark shadow cast across the entire opposing hilltop, as if a storm cloud were blotting out the sun above them.

"What would you wager that he's thinking?"

Aaron glances back to confirm the deep, raspy voice. Nathaniel, one of Jonathan's division commanders and most senior warriors, leans against the tree eating a pomegranate. Everything about him embodies toughness. His thick silvering beard covers a jawline that Aaron is positive is made of forged iron. His shoulders are the width of a normal man's wingspan. His words are carefully chosen and always referring to the mission at hand. Aaron is dumbfounded by how he can always be so intense.

Is he talking to me?

Nathaniel nods toward Jonathan. "What's going through his mind right now?" he asks.

Aaron is not used to being directly spoken to so the question catches him a little off guard. He looks back to the field. Jonathan hasn't moved. He knows exactly what Jonathan is thinking.

"Knowing Jonathan, I think he's probably trying to strike fear into them singlehandedly. I wouldn't be surprised if he charges." Aaron holds his breath, hoping he hasn't overstepped his bounds.

Nathaniel laughs. "You have done well by his side, which is obvious since you're still alive."

Aaron exhales, thankful that his response didn't provoke Nathaniel to the wrath he is so accustomed to witnessing. As the armor-bearer to the heir of the nation, he is rarely around his peers, instead he remains with the commanders, and being a child among men Aaron lives in constant inferiority. It's not often that he is spoken to, much less commended.

Nathaniel is revered as the most seasoned commander under Jonathan. His flesh carries over twenty-five years of combat scars that serve as homage to his experience, and his personality is naturally just as callused. To hear a compliment from a man who has seen it all and has survived, Aaron understands the weight of the situation all the greater.

Does he believe that this is the end?

"Those are heavy words coming from someone such as you, commander."

Aaron glances over his shoulder. Nathaniel's stern face has returned.

"Don't let it get to your head. Just keep doing what you're doing." Nathaniel leans forward and whips a pomegranate toward a group of soldier's sleeping by a tree, striking one of them on the hip. "Wake up, or I'll finish you off before the sea maggots ever cross the pass!"

Aaron jolts, startled by the deep, sudden voice of Nathaniel directly behind him. He sits even more still now, hoping that Nathaniel will somehow forget he exists. It is amazing to Aaron how he can look forward to combat as a break from this tension that he constantly feels when surrounded by such high-ranking warriors.

Aaron keeps his eyes fixed on Jonathan, hoping to stay far away from Nathaniel's attention. It doesn't work. Nathaniel kneels next to him. But he doesn't yell. He doesn't correct him, or belittle him. Instead, he just continues to watch Jonathan by his side, his heavy breathing sounding more like a bear than a human.

"You may wish you could be out with the others away from the commanders, but you're not one of them." Nathaniel nods toward the soldiers, complaining and sleeping under the trees. "You're not one of these worthless warm bodies out here just hoping to return safely. They just want to live in comfort. This life bothers them, the pain, the heat, the imminent death looming above. Their little minds are too weak to stay focused through the hardest part of war… the silence. But Jonathan picked you for a reason. The fact that you're still alive proves that he was right about one thing. You're not afraid of death. Do you know how I know that?"

Aaron feels Nathaniel's eyes now fixed on him, each heavy breath pounding against his skin. Aaron doesn't know what to say.

"Because you're not dead." Nathaniel says. "Many of these men are as capable as you. But when you fear death you hesitate. They all will and when they do, they will all die. Jonathan knows that. His years of knowledge far surpasses his age. He did not pick you to live for him, but to die for him. I know you do not enjoy this time in solitude surrounded by your elders. You'll deal with it. You need to keep your blade sharp. The silence never lasts." Nathaniel stands. "You hesitate, you die."

As his commander walks away Aaron senses that he was just listening to Nathaniel's intuition. Jonathan is up to something and it may not be long before Nathaniel's words are put to the test.

"Aaron!" Jonathan calls out from the front of the field.

Aaron's stomach sinks. He grabs his gear and sprints toward Jonathan, looking back only long enough to see Nathaniel watching him from the tree. It almost feels like he knows what is about to happen. Aaron knows, however, that with Jonathan, you can never be sure, but he senses that carnage is closer than it appears.

12

High above the cowardly Hebrews that have scattered and hid just across the ravine, the Philistine camp of Michmash is quite a different atmosphere.

Kilech, a Philistine boy known by only a few, cowers before the presence of the seasoned warriors surrounding him. Everywhere he looks grown men prepare for bloodshed. Carnage, violence, and death are a foreign concept to him. Dark images of what battle may be like materialize in his mind, images he does not look forward to experiencing. In reality, he understands that he is nothing like the men that surround him. He dreads the very thought of battle.

At the age of thirteen, Kilech is the youngest so-called warrior in the camp. Being the only unblemished male child his mother could bear, he was spared from becoming an infant sacrifice before the idol of Dagon, but seeing what he sees now, he would have rather died a blemished discard at birth than to be here.

He's not a warrior; he doesn't feel like a warrior nor can he pretend to be. Just looking at the men on this hill it's clear that he is not like them. Their eyes are filled with lust. They have a thirst for blood that Kilech could never understand. A thirst for blood, as if it's natural to them, as if they came out of the womb not nursing on their mother's milk, but nursing on the thick crimson liquid of dead Hebrews.

Kilech lets his mind wander. He misses the touch of his mother, her warmth, her loving hand. Here, even in the midst of summer it feels cold, and the only womanly touch is that of prostitutes that pass through the camp, sparking brutal fights among the men, like a pack of wild hyenas trying to share a kill.

Kilech questions why he ever learned to read and write when it appears that now he will just die as an extra body heaved before the enemy to spare a real warrior a little more time. Maybe he'll be lucky enough to be used as a shield and will remain alive long enough to feel the brunt of battle waged against him. Either way, he could escape now but this land is terribly undesirable.

He wonders why, surrounded by nothing but sand and rock, hills and wilderness, mountain and plains, the Peleshet tribes didn't just fight against the armies coming from the north that removed them from their own lands. The stories he has been told of the Aegean islands make him wonder why his people never returned to war over *them*.

Without warning, the unruly crowd of men around him turns into a mob of chaotic spectators. Kilech tries to keep up with the men circling around but his attempt fails, again. The crowd has encircled, leaving a void, a gaping wound in the center, and it is widening with every passing second.

Like the eye of a hurricane it forms, placing him inside for a brief moment, a moment of final peace before all hell breaks free. Instead of heavy storm winds, its warriors now surround him on all sides. Their bodies are marked with animal blood and their eyes are outlined with black charcoal from the embers of the fires that illuminated the camp the night before.

This ritual happens three times daily and the dread that accompanies the brutal custom never goes away. Kilech wants nothing more than to disappear into the tree line, but he fears the time for escape has passed. He can feel the wall of battle-scarred flesh closing in behind him and the feeling is nauseating. Everywhere he turns there is a barricade of bloodthirsty warriors in full rage. Suddenly, there is nothing but open space behind him. He finds himself once again isolated on the inside of the cage formed by possessed men shouting and chanting, anticipating the spectacle before them.

A burly warrior enters the middle of the ring with his sword drawn. As he shouts, spit flies into the air, and the frenzy of the crowd grows wilder. Only a week ago Kilech was home under his mother's care but now that seems worlds away. He attempts once more to back into the crowd, hoping to dissolve into oblivion, but it's an impenetrable force of iron and callused flesh behind him. The burly man swings his sword around recklessly all while searching each warrior on the inside edge of the circle. Turning closer now, his eyes scan down the line of men as his gaze crawls toward Kilech. Pressing backward, harder, Kilech digs his heels into the dirt, his shoulders cutting back into the crowd.

Something is fighting against him. Hands, two large hands, have seized Kilech's back. He tries to fight against the solid palms and fingers that dig almost as deep as his bones. He is pushing against them with everything he has, but the strength behind them is too powerful. As if trying to push his way through a mountain, he finds there is not only no give, but this mountain shoves back. His will is broken, the hands launch him forward. He tumbles across the dirt into the center of the circle, the center of attention.

Looking away from the burly man that now bears down upon him, Kilech catches a glimpse of the one who possessed such powerful hands. He can't believe his eyes. The disbelief, however, is short-lived as the screaming crowd of hardened warriors now has their first fighter for the night. And Kilech has his first fight of his life.

13

David tries to not make it obvious, but he can't take his eyes off Ezsri. The meat is as juicy as David has ever tasted. The fact that it is still warm surely doesn't hurt. But he doesn't enjoy it as much as he would have if Ezsri wasn't sitting across from him. All he can think about is what he will say if she speaks to him.

Ezsri eyes glance up. She smiles and takes a quick breath. It looks like she's about to say something.

Here it comes. Get ready, David thinks.

He has suddenly become aware of every muscle in his body, but for some reason he can no longer control them.

"So, are you ready to head outside and show me how to kill tomorrow's meal with a stone at seventy paces, or what?" Benaiah asks, bumping David's arm. "Mother, may David and I be excused from the table?"

What are you doing? David can't believe Benaiah's timing. *She was going to talk to me!*

Ezsri settles back into her seat as if the moment has passed, and then, as if she has thought of something new, leans forward toward David again.

"Wait, you killed this quail with a stone?"

David grins. "Well…"

"He says he did. We're heading outside to see if his claims are true," Benaiah says, laughing.

"You may be excused, but the chores won't be doing themselves, so I don't want you out there all night," Benaiah's mother says.

"I'm coming," Ezsri says, following Benaiah toward the door.

David stands slowly, picks up his plate, and lowers his head in respect. "Thank you again. I cannot thank you enough."

Benaiah's mother stares at him, her cheeks pulled tight into a half-smile. "Put it down, you are our guest. If anything, I should thank you for such a meal, and for bringing my son home."

David smiles. He has never felt so welcome, not even with his own family. He realizes that he still has no clue what their husband and father does for a living, or why they appear so prestigious while living in the small village of Bethany, but right now he doesn't care. All he knows is that his belly is full and for the first time he feels welcome.

Outside, Benaiah is already holding the sling, waiting for David.

"If you can hit the fig off of that branch, we'll start your training first. If not, then I guess you'll just have to show me how to miss a target with a sling."

David passes Ezsri at the end of the porch.

"Good luck," she says with a smile.

David never thought that there could be so much pressure in slinging a stone for fun. It is not life or death. He is not starving or protecting himself. It's just a piece of fruit and a challenge.

David takes the sling from Benaiah. He pulls a stone from his satchel and rubs it between his fingers, feeling the shape, the texture, the weight. Placing it in the pouch, he whips it into the air where it swings above his head. He can sense Ezsri's eyes watching him but he pushes the thought away, focusing.

Weight, balance, speed, David enters his oasis. With a flick of the wrist the stone whizzes through the air. It flies hard left, completely off target. At the last possible second the stone rips to the right and slices through the branch holding the fig, dropping it to the ground. Benaiah turns with a surprised look. David grins.

Benaiah returns his attention back to the field. "Looks like I'll be up first after all."

David turns around but Ezsri isn't on the porch. Instead,

Benaiah's mother stands alone in the doorway, visibly impressed. Or is she? Her grin continues to rise as if...

David's legs are swept from underneath him. A wincing pain shoots through his body as his back slams against the ground. He opens his eyes to a rather unexpected sight.

Well, I didn't see that coming, David thinks.

Ezsri stands over him. "Rule number one. Never let your guard down."

14

Aaron stands next to Jonathan at the edge of the open field, staring at the hill of Michmash across the ravine below. The cliffs before them are so treacherous they have each been named. The first, Seneh, a jagged cliff covered in mangled thorns, and the other, Bozez, a towering sheer wall that reflects the morning sun. These two rock faces and the ravine that separates them is all that stands between them and the raging thousands camped in Michmash.

The raging shouts of thirty thousand Philistine warriors have erupted, sending shrieking echoes of war chants throughout the valley. The thought of the entire encampment descending across the pass to the west and enveloping the hillside of Geba is unsettling to say the least. But Jonathan's face shows no trepidation. Instead, it appears focused.

He hasn't been staring this whole time, Aaron realizes. *He's been praying.*

"Do you hear what I hear?" Jonathan asks.

Aaron listens, hoping to hear whatever it is that Jonathan wants him to hear, but he can't divert his attention away from the sound of imminent death.

Probably not, Aaron thinks.

"What is it that you hear?" Aaron asks.

Jonathan takes a deep breath, inhaling with a grin as if the sound itself is refreshing.

"It's the sound of disorder." A grin overtakes Jonathan's face as he glances at Aaron. "Are you thinking what I'm thinking?"

Aaron looks into Jonathan's eyes, the rising screams of warriors shouting for bloodshed in the background.

Again, all that comes to mind is, *probably not.*

But Aaron can't let Jonathan down. He won't let Jonathan down. "Whatever you are planning, I am with you."

"Are you sure?" Jonathan laughs.

Aaron stares in amazement. This leader, this heir to the throne, stands across the canyon from an outpost of the largest assembly of enemy forces this nation has faced in his lifetime – with a grin on his face. If Aaron didn't know better, he would assume that Jonathan is mad. He thinks of Nathaniel's words, why Jonathan has chosen him, and he is convinced that it is for moments such as this.

"I would jump right now if you so commanded," Aaron says, looking to the edge of the cliff.

"I will need your descent to be a bit more controlled than that," Jonathan says.

The comment was lighthearted yet as heavy as a boulder lowered onto Aaron's shoulders.

Are we really doing this?

Jonathan shrugs, as if hearing Aaron's thoughts. "Perhaps *He* will be with us," he says, dropping his gaze from the sky above. He turns back to the empty field behind, the soldiers cowering under the shelter of the trees. "If I'm going to die, it will not be from fear." He turns back toward the steep cliffs leading down into the ravine. "And it seems there is only one way to the top." Jonathan's penetrating eyes catch Aaron's. "Are you prepared to become a legend?"

Aaron lets the reality of the comment sink in.

I'm going to die tonight.

He thought the moment would be more terrifying but the truth is, he feels exhilarated. Going on a suicide mission with Jonathan is far better than being mocked by the commanders in a constant feeling of isolation with no authority to respond. Aaron senses that a part of him is becoming just as crazy as Jonathan.

The voice that escapes his lips is hauntingly smooth. "I am with you until the end."

He surprises even himself with the conviction in his words. He realizes that he actually believes it. Ready or not, he is actually committed to do this.

Jonathan cups the back of Aaron's neck with his palm. His grin reveals a lust for more than just combat. He has a desire to fulfill a purpose and it drives every part of his being.

"Good. Tonight you will have a story to tell for the ages." He pauses. "Just don't spew your rations all over the slain or that will be all your generations will remember." Jonathan laughs as he edges over the rim of the cliff.

My uneasy stomach is the least of the concerns tonight, Aaron realizes.

Standing at the peak of Gilgal, a short distance east from both Geba and the mounting army at Michmash, Saul watches as the goat, the final piece to the burnt offering, is tied to the altar. The light of day is receding quickly and still there is no sight of Samuel.

This is surely the day he was speaking of, Saul thinks.

Saul looks to the hills, the sky, the rocky terrain, nothing has changed. Even the hot sun feels the same as it did that day. He remembers it like it was yesterday. It was here years ago that Samuel brought forth the assembly once more after anointing Saul as king. The nation had yet to come together under Saul's authority, and Samuel had made it very clear: Saul was the king they requested, the authority set by God, but Yahweh was still *the* king over Israel.

He looks to the blue sky, not a cloud in it, just as he remembers on that day, the day Samuel summoned thunder and rain to show his authority and Yahweh's power. No one stood in more awe than Saul that day. The man that anointed him as God's chosen had just brought rain in the dry season with the same words that established his kingship.

"What would you have them do, my king?" General Abner says, pulling Saul from his thoughts as he steps alongside him.

"He will be here."

"And yet he is not. Time is not on our side if we are, in fact, to seek the favor of Yahweh." Abner pauses before turning to Saul. "It is, of course, *your* decision, my king."

The years have passed and he has not forgotten Samuel's words. "If you are to ever return to Gilgal, it will be a dire time. Wait seven days for my arrival and I will sacrifice burnt offerings and peace offerings so that you may know the choice Yahweh has for you."

Here he stands in Gilgal, in the moment promised by the prophet. Saul senses the entire nation staring down on him. It is his decision to make. He weighs his options, wondering if he should let the moment pass him by and crumble under the pressure, or take action as a king should do in this situation and show them that he is, in fact, in charge.

It has been seven days, and still I seek the direction of Yahweh.

He pauses, gazing toward the direction of the opposing camp. The decision has been made. One way or another they must know what to do before it is too late.

His voice returns, stern but regretful, upon his only option. "Burn the altar."

15

David circles with Ezsri inside the fence. Horrified that he has been embarrassed by not only a female, but the most beautiful girl he has ever seen. He tries to remember what his brothers do when they test each other, but he realizes that it's completely different watching a fight and being in a fight.

"I told you I would teach you, I never said with whom," Benaiah says with clear joy in his voice.

David lets the anger build inside of him. He attacks first in an attempt to win the element of surprise. He grabs Ezsri's arm, pulls her closer, and wraps tightly around her waist in an attempt to lift her, but she counters. Her body weight drops, she passes underneath David's armpits and her right leg steps behind him, hooking his heel in the process. His balance is lost.

David finds himself on his back… again. This time, however, Benaiah is there to help him up.

"Hand to hand is not won in your head or in your strength. Those must be mastered before you are engaged." Benaiah pokes under David's rib. "It is won in your muscle memory and in your leverage."

David heaves over from the poke and Benaiah smacks him on the forehead as he bends forward. David stands up quickly, becoming more irritated, more frustrated by the second.

"And when you are angry, your judgment is clouded."

This time, David sees the poke coming. He attempts to block it but Benaiah uses his wrist as leverage to spin him around. Benaiah's free arm locks tightly around David's neck, blocking his airway. Benaiah releases quickly, just as David's vision begins to narrow.

"My father always said it is not any one move that you must

learn, but rather an understanding of why one moves."

"You're father always *said?*" David asks.

Benaiah shifts uncomfortably for the first time. "He died in the battle of Jabesh Gilead."

Jabesh Gilead? This is the dwelling of a warrior?

David knows the battle of Jabesh Gilead well, everyone in Israel knows it. Countless times he has heard the story of the Ammonites to the east of the Jordan laying siege to the city of Jabesh Gilead and requiring the inhabitants to make a covenant of submission. To show their submission they were to pluck out their right eyes for the Ammonite king.

It was the Ammonite King Nahash's challenge to the newly crowned King Saul. It was a move that could have toppled King Saul's reign and folded the nation under his command if he had proven an inability to provide protection or leadership in an already divided kingdom.

King Saul, however, responded. As David remembers being told, the people had noticed the king's eyes. They shimmered as if a diamond twisting above the waters of the deep, a window into his spirit as the covering of the Lord came upon him.

He slaughtered a yoke of oxen, and dispatched their remains throughout the land. It was a call to arms to the severity of the situation. The nation responded with three hundred thousand Israelites gathered at Bezek, only a half-day's march to Jabesh Gilead. One day later the Ammonites were overrun. Saul had rallied the largest fighting force since the days of Joshua.

"Your father was a warrior?"

Benaiah catches David's eyes scanning the large pasture.

"He was much more than just a warrior. He was a master of his craft," Ezsri says with a hint of charm in her voice. She brushes the dirt off of David's shoulders and remains standing next to him.

"He was the General of Strategy and Tactics for King Saul's largest military force ever assembled," Benaiah says. "He was the architect of the Jabesh Gilead victory and the one who trained King Saul's guard, and I will show you everything he knew."

Benaiah is the son of valiant Jehoida of Kabzeel?

David can't believe his ears. He has heard the stories and conquests of many of the warriors of old, but to meet the family, actual descendants of the warrior behind such a massive battle success, is exciting to say the least.

"You're the son of Jehoida?"

Benaiah picks up his gear and heads toward the house with Ezsri. "I have chores to catch up on. You're welcome to stay inside if you'd like. We can get in a full day tomorrow."

"I'll be fine out here." David says, pausing. "Why would you teach me all of this just to learn the sling?"

Benaiah stops at the porch, turning to face David. "Because one day it will be our turn to defend our land. What good would it be on that day to keep all that he taught to myself?"

David senses a trust, a loyalty, in Benaiah that is contagious.

One day he will be as valiant as his father, David thinks.

"I'll see you in the morning," David says as Benaiah and Ezsri cross the porch. Ezsri turns back for one more look. It's just enough to stir David's stomach.

Not wanting to impose or have his sheep feed on any more of their pasture, David rounds up his flock and leads them from behind the fence out into the open. He only has a short time to find a place to settle in before it is dark but, oddly, this is the last thing on his mind.

He has been seized by passion. He realizes that he has fallen in love with two desires in the same day. Something has been unlocked that he never knew was even there. The way Ezsri looked at him was exhilarating, but the rush inside that sparked a craving at the thought of the other was surprisingly just as powerful.

Warfare.

16

A scorching pain rushes to Kilech's head. It moves down his neck, back, and finally into his legs as he regains feeling. He is unsure if he fell asleep, or died, as his eyes open to a blur. The haze begins to lift, revealing the ground against his face. His eyes sting from the dust kicked up by the feet that continue to circle. Sounds begin to muffle with the ringing in his head. As his memory and vision return, it becomes clear. He is lying motionless in the dirt, surrounded by a frenzy of warriors. The fight is apparently over.

Suddenly, large, firm hands grab hold of his legs. The dirt begins to move. He is being dragged backward, facedown, through the crowd of people. He wants to turn to see who is dragging him, and hopefully to see where to, but he doesn't have the power to move.

He abruptly stops moving, and a silhouette approaches through the trees. The form of a man emerges as a blurry shadow from the dense brush. Kilech senses the man inspecting his weak and battered body. He can only listen as he feels a vile, heavy breath battering his neck.

"What to do with a worthless soul?" an old crackly voice says as bony fingers drag down Kilech's cheek.

Part of Kilech hopes that a sword will strike without warning and remove him from this new life, this new torment, but so far it seems to only drag on, every event worse than the last.

"Your blood is not even worthy to be offered before Dagon," the old man says before turning and walking away in disgust. "Take him to the cliff. Let his body strike fear into the enemy of what is to come. That is all he is worth."

Kilech suddenly realizes that he doesn't want to die. Before he can attempt to argue, his body jolts and once again the dirt and stones tear into his chest as he is dragged, this time toward the cliff, his final resting place. It is now only a few short breaths before he is hurled over the edge.

✦━◆━✦

As Aaron clings to the side of the cliff his fingers become filled with pain. The joints are locking, making it feel like his fingers are rods of iron, no longer moving the way they should. Looking over his shoulder, he can see the base of the ravine is only a crippling fall below. At this height he would no longer die, only mangle his body in such a way as to never walk again. The thought reminds him to not get complacent. He refocuses and slowly descends as Jonathan waits, watching, from the bottom.

Relieved he steps onto solid ground for the first time since daylight. He needs rest but it seems that rest is the last thing on Jonathan's mind. Jonathan has already turned his attention to the next towering wall of jagged rock.

The darkening blue sky looks like a winding river above as it cuts through the opening of the ravine.

This is as vulnerable as it gets, Aaron thinks. *Not only do they have the high ground but they could kill us with a few hurdled stones from their position.*

Realizing the strategic vulnerability at the base of the ravine, Aaron is glad to have the cover of the shadow cast between the cliffs. They will stay alive as long as they remain silent and in the dark.

"Peasants of Dagon," Jonathan yells, "come to the edge and let me see the servants of a dead God!"

Aaron is stunned. *What is he doing?*

Part of him wants to run. The other part wants to cover Jonathan's mouth and save him from himself, but Aaron does neither. Instead, he stands horrified. Worried that Jonathan has just sealed their fate.

Looking to Jonathan to see if he has lost his mind, Aaron notices that his typically relaxed and lighthearted demeanor is focused like never before. His eyes are intense just as they are moments before battle. If it weren't for this abysmal position of theirs, pinned on the canyon floor, Aaron would be more confident. But still, it seems that Jonathan has not lost his mind.

Hopefully, he hasn't.

Aaron watches as Jonathan waits patiently. His eyes locked onto the edge above.

"Be ready, brother. If these uncircumcised leeches come to us then we will wait here for the unfortunate few. But if they call us up," Jonathan turns to Aaron with a grin, "then we will go and we can be sure that Yahweh has delivered them into our hands."

Laughter echoes through the valley as silhouettes emerge, leaning over the cliff. "Oh, look, the Hebrew dogs have come out from their holes!"

A large burly man stands at the edge laughing, surrounded by soldiers.

If Jonathan wanted to become a spectacle then his plan has definitely worked.

But then it happens.

"Why don't you come up here and we'll show you a thing or two." The broken dialect is clear as the laughter continues.

Aaron's heart now pounds like the hammer of a tent builder as he drives the stakes into the ground. Before he can ask about the plan, Jonathan has already begun his ascent, climbing as if he's excited to charge head-on into a full garrison of Peleshet warriors. Over thirty thousand have encamped at the top of this cliff and the surrounding hills, and yet Jonathan is convinced it is a lopsided fight because Yahweh is on his side.

Jonathan had once said that Yahweh and the faithfulness of even just one warrior was greater than an entire army. As Aaron watches him climb he realizes that Jonathan truly believed what he said. And tonight it will be put to the test.

This is insane.

Aaron approaches the rock face. As the armor-bearer to the heir of the throne, he has no choice but to follow. Besides, he would rather die by the hands of a Philistine than by the hands of Nathaniel. He grips the jagged cliff. With the eyes of the Philistines watching above, they have already passed the point of no return.

No matter what happens, tonight will truly be a night for the ages.

17

Darkness has begun to creep across the hills as the sun dips behind Samuel's caravan, warning that the new day is approaching. Unlike the pagan civilizations which believe the day begins at sunrise, the Torah details Yahweh's creation of each day as beginning in darkness and ending in the light. Samuel knows his chance to arrive on the seventh day is coming to a swift close, and due to a flood of evacuations to escape the Philistine invasion he's running even farther behind. Finally, he sees his destination ahead.

It should be obvious that this is the time he spoke of years ago when confirming Saul as the king before the council, but there is always a chance that it has been forgotten in the chaos that Saul constantly faces.

If only he would trust in Yahweh, the architect of all life, he would be at much more peace in the troubled times, Samuel thinks.

He remembers when he, being both a prophet and a judge of the nation, drove out the attacking Philistines from a very similar military stand. Those, however, were Samuel's younger years. Now, it must be another. Hopefully, Saul will have remembered the victories that took place early in his reign and will trust in God to lead him in this victory as well.

The top of King Saul's tent appears as the caravan crests the encampment of Gilgal. The nauseating sway and numbing jolts finally come to a stop as the line of camels and carriages settle next to the king's tent but, oddly, it appears to be deserted. There is no General Abner and no guards, but more importantly, no King Saul.

Samuel dismounts and treks to the eastern side of the tent. When movement in the distance catches his attention, he realizes that even though he has arrived on time... *it is too late.*

The horrifying sight almost drops him to his knees. Samuel covers his mouth in shock. His withered fingers tremble against his lips. His legs barely hold the strength to keep him upright, but with Saul's act of complete disregard of Samuel's warning in full display before him, the terror turns to anger, propelling him forward. In the distance a flickering orange hue reflects a familiar silhouette of a tall, robed man.

The sacrifice.

Saul has obviously remembered, but in his haste he has done the unthinkable. Samuel finds himself rushing to face the king, his body moving with a speed that he hasn't experienced in years, full of a dread that he hoped to never experience. As Samuel nears the king he realizes he has completely lost his breath, but he fears that will be the least of what is lost here tonight. He stares at the charred goat amidst the flames, its body fading to ash as the flames consume the head, the last recognizable body part of the sacrifice.

My king, what have you done in the name of fear?

Kilech knows that at any moment the rocky ground over which he is painfully dragged will disappear and he will be hurled over the edge of the ravine. The closer he comes to death the more he realizes that he wants to live. He considers fighting back but the grip on his legs is too strong. There has been complete silence with only the ground gnawing at his ears since being pulled from camp, but now he can hear voices again in the distance. With all his strength, he cranes his neck to the side and wills his eyes open, longing to see the final moment of his life. Ahead, the hazy, dark tree line breaks into the faded twilight.

The voices grow louder, laughter fills the air. Suddenly, only twenty paces from the edge, the unimaginable happens. The firm hands release their grip on his legs, letting his feet slam to the ground.

Confused at the sudden stop, Kilech uses the last of his energy positioning his body toward the sound of the voices. Again, breaking the crusty seal of his eyelids, he catches a sliver of what lies ahead. His eyesight is blurry, but his mind is still sharp, and yet he still questions what he sees.

How can this be?

Amidst a group of guards, two dark silhouettes have risen up from the ravine below like ghosts in the night. They even stand like spirits from the afterlife and yet the guards at the canyon edge continue to laugh. They don't seem worried in the least. Kilech's eyes focus now, the blur coming clearer as a third figure materializes but, oddly, not a single one of the guards has noticed him.

Kilech tries to move, but to no avail. His body is broken. Whatever is about to take place, whatever these spirits have come for, Kilech realizes that there is nothing that he can do, nothing but watch the night unfold.

18

On the far side of the ridge from the town of Bethany, David settles his flock, which has continued to make noise. He was sure that Benaiah's family would be kept awake well into the night with the commotion, and the last thing he wanted was to overstay his welcome on the first day.

Now, however, he has a new concern. The sound of sheep echoing through the valley will surely entice predators to investigate. David retrieves his most effective weapon, the lyre. He's not sure if it actually helps calm the animals or if it just calms him. Either way, playing late into the night somehow removes him from more than just his circumstance. The weather, the noise, the threats, they all disappear as his spirit releases from the thoughts of this world.

It's times like these when David can fully express himself. All the cares of the world seem to fall away, his heart is uplifted, and he feels a purpose, a calling in his life, far greater than just lying in the dirt surrounded by a flock of sheep.

But even if this is all that I am called to do, I will do it with joy, David tells himself, believing that he must continue to remain positive even when he feels like his life is wasting away in a field.

While many of his peers are being trained by their fathers to one day take over the family trade, and others are preparing to one day become great warriors, teachers, or prophets, David spends many nights doing just this, seeking Yahweh. While it's easy to desire what he sees around him – the youth that are treated by their families as royalty, the children whose parents own vast amounts of land and cattle – he knows that all of it is fleeting. His greatest desire is not to hold a position esteemed by men, but to walk with the God of Abraham, Isaac, and

Jacob, just as the patriarchs did.

When the nights are long and his body is worn, he reminds himself that he is not as confined to schedules as others are. He has the time to sit in deep reflection and reverence the God that led his people out of Egypt, gave Sampson the strength to bring down the Philistine pillars, the God that led them back to the promised land of Abraham.

The stars now hang in the darkness, and once again David has been completely removed from time while playing. His callused fingers slowly pluck the last few chords until silence overtakes the night. The sheep have long been asleep. The trees gently sway in the breeze, rustling together with a soothing repetition. David sighs and leans back against a tree and closes his eyes. His body relaxes, his mind drifts, and slowly the natural sounds of the woods that surround him fade away.

The day's memories play across his mind like a chariot wheel spinning, each spoke bringing a new recollection. David sees the farm dwelling from the ridge for the first time. His stone slices through the branch. He notices Ezsri's beautiful face. His back smacks against the ground with a loud thump.

David wakes up.

He's unsure if it was a sound or just instinct that jolted him awake but he's sure of one thing. His senses are fully engaged as he stares wide-eyed into the blackness. The sheep have not been startled, but David hears a soft whisper on the breeze.

Get up.

After sitting motionless, overwhelmed by an imagination running free with the worst possible scenario, David pushes the lyre from his lap and slowly reaches for his staff. His hand grips the cool wooden rod as he glances over the sleeping flock. They are completely vulnerable without him. They need him and he notices that right now one of them is missing.

David knows that sheep don't often stray into the darkness unless they were startled enough to do so. The unshakable sense that something has frightened this lost sheep into wandering, and it now watches, or worse, approaches from the darkness, compels David to stand in the face of his fear. It is something he has become accustomed to, listening to the soft nudge deep down in his gut. He discards the paralyzing thoughts and jumps to his feet. Not one sheep has ever been lost under his watch and it isn't about to happen tonight.

As he once again treads toward the sense of lurking danger, he reminds the fear spreading throughout his body that although he may be young, he does not walk alone. With only a wooden staff in his hand and courage as solid as stone seated deep in his heart, David moves swiftly into the night, expecting to search… prepared to defend.

Samuel approaches Saul who stands focused on the sacrificial fire blazing in front of him. The crackling embers disguise Samuel's approach to Saul, but not to the guards. One by one they note the advancing Samuel and draw back from his impending wrath.

The initial sight of Saul performing the sacrifice brought shock to the eldest Hebrew prophet, but that has quickly turned to anger as Samuel considers the ramifications of this clear disregard.

There is no excuse.

Saul turns, clearly surprised. "My great prophet. I'm glad –"

Samuel is in no mood to mince words. "What have you done?" he scolds, interrupting.

Saul is visibly taken aback by Samuel's anger. He repositions himself to make his defense. "Do you not see the men preparing to devour our army?"

Saul's words sound more like a child's defiance than a king's strength. Samuel pauses, looking deep into his eyes. "Do you no longer listen to the words of a prophet?"

"You had not come in the seven days as you said you —"

"Today I have come, as I said I would," Samuel snaps back.

Saul stands tall, lifting his chin. "I did what I had to do as king. If I didn't burn that altar, Yahweh would not have favor upon me, and my army would be at the mercy of men."

"By the looks of it, they already are." Samuel glares at Saul to let the comment sink in. "It is only a prophet, not a king that is to perform and request favor for this sacrifice. The words given to me are not to be discarded."

Samuel glances into the burning fire, now a pile of black coals and bone where the animal once lay. The flames are devouring, yet transfixing. As they wave and flicker, Samuel hears the words he is to deliver.

"Tread carefully, my king, for your decisions will jeopardize the future of your reign. One will surely rise from beneath you to lead his people. One who will possess the heart, as well as the throne."

Saul lets the words sink in. The prophet that was raised in the temple of Shiloh under the great prophet Eli and descends the office of Sampson as Judge over Israel has spoken. The same man that drove the Philistines out of their lands, called down thunder and rain from heaven, and anointed him as king has just declared that his time as king has been jeopardized.

He's just getting old, Saul tells himself as he watches Samuel climb the hill toward the tent.

Even though the prophet's words seed deep into the recesses of Saul's mind, he buries them for now. There is nothing else left for him here in Gilgal. And he will not let this time pass from him. Not when he can prove a man like Samuel wrong.

He turns toward his guards and generals who have kept their distance.

"How many men do we have left?"

19

The light is all but gone. The adjustment of their eyes will slow their reaction, Aaron thinks.

His breathing quickens. Never has he stood this close to the enemy without being in the heat of battle. He studies each of them, knowing that soon all of them will be dead. Ten guards stand surrounding him, laughing and mocking. Not one of them has a hand near their sword. They are oblivious of the slaughter to come. More straggle over to see the spectacle.

Relax, he tells himself, attempting to slow the blood rushing to his core from his limbs.

He looks to Jonathan who stands calm but clearly focused.

One of the men, a large warrior with dark makeup outlining his features, steps toward Jonathan. The warrior looks him up and down as if to provoke a reaction. His eyes focus on Jonathan's sword.

"I was under the impression that only royalty carried iron in your godforsaken lands." His glance moves to Aaron for a moment but his attention returns to Jonathan. "It's about time you came out from your holes. Come, I will take you to our king. Surely, you have come to surrender your army," he says with a grin as he turns away.

"I plan to find my own way to Achish. But I have not come to surrender," Jonathan says.

The warrior turns around, surprised. "No? Then for what reason have you come?"

Aaron's pulse quickens even faster now. He feels the guards' bodies close, two behind, four to the right, and the rest to the front of Jonathan.

"To kill everyone on this hill," Jonathan responds.

Laughter erupts on the hilltop.

Aaron's stomach feels like a bottomless pit as the voices and laughter blend into a muffled echo. Time slows to a crawl as he scans each warrior, none of whom are prepared. Some lean back, leaving their necks vulnerable. Others turn their gaze to one another in disbelief.

Jonathan's right hand moves. Aaron reacts instinctively.

He spins, removing his sickle sword from his waist and striking the first warrior to his back. With one smooth motion he drops to his knee, removes the iron sword from the slain warrior's sheath, and chops the blade into the second warrior's inner thigh. Blood gushes as he collapses to the ground. Aaron turns back toward Jonathan who is unleashing chaos against the surprised and overwhelmed warriors.

Closing the distance between them, Aaron moves swiftly, letting his body take over what his mind would only slow down. A warrior reaches for his sword but Aaron is already in motion. The man's hand falls freely to the ground, having been sliced clean through, as Aaron finishes him by plunging the iron deep into the warrior's spine. He reaches Jonathan, but by now the others have had time to react. Fewer than ten men close in on their position; however, Jonathan's and Aaron's backs are now pinned against the cliff's drop and the enemy's drawn swords.

The element of surprise is over and the Philistines' eyes have most likely adapted to the day's strategic advantage of twilight. If there is any time for Yahweh to reveal himself, now would be the time.

20

Just across the ravine on the lower hilltop of Geba, Jokim sits watching the newly lit fire slowly consume the stacked wood. Each night, the Hebrews leave the shelter of the pomegranate trees to reunite in the open field under firelight. Prolonged days of boredom can take more of a toll on a young soldier than combat itself: the constant stress of what is to come, the constant despair of what is, and the constant thought of what has been left behind. It is a torture of war that often reveals the strength of the most important weapon of a warrior, the mind. Tonight is no different.

Jokim listens as the young soldiers complain about wasting their life under the hot sun, the terrible rations that are depleting, and the constant threat of death.

The thought becomes clear. *They're losing their direction, their will.*

The fire crackles as it catches a dry log. The murmuring escalates.

In an army comprised of multiple tribes, the infighting can be intense at times. Tonight, however, there is a single harmonious thought.

"Why are we even here?" a soldier asks, his accent clearly deriving from the Tribe of Benjamin. "There are thirty thousand men to our north. We have a handful of farming tools and a God that we have never seen to lead us. Give them the hill country, we don't want it anyway. Let us return to our farmlands."

Jokim watches as the soldiers erupt in agreement. With a Benjaminite king in Saul having set up his capital in the territory of Benjamin and the main front of the Peleshet establishing a foothold in the center of their land, the last tribe of the twelve that Jokim would expect to shy away from fighting this current threat would be the Benjaminites and yet here they are, not only agreeing but leading the charge.

These are the descendants of those that were set free from Egypt by the hand of Yahweh?

Jokim sits quietly, watching the youthful impatience on display. He is a well-respected farmer, well past the age of the young soldiers in his line, and of no significant rank. Only leaving his farm in the most troubled of times, Jokim lives for moments like these, the steady strength when the leadership isn't around. Young men have strong bodies but often weak minds. When their bodies are broken, their will is never far behind.

"Have we forgotten?" Jokim asks. His raspy voice is quickly drowned out by the chaos. He waits patiently until enough eyes drift his way, and it becomes apparent that the wise old man has a word to speak. "Have we forgotten The Hand that led our ancestors from the grip of the Egyptians? Let them have it, you say? Look around, you are standing in the land of Our Father Abraham, everything that you see was promised to you and now it is yours."

Jokim stands, turning toward the dark hill of Michmash, speckled with flames as if the star-studded sky descended upon it. "When I was a young boy living in Ephriam, I watched those that sit on top of the hill opposing us today march past my dwelling. I will never forget the disgrace that they brought to our women, our children. I saw unimaginable things, men that were not of this world, but rather the offspring of the fallen spirits spoken of by Moses and Enoch, the counter seed to Yahweh's promise of our redemption to come through woman. It now stands at our door, threatening to remove our race, and you think Yahweh will forget you?"

No one speaks. The fire slowly dies as the wind blows from the direction of Michmash. The breeze carries a faint, ghostly, yet humanlike shriek, followed by another that echoes across the ravine. A disturbing chill crawls inside of Jokim and settles in at the thought of the horrific sound's origin. Not one man moves, their eyes fixed to the cliffs.

Jokim can feel fear descending over the entire camp. He decides to break the silence.

"Whether you believe in your king or not, the spirit of Yahweh is upon him. He is also with us."

"How can you be so sure?" a voice asks softly.

"Look closely," he says, moving though the soldiers, keeping their attention on him. "A man's eyes are the opening to his soul. The king's –"

"The *king* has requested Jonathan's presence." The voice of General Abner cuts through the dark eeriness. "Why is he not at the head of his men?"

Jokim turns toward the general who emerges suddenly from the blackness. But a voice from the back beats him to the answer.

"General, regularly he departs from us to scout the land."

"In what need is a scout when there is no plan for an attack?" General Abner fires back.

Jokim returns his gaze to the blazing fires of Michmash. "Jonathan always has a plan for an attack, sir."

21

Only six hundred men remain? I have a guard detail, not an army, Saul realizes.

He grips the horse's reins tighter. With a swift pull of the leather straps, the horse gallops to a sprint.

Saul knows he can't afford to lose one more soldier by way of the exodus taking place amidst his army, much less wage a war. Trained or not, six hundred warm bodies will be torn apart by scavengers before dawn if the Philistines decide to attack. His only hope is that Jonathan has retained more men than himself.

It doesn't matter. Saul succumbs to the reality. Even if Jonathan's entire command of two thousand remains, there is still no chance of victory. Fear and anger twist together as if someone were braiding them tighter and tighter inside his skull. He now feels like his head is about to cave in as he closes in on Geba. The fear of being overrun in the night hardly compares to the embarrassment of arriving with nothing more than a band of stragglers.

I will have to assert myself immediately. Show that I am in charge of the situation. If I don't... Saul stops mid thought, deciding that he'd rather not think of the outcome after all.

There is a concern that Saul has kept buried deep inside, one that that lies so dormant that at times he forgets about it himself. It begins to bubble to the surface once again as the distant firelight comes into view.

Saul fears that the people will discover that he is nothing more than a common man, that he is a tall, handsome, and strong servant that is in well over his head.

I am unqualified, he thinks.

With the six hundred men well behind him, Saul approaches the camp of Geba, but he doesn't ride to the commanders. Instead, he decides to steer clear of the campfires surrounded by soldiers and gather himself with a moment of solitude under one of the many pomegranate trees far south of the cliffs of Michmash. The pressure in his chest is mounting, but for now, in the darkness, away from everyone, he can sit in peace and pretend even if for one moment that he has no responsibilities. That he *is* just a common man. That he is no longer king.

⊰══╬══⊱

David locates the lost sheep with help from the moonlight. As if a sign from above the blue haze pours through a gap in the canopy like a waterfall flowing down to the forest floor, spotlighting the helpless animal. The sight is a relief, but the moment is short-lived.

Noticing the gradual incline ahead of him, littered with boulders, David realizes that this is a perfect location for a predator to remain concealed, to observe… to hunt.

The opening in the canopy, he thinks, noticing the familiar landmark.

David tenses, realizing where he has stopped for the night. He's been here before, and he suspects the lone sheep was startled by a very familiar predator.

I've settled in the wrong crossing, he realizes.

With his once lost sheep in his grasp, he turns back toward his flock which lies forty-some paces away. His fears are confirmed by a very recognizable print.

The lion is no longer roaming, it is hunting.

The lion could have easily pounced, but it appears that today David has foiled its plan. This time it was prodding, testing its limits near the flock. One day it *will* decide to strike. And when it does, David knows that he had better be ready.

He ensures that every last sheep is now accounted for and decides to pack up his gear and prepare to move toward Bethany. Tomorrow, he will start early and train like his life depends on it. One day, possibly very soon, it just might.

⁍⸻⧫⸻⁌

Kilech watches in horror as the two ghostly figures carve their way through the entire Philistine force at the cliff's edge. It is the first he has seen combat, and his eyes are fixed on every detail. Iron and bronze collide, flesh and bone are crushed, and men that were laughing only moments ago now lie lifeless, face down in the dirt.

As much as Kilech was afraid of a life-or-death engagement with another human being, he finds that watching it is captivating, even exhilarating. He's never felt this fascinated and fearful all at the same time. The hand that dragged him here, the same hand that had pushed him into the ring to fight, now approaches the two warring figures.

What is he doing? Can't he see they can't be stopped?

Kilech watches as the same man, who only moments ago dragged him to his impending death, now unsheathes his sword, and with more courage than Kilech could ever fathom, approaches the flank of the figure to the left. The warrior, while in the midst of engagement, neither sees nor reacts to the oncoming blade. His sword drops from his hand, but suddenly the third figure reappears. He begins warring as if hidden behind a veil, a glowing silhouette of violence and speed. As this shadowy image joins their side, Kilech anxiously watches to see if one of the three ghostly figures that appeared as if from the pit of Sheol is not immortal, but a mere human after all.

22

Aaron drops to his knee as a ball of spikes chained to a wooden club whizzes past his head. The large bearded warrior winds up for another blow and Aaron slices his sword at the man's legs. Strangely, nothing happens. Aaron's hand has swung through the open air causing no damage and bringing forth a disturbing realization. He is no longer holding his sword.

How is this possible?

The warrior whips the mace above his head, preparing to chop down as Aaron, defenseless, scurries to regain his sword. Searching frantically, Aaron discovers the reason for his useless hand. A deep slice across his forearm has severed his control of everything below his elbow, but more importantly, he now notices the deliverer of the wound.

A warrior that Aaron had not accounted for has managed to approach undetected, as if he were waiting in the tree line before they even arrived. Now, it's too late. With the mace preparing to bludgeon his skull from above, and the emerging warrior positioned to eliminate any thought of escape, his fate appears to be sealed.

Time slows. Everything becomes crisp. Memories dipping as far back as his childhood race through his mind as the mace arches over the bearded man's head like an ax preparing to split a log into two. Aaron watches it draw closer, eyes wide open. He has decided that he will not cower in his final moment. Suddenly, his commitment to Jonathan captures his thoughts.

I have failed my duty as armor-bearer and will gladly take this execution as a result.

He takes a last glance to check on Jonathan, hoping that Jonathan's vicious fighting style will put his mind at ease. That the heir of the kingdom will survive even in his own failure.

But... Jonathan isn't there.

The prince, the son of the king, the heir of the kingdom is racing toward him with violent speed, a short sword clenched in his hand. He draws back and releases it, lodging it in the chest of the warrior that Aaron had not accounted for.

Immediately, Aaron reverts to his training and without thought plunges his shoulder just below the kneecap of the bearded warrior, while pulling the man's heel toward his chest. In a lunge forward, the warrior is thrown off balance, toppling backward to the ground. The thick spikes of the mace sink into Aaron's leg, but the pain is masked by an overdose of aggression.

Launching himself onto the warrior's chest, and with no weapons within reach, Aaron thrusts the palm of his only working hand between the eyes, in the depression just before the bridge of the warrior's nose, with all of his body weight, crushing his face. The pressure forces an exhale, the bearded warrior's final breath before his body goes limp between the straddle of Aaron's legs.

A gushing sound as if a spring released from the mountain pulls Aaron's attention to Jonathan who's removing his short sword from the sternum of the tree-line warrior. Jonathan, no longer full of humor, nods for him to get up, as the remaining Philistines attempt to capitalize on the chaos. He motions toward the cliff, his eyes telling a story of what is to come. Aaron has been by Jonathan's side for long enough to know what is going through his mind. With a renewed confidence that tonight will not be his final battle, Aaron stands.

23

Kilech's stomach turns in a twisted bundle of emotions. He just watched the most horrific series of events unfold only thirty paces before his eyes. Now, a feeling creeps in that he has never felt before. A hatred laced in anger emerges, quenching the fear that he felt rising through his frail body only moments ago. For a boy who wanted nothing to do with this lifestyle, this dark side of humanity, he senses it pulling him in.

The familiar firm hands that pushed him into the ring of warriors and carried him to the cliff with the intention of throwing him to his death have now gone limp. His intimate view of each killing tonight was a shock to his young mind, but this man's death, a man of his own blood that was so different from him in every way, somehow transcended the ordinary emotions. This was an awakening.

Kilech watches the Hebrew who had thrown the short sword into the chest of what he now reveres as an honorable and courageous warrior instead of the barbarian that he despised in life and could never become. Kilech is overwhelmed with the inexplicable feeling that a piece of him has just been lost.

He didn't even have to think, he just murdered him.

The two shadowy figures move together with a fluidity that Kilech has not yet seen. They easily maneuver to the flank, pinning the few remaining warriors against the cliff. One by one the Peleshet are hacked, kicked, and pushed from the edge. The peaceful night's breeze is suddenly filled with horrific cries that are silenced only by the crashing of their ironclad bodies smacking into the ground two hundred cubits below.

Kilech stares at the figure wielding the short sword, his heart welling up with hatred. Kilech has realized that he is in the enemy's land, threatening their way of life and desecrating their God, but all of that means nothing to him now. All that he can think about is vengeance.

✦━✦━✦

Nestled alone, far behind his army encampments positioned at the ravine, facing the rising mountain of Michmash, Saul sits peacefully concealed by darkness. For a moment he forgets that he is the king, that he faces a far more advanced, trained, and mobile force than ever before. For a moment he is just a man sitting under a tree enjoying the night. But that moment doesn't last long.

A subtle draft blows against his skin but the chill he experiences isn't coming from the cool night air. Looking over the few fires that remain in his son's military stronghold of Geba, his eyes fix on the distant hilltop of Michmash where the now faint shrieks of death wisp past him like spirits carried by the wind. The air howling through the bending grass around him, the tree leaves rustling behind and above, the whisper of souls swirling in the darkness remind Saul of the horror that surrounds him. He can't hide forever.

What could they possibly be sacrificing at this hour? he wonders.

The sounds are unsettling, even for a pagan culture that often sacrifices its youth. He exhales a slow, steady breath, focusing, listening. The ghastly tones cutting through the thin night air are too human to be the sacrifice of a goat or a ram, and too deep to be children. No, they are clearly the unmistakable howls of grown men.

Now more confused than ever, Saul forces himself back to his feet, but something's not right. The ground, the only stability left in his life, is moving, trembling, shaking, as if the earth has been rattled by the same chill that shivers inside his bones.

What on earth is happening tonight?

Kneeling low enough to place his palms on the ground, Saul feels the warm soil, hoping that he's not losing his mind. Again it happens. The ground rumbles as if its womb is being stretched to its limits. As if birth pains shuddering deep inside threaten a violent release.

I have to find Abner.

Saul mounts his horse and races toward the camp. The burning campfires that cover the hilltop of Michmash begin to go black. As the final flame is doused into darkness, the hill disappears into the night.

"My king!" Abner's voice calls out from the blackness.

Saul stops, having just breached the flickering light of the first campfire surrounded by Jonathan's soldiers. General Abner emerges from the dark.

"Jonathan and his armor-bearer have departed. We may have a short opening in the chaos to inflict maximum damage."

Saul reacts, knowing this is his chance. "Send all that remain to the pass! Flank their retreat and smash them blind!" He pulls the reins, turning the horse toward Michmash. "I'll lead the way!"

General Abner sprints off toward the soldiers who are already waiting for the order. This is no longer a dreadful waiting game for an impossible fight in which everyone will inevitably die, but a chaotic slaughter in which every man is eager to expose. As the screams of men and the rumbling of the earth mix to create a poetic blend of battle hysteria, the remaining few in the army follow their leader. Saul races to the front of the already moving formation, filled with pride once again.

The king has returned.

24

A searing pain shoots down Aaron's arm. For the first time since losing the function of his hand he is able to look at it closely. His flesh is flapped open, revealing his muscle underneath, but at least the cut is clean, so clean that he wouldn't have felt it if he hadn't lost the use of his hand.

"You'll be fine," Jonathan says cutting a piece of leather from a slain Philistine and wrapping the arm tightly. Aaron winces at the sharp sting as Jonathan cinches down the strap, a reaction that he regrets immediately.

Jonathan laughs. "You act like you've never had your arm almost hacked off."

The comment somehow relieves some of the pain. Aaron grins. "I just don't know why you had to butt into my fight. I had them right where I wanted them."

"If that's having them right where you want them then I understand why you're still unmarried."

"No, that's just because I'm ugly. But now with that gash on your cheek we may both endure the same fate."

They both stand in the midst of carnage, surrounded by the wake of their violence, impossibly successful violence, laughing almost uncontrollably. The adrenaline clearing their bodies is being released in the form of humor. It is immediately following the evasion of death that Aaron recalls his most joyful moments. Not only have they just tangled with the afterlife but the tremors that shook the ground have subsided, giving them both a chance to regain their bearing.

The commotion in the tree line, however, is beginning to turn wild. Like smacking a stick into a beehive, the swarming of thousands becomes a single monotone buzz, only it is grown men scurrying around, their grunts and their screams filling the early night with that monotone hum that only humans in disorder can create.

Aaron wipes the sweat from his face but he quickly finds that the liquid dripping from his brow is not perspiration. His palm returns covered in blood. The harsh taste of iron in his mouth, as if he just licked one of the Peleshet swords, leads to an interesting thought. He knows the warm metallic flavor well and it's not just the taste of another man's blood that causes his disgust, but possibly the taste of the offspring of the mighty men of renown, the blood of the Anakim, the giants.

Aaron wonders if it's all just a myth. After all, he has been in a number of battles with these Sea People and has yet to see anything that would resemble a race mixed with fallen angels.

"Do you think it's true?" Aaron asks, as they move toward the dark tree line.

"Do I think what is true?"

Aaron freezes at the sight of movement just beyond the trees, but Jonathan has already moved past and entered the darkness, unable to resist seeing the cause of the chaos.

"It's just a boy. Come on, we have to move," Jonathan says.

Suddenly, another tremor shakes the ground below them, this one more powerful than the last. The trees sway back and forth and the sound of thousands swarming only one hundred paces or so away erupts into an explosion of disarray.

"It's now or never," Jonathan yells, sprinting past the boy and into the thundering black forest.

Aaron hesitates, meeting eyes with the young boy. He's only a few years younger than himself, but he doesn't have the look of a warrior. He's soft, a nonthreat. A frail boy who's obviously been badly beaten, but his eyes aren't looking for rescue. Instead, they look as if they are filled with hate, as if Aaron is the one intruding on *his* land.

He wants to reach out to the boy but Jonathan has already gone ahead. Nathaniel's words begin to repeat in Aaron's ear and he is reminded to stay close. Reluctantly, Aaron breaks eye contact and heads into the chaos.

25

Kilech watches the savages vanish into the darkness, his mind replaying the comment.

I'm just a boy?

Hate boils up inside, filling him from his core, but exhaustion overwhelms his frail body. He blacks out, but before he knows it he is sprinting, swinging, stabbing. His revenge on the killer with the short sword is swift and bloody. But how did it happen so fast? How did he even get here, and why doesn't he feel any pain?

It doesn't matter. He feels so liberated and fulfilled. He is a warrior after all. But then pain and excruciating discomfort returns to his body. He no longer feels weightless, but heavy and constricted. The sound of birds chirping in the night grows louder, now surrounding him. The intense warmth of sunlight covers his body but it's still dark. The pain is almost unbearable as muffled voices approach. He can't make sense of any of it until the sunlight battering his eyelids forces them to open. Squinting in the morning sun, he realizes that his hands are wrapped around a warrior, but not the savage Hebrew.

This warrior is already dead.

The reality that the revenge was only in his mind immediately delivers a feeling of despair that quickly consumes him.

It was only a dream?

No longer concealed by darkness, he is now in the open after mustering all of the energy and power that he had last night to drag himself to the edge of the cliff where he wept in a struggle to understand his feelings over this man, this protector that had ultimately dragged him to… safety.

With his head still lying on the slain man's chest, his father's chest, his emotions still twisting inside, he contemplates the odd connection that the two of them formed in such a short time.

If he hadn't pushed me into that ring, or dragged me to the edge of the tree line, I would be dead, Kilech realizes.

The muffled voices are now crisp as if they are standing next to him, because they are. Two men, walking as they converse, stop only a few paces from his position. He slows his breathing so that his chest doesn't rise too much and draw attention. But it's not easy now that he realizes who is standing next to him.

⋘━┃━⋙

Samuel and Saul stand at the edge of the ravine at Michmash, looking back to Geba below. The birds singing their morning chorus replaces the horror of men screaming. However, the evidence of last night's slaughter still surrounds them. Samuel glances to the ravine floor where more lifeless bodies lie in an unrecognizable heap of mangled carnage.

Sensing a stirring in his spirit, he pauses to listen. Just as he did when he was a young boy growing up in the temple at Shiloh, he hears the voice of Yahweh and delivers the message just as it comes. He turns and locks eyes with Saul.

"Yahweh sent me to anoint you as king over His people. Now, listen to the words of God."

Samuel closes his eyes and lets the breeze beat against his face, calming his mind. In an instant his body is wrapped with warmth that descends from above like a soft, feathered wing. The words become clear, playing across his mind like an unraveling scroll.

"Yahweh says, 'I will punish Amalek for what he did to Israel while coming up from Egypt. Now go and strike Amalek and utterly destroy all that he has, and do not spare him but put to death man and woman, child and infant, ox and sheep, camel and donkey.'"

Samuel slowly inhales, savoring the weightless feeling. Then he opens his eyes and the warmth is gone. He is again aware of his aged body and the surrounding corpses. Samuel is possibly as surprised as Saul at the message, not to mention the destruction that is now visible in the daylight after Saul's impatience in Gilgal.

If only others could experience this Presence that overwhelms him in moments like these. Maybe then Saul wouldn't make the choices that he does so often. But Samuel is not so sure. After all, Saul has been anointed, just as many prophets and priests that are given a divine calling are anointed. Samuel is encouraged however, that Yahweh is still using him to speak to Saul, especially to fulfill an order from the Law, a directive descending from Moses to never forget Amalek. Samuel repeats the order as Moses also commanded. He wants to ensure that Saul will not forget.

"As the Philistines have been delivered to you this day, so shall be Amalek so that the divine words of Moses shall be ever true. That when the Lord your God gives you rest from all the enemies around you in the land that he has given us to possess as an inheritance, you shall blot out the name of Amalek from under heaven. Do not forget! Do not spare them, but kill man, woman, and child. Anything that has breath let it breathe no more."

Saul places his hand on Samuel's shoulder. "Great prophet, may your words be ever true. Surely I have found favor? Surely my kingdom will remain."

Samuel offers nothing more than a glance. He's not so sure that Saul should be so confident. They both know that Saul isn't the one that deserves the recognition for this victory but it will be the king that receives it. If it were up to Saul alone, Michmash would have still been a slaughter, but a much different outcome.

26

Over the wooden fence that wraps the sweeping green hillside, David can already see Benaiah waiting on the porch. His stance is rigid and his eyes are steady.

He's definitely ready to train, David thinks.

It makes sense that he would be the son of an iconic general. Everything about him evokes authority, power, and control. David watches Benaiah's body language as he approaches. Part of him wishes that he was more like him. That he could be the man of the house and just take charge of his life. He knows that he has been called to serve this flock, and no matter how insignificant it may seem, this is what he is to do. But sometimes his role in life seems so mundane compared to others, especially Benaiah.

One day they'll see, David thinks.

Inside, he knows that he has been created for a plan. No matter how insignificant it may feel, the one that walks with the God of Abraham is never let down. David is reminded of Samson's outcome. One of the original twelve Judges of Israel, Samson appeared to have everything that a man could ask for, but bad decisions led to his demise.

David wants to be sure that if and when his moment of truth comes that he will not cave to the pressure, but will be as a tree planted firmly by a stream of water, one that will yield fruit in season and its leaves will not wither. Today, he believes, will be the beginning of one more root grounding itself into the soil.

"Most would have run off after being beat up by a girl," Benaiah says with a grin.

"Most ponder too highly of what others think," David responds. "Plus, I would like to learn what to do so that it doesn't happen again."

Benaiah descends the steps. "Do you watch the beasts of the field often?"

"I have plenty of time to study them."

"I can tell." Benaiah steps close. "What does a ram do before it strikes?"

"It lowers its body weight," David answers.

"Do it."

David lowers. Benaiah grabs David's palm and pulls it to him, placing it under his chin.

"Drive gently," Benaiah says.

David takes a step forward and lifts upward, causing Benaiah to backpedal and quickly turn away from David's palm.

"Do you see the control, the power, you can generate from nothing more than position?

Before David can respond, the blade of Benaiah's hand, the hard muscular exterior from wrist to pinky, presses against David's nasal septum. A sharp pain shoots through his face, causing his head to snap back instinctively. He catches his balance.

"One finger in the right position can cripple an entire body, just as the mind of one man can cripple an entire army," Benaiah says, before walking into the field.

That's impossible, David thinks.

"How can one man cripple an entire army?"

"I'll show you."

David herds his sheep inside the fence and runs to catch up with Benaiah out in the field, but he's gone. David approaches where he last saw Benaiah and discovers him kneeling inside a matted down spot in the high grass. David immediately notices the paw prints pressed into the soil around the area.

Wolf prints.

"Notice where the wolves lie," Benaiah says. "Concealed against the tree line, they are close enough to watch my livestock and yet have a quick escape if they sense danger. The wolves that harass my farm understand more than just how to fight and kill. They understand how to use the terrain for movement, protection, and surprise. Sound familiar?"

"An army."

"An army, and what happens if the alpha is killed?" Benaiah stands, glancing back to the edge of the forest as if they are being watched. "The whole pack will dissolve."

The army will dissolve.

"Eventually a new leader will emerge, but for the moment they will be crippled," Benaiah says.

David pays close attention knowing that there is a world of knowledge that he longs to learn. But one day he hopes to reach a point where he can hunt and outsmart a predator as intelligent and aggressive as an alpha wolf. He knows that Benaiah, being the son of a general, has a different mission than he does. For David, it will take a perfect blend of military tactics and predator instincts to stay alive in the animal kingdom.

He stares out into the forest, committed to tightening his skills so that one day he can repay Benaiah and his family for their unwarranted hospitality.

27

YEAR 1028 B.C.
AGE 13

David's leg muscles flex under his tunic. The tight grip on the rope that pinches snug over his shoulder is weakening with each step. The early morning journey has been a long and tedious trudge over two steep ridgelines in his return to Bethany.

David's body is no imposing force but the added muscle over the last few years is definitely noticeable. The carcass that he painfully drags behind him, however, seems to have tripled in weight since the night's journey began.

The sprawling green pasture below finally comes into view as David crests the ridgeline that wraps the back side of Bethany like a towering city wall. The relief that the descent provides his muscles is almost as rewarding as his timing. The sun has yet to rise, and if he keeps this pace he will surely arrive before Benaiah makes his way to the porch, perfect for the surprise that he has been working on.

David grips the rope with renewed energy and presses on through the exhaustion with one thought driving his will.

Benaiah is going to be thrilled.

28

The Negev desert is a brutal land just south of Judah that acts as the gateway to Egypt. Its harsh mountains and extremely dry landscape serve as a border, a warning, for one of the most barbaric nomadic tribes and enemies of Israel, the Amalekites, known across the Arabian trade route from Babylon to Egypt as ruthless. The scribes in Amarna, the same scribes that documented the Exodus and the movement of Joshua into the Promised Land, also named these violent nomads.

Khabbati.

Plunderers, Samuel thinks, reminding himself of the Egyptian name as he steps over the unmistakable line where the foliage ends and the dry desert begins.

Not that he needs a reminder of their reputation. During the exodus from Egypt, it was the Amalekites that slaughtered many of the exhausted Hebrews, mostly women and children, who were lagging behind during the long, tiresome journey through these lands.

Moses warned the Hebrews to never forget and Samuel hasn't, nor will he. It was his last communication with Saul, to never forget. Since then, and with the miracle victory in Michmash, the king has been on a rampage, inflicting punishment upon every enemy, the last of which was Amalek.

No one travels this far south without an army, much less alone, and yet here he is, alone. Saul marched with no less than two hundred thousand by his side, ten thousand alone were the valiant warriors of Judah, and Samuel can see the evidence of their visit. Black smoke billows in the distance, ensuring his travels farther south should be relatively safe.

He crests the hilltop but the smoke is gone. There is no city, no homes, and no army. His mind races for an answer, but there isn't one. It makes no sense. Part of his memory has vanished. He can't even recall how he traveled this far south or why he has done it alone. He stands looking across the empty landscape, his mind muddled with no answer in sight.

Booming thunder rolls across the clear sky. Clouds quickly appear overhead and the thunder begins to speak. Samuel is stunned at the voice rumbling from the sky but he knows it well. As it fills the air around him, he recognizes the familiar voice of Yahweh.

"I regret that I have made Saul king, for he has turned back from following Me, and has not carried out My commands." Lightning cracks and the sky flashes white.

And with a gasp, Samuel awakes inside his cramped stone room in the city of Ramah, his eyes full of tears. The experience was so real, like it always is. But this time the message, the tone, was different. It was clear, Saul will be dealt with. Whatever he has done it must have been drastic.

Samuel rises to his feet.

I need to find Saul.

29

Beads of black sweat slide down Saul's arm and drip from his elbow. His dry linens stick to his damp skin with his every move. It's a feeling that he typically detests, but today, even as the black soot that fell from the sky coats his body in a dark grimy paste, he doesn't mind. Today, it is the ashes of the enemy coating his flesh in victory.

He would have rather bathed following the battle, but the people must see that he was part of the carnage. No longer will the army lose confidence and turn from him. The nation will hear of this slaughter and they will know that Saul, their king, led them into victory against the wicked.

Pride wells up inside of him as he thinks of the monument that he ordered on his route home to be erected in Carmel in honor of what he had done to Amalek. But nothing could bring more pride than gloating to the man now approaching from the distance. He owes everything to Samuel. And yet, Saul reminds himself, he is still the king and must be perceived as such. He stands tall, arching his shoulders back.

"Victory," Saul says. "We are just as you said we would be. Blessed are you for I have done what you've said."

Samuel's face doesn't brighten in the least. Instead, he actually scowls.

Saul can't believe his eyes. *He's angry?*

"Have you?" Samuel asks, his focus diverting from Saul. "What then is this bleating of sheep in my ear?"

I have laid vengeance against Amalek and he's concerned about sheep? After all that he has accomplished, Samuel's attitude is extremely frustrating. Anger boiling inside begins to take shape, uncoiling into a string of regretful words. They slip to the edge of his tongue, but he withholds them, concealing what is actually swirling on the inside. Exhaling, he regains his composure.

"The people have spared only the best for a sacrifice to the Lord, of course," Saul says, hoping for some acknowledgment. Samuel's countenance doesn't waver. "I can see that you are not pleased. What of my kingdom would you have me give as my repayment?"

"It is not what I will take that should be of your concern." Samuel turns toward Saul. "I say unto you that to obey is greater than to sacrifice. To listen is greater than the fat of rams. For you have rejected the Lord this day and this day the Lord has rejected you as king."

How dare he ignore what I have done here!

Saul reacts on impulse when Samuel turns to leave. His mind warns him against it but it's too late. The anger, the pain, and the insecurity all rush to the surface in a second's display of recklessness. Saul grabs the hem of Samuel's robe and instantly regrets it.

Samuel stops but doesn't turn. His calmness is more terrifying than a violent man's anger, especially when Saul realizes what he has done. He feels the frayed piece of Samuel's hem still pinched between his fingers.

Samuel remains still with his back to the king when he delivers his message with firmness. "As you have torn my garment so has God torn the kingdom of Israel from you this day and has given it to a neighbor of yours. One who is greater than you, the strength of all Israel."

Saul drops the torn cloth and feels not only the garment but the kingdom slipping through his fingers. Samuel's prophecies come rushing to his memory. From Saul's anointing to become king, to Amalek being sieged, Samuel's words have yet to be wrong. Saul knows that he can't let Samuel leave with only that being said. There must be another way.

"So I have sinned. Honor me now, I beg you! Take from me what you will."

Samuel looks off toward the land that has brought forth such heartbreak and destruction to his people. The instruction was clear. Blot out the name of Amalek.

"Bring forth Agag," Samuel says.

He watches as Saul orders the King of Amalek before him. Saul's countenance has relaxed.

He thinks he's getting a second chance.

With a soldier on each arm, King Agag is brought before the notorious prophet and Judge of Israel. Samuel knows how he must be perceived now that he has long passed his youth, and the grin on King Agag's face confirms that thought. He drops to his knees, seemingly thankful that a prophet has summoned him instead of a bloodthirsty king.

"Surely the bitterness of death has passed, great prophet," he says with a mocking conceit laced with the harsh Amalekite dialect.

Samuel looks into the king's eyes. The oral stories that were passed down of women and children slaughtered, raped, and terrorized by this very bloodline boil up inside of him.

Do not forget, he tells himself.

He unsheathes King Saul's sword when he pulls it from his hip, surprising even the surrounding soldiers. His old age has removed him from leading the charge of war but he has not lost his edge.

"As your sword has made women childless, so shall your mother be childless among women."

Samuel raises the sword. It's heavier than it used to be. He focuses on Agag's neck but can't help but notice the dumbfounded look on his face. Maybe this will send a message to Saul. It seems to already have sent one to Agag.

Gripping the handle tight with both hands, he strikes downward with precision and force.

30

Blood oozes onto the chopping block as the knife chops down through raw meat. David watches from the porch as Benaiah's mother squeezes the red juice from the goat breast in preparation for the night's meal. Instead of barging in and interrupting as Benaiah's family finishes their routine chores, David dips out the front door and lowers down into the shade, alone.

From the porch, his view of the rolling green hills wrapped by the sprawling fence is a reminder that although he may be often overlooked there is still good even in the hard times. He can always find the good in things. He has realized that it just depends on perspective.

His life, once full of solitude, has become a perfect blend of self-reflecting and self-testing of his young strength. He has learned a lot over the last few years about his body, his mind, and his faith. Gratefulness has become the key to his joy, even in the darkness when he feels as if he's wandering the wilderness of life like the Israelites on their return to the Promised Land. Something deep within him screams to be let out, but what?

The day has finally come for Benaiah to leave. He will soon be gone, fighting with the armies, doing what he does best, and David knows that all will quickly return to normal for him.

The thoughts creep in, slowly they begin to take root and drag his mind down into darkness. Thoughts of loneliness and mediocrity, a life lived in the shadows or worse, a life forgotten, now weighs down his spirit. The speed at which fear can grip one's thoughts always surprises David.

It's much like the ten spies that all scouted the same land and returned with conflicting outlooks. After forty years of wandering the wilderness and four centuries of slavery, the Hebrews were ready to return to the land full of milk and honey, their Promised Land, their home, but the spies returned with a horrific report of giants that scoured the landscape. Fear swept through the entire camp.

Only two of the spies are still remembered today. David believes it is because they were the only two in the camp without fear. It is the reason Joshua and Caleb remain two of his favorite figures.

David's heart quickens in his chest. The thought of those two names, immortalized now throughout history, sparks a passion. Deep down he knows that he would have stood with them, strong and unwavering against the giants, standing strong with Yahweh, but those days are gone. Besides, no one will know his name; shepherds are not spoken of throughout the generations.

The darkness creeps in again.

David plucks a chord and lets the vibration penetrate his chest. Using the best weapon he has against fear, he places his lyre tight against him. Again he plucks a chord. The vibration overtakes his focus and his fingers react on muscle memory. He lets go and focuses on one thing, thankfulness.

As usual, his playing transports him from the porch to a place far from the worries and fears of this world, a place where comfort and peace abound. It is refreshing but short-lived. The sound of a sandal sliding against the wooden threshold draws David back to the porch. Benaiah emerges from the doorway and sits next to him quietly, attempting to not disrupt him. Now aware of his audience, David slows his play to a halt. They both stare out into the field without a word spoken.

Benaiah shifts uncomfortably before breaking the silence. "David, why have you never stayed within the safety of our gates?"

David knew that has always bothered Benaiah, but he would rather not get into the lengthy explanation. He decides to ask a question that he's wanted to ask for years. "What was your father like?"

"I've taught you everything he ever taught me," Benaiah responds without much thought.

David lowers the lyre. Sensing that Benaiah's pain is as callused as his own, he prods again, searching for the answer. "No... I mean, what was he like?"

"He would have wanted you to stay within our gates for a night," Benaiah says, standing. His attention is diverted as he leaps off the porch and runs to see the hanging carcass that dangles from the fence. "You stalked this?"

"I would have loved to have met him," David says, standing to join Benaiah.

"He would have been proud of you, David." Benaiah slowly turns the dangling wolf. "You know, he used to say men are much easier. They just require different bait." His hands comb through the fur as the wolf turns, as if he's inspecting it. "You can become the predator as opposed to the prey simply by the bait you choose. If you choose correctly, the predator will be so focused on what is in front of him he will neglect what is to the side of him.

Benaiah stops spinning the wolf in time to notice the long laceration across its neck. But David's attention has been diverted. Benaiah's mumbled words fade off, having failed to keep his interest, but Ezsri's grin from the doorway is more than captivating. His stomach feels like its crawling up into his shoulders, and his legs have become feeble. He grins, holding enough of his smile back to appear relaxed instead of how he truly feels in her presence. Awestruck.

"David?" Benaiah snaps, attempting to break David's trance.

David senses the quick movement from Benaiah and anticipates his strike. He parries his hand downward and blocks Benaiah's incoming fist.

"I understand what he meant," David says, beating Benaiah to his own punchline. "And sometimes playing vulnerable can be just as good for bait."

David glances toward Benaiah who still hasn't found the words to respond.

"You have taught me very well," David says with a smile.

31

Traveling south on the hill road toward Hebron, Samuel begins to recall the familiar sights of Judah as he travels through the most southern tribal territory. It has been years since he has ventured this far south. But the view of Mt. Moriah, a city rich in Hebraic history, in the distance is a sure sign that he is getting close to his destination. The caravan slows as a few of the merchants depart the now dwindling line of travelers. Samuel straightens a bit, knowing the severity, the danger of his current mission. The next stop on the trade route is Beit Lehem, the house of bread, Bethlehem.

Samuel listens to the numbing rhythm of camel feet pounding the ground below him. His mind is deep in thought. For the last few days he has let the dismal future of the nation weigh him down. Without the people willing to be led and without a king to lead them, he can only imagine their fate once he passes on. He is well aware that this life is not his final stop. It is a testing ground, just as Job experienced, for the eternal life that follows. God has rejected Saul as king and now it is Samuel who must head south to establish Yahweh's will.

His chest tightens under the burden of what he is about to do as he lays eyes on the small town nestled amongst the ridges.

If Saul finds out what I'm about to do, he will have my head, Samuel thinks. *Nevertheless, I must do what I have been told. Find the boy.*

⊹⟫⟨⊹

David stares at Benaiah, wishing that the time hadn't come but knowing that it's finally here.

"Well, I guess this is goodbye," David says, standing firm.

Benaiah laughs, placing his hand on David's shoulder. "I'll be home before harvest. I have a responsibility here you know."

David attempts a smile, but he's not sure it worked. The last four years have been a blur, and now he will again be on his own to study and train in the forests.

"I'll look forward to it. Take it easy on those warriors at the palace. They won't be expecting a boy to fight like a man, you know."

Benaiah laughs. "I will see you soon."

David looks to the porch. Ezsri leans against the threshold, watching, possibly waiting for her goodbye. Every fiber in his being tells him to go say something. To tell her how beautiful she is but it's too late. It would be dishonorable to Benaiah, the man of the house, not to mention awkward at this point. This period of his life is over and there is no use hanging on. He doesn't hold back the disappointment in his face as he turns toward the hillside.

Something tells him that he won't be back, so he focuses forward, straining against a tempting glance over his shoulder for one last sight of Ezsri. Besides, the sun is almost centered in the sky and Bethlehem is still a few hours away. He reasons for a moment and then instinct takes over. He turns for nothing more than a glimpse, and he's glad he did.

She's still looking.

Samuel dismounts and approaches the small town with a heifer tightly reined by his side. He knows that no one could possibly know why he is here, or the severity of the situation, but still he would rather remain undetected.

Maybe no one will notice my presence, he tells himself.

Just as the hope of remaining unrecognized passes through his mind, he spots a group of elders congregating ahead, and his optimism vanishes just as quickly as it came. He takes a deep breath and recalls what Yahweh instructed him to say.

The eldest of the town hesitantly steps forward to greet Samuel. The others are visibly shaken by his presence.

News travels fast across this land, Samuel thinks, recalling his most recent action against an Amalekite king.

"Please, let your presence be not of despair. Have you come peaceably?"

"I have only a word. It is not my choice to decide its reception," Samuel says, hoping he portrayed more confidence than he felt.

"Who are you here to see, great prophet?"

Samuel pauses feeling more transparent than the seawater along the coast of Dor.

There is no way that they could possibly know why I'm here, he reminds himself.

Still, the words escape him. Being a prophet and a judge he is used to saying that which is difficult, demanding, and even grim. This attempt at being discreet is foreign, to say the least. He knows that if he says what his true intentions are that Saul will kill both him and the child he seeks.

I'm here to anoint the next king of Israel, is all he can think to say. He stands motionless, at a loss for words.

Then, as if provoked from above, the heifer to his side tugs the reins, reminding Samuel what Yahweh instructed him to say to ensure that no one finds out the true reason of his visit.

"In peace I have come to sacrifice to the Lord. Come with me."

Samuel hands the reins of the heifer to the eldest and enters the village.

Now to find Jesse, the son of Obed.

32

David maneuvers his flock through the dense forest, every step coming closer to his least favorite location that he has named "The Crossing."

The large cedar trees that shade the landscape in a dark haze, even under the midday sun, are a sign that he's not far from the dangers lurking ahead. After years of trekking around, avoiding The Crossing, he decides that today, with the fast-moving sun above, he has no other option. The rumbling of thunder off in the distance to the east is a clear indication that the typically predictable weather is about to take a turn for the worse, and The Crossing happens to be the clear-cut path from Bethany to Bethlehem.

Each step becomes slower, more mindful than the last, as instinct takes over. As the gradual incline of the hillside, littered with boulders, appears, his senses have heightened to an all-time high.

His breathing steadies, his eyes scan every cleft, and he listens for the most subtle movement. It doesn't take long before his fears are confirmed. The territorial lion has not migrated over the years. It has remained somewhere in the darkness, leaving only paw prints as evidence.

David leans down, placing his fingers into the indention in the soft soil.

They're fresh.

Tracking the prints with his eyes, he follows them to exactly where he was hoping they wouldn't go, up the incline, vanishing into the rocky overlook.

There is no turning back at this point. With a storm approaching from the rear and a lion watching somewhere from the front, David knows that to turn now would be choosing suicide. But to press forward would be begging for it. He scans the area for any advantage the terrain will provide him. With not enough brush to hide his flock in the midst of the cedar trees, he boldly improvises. He settles his entire flock out in the open, perfectly visible from the hillside of boulders. David prepares for the inevitable. Today, he will put his training to the test.

The heat of the fire is unbearable with his priestly garments layered upon his body. Samuel takes a step back as the sacrificed heifer is engulfed with flames. The elders have arrived, and as with a small town where there is not much entertainment, the presence of such a highly esteemed judge and prophet has garnered a growing crowd of locals.

Just what I need more spectators, Samuel thinks as he fears the repercussion of anyone finding out his true intentions.

He has begun the very specific process of consecrating the elders and the town when he lays eyes on those he has come to see. Jesse, the son of Obed, and his boys, stand on the fringes of the gathering. Their presence halts Samuel for the moment as he gazes over each of them, his mind wandering freely, trying to decide which one it could be. The crackle of the fire quickly reminds him that now is neither the place nor the time.

Samuel cuts the sacrifice and partakes of the meat, as the high priest does during the end of any consecration. He stays in reverence longer than usual and when he opens his eyes and stands up, the crowd that gathered has mostly dispersed. Samuel grabs Jesse's arm before he can depart.

"Thank you for coming," Samuel says. "Now, join me for a moment with your eldest in the shrine."

Samuel enters and stands in front of the altar toward the back of the shrine, waiting for Jesse's eldest son to enter. He unslings the horn filled with oil from his neck and clears his mind. Often, the horn filled with oil is used to separate one called to fulfill a divine office as chosen by God, such as a high priest, a prophet, or a patriarch. Today, however, only Samuel and Yahweh know the reason for this anointing. That the oil poured from this horn will not be for any of these, but for a calling much greater, so great in fact that there can only be room for one anointed among the nation.

The anointing of a king.

The door creaks open and Jesse, the son of Obed, the father of the child that Samuel has traveled here to find enters with his eldest son.

"My son, Eliab, great prophet," Jesse says proudly.

Eliab is tall, his muscles are defined, and he walks with confidence. In his early twenties he has already seen battle and is ripe in age to learn the office. By all accounts he looks the part. Knowing that he is a perfect fit, Samuel reaches for the horn of oil.

Surely, this is the son, the one I am to anoint as king, he thinks as he prepares for the consecration.

33

Thunder rumbles in the distance, reminding David that he is running out of time. With his wooden staff clenched under his arm and a sharp stone pinched between his fingers, he prepares for the encounter that seems to be inevitable. He slides the edge of the stone across the bottom of his staff in rapid succession to sharpen the tip of a makeshift spear. The cedar trees towering high above have just begun swaying under the gusts of the storm blowing in, and the sound of bleating sheep echoes like a dinner bell calling for an easy meal.

The bait has been set.

David glances up. Beams of sunlight shower through the canopy to the forest floor. The time of day and the season, he remembers, puts the arcing sun on a direct path to the opening in the canopy directly above.

The beast finally emerges through the thin golden rays. The unmistakable shadow of the intimidating hunter prowls from the distance. It is the same scenario playing out before him as it did four years ago. This time, however, he knows that the lion won't be hesitant. He will go for the kill. David slows his breathing and watches through the brush.

Keep coming.

⊹≒⟨⟩≒⊹

Samuel stares at Eliab. He lifts the horn of oil to anoint the young man but an image of Saul's face flashes before him. Samuel freezes, his arm locked, outstretched in the air. The Presence of Yahweh overwhelms his body but not with warmth or comfort as usual, but instead, a cold shiver sweeps across his bones and for good reason.

This is not the son.

Without warning, as a true prophet, the words escape Samuel's mouth and he is reminded that this is not his decision to make. "It is not his stature or appearance that I have come to see. Bring to me the next in line."

Samuel lowers the horn back to his side and sits down, knowing that he has just spoken the words of God. Yahweh has made it clear. This decision is not to be taken lightly or with only what can be seen by the eyes.

Jesse cracks open the door and waves the next son to enter. Abinadab stands before Samuel, then Shimea, Nethanel, Raddai, and Ozem each take their turn, and Samuel rejects them in succession as they appear. Finally, Jesse calls in the youngest and final son.

He enters slowly, hesitantly approaching Samuel who knows instantly that this is not the son. Samuel doesn't even stand.

This doesn't make sense.

The instruction was clear and yet all seven sons failed to be the chosen one. Samuel sits quietly, clearing his thoughts. He knows that this trip wasn't an accident. It *is* one of Jesse's sons, but which.

"The Lord has chosen none of them for his anointing today. All of your sons are here?"

Jesse's long, awkward pause is reassuring to Samuel.

Jesse clears his throat. "Yes... well, there is yet the youngest. He is tending the…"

"Send for him." Samuel's voice makes it clear that he is agitated. And yet inside, relieved.

34

Stretching farther than the eye can see in both directions, the white sandy coastline of Ashdod is one of the longest continuous beaches of Philistia. Its port is a strategic necessity, allowing access for incoming supplies and a thriving fishing trade, but more importantly, raider ships returning from plunder with newly acquired riches. One of only three main Philistine city-states located on the shore of the Great Sea, it has become Kilech's favorite place to spend his time.

He digs his feet deep into the sand, closes his eyes, and listens to the ocean waves crashing against the shore. The occasional squawk of a seagull flying overhead makes him feel at home, but he's not sure why. He has never been to the Aegean Islands but he imagines that they must be exactly like this.

The stress of his daily requirements evaporates in the warm breeze. He has tried to become a warrior but his effort has only brought more disappointment. Shortly after his escape following the defeat of Michmash, Kilech was rescued by a retreating band of Philistines heading for Ekron. The bruises and blood that covered him led the soldiers to believe that he was a fearless warrior, but Kilech knew there was nothing farther from the truth. He wasn't, however, going to let the truth stop him from being rescued.

The image of that man, that demon man, killing and murdering directly in front of him has yet to allow him a single night of restful sleep even after all these years. Although he has been deemed, and is still considered, a worthless warrior, it hasn't stopped Kilech from training.

One day I will get my chance, he thinks.

Just as the naked flesh of women consumes the minds of the warriors throughout the day, revenge eats at his every thought. It is the only force that can carry him through the daily anxiety that builds with every order shouted. He knows that he is not built physically or mentally like these men. The loudness, the anger, and the abuse are often more than he can handle. And if it weren't for the fact that he can read and write he is certain that he would have been sent to Gath.

Gath, the fifth of the city-states, is known for its ruthless and barbaric practices. Often, warriors that are deemed worthless, pathetically weak, or timid, essentially those that are identical to Kilech, are taken there to become a blood-tasting. The ritual is meant for the young warriors that show significant promise, but have yet to see the field of battle. They are often brought the weaker, useless men to kill as a passage, an initiation into their brutal way of life.

Kilech thinks of the young boys that have already spilled blood, often innocent blood and yet here he is at the age of eighteen and he still has yet to even strike a man. It's embarrassing. It does not pay to be intelligent. He knows how the men look at him.

"Scribe!" a voice shouts from behind.

Instantly, the anxiety rushes back to his chest. The tranquility of the beach is over. He turns and sprints toward the silhouette in the distance that continues to shout for him.

"You better run to me as fast as you retreat if you ever want to escape from another battle, you worthless Hebrew sympathizer."

Hebrew sympathizer?

Kilech has been called many things, but a Hebrew sympathizer is blasphemy. Even though the words dig deep he does what he always does. He keeps his mouth shut and shows no emotion.

"Yes, sir?"

Now standing face-to-face, the man is no longer a silhouette. He is old and leather-skinned, with eyes that have no life in them, eyes that stare directly through Kilech as if digging for his most protected secrets. His coarse face is covered in old scars and his thin frame somehow appears more powerful than that of an ox.

Please don't kill me, is all Kilech can think.

"Grab your gear, we're heading south."

South?

"Yes, sir," Kilech says.

He turns to leave but the man grabs his arm. Internalizing his pain, Kilech focuses on not collapsing to the ground. Even if his legs give way, he is convinced that the firm grip on his arm would keep him upright.

"You had better be moving with a purpose, scribe. King Achish requested you, not me. If you hold me up, trust me, you'll beg to become a sacrifice."

Kilech's body goes numb. *Achish? What evil have I done to receive such an order?*

His mind screams *RUN,* but for some reason he doesn't, or maybe he can't. He stands motionless, his mind and body disconnected, one pleading for death, the other terrified of it. Both are in complete shock at the command, the now inevitable future. A future that not only requires reporting to a king, but the king of the most feared Philistine city in the land.

Gath.

35

Abinadab searches for answers as to where David might be as he races deeper into the dense forest. David was set to be home just past midday and that time is rapidly approaching.

He can't be far.

Abinadab wants to shout for his brother, but he knows better. This far from home he fears announcing his position to a possible Amalekite scout or Philistine mercenary moving through the area. He knows the farther you stray from civilization the more likely you are to come into contact with an enemy that is always scouting. He reminds himself that his youngest brother does this daily, with dozens of bleating sheep, without fear. But the fact that the judge and prophet of the nation is waiting for his presence compels Abinadab to overcome his better judgment.

"David!" he yells as he pushes deeper into the brush.

He continues to shout David's name until a rustling catches his ear. He stops dead in his tracks, attempting to listen, but he's breathing too loud to hear anything. He raises his axe and creeps toward the brush where he heard the sound. With his panting heavy, his heart pounding, and his grip on the weapon strained, he quickly swipes aside the branches, revealing the cause of the jostling leaves.

Two surprised rodents dart away from his feet, vanishing into a dark cave he now faces. With a hesitant voice, Abinadab calls into the cave for David but only an echo responds. Stepping back, he exhales, thankful that there was no real threat. But before his tense muscles can relax, he hears a snap beneath his feet and it's not a stick. Hesitantly, he glances down.

The leaves have shifted, revealing a large spread of bones around him. The ribcage which curls up like a claw is massive. It's the obvious remains of a bear, but with a skeletal structure so large and perfectly intact that Abinadab wonders what could have killed it. He leans down and picks up the large skull. He doesn't have to look hard to figure it out. Lodged deep between the eyes is a smooth stone, one that looks eerily familiar.

"David!"

✦══✦══✦

Prowling slowly down the boulders, the lion nears David's position. David, staring through the brush, knows that he is concealed, but it still feels as if the lion's eyes are penetrating the foliage with a stare that David will never forget. Maybe the lion remembers him and is back for revenge? David knows better. The lion's attention is certainly fixated on the easy prey.

Stay still, stay steady, David tells himself.

David draws long, slow breaths. He relaxes his grip on the staff to conserve his strength if the opportunity to strike presents itself.

The rays of sunlight still move in a twinkling shower of orange brilliance. Each beam stretches toward him, like the sun shining to the sea floor, as it rises toward the open canopy.

Twenty paces.

The lion passes the line of no return. The stalking is over. He is moving in for a kill.

Fifteen paces.

David is closer than he has ever been to an animal of such sheer power. He is astounded by the stealth of something of such size. It is the perfect hunter. David watches closely, preparing… studying.

Unexpectedly, the lion stops, his paw raised just above the ground. Apparently, something has caught his attention. The foliage surrounding David suddenly feels transparent as the lion's eyes lock on him as if he were completely exposed. He holds his breath, his chest pounding. He stands perfectly still, trusting his instinct.

A rustling of sticks and leaves behind David quickly overtakes the silence. Something is approaching from his rear.

"David!" Abinadab's voice rings through the forest.

Abinadab? David can't believe his ears. *What is he doing?*

His soul screams to flee from the shell of his rigid body, tearing, clawing, attempting to escape to protect his brother from the danger, but there is nothing that he can do. Not now.

The lion stands perfectly still, his eyes scan slowly under his lowered brow.

"David!"

David recoils at the sound of his brother's voice.

Just stop! David's mind can't scream loud enough.

His conscience is thrashing inside like a caged animal, but he knows the only way to save his brother is to remain silent… and wait.

Abinadab finally stops but it's too late. He stands directly between the lion and its prey, the sheep now bleating in response to the new threat. Abinadab looks as if he has run into a solid rock wall as he makes eye contact with the beast. It lets out a low, booming snarl that rumbles across the forest floor, a reverberating threat of what is soon to come.

Abinadab has just become the prey.

David tightens his grip on the staff as the rays of sun slowly climb toward the hole in the canopy. His gaze returns to the lion, its muscles now contracting, and its claws gripping into the soil.

David is out of time.

The lion pounces, letting out a thundering roar, and David fears that he won't be quick enough. Abinadab has pulled the lion's approach too far past David's ambush point. If he charges now, he will be exposed for too long, giving the lion just enough time to adjust.

Quickly processing his options, he realizes that there is only one.

David reacts, emerging from the brush, his strength coiled behind his staff. The lion is fast, massive. He'll never get a clean strike. Abinadab is frozen with fear as the lion hurls through the air. David prepares to thrust the staff when the lion suddenly disappears.

The sun reaches the open canopy in the trees, pouring a luminescent barrier of light from above like a wall of shimmering gold, concealing David's charge across the open ground, but also turning the muscular killer into a ghost.

Right on time!

In a full sprint, David focuses just forward of Abinadab's throat, attempting to intersect the lion's trajectory. The golden curtain of light will either be an asset or certain death. David has no time to fear, no time to miss. He closes his eyes and imagines the lion barreling down. He thrusts his staff with all of his might into the air, but feels no resistance.

A miss?

Then, in an instant, it feels as if the tip of his staff connects with the side of a mountain. Opening his eyes, David sees the lion emerging from the light. He thrusts hard until his arms are fully extended. The force of the lion's weight rips the staff from David's grip and something hard, something forceful, hits him from the side, sending him to the ground.

A terrifying series of roars emanate from inside the dust cloud next to him where Abinadab once stood. All David can see is the top of the lion when the plume clears. It is directly on top of his brother, who is now covered in blood… when the chaos turns silent. David fears the worst.

You killed my brother, David thinks.

The thought releases a rage inside David that he has never felt before as he races toward the lion.

With unprecedented strength, the beast lunges forward, grasping the nearby sheep in its jaws. It staggers to stand, clearly shaken up, but before it can move David is upon it. With its thick mane clutched in his fist, David takes hold of a branch at his feet and swings. Again and again he swings until the lion's warm crimson liquid covers his flesh and the sheep is released.

The lion no longer resists, and with one glance it is obvious why. The staff has penetrated the thick neck, severing the vessel carrying its life's blood and lodging itself up into the jaw, hindering the lion's most fatal weapon.

As the lion's muscles relax, David emerges from somewhere he's never been before. The rage that arose without warning and consumed him now crawls back from wherever it came. His years of training and protective instincts have for the first time erupted in an untamed display of violence.

A groan from Abinadab pulls David's thoughts to his brother. A rush of power surges through David's body. He grabs Abinadab's shoulders, pulling him up with relief. His brother winces in pain. Deep claw marks run down his arms. Dark red blood oozes from under his tattered clothing.

"You all right?"

Abinadab slowly nods his head, staring at the lion that lies motionless. His mouth opens but he is unable to speak.

"You almost got yourself killed," David says, patting his brother on the back.

Abinadab stares at David's staff lodged deep in the lion, then directly into David's eyes. He seems to gaze straight through him. His throat quivers as if he's about to throw up.

Again Abinadab's mouth opens. This time he is able to push out the unsteady words. "You need to go home."

36

Black clouds roll across the southern hill country of Judah in the distance. Saul watches from his balcony, unable to shake the feeling that it is a foreboding sign of what Samuel had declared.

The rains are coming and the storm is bringing about the darkness.

Yet, it is south, far south. It seems only the winds will reach Gibeah. Possibly it *is* a sign. Maybe there is still a chance to save his throne. Perhaps Samuel was giving a severe warning of a rising danger.

A motion below catches his eye.

What is he still doing here?

"Abner."

Abner stops. He turns around slowly. "My king?"

His cousin and commanding general was supposed to have already returned to his living quarters. But Saul knows how committed he is and it appears that he is still roaming the palace, keeping the guards in line.

He never stops.

Saul could use the experienced general's thoughts anyway. He always has a plan for war, and right now Saul just needs a plan. He motions for the general to join him.

The stone room inside the shrine of Bethlehem continues to darken as the rain now batters against the roof. Samuel feels a pull on his spirit as if the winds have shifted their direction. He knows that something is coming. He leans back, eyes closed, and enjoys the moment. His fear of Saul finding out what is taking place drifts away finally and his body relaxes.

The door swings open, filling the room with an encroaching shadow of darkening skies. A boy enters, out of breath, his drenched, ragged clothes soon forming a puddle under his feet. Samuel's first thought is that he must be a wanderer, a boy lost along a journey and looking for shelter, but the heat that has engulfed his body is sending a much different message.

This is the one.

A burning peace that nestles deep in Samuel's gut confirms that this young, ragged boy is the chosen child that he has traveled here to see. He knows that this is a secret that for now will remain with him only. No one can know the truth, not yet. This boy wouldn't make it a day if word got out. The kingdom would descend upon him before he even got cleaned up if anyone were to hear of an anointed king.

Samuel stands with the horn in hand. The boy wipes his hair to the side as he steps forward. He is ruddy and unpolished but it has already been made clear that the outward appearance means nothing. Samuel notices some of the brothers failing to hold back their smirks.

As he raises the horn above the boys head, the smirks disappear.

"This is he, the one not I but Yahweh has chosen."

Samuel tilts the horn.

✦══╪══✦

Yahweh has chosen?

David has no time to react. He feels the first drop of oil, followed by the flow of warm liquid pouring over his head, and then it happens. The smooth liquid is penetrates through his skin faster with each passing moment until his entire core ignites with a blazing heat like the morning sun is burning him from the inside out. His body feels cleansed and his mind refreshed. He senses a father's love that sadly he has never felt before, but still it seems oddly familiar somehow.

What is happening to me?

The feeling of weightlessness is a welcome sensation, since his legs are exhausted. Mundane thoughts pass away and a joy, an unexplained exhilaration toward the future, explodes within. The years of longing for an encounter with the creator of all existence appears to have finally taken place and in the most unlikely of ways.

The closest that David has come to this experience is when he has played the lyre for hours. But this occasion is on a whole new level. It is as if something is being placed upon him. He can almost feel the coat or blanket wrapping him when his senses return to this world.

Voices mumble from the corner of the room.

"David, the one?" one voice whispers.

"The one for what?" another says.

David's brothers murmur against the wall. He would look but the numbness in his body has yet to fully dissipate. He has no idea what, but something significant has just happened and he does not want it to end.

Abinadab stumbles into the shrine, not realizing the silent reverence taking place until he has caught every eye. Awkwardly, he gathers himself and searches the shadows for his brothers. They are standing motionless in awe, but their blank stares are quickly diverted to his open wounds and bloody clothes. Abinadab ignores their hand gestures as each of them motion him over. They obviously have questions; Abinadab knows that he surely does. He is still in shock at what just happened with the lion. Maybe more unbelievable is the oil dripping down David's face.

What is happening?

Abinadab stares, watching David as he tries to put all the pieces together in his mind. Then he witnesses something that makes him question his own eyesight, a flash of color across David's eyes that is more telling than anything he could ever want to accept. He won't accept it.

It is an instant that explains everything without a single word being said. The prophet, the oil, the private anointing, and now David's eyes confirm the unthinkable. Abinadab pretends that he never saw it, but he has a feeling that the look on his face is telling a very different story.

David a king?

37

Gazing from his view high above the territory of Benjamin, Saul looks off, mesmerized by the lightning flashes in the storm clouds to the south. Abner enters the balcony and steps to his side.

"Samuel has led me to believe that my throne is in jeopardy," Saul says.

Abner leans back. "Is that right?" The lightning strikes over Judah draw both of their eyes to the distance. "I will keep an eye out for Jonathan. If anyone is to threaten the throne it is your son. One who possesses the heart of the people."

Possesses the heart, the words sit heavy on Saul as he recalls the exact phrase used by Samuel.

He knows that Abner is right. If anyone is going to rise to power and threaten his throne it will be Jonathan. Saul turns to Abner.

"Good."

Abner prepares to speak but Saul notices that he stops short. Something about Saul has caused Abner to pause. He knows that Abner, a seasoned general and warrior, has never had a shortage of words. Abner stares just long enough for Saul to notice the intensity with which he's looking into…

My eyes?

Abner breaks eye contact quickly but not before throwing Saul's conscience into panic.

"What do you perceive, general? You are my most trusted."

Abner glances back, looking lower. "What else has the prophet spoken, my king?"

"Only that the true king is to be threatened. But the challenger is surely to be sought and killed. I, of course shall reign forever."

"Is that all he has said?"

Saul is not used to the slight of speech from Abner. He is usually razor sharp, and right now he would prefer it. "What has provoked your questioning, general?"

"I just perceive that you are grieved, nothing more."

Saul becomes concerned. *How can he perceive that?*

Suddenly, a rush of anxiety crashes over him, rattling his normally steady hands. Abner seems to notice.

"That will be all, general," Saul says, heading for his room.

The spacious room abruptly narrows, blurs, and begins to spin around him. He loses his balance and collapses, crippled by a perfect blend of fear, depression, and anxiety that strikes with a single arrow. His world quickly blackens, his breathing labored. His chest feels like it is being crushed by an invisible boulder.

What is happening to me?

"My king –" Abner grabs him to help him up.

"Get out!" Saul can't contain himself. The pressure squeezing his skull is now too much to bear. He swings his arm, breaking Abner's grip on him. "I said get out!"

His body reacts on impulse under the intense pain. The sound of a door closing seals him into solitude. In an instant he is alone, lying in a heap of misery. The blackness has snuffed out even the faintest of light.

My God, what have you done to me?

38

The silhouette of a tree appears with a flash of lightning as David snaps his wrist forward, releasing a stone. Immediately, shards of wood explode as a branch falls to the ground. David drops another stone into the sling. His mind is searching for answers as his body does what it knows best. His muscle memory has taken over, slinging stone after stone without much thought.

What happened tonight? David wonders.

Another stone, another thud, another branch falls to the ground. David is slinging harder now, paying no attention to the strength of his release.

I know I felt You like never before, he thinks. *What have You called me to be?*

David looks at the stone in his hand. It has become second nature to reload stone after stone without looking. Frustrated, David rubs his callused fingers, wondering what he has been preparing for. He senses that Yahweh is training his hands for more than just the fields, but it just doesn't make sense.

The feeling that he just experienced was like no other. It was far deeper than he has ever felt strumming the lyre, most of all he felt a change. Like the easterly winds blowing in a new season, Yahweh has swept over him. David is sure he felt what others described as a mantle, a calling, being placed upon his shoulders. A separation has taken place, but for what?

As he stands drenched from the night's rain he again feels normal. The overwhelming feeling did not stay, nor did it noticeably change anything except now he is completely segregated from his brothers. The looks on their faces, first laughter and embarrassment, then confusion and anger as the oil poured down his head. He already feels completely separated even from his father. Out of all of his brothers, he was chosen, but for what and why? His mind is overwhelmed with questions. How can a shepherd be used for anything other than herding?

Why can't I feel You close now? Why did You depart so fast?

He turns his attention back to the sling and hurls one more stone through the air, this one powered by frustration.

"Who else knows?" Abinadab asks.

The sudden question startles David. More than being rattled, he's disappointed in himself for being too distracted to be aware of his surroundings. The last thing he wants right now is to talk. He holsters his sling and walks to the tree to pick up his stones.

"David!"

"Knows what?" he snaps back.

Stones are littered all around the tree. One in particular catches David's attention. His last throw has lodged itself deep into the trunk, splintering the wood around it. It serves as a reminder of how powerful he has truly become with his weapon of choice.

"Who you are. And what was that all about? Why would the prophet seek you to be anointed?" Abinadab says, approaching the tree.

"I'm your younger brother and a shepherd. Haven't you heard? That's all I am. It's all I will be. If there is anything more, only God knows. Now I must tend to my sheep as a shepherd would."

"All of your stories were true." Abinadab's tone is sincere. "One day everyone will see what I have seen."

David doesn't know what to think anymore. He feels more alone than before, more confused, more separated. His brothers are warriors, his friend has left for duty, and he is still in the same place he was years ago, possibly the same place that he will always be.

Abinadab's comment was heartfelt, that he could tell, but right now he knows what he needs more than anything.

David heads off into the darkness alone, illuminated only by the distant flashes of lightning. There is only one thing that will comfort him and he knows just where to find it.

39

The silk drapes hanging at Saul's window suddenly blow open with a violent gust of wind. Like a kite losing its push, the drapes fall, and then stop abruptly. They come to rest around an object, an outline of someone standing behind, concealed. The human figure moves forward, creeping out from beneath, letting the fabric slide from their shoulders and fall.

Saul waits, his eyes wide open, his body rigid with fearful anticipation. He watches, waiting for whatever it is to emerge but… nothing. Nothing emerges. He looks around the room, confident of what he has just witnessed, but there is no explanation. Something, someone not made of flesh and bone is standing in the darkness watching him as the lingering breeze ripples his sheets across his body. Maybe it's a spirit, or possibly his vivid imagination playing mind tricks. Maybe he's having another nightmare. Whatever the case, Saul is convinced that he is not alone.

The door to the main hallway creaks open, sending Saul's already throbbing pulse into an irregular beat, double, possibly triple its usual patter. He shifts his gaze, slightly lifting his eyelids to get a glimpse of who is entering at such a late hour. Whoever it is, Saul knows they do not bring good intentions. A silhouette enters and stalks toward his bed.

Jonathan! Saul's heart is crushed.

Saul expected it and yet it still comes as a surprise. How could his own blood seek to murder him? Another figure enters the room behind Jonathan. A woman, her eyes a haunting amber, stands in a cloak watching his son from the doorway. A grin rises on her face as the heir, Saul's own child, unsheathes his sword.

This isn't real! Saul's mind screams out, but to no avail.

Saul is no fool. He grips the blade handle under the sheets to his side as Jonathan raises the sword, his body now pressing against the bed. Saul knows there is no time to waste. He lunges up, grabbing Jonathan behind the neck, pulling him down, thrusting the blade into his chest.

You're losing your mind! Saul knows it's true, but it's too real to stop now.

Saul lets out a shout as he plunges the blade into his own son. Jonathan relaxes, the full weight of his body now pressing down on Saul. The cloaked woman's eyes turn black as she recoils against the wall, vanishing into a breeze that lifts the drapes once again. Saul knows there is nothing he can do. Tears begin streaming down his face.

"My king!" Abner shouts, blasting through the doorway with his sword drawn.

Breathing heavily, Saul scans the room. "Jonathan! He..." Saul, still sitting in bed, grasps his blade in disbelief. "He was just here. He was trying to kill me."

The empty room tells a different story. As Saul's breathing calms, he finds himself unwilling to accept that it was all in his head. No, this experience was a premonition. One sent to him by God, a god, the gods. It doesn't matter who. Not at this point. What matters is that it was sent to protect him, to warn him. Now something must be done.

He stands. "We must finish this."

Abner steps forward, his hands cautiously held out. "Calm down. No one is trying to kill you. Not tonight. You're having night visions, nothing more." Abner places his hands on Saul's shoulders. "Lie back down. I'm not going to let anyone kill you."

Saul looks around the room. His general speaks the truth. It is only the two of them. Saul tries to relax, but then he sees the outline of the invisible figure watching from beneath the drapes.

I'm not losing my mind.

40

David's mind is spinning as he returns to the field that he named Maaneh, the place of his answer. It was here that he met Benaiah, but more importantly it was here that he believed God had left him hungry. Both the quail and Benaiah's mother's home cooking was a sign to remember that even if you don't see Yahweh's hand, he is still in your midst.

Standing now next to the trickling brook, David lets the worries of the world drift away with the current. There are more questions than answers, but just as with the quail he understands that he will never figure it all out. All he must do is trust.

He kneels down on the bank, removing a smooth stone. Cupping his hand with the stone in his palm, David lowers it into a riffle in the brook. The clear water flows in a rhythmic trickle over the top and into the pool downstream where the water becomes smooth as glass and appears to stand still. The sound is calming. He leans back into the refreshing green pasture. He needs this time alone, away from the constant barrage, to renew his mind.

Whatever You have called me to do, in Your Name I will do it.

Closing his eyes, David feels the soft breeze against his skin. His thoughts are at peace. He will not change course now. It may look grim but he knows that the time will come and when it does he will be ready.

41

The constant patter and bouncing of the camel underneath Kilech slows to a crawl. His senses gradually emerge from the nodding, drifting in and out of sleep. His eyes open and he scans the darkness, attempting to understand what has caused the change in speed. As his eyes adjust he notices the steep grade as the small convoy now carefully descends down into the black valley.

Fires speckle the landscape below, like torches illuminating the way into Hades. Booming war drums blend with the shouts of a tribal cadence. The cries and shrieks of grown men rush a sudden and unwanted feeling deep into his gut. It is the darkest hour of the night and the city is raging with violence.

Kilech has heard the legends of Gath and he is hoping that they are just that, legends. The city itself has warriors that are fiercer than the soldiers of any other city-state, but outside, beyond the darkness, is a breed of warriors unlike anything Kilech has ever heard of. They are so frightening and dangerous he has been told that they are separated from the main populace. They are essentially caged, like animals. Unleashed for one reason, war.

The fear that twists in Kilech's stomach at the thought of reporting to the king is only softened by the hope that King Achish will be secluded far from the bloodshed and hopefully in a palace nestled safely in the city.

Kilech turns around and notices the fading lights upon the hilltop. His throat tightens as he realizes his greatest fear is coming true. The city is already behind him.

Where are we –

"We aren't going any closer," a deep voice says from the

darkness. "The rest of us are traveling back to the city."

Kilech doesn't move. He's waiting for someone else to move, someone to laugh because this is a joke, surely this is a joke. But no one moves and no one laughs.

"So get off," the voice yells. "King Achish will be the one with everyone around him inside the big tent."

A foot presses into Kilech's back sending him off balance and onto the ground. The convoy wastes no time turning back up toward the ridge.

They weren't joking.

Kilech had overheard rumors that the army was preparing to move into Judah, but he never considered that he would become a part of it. As the last camel vanishes over the crest, Kilech's gaze turns back toward the ominous sounds of his awaiting horror, the outskirts of Gath.

He presses forward, and with each step his legs get heavier, the drums louder, and the cries more violent. He pushes his hands against his legs to steady them. His body shivers but he's not cold, it is only the dread consuming him from the inside out.

As he nears the chaos surrounding the fires, he spots the large tent that he assumes must be King Achish's. The fright that devours his heart is quickly replaced with a sharp sting shooting down his spine. His back ignites in a blaze of pain as he falls to the ground. Then everything fades to black.

42

Saul looks on as the nation's youth train in hand-to-hand combat in the palace yard. Three hundred boys have reported to be tested and battle trained, hoping to join the army and complete their passage as men. After a rigorous physical examination, two hundred and fifty remain, having been deemed deployable.

As the boys spar, one of them in particular continually stands out above the rest.

Saul can't take his eyes off him. He reminds him of someone familiar but he can't place who.

With an army solely comprised of citizen-soldiers, there is no formal lifelong training. The youth must possess a natural fighting sense by the age of thirteen, or else they will most likely be relegated to the front lines and live a very short life.

This boy, however, seems trained, seasoned.

"It's rare to find a child with such fundamentals," Saul says.

General Abner leans forward. "That would be General Jehoida's son. He will be ready for the ranks soon."

General Jehoida? Saul immediately recalls the boy's father. His mind drifts as he watches the child. Each counter, each strike, brings Saul back to when General Jehoida was in battle. The moves are identical. The boy is a younger, more energetic spitting image of his father, a man who was a valiant, fearless warrior.

"Soon?" Saul says, surprised. "He fights with the same spirit that his father did."

The boy slams a young warrior down, surprising him with his speed and strength.

"From the looks of it, he could fight in the ranks today." Saul laughs at his own comment, enjoying the young aggression. "Bring him here."

General Abner sends for him. As he does, Saul's attention is diverted. Jonathan enters and immediately begins adjusting techniques and instructing. Every eye watches him, the young and untested, as well as the seasoned and battle-hardened alike. Saul can tell that they are mesmerized by his experience, fearlessness, and charm.

He has it all, Saul thinks.

Jonathan's laugh spreads like a wildfire. Every one laughs at his jokes and straightens when he turns their way. Saul can't remember the last time anyone gazed at him the way the warriors look at Jonathan.

They respect him, he realizes.

General Jehoida's son kneels before Saul. "Benaiah the son of Jehoida of Kabzeel, reporting as ordered, my lord."

Saul is oblivious to anything but Jonathan. He watches his every move, his mannerisms, his smile, his command of attention. "How can a father not trust his own son?"

"My king, my wish is to honor you even until death as my father has."

Saul refocuses on the boy kneeling in front of him. "Not you, my son." He forces a laugh to lighten his pain. "I speak of the evil that plagues my mind."

"Then, my king, may your mind be renewed and may you live forever," Benaiah says.

A faint but natural smile emerges on Saul as he studies Jehoida's son. The boy is talented but obviously still innocent, still optimistic. "If only it was that easy."

"Perhaps I may have a solution, my lord."

"Do not speak to the king unless spoken to," General Abner says, moving to intervene.

Saul stretches his hand forward, holding back the wrath of his general. He is intrigued more than anything at Benaiah's tone. He truly believes he may have a solution.

"I'm listening."

Benaiah hesitates, glancing to Abner before turning back to Saul. "I believe it would do your mind well to hear the music that calms the soul."

Saul will try anything to alleviate the pressure, to reduce anxiety, to calm his soul. His thoughts have become constricting, squeezing from his pores as if he were in a wine press. "What have you heard of such music that calms the soul?"

"I have heard it played many times and no better than by the son of Jesse."

"A warrior as yourself?"

"He is a brave warrior. He is a shepherd, but a well-trained shepherd who speaks well, presents himself properly, and is a more skillful musician than any. Most importantly, the Lord is with him."

"That is quite the report for a shepherd. You must truly revere this boy?"

Benaiah returns his gaze to Saul. "I do."

Saul nods to Abner. "Bring this well-trained shepherd boy to me."

43

Kilech's consciousness creeps back ever so slightly, making him aware of the throbbing pain shooting through his body. A faint light appears, slowly growing brighter as his mind emerges from blackness. A blurry, hooded man's face materializes as the room focuses around him.

I'm in a tent?

He feels the grip of two large hands and instantly he is on his feet. In front of him sits a man robed in white. His bony face is pale and his recessed eye sockets are either filled with a shadow or are painted black. Either way, they're terrifyingly dark. Kilech stands in horror as the king of Gath rises from his iron and gold throne.

His slender, pale fingers grip Kilech's shoulder. "Kilech of Aphek, son of Maleph, welcome to the city of immortals," King Achish says with a grin.

Hooded men open the tent entrance, welcoming in the escalating shrieks and horrific cries echoing from the darkness beyond.

"I requested your presence for one reason," King Achish says as he walks through the doorway.

Kilech wonders if he should follow. With one look at the hooded guards, and the pain shooting down his neck, making itself known as a reminder of their unsympathetic ways, Kilech decides it would be wise to stay close.

Outside, Kilech gets his first real taste of the ominous creatures of Gath. A fire rages, shining against shadowed warriors as they chant. Kilech watches as children, no older than nine or ten years of age, butcher a defenseless man. Parts of his body are thrown into the fire and more roars ensue from the crowd. Their faces, splattered with blood, are a clear sign that this has been an all-night event.

Kilech grows sick, his stomach turning more with each frightening sight. This place is somehow even darker than the rest of Philistia. It occurs to him that this just may be where the darkness of nightfall is born.

The king's voice wavers as if he is on the verge of laughter. "I want you to record the slaughter that is soon to sweep our enemies."

Kilech attempts to catch a glimpse of Achish's facial expression, but his attention is diverted. A wave of warriors disperses, running like rats scattering from a swooping falcon. Unable to imagine what could force such violent men to flee in terror, Kilech strains to see the answer through the dark.

Without warning, a body soars from somewhere and crashes down into the blaze. The fire engulfs him, illuminating a massive, shadowy figure that now emerges from behind the crowding soldiers. It becomes clear. The man did not fall from the sky. He was thrown by this thing, this savage… this monster.

It's Dagon in the flesh!

With ease, the now burning man is lifted from the fire and thrown like a flaming arrow, into the crowded soldiers. The quick flashes of the fire's orange glow only highlight the beast's striking gigantic frame. Kilech is astonished by the sheer power of this foreign deity. Saliva spews as a deep bellow rises over the sounds of chaos, rattling Kilech's chest.

The bony fingers of the king wrap around Kilech's neck, turning his focus toward his malevolent grin. "And that is only the brother of our great champion. Generations will read your writings of the victory that is upon us. Now follow me. The ritual is coming to a close. We move into the enemy's lands tonight."

44

David musters the flock tighter as he nears the gate of his family's dwelling, preparing to secure the sheep after a long journey back. On a late return home such as tonight he would typically sleep outside to avoid disturbing the family with his arrival, but this evening, in the darkest hour, it surprisingly appears that not everyone is asleep. Outside, at the foot of the porch stairs, he spots silhouettes, six of them, standing under the moonlight. As David encloses the final sheep behind the gate, he hears his name called.

He pauses, unsure if he heard correctly. He hears the voice call again and this time it's unmistakable. It's the deep, bellowing tone of his father.

What could possibly be so important that he would be awakened at this hour?

David knows that there is nothing that could save him from his father's wrath if somehow he is the cause of this midnight disturbance.

As he nears the men he notices the chariot that he saw off in the distance as he left the tree line.

A chariot? The only chariots that look like that are – His heart drops as he eyes the marking crested on its side. *The king's seal.*

The men turn as he approaches. Their royal purple tunics and bronze breastplates make it clear that they are in fact the king's personal guards.

"David, these men are here to see… you," his father says, his voice revealing a surprising hint of concern.

Me?

David wonders what could possibly be so important that the king's top men would arrive in the middle of the night, requesting him.

The larger of the two men eyes the pouch hanging across David's back. "Bring the satchel," the man says. "We leave immediately."

David realizes that whatever the importance of this midnight visit, he will soon find out.

45

The valley of Elah or "Valley of the Terebinth" is known for its large terebinth trees that line the winding brook which serpentines through an expansive flat vale. Large oak trees stand along the edge of its water like monuments guarding the lush green landscape. The valley leads from Gath to Bethlehem through continuous valleys and rising hills.

Along this path is the city of Azekah. It is the first city along the Elah Valley and it stands as the gatekeeper from the coastal plain to the hill country of Judah. It also conveniently serves as one of the hubs for Hebrew scouts to replenish when working behind the enemy lines of Philistia.

Henick looks over his shoulder. The burning lights of Azekah upon the hill have long faded in the distance. Being this far from the protection of any city walls would cause overwhelming anxiety for most, but Henick has lived alone in the land for years, even traveling through foreign lines to deliver essential communications. When the opportunity arose to make some extra money scouting the valley, he jumped at the chance.

Scouting can be a boring, uneventful life, but there is always that one chance, the chance that the painful silence will explode into a frenzy of activity. And when it does, when the inevitable finally takes place, Henick knows he is the best in the business. Scouts don't get paid to lie in wait, they get paid to react and stay alive.

He lies quietly in the brush, concealed by the ever-blackening night. The soothing, repetitive flow of the brook is lulling him to sleep. There will be plenty of time for that in the daylight, but right now sleep is not an option. He pinches a blade of grass, pulling it taut before gliding the back of his hand against it. The thin edge slices his skin like a blade of iron, which shoots pain through his body, refocusing his eyes. It only lasts for a moment but there is plenty of grass. A city, a nation is trusting his watchful eyes. The back of his hand is hardly a sacrifice.

It's not long before his mind again begins to slip. His face feels heavy. His arms numb. The sounds of foreign scouts sneaking past grows in his ear until... his eyes shoot open. *Was I sleeping?*

His heart pounds so hard he fears that if someone were out in the darkness that the heavy beating in his chest would give away his position. It couldn't have been more than an instant. He doesn't even remember closing his eyes. The uncomfortable sense that someone is standing over him, watching him, is overwhelming.

Glancing over his shoulder, he is relieved to find that his quick nod was only that. The lost sense of awareness and control over his surroundings that takes place with a single momentary lapse in attentiveness can cause a paranoia that often lasts throughout the night.

Over time his eyes begin to play games. Things that were there all night seem to look new. Objects appear from shadows, and even the illusion of a human form moving toward him takes shape. Then two more shadowy figures materialize in the valley, the moon casting an eerie darkness at their feet.

Henick squints. *You're seeing things,* he tells himself.

But the burning fire rising from his stomach is screaming a different message. He is wide awake, his mind is fully alert, and his eyes are focused. He slowly reaches for the dagger on his hip as they near his position.

He is surprisingly calm, his breath slow and steady. He grips the handle and prepares to attack, but there are more dark shapes emerging around the bend in the distance. His heartbeat thumps, but he remains steady. This is, after all, what he does best. He lies still, patiently waiting, curious to see just what size force is on the move.

The scouts pass. Henick remains like a stone against the ground as the army emerges around the bend in a flood of silhouettes. The army fills the entire valley floor like thick oil in a bowl. Henick doesn't move. He's hoping that the end of their movement will come soon so he can race up the hillside and cross the valley ahead of them, undetected.

Amazed at their silence, he studies their movements. Then, shadows emerge that rise above even the terebinth trees. The dark figures approach as if the oak trees that line the valley have come alive, but they have not. No, these massive black shapes are of human origin, but their height rising to the sky is anything but worldly. Henick has to hold his breath in fear of gasping at the horrendous sight. He can't take his eyes off of it, off of *them*.

They have unleashed the sons of Anak upon us.

Henick has heard the stories that have been passed on from generation to generation of this antediluvian breed. The twelve spies that were sent by Moses and were recorded by both Moses and the Egyptian scribes reported giants roaming the land that made the spies look like grasshoppers. Joshua later went to war and expelled them, except for a small remnant, part of which Henick now watches in awe as they near his position.

He is in disbelief that this moment is truly taking place, that his eyes are really seeing this ancient descendent of the Nephilim walking in his midst. But the thought is quickly replaced with a longing to understand the purpose for which these beings have come. They have walked this land before. This time, however, Joshua is long gone.

Even if the Hebrews can gather, who could stand against this evil?

Regardless of the horror before him, he only has a short period of time to duck behind the spine of the ridge and race across the valley undetected. Right now, however, he can't move. He is frozen in fear.

My God, what have I just seen?

46

David has never traveled this far, this fast. Moving across the dirt path, pulled by two horses, he feels as if he's soaring just below the clouds. The sights are far different up on the high road. The view is amazing at this time of night as they approach the distant hilltop overlooking Mount Moriah. David, not having to tend his sheep, is free to just gaze across the valley at the majestic mountain.

The burning lights of Jebus faintly dance from afar but David's mind drifts to the history of that divine mountaintop. He envisions Abraham a thousand years ago, before even the Egyptian captivity, walking with his son Isaac to the top where he would ultimately present a sacrifice and establish a Hebraic covenant, a promise with Yahweh for his people. Abraham was prepared to offer his son to God, and now because of his faith, many of the Hebrews, including David, wait for Yahweh's part of the covenant to be fulfilled.

Today the Jebusites control the mountaintop, but David knows that it is more than just a perfect location for a military stronghold. It is a promise from the beginning of mankind's restoration. Yireh or "Yahweh to manifest himself," as Abraham called it, was a name added to the already infamous city ruled by Noah's son Shem, or as many know him Malchizedek, the king of Shalem. He was the ruler of this land, the high priest of which greeted his descendent Abraham with open arms and blessed him in this land, Shalem, or "to consume the authority of chaos."

Even though the Jebusites captured the city and named it Jebus while the Hebrews where enslaved by Egypt, David knows that one day it will be restored to its original owner and name. Still, today his people call it as Joshua did by its ancient name, a combination of the two historical names of their forefathers, Yireh and Shalem, Yerushayalim.

Many simplify it as the "foundation of peace," but David knows it's much more than that.

Jerusalem.

Yahweh to manifest himself, to consume the authority of chaos, he thinks.

Something divine has happened on that mount when Yahweh manifested himself as a man before Abraham, stopping him from sacrificing his son, but what is to come? If Abraham has finished his part of the covenant, then what is Yahweh's part? Thoughts continue to cycle through David's mind. Will Yahweh again manifest himself in the form of a man, on that summit? David has sensed him, but never has he laid eyes upon him.

The chariot jolts over the stony path, bringing David's thoughts back to the night's events. He is halfway to the capital city of Gibeah at the darkest hour of the morning, and he still has no idea why. On the outside David is calm, relaxed, but on the inside he is consumed with possibilities, outcomes. He takes a deep breath and glances to the heavens that beam down with speckled light.

I could sure use Shalem right now.

47

Henick sprints down the back side of the Elah Valley as the orange glow from the flames, now rounding the corner, dance across the ground. He looks back to the open valley floor speckled with trees. There is not enough time to reach the other side without the risk of attracting the eyes of Philistine scouts. The last thing he needs right now is to be hunted.

Remaining alive to warn of the approaching army's position is too important to risk. If his message doesn't reach Gibeah by morning, there may not be a capital by nightfall. Instead of making a run for it, he will have to wait until they pass before he crosses the valley.

He moves from the open vale toward the thick brush of the hillside but the footsteps are upon him. His shadow grows with each closing step of the torches and he knows that he's out of time. He abandons all plans to distance himself from the oncoming path. Henick drops into the brush as the first dark figures emerge from between the hillsides and enter into another vast expanse of the valley floor.

Henick lies perfectly still. The blazing torches cast repeating shadows over him as the army passes close enough for Henick to smell their filthy bodies. The ground vibrates with each additional rank that rounds the corner and enters into the opening. The vibration escalates into a rumble as the flames burn brighter. The drums begin. Low, booming echoes reverberate across the valley floor as the flickering shadows grow larger.

Henick closes his eyes. He can feel the darkness seeking him out, breeding fear into his heart, as if it knows right where he is lying. The drums become violently loud as a thundering rhythmic sound of footsteps strike the ground. Henick opens his eyes just in time to witness a bare foot, the size of a mountain, slam down only half a pace from him. The thing's sweat splatters across his face. He can taste the salt on his lips.

The oversized bone structure is contorted with six toes and coarse dark hair. The foot compresses as the weight of the massive body crushes it into the earth. The beast moves past but the army appears to be stopping. The drums continue to pound as the warriors begin hacking down trees and stacking the wood in preparation of building a fire. After a few moments, it's clear. This isn't just any fire that they are building. It's an altar.

This is not what Henick was expecting. He lies back and exhales. *It's going to be a long night.*

48

"Shepherd," a voice calls out.

David opens his eyes, squinting as the bronze trim lining the walls of the room reflects the morning sun across the floor. He rubs his face, realizing that he couldn't have been asleep for very long. He's exhausted.

"Shepherd," the voice is stronger now that David is fully awake. A soldier stands at the doorway. "Your garments are beside you. You may change and prepare across the hall."

David feels the stack of cloth under his arm, a perfectly folded cloth tunic and shirt. He looks down over his own garments which are dirty but work just fine.

I don't see why I need new clothes, David thinks.

Regardless, understanding an order when he hears one, David grabs the clean linens and heads across the hall. The sound of laughing and giggling stops him and he focuses his eyes, his attention to the children, all roughly his age, who have stopped in mid-conversation at the sight of him. Their eyes drift over his garments, which now look filthy compared to the clean white silk that is draped across their shoulders.

Maybe changing isn't such a bad idea, David muses.

He watches them as they pass. No, he watches her. The girl on the right, the one with the jasmine tucked behind her ear has captured his full attention. She drifts down the hall weightlessly, as if she doesn't have a care in the world. Unlike Ezsri, this girl looks as if she has never had a callus, much less toiled in a field, but her seductive, flowing movement, long hair, and a tantalizing glance back at him sparks yet another unknown desire. Then, confusion reigns as the children disappear into… a wall? It must be a hidden passageway. David moves closer to take a better look.

"Shepherd." The soldier's voice prompts him to turn back and enter the intended room without further inspection.

Inside the bathing room, David puts on the clean garments and cups his palms into the water bowl. His hands drag slowly down his cheeks revealing his reflection. His clean face stares back at him, rippling in the water.

In a few short moments you are going to meet Yahweh's chosen king, he tells himself.

He knows the history, the accomplishments, the victories, and now he will actually meet the man himself.

A fist pounds on the door, startling him. The soldier hollers, "Shepherd."

David takes a deep breath before emerging from the room. He follows the soldier to the large wooden double doors at the end of the corridor. The soldier pounds on the door twice, then nods to David before he turns back down the long, narrow hallway. David takes one last inhale, and wipes away the small beads of sweat that have begun to form on his forehead. With a creak, the large doors swing open, revealing the king's lavish bedroom.

David's insides leap at the sight of King Saul staring out the window.

"I didn't ask for this you know," King Saul says. "This luxurious room, this palace. They insisted that I have it. It would project more power, they said. But I'm used to the fields, much like you." Finally, King Saul turns toward David, whose legs stiffen. "I was… am, a farmer, but I am also a king."

King Saul glances at David's satchel, draped across his shoulder. "And I hear that you are more than a shepherd."

David stops mid-breath. He has no idea what the king is referring to.

How do I answer?

In an awkward realization that he still has no idea why he has been summoned here before the king, David doesn't respond.

King Saul nods toward David's satchel. "I hear you are quite the musician?"

David is relieved to find out that he may be of use, but he believes it is always better to under commit and over achieve. "I am not a musician by trade, my king."

"I will decide that." King Saul returns his gaze out the window. "Do not be nervous. I am not that kind of king. Just play as you would any other day."

King Saul's words help to comfort David's nerves. In the wilderness, he is in control, fearless even, but in this palace, in the king's sleeping quarters, he feels completely vulnerable. This is not his element in the least and David is sure that it is obvious to anyone who lays eyes on him.

David does the one thing that he knows will make him more comfortable. He removes his lyre and lowers himself against the wall. As his hands grip the smooth wood of the instrument his nerves immediately settle.

David's fingers connect with the first chord and immediately he knows that something is different. A heat that startles him rushes over his body. David stops, opening his eyes to look around the room, but nothing is out of the ordinary and King Saul doesn't seem to have noticed.

David recalls the anointing of oil and the warmth that he felt. He hasn't played since, and obviously the intensity of the Presence he feels has increased. After realizing that he has completely stopped playing, he continues. Time evaporates as the overwhelming presence comes with more than authority than before. The more he plays, the more it envelopes him, and the more power it brings. The melody flows from

David's fingers playing a mesmerizing tune that he has never played before.

Something has definitely changed.

49

The low, pounding drumbeats ignite once again. It has been a long night, but an even longer day. Henick has not only lain exposed in the crisp night air that continually gusts through the valley, but also the scorching midday sun that pounds from above with relentless heat. A perimeter of soldiers with their eyes focused outward has kept Henick in his prone position for much longer than he ever could have anticipated.

He has had to relieve himself three times, each time creating a pool of urine that soaks into his tunic while he remains perfectly still. Thankfully, it has only been urine that has soaked into his cloth thus far.

As night falls and cool air settles into the valley once more, the pagan altar comes to completion. Knowing all too well that the young soldiers placed on outer perimeter duty will hardly be able to keep their eyes off of the coming night's festivities, Henick decides that tonight will be his escape and by morning the nation will know that they are at war.

Saul approaches the double wooden doors at the end of the hallway, finally returning to his room after another challenging day as king. At least he's at home and can sleep in his own bed, he reminds himself. But then he remembers the shepherd. No one has seen him, nor have they checked on him. Saul questions his own sanity, having left a stranger, a youth, alone in his room.

As he nears his sleeping quarters he realizes that the shepherd boy has been left alone the entire day with only one order, to play. His mind fills with thoughts of what this boy could be doing with no supervision. Surely, he would be curious to know what the king keeps in his most personal space.

Imagine what he could be rummaging through.

Saul's pace quickens. His mind fills with the possibilities of what this rough young Judean could be destroying or stealing. Without hesitation he pushes the doors open, fully expecting to catch the boy amid blatant wrongdoing.

But the boy isn't rooting through the room. The bed sheets aren't even wrinkled. The shepherd is still sitting in the same corner, still playing as fervently as he was this morning.

Saul relaxes, letting his tension release as he steps into the room. Immediately, something feels different. He has passed through a curtain of warm serenity that wraps his body, calming both his mind and his thoughts.

Instantly, he feels convicted about his rash assumption concerning the boy's integrity, and Saul knows that there is only one thing that could convict him of his thoughts. He hasn't felt this way for some time now but he knows this sensation well.

The Presence of Yahweh is here.

He stops short of the bed, pausing to admire the boy's skill. He plays like no other musician that Saul has ever heard. Passion pours from his fingers, through the chords, and into the room. Saul watches intently but the boy seems oblivious to the fact that anyone is in the room with him. The soft melody continues flowing, luring Saul's mind to rest. Something that he has been longing for, but one question lingers in his mind.

Who is this boy that commands such a presence?

50

Kilech stands astonished as the warriors of Gath completely disregard the enemy's land. After marching through the night they have settled camp beyond the Hebrew city of Azekah, in the tribal lands of Judah. He watches as the raucous crowd straps a young man high atop the stacked boulders of the newly built altar of Dagon in the middle of the Valley of Elah.

They're begging for a war, Kilech thinks.

Their excitement at killing one of their own has always disturbed Kilech, but tonight seems even more disturbing. As the fire is lit, he turns his eyes away from the brutality to come and focuses on the hill. He cannot take the sight of one more horrified expression as another man prepares to be burned alive. It is a sight that has already seared unforgettable images into his mind, faces that he sees every time he closes his eyes.

He can hear the fire ignite, sending the screams into a faded shriek that lifts into the night sky. Then, something catches his eye. A dark figure races up the valley wall toward the ridge. Kilech's first thought is how he wished it were him running, but then his curiosity takes over. The thought of someone escaping after marching this far doesn't make sense. Who would want to run off in enemy territory? There could be only one explanation. It's not enemy territory for him.

A scout.

"Scribe," a voice calls out from inside the king's tent.

The man running is no longer a concern to Kilech. His thoughts have focused back on his own misfortunes. He opens one tent flap and enters.

Inside, large armored warriors block the path to the back. Kilech stops, unsure what to say, where to go, or who called to him. One at a time, the guards move to the side, revealing two women seductively clothed and chained to the ground. Kilech trudges toward the king's dark iron throne layered with animal skins. All eyes seem to be piercing through him as he walks the path formed by the warriors.

They know that I'm weak. I can no longer conceal it, not with men such as this, he tells himself.

With each step toward the king, a tremble of nerves grows under his skin. It rises up his thigh even as he focuses, attempting to control it before everyone sees the truth, the fear rattling his body. He looks to King Achish, hoping for a hint of how he should approach the throne, but somehow the king is looking directly through him. The king stares toward the tent door. His lips curl into a devilish grin as the flickering firelight is consumed by the unforgiving black pits above his cheeks, the endless sockets that somewhere deep within contain his charcoal eyes. Kilech no longer exists.

He wants to look, to see what has such a grasp on the king's interest, but a tablet of brown papyrus paper catches his attention. He lowers his knee in respect and moves to the tablet, feeling a sense of security with it. All eyes are focused on the tent door now. An eerie silence fills the inside, and suddenly Kilech no longer feels alone in his misery. Even the large intimidating guards begin fidgeting, revealing their nerves have just taken a turn for the worse.

What is about to come through that door?

Time seems to stand still as every eye stares. Every mouth is silent in anticipation. Finally, the tent flaps open as one man on each side holds them high. A shadow approaches, quenching the view of the distant fires one at a time until the entire opening is saturated by his presence.

The ground rumbles in the rhythm of long strides that draw near. The being that materializes in the flickering light of the tent is anything but human. The once intimidating and masculine guards now resemble children as they stumble to get out of his way.

The ghastly beast that enters is not a man, but a creature. A massive creature that Kilech could only imagine was formed in the darkest recesses of the earth. The being is bent at the waist which is the height of a common man. His knuckles almost drag across the ground in order to fit his grisly frame through the tent's double doors. His eyebrows are thick, giving him a constant scowl. Scars so large they would have killed any other man look like mere scratches on his massive body. Even his breath tumbles from his lungs like a lion signaling a warning. It appears that a wild animal has just entered the room and everyone is worried about its predictability.

"Goliath," the king says with a cunning tongue. "Welcome."

The giant's scowl remains, obviously not fazed by any man's title or position. His eyes drift to the half-naked women chained to the right and left of the throne. Which draw the beast's gaze far too close to Kilech. He holds his breath as if that might help in some way, and he can feel his body stiffening, his breath drawing from his tight chest as through a pinhole. He would do anything to remain unnoticed by this monster.

"Yes, they will be yours as well as many more. I know how important it is for you to pass along your seed. It would be my honor for you to have your way with our women, you being an Anakim among Peleshet."

Goliath's eyes scan the women who now cringe and recoil from him as he lifts his nostrils, sniffing their scent. "Go on," he says.

Kilech jolts at the deepness of his voice. It roars with a harshness that booms from his lungs. Inside his mouth even the darkness twists uncomfortably like maggots squirming for an escape, and the smell when he speaks rivals the worst of dead animals rotting in the sun.

King Achish's stern face returns to a grin. He knows that he has

Goliath's interest. "Our enemy is conceited enough to believe that they are created in the image of God. But you, Goliath, you are not an image of God. You *are* a God. The Anakim blood that courses your veins is not of this world and you will prove it. Not to us, not to them, but to their God. It will be our giant god versus their invisible God. And you alone will reap the rewards when they bow before you, or when you kill them, whichever comes first."

Kilech hesitantly glances toward the monster. He doesn't look concerned in the least.

Goliath stares at King Achish for a moment, as if letting him know who's really in charge. He turns back toward the door and lets out a shockingly loud response.

"Send the women."

Cresting the top of the ridge, Henick looks back to the valley below. His plan has worked to perfection. The wall of the valley has become a black shadow in contrast with the blazing altar and with the night's pagan events carrying on, he has become a ghost. The route behind him looks secure. No one appears to have followed. His path to Gibeah in the tribe of Benjamin should be unhindered, and by morning the message will be clear.

Israel is at war.

51

The sunlight glistens from the windowsill, forcing Saul to wake. He rolls to his side and rubs his eyes to clear his vision. It comes as quite a surprise to hear the peaceful melody still flowing throughout the room. He fully expected the boy to have taken a break, but as Saul leans forward it becomes clear that he has not stopped all night.

The boy's head and shoulders are slumped. His fingers are raw and crimson blood beads down the strings in long steady drips.

"Shepherd," Saul says, humbled by the boy's devotion. "Enough. You have honored me greatly."

Saul stands and takes the lyre. "I have never seen such devotion. What is your name, shepherd?"

The boy's eyes lift to the king as he stands then lowers to his knee in respect. "David, my king. Son of Jesse of Bethlehem."

Saul reaches out his hand to help David stand. "I will be glad to…" Suddenly, a fist pounds on the door, startling him.

The door swings open and Jonathan enters, speaking clearly and concisely. "Father, the Philistines have crossed to Azekah. The entire army of Gath is in Judah."

Saul pauses, the rage that would typically consume him from his door barging open without authorization is nowhere to be found. It is a welcome change. He hasn't had an unexpected relapse of anxiety even with news of an invasion. Surprisingly, Saul is steady, clearheaded, and focused.

"Have they now?" he says, almost eager for the challenge. "Our army should already be fully gathered for the spring, is it not?"

"It is, Father," Jonathan says, still breathing heavily.

"Then send the order and prepare the young soldiers in training for the march as well. This will be a warm welcome to their glorified view of a soldier's life. Prepare them for the march south."

"As you command, my king." Jonathan races out of the room just as General Abner enters.

Saul tilts his head back and inhales the aroma of peace that has descended upon his room like the morning mist. The Presence lingering in the room has not only calmed him, but also seems to have empowered him. His eyes find the lyre, and then slowly track to David.

Realizing that this boy commands the power of Yahweh, a power that has otherwise become deficient in his life, Saul knows that this musician must remain by his side.

"David, I could use a boy with your devotion right now. Come, you will carry my armor by my side." Saul grips David's shoulder like a father would.

David glances up with a smile, seeming to appreciate the gesture. "As you wish, my king."

52

The last few days have been more than exhausting for Henick. After traversing the grueling terrain of the hill country throughout the night, and being deprived of sleep for almost three days, he can finally relax. The crucial warning has been delivered to the nation's capital and now it is up to her people to defend it. Pressing his back into the stone wall at the base of the king's palace he feels the tension in his muscles release for the first time since reaching Azekah.

His mind drifts to the monsters entering the valley in the darkness, the smell of fire and burning flesh, the screams echoing between the hills, sights and sounds that continue to haunt him.

The giant enters the valley, stops, and turns toward him. "Messenger," the giant says, staring directly at him. Again he calls out, "Messenger."

Henick jolts awake, opening his eyes to find himself still safely at the palace. He didn't realize that he had fallen asleep.

"Messenger," the same voice calls out once more.

He turns his head, noticing a figure standing to his side. The morning sun beams over the man's shoulder, casting his face in shadow, but his attire is unmistakable. Jonathan. Henick jumps to his sore feet.

"Your Highness." Henick's voice cracks with exhaustion.

"You have served us honorably and your courage has protected our lands, our people. What payment do you request?"

The question of payment comes as no surprise. Henick, not being born within the twelve tribes, serves more as a mercenary than a soldier. Trust is always an issue when dealing with foreigners. But Henick is a native to the land of Canaan and has embraced the God as well as the traditions of the Hebrews. He would love nothing more than to be welcomed as one of their own.

"I do not request payment, only to fight one day by your side."

"Then grab your armor. My senior commander will gladly take you under his charge. You will report to Commander Nathaniel of Reuben." Jonathan looks Henick over with a proud grin. "I will inform him that you must receive some rest on the journey south."

Henick kneels. "For the nation, for Yahweh, I will sacrifice."

Jonathan nods, and as he turns, Henick questions his decision. It is true. All he has ever wanted is to fight side by side with the Hebrews, to be accepted. But now, barely able to muster the energy to stand from the kneeling position, he must turn back and head once again into the nightmare that waits.

⊱✦⊰

David descends the stairs to the courtyard at the base of the palace with the King's armor in hand. He notices that the scaled bronze armor is not like that of the lightweight leather that the rest of the army wears. Commanders rallying their troops are fitted with a few bronze scales but the king's armor in David's hands is made of solid bronze. The weight will take some getting used to. His shoulders are already burning as he reaches the courtyard.

How does anyone fight in this?

David glances out to the fields where hundreds of soldiers are gathering. At the front, where he was instructed to stage the king's armor, is a boy not much older than himself, kneeling before Jonathan, the heir to the throne. The boy is rugged, muscular, and dirty, but more than his physical features David notices his weaponry, multiple carved wooden knives, less than a full span, line his belt. He does not appear to be a soldier, nor does he carry the standard long weapon or farm tool that the ranks typically choose. It seems clear that he is anything but standard.

Maybe he's a spy? David thinks as he approaches the formation.

"Armor-bearer," a voice calls out.

It takes a moment for David to realize that someone is referring to him, but finally it registers and he turns to see a warrior staring back at him. The soldier does not have an imposing stature but his eyes are sharp, like the tip of a blade; they warn of the lethal weapon within.

"Yes, you. You are carrying the king's armor, are you not?"

The man leaves Jonathan's side and approaches David. "You can drop it there." He points to the large boulder next to the courtyard's stone wall. "That is where the king's armor is staged, always at the head of his men and never on the ground."

The man lifts the chestplate from David as if it were weightless. He places the helmet inside pulling it up through the neck-line like a handle. "You may want to carry it this way from now on." He smacks David on the back. "I'm Aaron. If you need…"

"I hear you're mine now," a voice cracks from the distance, immediately silencing the murmur of the gathering soldiers.

A large, burly man pushes his way through the ranks, hollering at the soldiers to his sides as he approaches. He emerges at the front of the formation, his scarred face covered with a thick silver beard.

"Fall to the front," he yells, while eyeing the boy who has remained kneeling even as Jonathan turned away from him. The rugged young spy jerks a nod as if he were startled just before falling asleep. "And grab yourself an actual weapon. I'm sure you can find a spare rake or an ax lying around. Anything will be better than those sticks on your belt."

The large bearded man turns to Jonathan and lowers his head in respect. "Your desire is my command, your highness."

"Now let's move, sweetheart." He grabs the rugged boy by the shoulder, lifting him from his kneeling position, and thrusts him toward the ranks. His loud, degrading shouts continue as he plows toward the back of the formation. The chaos and uneasiness subside as he departs.

Aaron grins and turns toward David. "That would be Nathaniel. If you don't want that fury coming your way, then you should learn your responsibilities quickly."

David stands in awe. Not at the spectacle that just took place, but at the small-framed armor-bearer that is currently assisting him with his new position. He has heard of the feats of this man. He has heard the exploits, the legends of the things that this man and Jonathan have accomplished. Namely, their single-handed victory as they defeated an entire army on the hill of Michmash. Now, here he stands directly in front of him.

"Did you hear me?"

David freezes, realizing that he was too caught up in amazement to hear anything.

"I said always stay on the right side and..." Aaron stops to look over David's shoulder. "It seems we are preparing to move."

David turns just in time to see King Saul descending the staircase. Silence sweeps the army. David realizes that only a few days ago he was irrelevant, wandering in the wilderness with a flock of sheep, and now here he stands talking with legends, standing at the head of an entire army, and waiting for the king of the nation to lead them into war.

How did I ever get here?

53

DAY 1
BATTLE OF THE ELAH VALLEY

The march is long and tiring and the dry hill country has taken its toll on every soldier's morale already. Their tiresome moans and frustrated grumbles can be heard across the hilltops, and Aaron fears that at any moment the wrath of Commander Nathaniel and General Abner will be unleashed to rein in the focus of the masses. These are the times when it pays to be the armor-bearer, walking with Jonathan as he strays from the ranks to gather his thoughts.

Aaron stays close to Jonathan's side all the way to their destination, which looks to be just ahead. As they reach the edge that overlooks the Valley of Elah, Aaron's stomach turns. Cresting the hill, the landscape drops sharply, stretching across a large plain until rising back up toward the sky into the opposing valley wall.

Soldiers cover the far hillside. Their eyes are circled in black and their screams echo across the canyon like demons scurrying throughout the valley. The vale below is littered with the black, charred remnants of fires that burned throughout the night. An altar, hastily erected to their pagan gods sits as the centerpiece. Aaron's anxiety is quickly overtaken with disgust.

"We should just charge them and get this thing over with," Aaron says, glancing at Jonathan.

But Jonathan doesn't respond. He stares off, deep in thought, as if listening to the wind. "No," he finally says as he scans the valley. "Something is different."

Jonathan's gaze focuses on the altar erected in the valley, its platform charred with black soot. "Look at their altar over there," he says, nodding toward the boulders stacked into the air. "They've defiled our God." Jonathan's eyes drift across the valley, not settling on anything specific, but taking everything in at once. "The smoldering fires burning our terebinth trees… It is obvious that they have a complete disregard for our land."

His gaze shifts toward the opposing valley wall where the entire army of Gath has formed. "And their battle lines are fresh, having settled in while we marched. But that is not why they are convinced of a victory." His eyes again wander the landscape. "No, they chose this position for a reason. All of this is for a reason."

Aaron looks out. The wide expanse between the two valley walls creates a perfect view of the broad plain between the hills. It's a natural theater. "For its view," Aaron says, now understanding Jonathan's intuition.

Jonathan nods. "I'm afraid the messenger may not have been exaggerating. Whatever he saw that night, marching in the darkness, they fully intend to reveal it. We're being lured in."

Benaiah watches the soldiers ahead of him gather around the edge of the hilltop. By their reactions, the sight across the expanse isn't pleasant. The long, hot journey south ignited quite the murmuring, but by the looks of the soldiers at the edge, whatever is on the other side of the valley is far worse than anything that they encountered so far. Benaiah figures it must be bad; they have all gone silent.

He makes his way through the soldiers to gaze over the expanse for himself. The moment feels unreal. The enemy, the Peleshet, is standing within sight. They are so close and willing to fight. He can't help but grin. He has waited, dreamt, longed for this moment since he was a child. Since his father's sword was returned to his grieving mother. Now, however, as the enemy drums pound louder, and their cheers resonate through the valley, it's not quite how he envisioned the beginning of his first battle.

He looks to his right and left. Every soldier around him gazes with terror in his eyes. They have all passed along the tales of giants marching in the darkness, waiting in the Valley of Elah, and now it seems they are already defeated before the battle has even begun.

Benaiah is confident in his skill and has been longing to test it, to fully unleash it, against men twice his age. But with fear surrounding him, there is little that he can do alone. The enemy is chaotic, possessed even. Their lines are strong, deep, disciplined, and ferocious.

His focus shifts back to the men surrounding him. These men, these soldiers, these so-called warriors, are nothing but timid boys in the face of such a threat. There is no order, no discipline. These men wield farming equipment and only train when their work is done. He doesn't even have to consider his decision. Fear or not, you do not back down from an enemy at your door. He knows what he plans to do. Move toward the elite fighters and fight like a cornered animal. Fight like the savage dog that he is.

Benaiah watches as the opposing enemy makes a mockery of their army with their shouts and cheers.

Cheer all you want, you will remember my name when this is over.

54

Abinadab reaches the edge as the shouts of the enemy increase, provoked by the growing number of Hebrews converging to observe. It's like they have been enthusiastically waiting for this moment. They are not slaves forced to do their king's bidding like other armies. No, they enjoy this life.

Abinadab scans the enemy ranks as the deep battle drums pound across the valley. The massive number of soldiers in black attire creates a large, ominous shadow, as if the entire valley wall were cast in darkness.

He glances to his brothers. Not one says a word. He knows they won't say it, but they are as fearful as he. They have all experienced combat at one time or another, but this appears to be on a whole new level.

"They're provoking us," Eliab says, breaking the silence first.

This is suicide, Abinadab thinks.

"We're not really going to walk into this trap, are we?"

"Well, look who it is." Shimea says, turning around. "All hail. Prince David has returned to his minions."

Surprised, Abinadab turns to see David slowly making his way toward the edge. David seems as stunned as they are, but grins when he sees Abinadab and his brothers. His pace quickens toward them and Abinadab feels Shimea's gaze swing from David to him.

"What? You can't tease him now that he's *royalty*?" Shimea says, laughing.

Abinadab gives a lopsided grin. He's eager to see him but holds back his excitement, fearing Shimea's lack of understanding. The bond that Abinadab now feels toward his younger brother will be hard to explain.

Just before David reaches them, a voice calls out, halting David's movement toward them.

<hr/>

"Shepherd."

David stops midstride. The voice is deep and sends a shot of fear though his body, almost turning his limbs utterly stiff. He was so close to his brother, to the edge of the valley. King Saul's voice is commanding, but it's David's respect that turns him around instantly. He quickly glances back. His brothers look disappointed, even angry. He understands how it looks. He's leaving them at a crucial time, and he swears that for an instant, he saw true fear forming on their faces.

He so desperately wants to look over the valley and see if the rumors are true. To see if the enemy really set up an altar and defiled Yahweh in the face of his people, but he has orders.

David fights through the crowd, emerging toward King Saul. The king slows his movement toward the edge but doesn't stop. With General Abner accompanying him, King Saul never even looks at David. "Your time will come, as for now return to your father's house and do as he commands."

King Saul's demeanor has changed. He is cold, his emotion again bottled deep inside. David feels expendable, unlike this morning when he felt appreciated.

"As you command, my king."

David bows and moves past the king only to look back and watch him and his general walk toward the edge. It's clear that the king has forgotten all but what lies before him, relying on only what he can see. He is listening to what his circumstances are telling him, and the stress is visibly noticeable. It's the same look his brothers had... panic.

He looks to where his brothers were, but they're gone. The last thing he remembers was the fear in their eyes and the anger on their faces.

I didn't leave you, he thinks as he turns back toward home.

A sensation rises in his gut, one that he knows he can't control: an overwhelming flood of protection, as if he were looking at his flock in danger. The men, the boys, the soldiers, they're all terrified of their fate.

This isn't the shepherd field, this is war, the voice in his head says. *What could you do anyway?*

David walks away alone, helpless to defend them. He's been given a direct order by the king. He realizes that as quickly as his opportunity came, it has vanished, just like his brothers did behind the crowd of soldiers.

55

DAY 17
BATTLE OF THE ELAH VALLEY

Benaiah fights through the enemy lines. The grueling nonstop skirmishes have made these last seventeen days feel like five years. Each day, the engagements get harder, or maybe he just gets weaker. The ground is soaked with bodily fluids, making it difficult to gain a strong foothold and strike with any kind of precision. He has adapted his style to the slippery surface, but the constant focus on his legs is wearing him down mentally as much as physically. Exhausted, he pushes on, knowing that the moment he stops, he dies.

Only a few weeks ago he was eager to experience war. Now, however, he has learned the hard way. War is not to be desired. It is not enjoyable, but he has confirmed that even at his young age, he is good at it. War is his trade. It is what he was born to do.

Refocusing, he grips his sword. A Peleshet soldier sprints toward him, the tip of his sword aimed forward, prepared to strike. Benaiah reacts. He sidesteps and thrusts his blade into the oncoming soldier with one fluid motion, killing the attacker with ease. In his peripheral vision another appears. Benaiah tugs at his sword but the blade is stuck. He jerks hard but it is jammed between his victim's ribs as the Peleshet warrior falls to the ground, pulling him toward it.

Benaiah gives one last hard jerk to free his sword, but the slain soldier has twisted upon falling, locking his blade, tightly pinched, between the bones. As the enemy sword slices down it seems that Benaiah, no matter how skilled, has killed his last Philistine. He will reap his revenge from the afterlife.

Benaiah closes his eyes, prepared to join his father. He winces as he visualizes his death. He is prepared to take the painful blow. He is prepared to die a long and agonizing death, but the screams and clanging continues in his ears. Still, no pain overtakes his body, no surprising blow strikes him. Confused, Benaiah opens his eyes and sees the armor-bearer Aaron pulling his sword from between the attacker's shoulder blades, letting the enemy soldier fall on his face at Benaiah's feet.

Aaron's attention snaps toward Benaiah. "Get it together! This fight isn't over!"

Benaiah refocuses. Pressing against the corpse with his foot, he has the leverage and time to remove his sword. With Aaron's display of courage and fearless attitude, Benaiah knows beyond a shadow of a doubt that he made the right choice.

Move through the ranks and fight with the elite warriors.

The chaos of the skirmishes in the field calm and the men disengage as they do every day at this very hour. Once in the morning and once in the evening, the carnage ceases and all eyes turn back to Saul.

He begins to shift awkwardly in his seat, knowing that he still has no answer for the escalating crisis. Each day the champion, the challenger, approaches his men at the base of the valley. The giant strolls across the field, stepping over the brook with no regard, and defiles the living God.

It's clear that the champion knows the fear he strikes into the men. Saul can even feel it as he sits high up on the valley wall. Every time this monster appears Saul knows that he not only loses authority but something even more damaging.

Hope.

Saul feels General Abner's eyes upon him.

Abner leans in. "You know this will not stop. We need to send someone out. We are low on supplies, and the morale at this point is nonexistent. The men are just trying to survive."

"So what would you like, a sacrifice? Because that is exactly what whoever we send out will become," Saul says.

Abner turns toward the field. "Then we just wait, until we are depleted enough for them to come cut you down? Then where will our nation be? We are already divided."

Saul lowers his head into his hand, rubbing his temples. "We have a resupply coming within the week."

"That's just prolonging the inevitable. The army is looking to you for guidance. They need a plan. We must send someone out for him to fight."

"And then what? Become their slaves when we lose the challenge, when another Hebrew gets slaughtered?"

"It will buy us time. We can arm the slaves that we hand over, formulate an attack, and open up a fighting chance."

Saul can no longer take the pressure. He can feel the entire army's eyes bearing down upon him. His generals, the enemy, this giant, all looking for answers, but he has none. There is nothing that he can do. He would rather be stripped naked and mocked than suffer this vulnerability. Men are dying every day and he has no answer to this madness. The tension builds inside of him until it finally explodes.

"I will not send out one more human to be sacrificed in this valley at the hands of this evil!" Saul immediately covers his mouth realizing that he has caught the attention of the soldiers in the rear ranks.

I'm losing it, Saul thinks.

Nathaniel approaches from the formation. "My king." He lowers, but is quickly up to his feet. "He is far closer than he has ever gotten before. He is not fearful in the least, and my concern is that one day he will attack our men and wipe out the first rank singlehandedly."

Saul sits quietly. On the inside he is crumbling. If only he could run and never stop, never look back. If only he could disappear, but he can't, and his men are looking for answers. He will just have to pretend that he has a plan.

"Reline the front with those that are fresh from the rear. Send a detachment to cut off their resupply through Azekah. Let the men know that I will not sacrifice any of them before the champion."

Nathaniel takes a breath. Suddenly, he bends, thrusting a violent cough from his throat. He quickly covers his mouth with a small cloth and heaves a few more times. Finally, he clears his throat. "With all due respect, my king, we are highly outnumbered. The forces –"

"Enough. Let them know that resupply is on its way and without a resupply of their own the enemy can't live forever."

Nathaniel departs, but he's never any good at pretending to be pleased when he clearly isn't. Saul knows that he is pinned into a corner with no way out. He is aware that he is not fooling anyone. Every man on this hill can sense that there is no escape. That they are drifting toward their demise one day at a time.

He watches Nathaniel return to his command over the ranks, as he does so professionally, no matter his opinion. His leadership is desperately needed and, selfishly, all Saul can think about is the blood on Nathaniel's hand cloth.

His cough is getting worse and I can't afford another setback.

56

DAY 40
BATTLE OF THE ELAH VALLEY

After weeks of harvesting the barley fields, David is finally ready to thresh the crop. He hammers the stalks with a wooden mallet, separating the grain. For hours he stands hammering without stopping, but no matter how hard he works the load continues to pile up. His father winnows the chaff after David separates it by throwing the mixed pile of grain and thin hulls into the air, letting the wind blow the chaff away from the heavier grain that falls to the ground.

There is never much talking, but the time spent alone with his father is something that David cherishes. His father is a hard worker, and David does his best to make him proud. Even if he will never say the words, David knows deep down inside that he must be.

The sun beats down on David who stands only a pace or two from the shade afforded by the stone structure under which his father stands. After countless hours of work, his father suddenly stops. He stares off into the fields as if listening to a sound, far off, that no one else can hear. Gazing west, he stands rigid, as if held captive by his mind.

David can only imagine his father's thoughts. He often wonders what his brothers may be going through, what they may be witnessing, if they are even still alive. He stops pounding on the wood block, deciding that his father may need a word of comfort, but before he can open his mouth his father speaks.

"Take this ephah of grain that I have roasted. Go inside, gather the bread, and take it to your brothers. I need to be ensured of their well-being."

"Yes, Father."

"And David," his father pauses.

David turns, waiting for his father to say it, his heart longing to hear the words. He feels pride well up inside, knowing that his father cares for his safety as much as his brothers.

"Also grab ten portions of cheese for their commanders. I want to ensure they are taken care of."

David stands speechless, unable to find any response. It isn't what he had hoped would be said. His heart is crushed.

Don't worry, I'll be safe, David thinks.

He dips his head in respect and mutters quietly, "As you wish."

57

David's heavy breathing fills the silence as he sprints through the dense forest. He wields his arms as shields from left to right in front of him for protection but he's moving too fast. Pine needles and branches smack off his face, thorns tear at his legs. He can only imagine what his eldest three brothers are experiencing. He can only hope they are all still alive. The thought of them waiting on the supplies that he carries only pushes him harder, faster.

He descends through the brush, leaping over stones and fallen trees with ease. His supple leather sandals are perfect for speed and grip. His lightweight cloth attire keeps him cool as he runs. He is agile and quick, and the thought of returning to the battle spurs on his final push.

The smell of pine and cedar is quickly overwhelmed by the stench of something rotting. The sound of flattening grass and brushing tree limbs is quickly replaced by metal clanging against metal, screams, and the rumbling of thousands trampling the ground ahead. Finally, David will see what his brothers have been seeing, but most importantly, he will see what the enemy has done to defile Yahweh.

The putrid smell turns his stomach as he moves out of the tree line into the open field of carnage. For forty days the sun has beat on the rotting corpses that mound high into the air. In the evenings he has been told, the dead from battle are piled together out of respect and cleanliness.

Others believe that they are moved so their spirits won't continue to haunt the battlefield. Regardless, David has emerged right in the thick of the mounds. He hurries to navigate through the twisted flesh by leaping from one clearing to the next, but they are few and far between.

Leaving the putrid smell and sight of the decomposing soldiers behind him, David now ascends the hill, searching, his eyes scanning the landscape for his brothers. The eerie thought creeps in that possibly he may have just passed them, stepped on them, in the piles behind him. He pushes the grim possibility out of his mind and climbs higher to get a better vantage point.

At the top of the hill, where wagons that have only recently delivered resupply are staged, David drops his supplies with the baggage keeper and moves methodically down toward the valley floor where the battles are raging. His eyes scan until, finally, he locates Eliab, then Shimea.

Where is Abinadab?

Frantically searching, David scans back and forth as he descends faster and faster, leaping down the hill, eagerly looking for his brother. He figures Abinadab must be with them. He has to be with them.

Finally, he spots all three, Abinadab included, engaged with the enemy. Together, they quickly take down a small pocket of Philistines that have strayed to the flank.

"David?" Abinadab notices him first.

David hurries down to meet them in the field where they have been fighting. He loses his footing and it almost sends him to his back, but he catches himself before falling. He glances down at the grass which has been churned up and coated in a slimy pink substance. The ground is as slick as the fish table at the market when a new catch is dumped and he can feel the gooey substance squish between his toes as he nears his brothers.

The liquid splashing on his feet is the last thing on his mind, now that he has found his brothers and knows that they are safe.

"David! Why are you here?" Eliab's voice is stern, actually, he sounds… angry.

David is confused at Eliab's tone, but then he notices how much the three of them have changed in such a short period. Their eyes are shadowed, their faces are aged, and they have lost noticeable weight in only forty days. They stand hunched, visibly exhausted.

"Father sent supplies for you, and for your commanders."

"Where are they?" Eliab says, his eyes searching David's empty hands.

"I left them with the baggage keeper until I found you. I was worried."

Shimea turns, disappointed. "A lot of help that does –"

His words fade as his attention diverts across the brook. His eyes lock onto something across the way and his entire face distorts. Something horrific has just caught his eye. And that horrific something must be coming closer.

"Go." Shimea reaches blindly as he backs up, feeling for David. He grabs hold of him. "Now! Run!"

The skirmishes shift suddenly into a chaotic mass retreat. The clanging metal and screams turn into a series of shouts and hurried trampling as the entire army has turned for the hill. Before David can comprehend what is going on, Abinadab grabs his other arm.

"Hurry," Abinadab shouts.

Whatever is coming, it has the entire army scurrying in fear for their lives, as if sprinting to survive a stampede or an avalanche. The chaos began with no warning, and David is trying to make sense of it all.

"What's happening?" David shouts back.

Finally, they reach the base of the valley wall and turn back. David is eager to finally lay eyes on whatever has caused such a stir, but he can't make out a single thing. Surrounded by grown men, David is too short to see what is approaching, but whatever it is, it commands the entire army to stand in eerie silence, watching. Their gazes lower to the ground, as if hoping not to be noticed – or chosen.

Abinadab leans over and whispers, "He comes out twice a day, once in the morning and once in the evening."

David stretches tall, moving his neck from left to right to peer around the men that stand in front of him. Still nothing. He has to know what could cause such fear in so many. Unwavering, he pushes his way to the front to see what the spectacle is. He can hear booming shouts from the field, but has yet to make out the words. The voice, however, makes one thing clear.

It's just a man?

David's brothers follow close behind him as he breaks through the front of the ranks.

For the first time, David now sees what the rest of men have been running from, and the rumors are apparently true. Now, he stands only a few hundred paces away from the one who holds his country's entire army in fear. He can finally put a face to the being that has held his nation at bay for the last forty days.

58

The giant nears the front line a few hundred paces away. He stands easily twice any man's height and walks with a confidence that even kings don't possess. Soldiers fall over each other in waves as they back away in terror. The massive humanlike being turns, having proven his point his eyes searching closer to David's position as he begins to move, stalking down the line, closing the comfortable distance between them with each step

Fear falls like a blanket covering each Hebrew, sweeping like a gust of wind through the ranks, infecting every last soldier. Even David feels it. Then he notices the altar that was erected before the battle began. The fear that was creeping in has been suddenly rinsed by a new emotion.

He closes his eyes, removing himself from the present. Something begins to boil inside of him. It starts small, a seed of anger. And then it grows until his entire being is consumed with retribution. Like a dog on a scent, he becomes single-minded, his eyes open, focused on the large beast that he now hears called by the name Goliath.

He looks behind him, the men, the soldiers, all of their faces are knotted in terror. It's obvious that they are more afraid of death than standing up for what is right. The giant continues to shout obscenities against Yahweh, each word digging deeper into David's heart. He can't take his eyes off this monster. He's arrogant, defiant, and blasphemous. Someone needs to silence him.

"What happens if someone kills him?" David asks without diverting his eyes from the approaching beast.

"What did you say?" Eliab snaps back, his tone that of a scolding father.

David still hasn't taken his eyes off the giant, nor will he. Something has been lit deep in his gut. "I said, what happens if someone kills him?"

"Great riches, my friend," a soldier says with a slight chuckle. "You're father's dwelling will forever be free –"

"And the king just added his daughter to the prize," another says, fueling the banter.

David feels the eyes of the surrounding soldiers upon him, but he doesn't care.

How can no one in all of our army stand against him? David wonders. *How could they listen to this for forty days?*

The continued blasphemy spewing from Goliath's mouth is beginning to coil David's skin. "He is nothing more than an uncircumcised Philistine. Who does he think he is to defy the living God?"

"Well, why don't *you* kill him?" another soldier says, causing murmuring and laughter.

For a moment the soldiers have eased. David notices that the king's son Jonathan and his armor-bearer have made their way toward the commotion, but Eliab quickly steps forward blocking their view of him.

"David, go home. You're embarrassing yourself," Eliab says, his voice trembling in anger. "Who's watching your sheep anyway? I know why you really came. Your heart is corrupt. You just wanted to see the carnage."

David can't believe his brother's contempt. Can he not see the *physical* defiling the *spiritual*, the *earthly* defiling the *heavenly*, a *man* defiling *God*? Has he become blind?

"Am I wrong? Should men be afraid of a man?"

"How would a boy know?" someone yells from the crowd.

Laughter erupts again, this time louder.

Suddenly, a thunderous roar shudders throughout the valley. Everything stops, even the birds go silent. The giant's head turns, his eyes seeking. Systematically, he scans every last soldier, searching for the one behind the disturbance. A dark cloud of fear descends upon the ranks.

As the giant draws near, David can finally get a better look at the arrogant mortal. There is not a man in the army that stands taller than Goliath's waist. His shoulders carry a fully scaled coat of bronze armor. David estimates that their width must be that of two men side by side. Upon his bull-shaped head he wears a bronze helmet, and matching greaves wrap his shins. A javelin, strapped between his shoulder blades, is long enough and sturdy enough to wipe out the first four ranks if it were swung as a club.

David watches the way the giant moves when he bellows. His body is agile for his size, and his voice is as deafening as an enraged ocean. The giant is only twenty paces away now and closing the distance fast. Each step seems to provoke his anger more. The safe distance that David once enjoyed has vanished, and Goliath's line of sight rapidly approaches his position. Any moment now they will lock eyes, and David begins to feel what the soldiers have been feeling. A surge of dread rises up in him as Goliath is now close enough that the stench of his breath sucks the air from David's lungs.

His empty black eyes move toward David, who suddenly finds that he is standing alone. The soldiers have all stepped back, abandoned him, leaving him to deal with his own consequences. His face pales as Goliath sets his attention on him.

Unexpectedly, a large, firm hand grips David's arm, pulling him back into the crowd.

59

It's beginning to fall apart right in front of his eyes. Saul watches as the army turns frantic. Chaos spreads through the ranks when the giant is unwilling to wait any longer for a challenger. Saul has feared that this day would come, the day that the giant decides to take matters into his own hands.

Soldiers stumble over each other, the masses erupt, and Saul knows that he will have to make a decision soon. By the looks of it, it may be too late. He squints, trying to make out what the commotion is. Someone is approaching through the crowd.

The wide, burly body can't be mistaken, even from this distance. Nathaniel emerges from the crowd, his pace quickening with each step. Saul fears the worst. He braces for whatever Nathaniel is about to deliver. Whatever it is it can't be good.

Whatever it is, I don't have an answer for it.

"My king," Nathaniel pauses to catch his breath. "The men say that there is one who will fight the champion."

Saul's body goes numb. *Tell me I heard that correctly.*

"There is one that *will* fight?" Saul asks, clarifying.

Nathaniel nods that there is.

Without hesitation Saul gives the order. "Send him."

David follows the king's general up the hill. General Abner doesn't say a word. He doesn't have to, his face says it all. He's embarrassed and David can't blame him. He can only imagine how this must look. How it must feel to be a general with decades of warfare, and the scars to prove it, only to march a boy, who claims to be confident but without a single day of experience, into a life-and-death battle that will decide the fate of thousands.

David hopes that the words, the claims that he spoke out of emotion, out of disgust for the giant's blasphemies, won't come back to haunt him. He is now being singled out and must back his claims, claims that with every step up the hill seem all the more absurd.

Out of the entire army, out of the entire nation, he is the only one qualified to fight the giant? Who does he think he is? His skin crawls, his muscles scream to run. He is now questioning everything that he has just said in that instant of emotional courage. The moment has become blatantly real.

What are you doing? his mind begins to question. *You saw him. You're going to be slaughtered, in front of the entire army!*

David feels like his legs are dragging tree stumps, as he climbs closer to King Saul. His mind has become overstimulated as all of his senses converge into a blur. Before he knows it, he is standing before the king.

"Shepherd, I have not sent for you." King Saul's eyes drift down toward the soldiers. "Return to your home as I have commanded."

"The soldiers say that this is the one that will fight the champion, my king," General Abner says.

"A boy?" King Saul's eyes bounce to David, but his gaze quickly returns to the valley. "Shepherd, he was a champion before you were born. He will tear you limb from limb. Another will fight in your place."

David can feel the king's contempt for his absurd actions.

"My lord, there is not another that will fight," General Abner says, pausing due to Goliath's uproar from the battle lines. "And the champion now expects someone to present themselves."

Before King Saul can respond, another outburst draws his attention back to Goliath, who has now entered the ranks of the Hebrews, looking for his challenger. It is becoming clear. He won't stand down anytime soon. The giant wants to be fed.

David has been given the option to turn and walk away from this situation, but something holds his feet firm. As badly as he wants to close his eyes and disappear, he realizes that he can't. He has let his mind stray, focusing on the temporal, on what he can see, and he has paid for it. Fear has crept in. Now it is time to remove it once again.

Memories stream back to the time spent in the wilderness, the dangers, the close calls, and the small victories, each in its own way leading him to this moment. With each memory comes a rush of confidence that buries his timid outlook, once again bringing him to a place where he relies not on what he can see, but what he can sense.

Knowing that the king is in a vulnerable position, and having witnessed the fear of the soldiers firsthand, David doubts that any of them will volunteer. The king is cornered into a single decision. One that David knows Saul does not want to make. So, David decides to help make the decision easier. He steps forward with new vigor in his voice and stance to plead his case.

"My king, I understand I am but a youth. But, as a youth, I have defended my sheep with my life. As a youth, I have defeated both the lion and the bear. And with your permission, my king, as a youth, I will defeat this uncircumcised Philistine."

With each word spoken, David believes in his own case all the more. No longer are his feelings in charge. His body and his mind are both pushed forward with the understanding that this is not his fight alone. The outcome looks bleak from man's perspective, but David has never been able to face danger without help. It is this keen ability to trust in more than his eyes can see that has kept him alive. He pushes through the fear, again believing that today will be no different.

He glances off to the valley that is filled with a dark haze, like a shadow of death, and an almost tangible panic, and he imagines that heavenly figure, that warrior that was promised to go before him in the battles, to conquer the impossible, waiting for him to come down through the fog of the unknown, waiting for one with courage to defend against evil.

King Saul closes his eyes and lifts his chin toward the heavens. He exhales a measured and steady breath as chaos churns in the air.

"They cheer for a challenger," King Saul says, his finger methodically tapping his face. "What am I to do? The champion now expects a fight." Saul is visibly distressed and the constant shouts and jeers of the giant are not helping.

He's breaking.

"You leave me with no other choice." Saul's eyes open, refocusing to David's face. "The armor you have carried into battle you shall now wear. The army looks for someone with courage. May they find it in you, David."

David feels his entire body tighten. The decision has been made. There is no turning back now. Yahweh has brought him here, and now *He* must carry him through.

The armor is brought before David and placed upon him. One man pushes and another pulls as, one after the other, they prepare him for the fight, each of them avoiding eye contact, their faces visibly somber.

They think that I'm a sacrifice, David realizes.

No longer treated as a human, but an object, David endures the preparation. With every moment that goes by the crowd grows more unnerved. Each piece of the king's armor is strapped, clasped, and placed upon him. The brass digs into his collar bone. The greaves hang loosely around his legs, smacking his shins with every step he takes. Every bit of the oversized armor is cumbersome and heavy. There is not a chance that he would ever wear it on a march, much less into a battle or a fight to the death. He can't do it. There is only one thing that he needs with him anyway. He clears his throat and steps forward.

"I cannot wear the king's armor," David says, sounding ashamed. "I can only carry what I have tested."

King Saul's eyes fill with remorse as he stands, reaching his hand out to David's shoulder. After a long, silent pause Saul pats David on the side of his arm. "So be it, David. May God be with you."

60

Nothing tells him that he will survive, but he knows he will, and he believes that he has made the right choice. No matter the circumstance, no matter what he feels, he is confident that Yahweh will not turn His back on a righteous stand. David reminds himself that he is nothing more than a vessel that allows the God of Abraham, Isaac, and Jacob to demonstrate His power through him.

He sets his eyes far below on the brook that serpentines through the valley floor, gracefully weaving in and out of the terebinth trees. He descends into the deep valley gorge, trudging forward with ever-increasing resistance. His flesh is fighting for survival. The moment barely seems a reality. The blood that has been retracting from his limbs to protect his core, as often happens in extreme danger, has left his body virtually numb by the time he reaches the brook. Even his hands have a slight quiver. It is the first time that David has ever experienced these reactions. His mind is sharp, but he must find a way to subject his body.

The light rhythm of the brook and the trickle of the water lure his mind back to the stillness of the field. It becomes his sole focus and the cheers of thousands fade into a muffled roar. His mind transports him to the field of manna where he was provided for when he was hungry. To the wilderness where he was protected, even though he felt vulnerable, and the nights under the moon, when the unworldly figure sat with him even though he felt alone.

He has felt the Spirit many times before but only on a few occasions was it not *an* angel, but *the* Angel of the Lord. A faint voice somewhere deep inside whispers that this very figure which has encamped around David, a presence that he reveres, even fears at times, is the same figure that wrestled with Jacob. It is the same figure that appeared before Abraham and Moses as Yahweh himself, Yahweh in the form of a man.

This man, this Angel of the Lord, was promised to be the one that would go before the children of Israel and deliver their enemies before them if they would only obey and trust, for his name was in God, because… he was.

Over David's shoulder to the west, the blackened boulders of the pagan ziggurat, the sacrificial altar erected only weeks ago in his homeland of Judah, rise into the air. The seed inside David that the giant's blasphemies had planted is sprouting. A rage, once buried, is now thriving, fueled with every last defilement on display.

The giant's roar coupled with the thundering cheers of thousands is magnified by the valley walls. The deafening noise draws David's attention back to the chaos, but his eyes focus, his mind sharpens and, suddenly, he no longer feels anxious. Most importantly, his purpose, his calling that has felt dormant for so many years is now wildly alive. He knows that this is what he was born to do.

The Angel of the Lord encamps around those who fear him, and he delivers them, David reminds himself one final time.

He rubs a smooth stone between his fingers. The stone is dense and will fly straight as an arrow to its target. The weight will ensure that the wind will have no effect on its trajectory, and as his experience has taught him, its snug fit measured inside his palm will cause a violent snap as it releases from the worn leather pouch. He places the four perfect stones in his satchel, keeping one in his hand, and removes his sling.

You protected me when I was hunted, fed me when I was hungry, and found me when I was lost. Now grant me strength to stand.

He knows that courage does not come with comfort. He steps forward, pressing, forcing his muscles through a veil of resistance, through the tangible curtain of fear and self-doubt.

KING'S BLOOD | 193

It is his body's last attempt to avoid the danger. David confidence in his craft and in his God brought him here today, started the movement toward the blasphemous challenger, and initiated an escalating series of events that now must be dealt with. They must come to an end.

He steps forward. The instant his sandal connects with the earth the last remaining drop of hesitation shatters like a vase of pottery against stones. He continues forward, leaving the shelter of the tall trees. As the sunlight connects with his ruddy skin, exposing him before the crowd, a warm covering wraps his flesh, but it's not from the sun. Like veins filled with boiling blood, it courses its way toward his hands, his fingertips, and a belief settles deep inside his heart.

I'm no longer alone.

David glances at the thousands cheering from the hills above him. The Hebrew hillside is loud, but uncertain. No challenger has yet to appear before the champion because his nation's army is comprised of men with broken spirits. He can see it in their eyes. David no longer sees an army of soldiers but a flock, his flock, standing on the hill, and to their front a lion roars at them, threatening them. His ears pin tight like a dog backed into a corner. His eyes glaze with a chilling focus. His body ignites with a rage, a belief, which flashes up from somewhere deep inside as the scalding blood courses through his veins, thick and alive like the oil that poured down his face. The seed has fully flourished.

"To whom vengeance belongs, show yourself on my behalf," David whispers as he emerges into the field of battle and every surrounding eye falls upon him.

⊰⊱

The crowd of soldiers squeezes tighter. Elbows, hips, and shoulders, combined with metal armor, press against Abinadab, pushing him from all angles. He tries to focus on the hilltop, searching for David, but he sees no trace of him in between the jolts of the crowd. King Saul, his generals, and the commanders… David is in the midst of none of them. *Where did he go?*

The crowd suddenly calms and Abinadab senses a wave of anticipation sweeping through the ranks. Every head turns toward the west. He lowers his weight and pushes back down toward his brothers, toward the front of the ranks. The opposing side erupts with cheers, and now something has even caught the attention of the giant.

Abinadab emerges though the sweaty entanglement of bodies and joins his brothers at the front just in time to see what has caught the valley by surprise. His heart stops as he sets eyes on his youngest brother now emerging from under the tree-shaded brook. David, completely exposed, is walking in the center of the valley plain – and directly at Goliath.

"What is he doing? He's going to get himself killed," Eliab mumbles and unconsciously moves toward the field. "David, run!" Eliab screams as he breaks free into the open. "He'll rip you apart!"

Soldiers grab Eliab, pulling him back into the ranks. A break in either army's ranks while challengers are engaged in single combat is one of the worst breaches of protocol that could ever occur in combat. Even though victory at all cost is the goal for any battle, there is still a thin code of honor that must be upheld.

Eliab finally stops resisting and calms, acknowledging that there is nothing that he can do to save their youngest. Abinadab notices his brother's quivering lip and realizes that he has no idea who their younger brother is or what he is capable of. Even Shimea, who is by far the hardest on David verbally, has a tear trickle down his dry, blistered face. They seem to think that they already know the outcome.

Abinadab can't help but grin. He sees the thin rope gripped in David's right hand and instantly knows David's ploy.

He places a steady hand on Shimea's shoulder. "Calm yourself, brother. Today the world will see the youngest among us as only I have seen him."

Movement in Abinadab's peripheral vision catches his eye. The heir to the throne, Jonathan, is standing to his right, staring at him with piqued interest. They both glance back to the escalating confrontation.

Eliab's outburst has caught the attention of not only Jonathan but also Goliath whose gaze follows Eliab's and drifts toward David who is approaching the field of battle from his side.

I surely hope he's as confident in himself as I am in him, Abinadab thinks as the moment becomes surreal.

He realizes that he is either about to witness the greatest defeat in history or his youngest brother's brutal death.

Come on, David, prove me right.

61

Goliath has finally noticed him and his expression is exactly what David expects.

The massive giant scoffs, disgusted. He turns to the battered ranks of the Israelites. "Am I a dog that you would send the crumbs of the earth for me to eat?"

Goliath is clearly repulsed and the tone of his voice has just turned the valley silent. His saliva spews into the crowd as his oversized jaw jostles under his drooping cheeks, the weight of which seem to tug at his eyes, giving him a constant grimace.

Both armies hang on his every word. The battle has just become a spectator sport.

Goliath turns toward David with a snarling scowl, his yellow teeth showing for the first time. "May the gods use me to deliver your flesh unto the fowls of the air and the beasts of the field."

David hears the cackle of laughter mustering across the Philistine army to his right. To his left the Israelites stand in horror. Not one of them moves. They are consumed by fear and David decides it is time to remind them all why they can stand in assurance. They, after all, are Yahweh's chosen people.

David can't believe the nerve of this oversized fool. It is becoming increasingly clear that this *champion* has no idea what he is walking into. David pushes him deeper, deeper into an anger that he won't be able to ignore. With the pagan altar to his back he knows that he has to reel in Goliath. He must plant his feet firm and provoke with confidence.

David's voice explodes across the valley. "You come with armor and weapons of war. I come to you as a servant of the One you have defiled."

The snickers halt and it is obvious that he has just shocked both sides with his bold response.

Goliath's face tightens with contempt. His eyes fill with a darkness that could only be harnessed from the afterlife. The anger builds under his dark brow until he unleashes his wrath upon his shield-bearer, striking him with a downward blow. Soldiers gasp and turn away from the brutality, but Goliath's not done.

His sword slices through the inside of the shield-bearer's shoulder penetrating deep into the man's chest, lodging at the base of his sternum. David ignores the sickening sight and instead takes notice of the perfectly impulsive rage of the champion. The champion who has just lost the protection of his massive shield. The reel in has begun.

The sight of a boy as his challenger has clearly hit a nerve. His mindless reaction shows how disrespected he feels. He's trying to prove a point.

Perfect, David thinks, preparing to now exploit it.

Goliath rips the sword out of the shield-bearer, twisting it back and forth as he approaches, letting the sunlight sparkle against the bloody mess. "Then when your master arrives I will strike the both of you down." Goliath turns toward his army. "And I will declare *my* victory!"

David closes his eyes as the valley erupts in cheers. He lets the chaos fade away.

Cheers don't win wars.

As it was with the lion, his breathing is steady, his mind is focused, and the approaching predator is overconfident, severely overlooking the threat in David's hand.

David feels the words welling up inside of him. They pour out of his mouth with a power so forceful that it surprises even himself. "You will declare nothing, for today your head will be removed from your body. And I will carry it as a trophy for what has been done on this day."

Goliath's wide frame shudders with anger, as if demons from Sheol where unleashed from within the prison of his soul, held back only by his flesh as they frenzy inside of him at the brash response. His veins swell, his muscles tighten, and like an untamed beast he lets out a ferocious roar as he storms toward David, completely abandoning tactics. The bait has been set.

Perfect.

The stone has since dried in his hand. The curve will be minimal. David feels the weight, the smoothness, and the angle one last time. His years of practice have made him a master of the craft, each miss bringing him closer to perfection. Every stone he ever hurled was preparation for this very moment.

Slight lift, high and to the right, he calculates each long stride. *Now!*

David sees his opportunity and pushes off into a dead sprint toward Goliath. Each one of his calluses fits snug around the worn rope. His body goes into muscle memory as he whips the sling above his head. He no longer thinks, only reacts.

The gap between them is closing fast. David sets his eyes on the slight opening between the giant's eyes and below the brim of his helmet, nothing else exists. With a quick flick of the wrist, the stone snaps from the worn leather pouch, scorching through the air toward its target. David slows to a stop, watching the stone hurl from end to end. The valley stands still as Goliath's long stride carries his body… up… and to the right.

A loud crack echoes between the valley walls. The growling, snarling roar of the giant is suddenly replaced by a final gasp. His momentum carries him forward, face forward, crashing into the ground at David's feet. The gigantic body, which is now limp, hits the ground with the impact of an ox falling from the edge of Michmash.

Dust coils into the air and a dry grit peppers David's lips. The dark cloud envelops him, but David stands his ground, never flinching, only wiping the sting from his eyes. Goliath's sweaty, oily body has been coated in the brown dirt that now fades to a dark red liquid.

David follows the crimson trail to Goliath's head. The sight is shocking at first glimpse. The stone traveled with such force that the elongated skull has completely caved at the forehead. Shattered bone fragments protrude where the eyes once were and a large black hole oozes a thick, red liquid that mixes with other fluids before draining across the giant's face.

David glances up to the thousands that now stand in stunned silence. Proven, his God will not be mocked.

With the attention of every eye in the valley bearing down upon him, David delivers on his promise. He wraps his fingers tightly around the hilt of Goliath's sword. His muscles strain, each fiber in his arms exploding with the effort to lift the long slab of iron. With a thrust of power he launches the sword off his shoulder and directs its path as it falls. Like a mattock into the dirt, he thrusts a perfect strike between the stones, directly toward Goliath's neck. The blade impacts, slices through, and plunges into the earth.

62

Kilech watches in awe, horrified. This army that once walked with such malice and arrogance behind their champion now stands in shock, having witnessed the unthinkable. As thousands are captivated by this rugged boy lifting the head of the giant into the air, fulfilling a promise that he proclaimed only moments ago, Kilech can't help but wonder what power this boy must possess.

He's reminded of the legends that his elders passed along. The Ark of the Covenant that brought plagues to his people when they stole it, the exodus from Egypt and the impossible pass through the Red Sea, and now this boy. What is this invisible God of theirs to Dagon?

The boy has disappeared into the flooding ranks of his people, ranks that now clash with unimaginable force into the retreating Philistine soldiers. The boy emerges moments later from the valley floor with the head still grasped in his grip. Kilech immediately fears for his people, for himself.

What purpose do I have if there is nothing to document for the generations?

Once again the dread of being surrounded by these savages seeps up under Kilech's tongue. His throat fills with the acid that always bubbles into his mouth accompanied by worry. King Achish to his right has yet to move, yet to speak, and Kilech fears that one movement will remind the king of his worthless existence.

"Who is that boy?" King Achish's voice snaps the silence, but only with a whisper.

Kilech, unsure if the king is speaking to him and without having an answer, keeps his mouth shut.

King Achish turns toward him. "Scribe, what has been done here today must be remembered. All should know what happens when you are not in Dagon's favor." He calmly moves his gaze back to the valley. "We will use Goliath's misfortune to corral his brothers into action for us. You will write what I tell you to write and together we will make history tell *our* story."

The anxiety slowly starts to drain as Kilech now feels needed, even trusted. He turns his gaze back to the Israeli ranks and locks onto a familiar face. The man that killed his own blood, the one that moved like a spirit in the night on the top of Michmash, slaughtering everything that had breath... the heir to their throne is within sight. His face has been ingrained into Kilech's mind. He watches him with narrowed focus, his hatred boiling up with each passing moment.

"Get on the chariot." A hand grabs Kilech and pulls him toward the peak of the hill. He looks back toward the now escalating sound of feet thundering across the valley.

The timid army of Israel has just received a dose of empowerment, putting the entire war culture of Gath and all of its soldiers on the run. The wave of Hebrews is now climbing to the top of the valley wall.

The boy has done the impossible all right.

Abinadab celebrates with his brothers as they all reach David, who is now pressing against the wave of soldiers charging across the valley. Everyone feels the need to touch, thank, and stare at his younger brother. David doesn't seem affected by it in the least, almost as if he doesn't even notice the praise. His eyes are intense. It appears that he has yet to finish his mission, whatever that may be. David is not relishing the moment as many would expect. With every step he takes through the crowd and up the hill, Abinadab becomes even more intrigued by

David's actions.

⊹⊱══⊰⊹

King Saul looks on, his eyes widened with amazement. His men are charging up the opposing valley wall, hacking down the Peleshet with aggression, a roar of victory on their breath. The giant is dead and all because of this shepherd boy, this musician, and now, apparently, this warrior.

Saul was all but certain the boy would be slaughtered, leaving him with a new set of problems, but somehow the shepherd succeeded.

How did he ever do this?

Saul needs to find out more information. This… warrior has something that he obviously needs.

"Of what family is this youth?" Saul asks.

General Abner's attention turns to David approaching through the crowd. "You shall soon find out, my king."

David emerges out of the chaos, the giant's hair gripped tightly in his hands, dragging the head behind him. Jonathan is now by his side, clearing the way. King Saul stands, waiting respectfully.

"You have slaughtered the champion valiantly. What is the name of your father's house for which you fight?"

David drops the massive head to the grass then kneels. "I come to you from the house of my father, Jesse, the son of Obed."

King Saul gently takes hold of David's arm, lifting him back to his feet. "You do so no longer. From now on you will fight for the name of the king."

63

As the chariot crawls forward over lush green grass, David is still living off the rush from the victory in the Elah Valley. The giant fell only hours ago, yet the moment already feels unreal. With a quick glance to what lies between his feet at the base of the chariot, the grim reality returns. The mangled head of Goliath, with dried blood still stuck to its face, would look back at him if it still had eyes, bouncing and jolting as the wooden wheels roll over the uneven terrain.

Following his brief interaction with the king, David had only one request in regard to King Saul's offer. Seeing that David was lugging the bloody trophy tight to his side, Saul offered to place the head of Goliath wherever David saw fit. Now, David is nearing the border of the Tribe of Benjamin. Just south is his hometown of Beit Lehem, but David has no intention of heading home with this symbol of wickedness.

The chariot stops far short of David's final destination. They have approached Jebusite territory and King Saul's men know what will happen to them if they continue. No one approaches the mount and returns alive. After today's events, however, David has little worry for his safety.

This must be done, he thinks.

He drags the head out of the royal chariot. He is just glad that King Saul granted this royal escort for David's personal mission.

When he was a young child, he would stare off toward the north, toward Mt. Moriah, the mount of Yireh, and Shalom. He feels a yearning toward it, a destiny, and after the rush of today nothing is going to stop the fulfillment of his desire.

He strolls through the thick brush toward the hill without coming into contact with any outsiders, but as he begins his ascent of the mountain base he begins attracting the eyes of the Jebusites. He reaches halfway up the mountain, and all eyes are upon him, but no one says a word as he passes through. Maybe it has something to do with the warm liquid dripping from his hand, or the thick, coarse hair wrapped tightly between his fingers. But it certainly has everything to do with the gigantic, scowling human head he's dragging behind him, the one with the wound the size of a fist in its face.

David knows how fierce he must look, and he uses every bit of it to his advantage. He feels that the Spirit of God has led him here, so who is going to stop him?

With each stride bringing him closer to the top, his emotions well up in his throat, like an olive press squeezing his lungs tighter with each step. He realizes that ever since he can remember he has dreamt of walking up this path, taking the same steps that Abraham and his son Isaac, the promised child, had taken. He crests the top, glancing back to gaze upon where Isaac would have arrived on a donkey, carrying the very wood on his back on which he was to be sacrificed.

David glances around the panoramic view, envisioning what Isaac must have felt after being saved, resurrected from sure death only three days into their journey. On this hill, the same Presence that stopped Abraham is here with David today, and it was in the valley shrouded with spiritual darkness.

He stands in the very spot where Abraham cut a covenant between man and God and received from Yahweh the promise regarding his own sacrifice. He stands in the location where Isaac was saved and God promised to take his place.

"Here I will bury the seed of evil, as a symbol of your promise. And to show the nations that not I but you killed the giant, through your servant."

David covers the crushed head with the last bit of dirt. The words of Moses spring up, sending a chilled wave across his skin.

He will crush your head and you will bruise his heel.

David wonders what more could take place on this very mount, a mount that has already received the fulfillment of so many promises.

One day, we will take it again, David thinks. *It will again be ours.*

It has been hundreds of years since a Hebrew has witnessed this beautiful view. David is the first Israeli to stand atop their sacred mountaintop since possibly before they left for Egypt. His journey straight to the top has emboldened him even more. He's not sure how but something deep down inside tells him that he will be back.

This won't be the last time I stand here.

He turns for one last glimpse as he begins his descent. Every major event that has taken place on this mountain has claimed a name and today will be no different.

Today it will be easy, "the place of the Skull, Golgotha."

64

King Saul waits in the dining hall, his advisors, his court, and his family stand with him, anticipating the arrival of the new champion. The table has been prepared with the king's best. The room is filled with the aroma of fresh charred meat and ripe fruit. Not one detail has been overlooked.

The door creaks open and a hesitant David enters. No one speaks. Everyone in the room, including Saul, stands. It appears that everyone is admiring the boy's timid humility, but also his transformation. His clothing has been changed, he's washed, and his hair is trimmed, revealing a young and handsome youth.

Realizing that the boy's reception upon entering the room has been gazing eyes and silence, Saul does his best to put David at ease.

"Come, eat, all of this is for you, my son." Saul guides David with a gentle hand toward his seat.

Saul watches David sit awkwardly, staring at the vast quantities of food that is laid out before him. Saul recalls to when he was young and understands David's hesitation.

"David, here you are not the least among us. Here *you* eat first."

⟰

The intimidation that David feels in a room surrounded by leaders and royalty is nothing compared to the feeling that emerges with a single glance across the table. Young, beautiful eyes watch his every move. He breathes steadily before glancing back at her. Her grin grows into a smile as she watches David reach for his food.

David is not a graceful eater, he knows that much. Still, he decides to go for it. First, her nose scrunches, and then cute dimples emerge as she bubbles into laughter, watching David take his first bite. The smiles and laughter trickle down to the end of the table. David is horrified and glances to King Saul, hoping for some relief, but it doesn't come from the king.

Directly across from David, on the right side of Saul, Jonathan, the heir, puts down his utensils and grabs his food with his bare hands. "May we all be so lucky to eat as the champion eats."

King Saul laughs, dropping his utensils and picking up his food with his hands. David can't believe it. He didn't even notice the hardware next to his plate. It has been far too long since he has eaten a civilized meal at a table. He glances back to what had captivated his mind to this point in the first place. How could he be so lucky?

Of all that could be his focus right now, only one of them has his attention. He remembers her from months ago when he first entered the palace. The silky black hair accented with the light tint of a jasmine blossom tucked behind her ear, the gentle motion of her body when she walked, her softly toned skin, and exotic eyes, like a wildcat eyeing its prey. And now she's here, again.

One at a time, each person sitting at the table begins to eat with their fingers. The quiet stuffiness of a royal dinner vanishes as the attendees relax, giving in to childlike laughter. Banter and stories are exchanged and David is at the center of it all. He is flattered at the attempt of such highly respected individuals to make him feel comfortable, but it wasn't needed. His eyes drift back to the girl sitting next to Jonathan. She has to be ten, maybe fifteen years, younger than Jonathan and only a few years older than David. She couldn't be Jonathan's wife. Possibly a concubine?

The image of Ezsri flashes before him. Her beauty, intelligence, and toughness are unmatched, but this girl, this woman, she lures his eyes with nothing more than a tempting glance. Her eyes have a language all their own and their message is clear.

David turns his head but his eyes stay fixed on her. She is making it obvious that David is the object of her attention. Gracefully, she places a grape on her tongue, dragging her finger across her lip. Her eyes never leave David's and now only one thing is on his mind.

I need to find out who she is.

He breaks eye contact, shocked, having felt a desire that he has never experienced before. His gaze bounces directly to Jonathan whose own glance is piercing straight through David's thoughts. David jolts back, his heart pounding in his chest, worried that his interest has just become public knowledge and he has yet to find out to whom, if anyone, she belongs.

As dinner winds to a close, Jonathan nods, as if to say, "Follow me."

David intends to do so without hesitation, knowing the history and reputation of the king's son. He is a violent man, a warrior like no other in all of Israel, and his feats are that of legends. David just hopes that he hasn't crossed any lines, because Jonathan is the last person that anyone would want to provoke.

David slips from his seat and follows Jonathan out the door, unnoticed, as the dinner party guests begin mingling. As they make their way quietly down a hall lined with flickering torches, David quickly realizes that he would gladly be uncomfortable in the presence of many than nervous in the silence of one – Jonathan.

65

David enters a dimly lit room with Jonathan. As he enters, Jonathan closes the door, sealing the two of them inside.

"I noticed you had a hard time taking your eyes off of the female beside me," Jonathan says, standing rigid and firm in front of David. "Did you guess her age? She has you by a few years."

David can almost smell the confidence radiating from Jonathan's pores. His body is tight. His wrists are thick and his waist slim and defined. The scars that riddle his body speak volumes of his experiences, and his eyes reveal a life of killing almost twice the years of David's existence.

David doesn't respond. He stands in timid awe of the warrior before him.

"Do you know who she is to me?" Jonathan asks. "I would protect her with my life. Do you know why?"

David clears his throat. "She is your wife?"

"No," Jonathan's stern gaze collapses into laughter, "she is my sister." He smacks David on the arm. "I could have kept you going for a lot longer, but you just had a pretty big day, killing a giant and all."

David grins. His body relaxes, relieved. And then the reality of what Jonathan just said hits him. "Your sister, you mean – "

"Yes, Michal, is the one father promised to the victor over the champion. There is a reason that only a champion of combat could take her in marriage. She is a handful." Jonathan laughs.

She will be mine?

The thought is intimidating. She is gorgeous, mature, and with only a look, can pull feelings from David that he didn't know he had. Suddenly, reality hits him. The palace, the dinner, and the daughter, it all seems too much, too quick, and all for nothing more than following Yahweh's leading.

"I don't deserve any of this."

"So I would have thought," Jonathan says as he slides the royal robe from his shoulders, placing it around David, "until I saw your brother's eyes. While every soldier there saw a youth preparing to be slaughtered, your brother saw a champion. I see a champion. Anyone willing to lay down his life with such courage for our people, my father counts as a son, I count as my brother."

Jonathan lowers to his knees. He loosens his belt, removing his bow and placing it at David's feet. He removes his sword from its sheath. With both hands, he lifts the sword toward David, presenting it to him.

"A son?" David retracts his outstretched hands, denying his natural reflex of accepting an offered gift. "I couldn't possibly. I am not counted as much in my own family. What right is it of mine to call myself a son or brother of royalty?"

"It is not your right to decide. It is my father's." Jonathan nods for David to take the offering.

Humbled, David grips the cold leather straps wrapped tightly around the iron handle.

Jonathan stands, placing his hands on David's shoulders. His demeanor is intense. The youthful personality that was just displayed is almost a past memory.

"Yahweh has brought you here and I am humbled in your presence. As you breathe, so shall I breathe, and as you live, so shall I live. Until our final hour, we shall be more than brothers. We shall be one. Even beyond death, my name shall be considered yours, and yours mine."

David is overwhelmed by the love shown by such a strong warrior. Jonathan is a commander of thousands, a violent fighter, and the heir of the kingdom, and he not only kneels but commits his life before him?

David imagines the ancient blood covenant, in which an animal is split in half, and the two individuals commending their lives to one another walk a figure eight, meeting face-to-face in the middle of the sundered animal. It is a significant promise, a symbol that only death can break their loyalty. It is commemorated as they sprinkle the animal's blood on a tree planted as a symbol to never forget the covenant. And now, David has just cut a similar covenant from King Saul's very son.

"May God do so to me and more also if anything but death parts me from you," Jonathan says.

"So to me and more also if anything but death parts me from *you*," David responds, almost fainting at the implications of his words.

The moment is not taken lightly by either of the two. They have just committed their lives to one another as an oath under God. And David has just entered into a covenant with the heir of the kingdom. Again he stands in awe, with no other explanation of how he ended up here other than Yahweh's grand design continuing to unfold.

His eyes drift about the room. The fires flickering along the walls, the violet silk sheets draped across the bed nestled in the corner. The room is the most elaborate sleeping quarters he has ever seen. It is fitting for royalty.

"All of this is overwhelming. The palace, your family, your kindness, even your room is faultless. I would be pleased to sleep with the animals just to enjoy the shelter."

Jonathan grins as he heads for the door. "This room is perfect for resting after long days of testing your body. Now I wouldn't stay up too late if I were you. I'll be back in the morning. Tomorrow is the beginning of your official training."

"Wait. You'll be back?" David asks. "I can't take your room."

"David, this isn't *my* room. It's yours."

66

Swords clang and the sweat of exhausted men sprays into the air as soldiers step forward one at a time, each one of them testing their ability against the greatest. Parrying, blocking, and striking with lion like reflexes, David outsmarts and outmaneuvers every last one of them. He moves with strict discipline yet flows like the animals of the wild. His unorthodox fighting style is hard to match, impossible to teach.

Exhausted and out of breath, the last soldier lowers to the ground in agony as he reaches for his cramping side. Saul watches as David forces every last one of them back to their feet. His instruction is swift, personal, and devoted, working with each one until they understand the cause of their failure.

Saul is proud of what David has become. He is a master of the craft, a student of the law, a devoted soldier, but most importantly he has integrated into their family. Even though he is not of Saul's own blood, he lives as if he were. There is no one more loyal than David has been.

As the soldiers pair up, each to an equal opponent, to rehearse the day's techniques, Saul notices Jonathan standing at the edge of the hilltop. Jonathan motions David toward him. After David crosses the field, the two warriors stand facing the rolling hills. Their conversation is full of hand motions and gestures that lead to laughter. They are always together, always talking, always laughing.

Saul wonders what they could be speaking of. What could be so funny during the preparation for the warring season? If only they knew the stress that was on his shoulders. If only they could taste one bit of it. Over the years they have become inseparable, like brothers, or rather like father and son, uncle and nephew. After all, Jonathan was in charge of divisions before David was even born.

He had felt much like a father, but as David grows it seems every day that Saul becomes more like a grandfather, enjoying the little moments of growth. Saul would surmise that David's growth has not been little moments but massive leaps. He has a gift of war that has blossomed since the days of the giant, and Saul is thankful that Yahweh has granted him such talents to be subjugated under his command.

"What do you think of their relationship, my king?" Abner says stepping to Saul's side on the staircase.

"I was just thinking how wonderful it has been having David under Jonathan's wing. Jonathan is smart. He knew before all of us what David would become. It was wise of him to align himself so quickly to an incredible warrior."

Abner hands Saul a rolled up ball of khat leaves to ease his mind. Saul shoves the dry green leaves deep against the corner of his cheek as Abner has always done to relieve the stress of the coming season, but he's not so sure it works.

"As long as he *stays* under his wing, my king."

"If David were going to make a move he would have done it by now, but I don't think he could if he wanted to. He has too much love for us, we are his family," Saul says.

Abner doesn't respond. Instead, he appears to purposely let Saul sit in his own silence to consider the general's comment. Abner's seed of doubt has caught him off guard. A part of him has always wondered if it were possible. What if Abner's suspicions were correct?

His thoughts manifest to his mouth. "Unless, of course, Jonathan was scheming all along to use David's talents to rob me of my position."

Saul has said it out loud. With David's intellect, the possibility of

David becoming Jonathan's pawn has never felt possible, but saying it out loud has brought about new perceptions of the possibility.

"I am not only here to guide the army, but also to guide you. To remind you to never become complacent. Everyone is after your throne," Abner says, seeming to know Saul's thoughts.

Saul squints, straining to observe David and Jonathan across the field. "I love them both as sons. I cannot, I will not, bring the sword against them without cause."

"I do not prescribe the sword, only to take advantage of what you've been given. The rest will sort itself out in time."

"And what have I been given?"

"An ability to gain more alliances and expand our influence," Abner says. "David could be our greatest political ploy to garner greater backing from the tribes, especially Judah. Use his gift in peace to unite the nation and strengthen our presence among the tribes, and we will be unstoppable in war."

Saul considers the implication, David *has* been a gift and with his unparalleled tact he could pull the entire tribe of Judah into support of a Benjaminite king, something that has eluded him for his entire reign. He knows that his humble origins and aversion to public exposure has hindered the nation from accepting him as the single representation of their twelve tribes.

David would thrive as a delegate of their message, just as he thrives as a delegate of their power. It is the tribe of Judah, after all, that send their brightest and toughest from the fields each year to fight. They are a kindred breed of warriors with a territory large enough in size that with full support would be followed by many of the other tribes, some of which have sectors that haven't sent men to war for years.

Saul's mind drifts to the words of Jacob some seven hundred years ago regarding the ruler's staff not departing from Judah. Could he truly be looking at the very son of promise?

If he is, wouldn't Samuel have anointed him already, Saul thinks.

The possibility is all the more reason to garner support from Judah. Saul realizes that now more than ever he must overlook his own shortcomings and public disdain, and capture the heart of the people.

"If they have been creating an alliance under our eyes then maybe we should place them in competition with one another and see how Jonathan handles his apprentice as an equal, a rival," Abner says, resting his hand on Saul's back.

Saul nods, confirming. "Place David in charge of the division opposite Jonathan and make it a promotion, nothing more."

How quickly his thoughts have drifted from family leisure to the political prowess that has kept him king.

"I will inform David of his promotion immediately, my king. I will ensure to make it public so as not to waste exposure in terms of our loyalty to Judah."

"No. I've decided that I will tell him."

67

Warm liquid slaps across Aaron's face. He recoils in disgust, regaining control of his sword before the next onslaught of flesh and bronze attacks his position. Planting his feet on the ground and realigning his grip, Aaron swipes the fluid from his eyes and spits the warm metallic saliva from the corner of his mouth. There is no time to contemplate the taste or the smell while Jonathan is engaged by his side. The warring season has begun and it already feels more intense than the last.

Aaron spots an enemy combatant charging with reckless abandon toward Jonathan. If he charges now, he will have just enough time to intersect with the enemy sword, giving Jonathan the time he needs to cut down the last remaining pocket of soldiers. Aaron presses off but a hand grips his leg, sending his face into the mud. He strikes the arm, separating it from the body with quick precision, causing the grip on his calf to fall limp, but the damage has been done. His opportunity was narrow and now he will never reach Jonathan in time.

Helpless, he crawls like a snake on his belly, trying to get into a position to intervene for Jonathan. He shrieks, but his opportunity has truly passed, and Jonathan, being fully engaged, has no chance to look, even if Aaron's voice hadn't been drowned out by the chaos.

Aaron reaches out, twisting onto his side, his sword pointing toward the sky, but it's no use. The boulder next to him has become a perfect shield for the enemy. He screams as the enemy thrusts for the kill. Mud splashes into his eyes, and he hears the all too familiar bone-crunching strike as a sword plunges through the human anatomy. His throat swells with pressure, his remorse overwhelming him. He turns away, unable to look, grimacing at the possible fate of his sole reason to live.

Aaron squeezes the sword's grip tightly. If Jonathan is dead then every last one of them will die, and Aaron will die with respect. He prepares to leap to his feet, but the sound of battle fades softly, replaced by laughter. Aaron glances up and is shocked at the sight before him.

68

David stands over the enemies' mangled bodies with his hand stretched out. Jonathan grabs it and David slings him back to his feet.

"Sorry, brother," David says. "But if you remained standing, this would have been plunged into your ribs." David taps his blade against the enemy's weapon.

Jonathan laughs. "I had the situation in hand."

"It sure looked that way," David says with a smirk.

David's attention is drawn to an aggressive, yet efficient, warrior fending off an ambush in the distance. The Hebrew that catches his interest moves with grace, emerging from a dark, concealed crack between boulders. He has a striking precision and fluidity that David has rarely, if ever, seen.

The warrior slices his way through the ambush, using the element of surprise and speed, as if it were the only way he knew to fight. The enemies fall, silent, and the warrior scours their bodies, removing their smaller, more subtle weapons, adding each to his own arsenal and leaving behind their larger, more cumbersome swords.

David has noticed his unconventional fighting style but he doesn't catch a glimpse of the soldier's face. The only defining features are the backs of his hands, which are covered in small, consecutive scars. David wonders what could have caused those marks. They surely aren't from a sword blade. The soldier moves back into the ranks as if nothing happened, like a ghost haunting its target and then returning to its original form back in the shadows. David knows one thing. He will see him again because he could use a warrior with not only those skills, but also the crafty approach.

David turns his attention to Aaron who, having fallen on his way toward Jonathan, seems to be relishing in a mud bath.

"No time to relax, Aaron, we have a battle to win."

David grabs Aaron's arm, lifting him to his feet. He appears to be on the verge of tears. David was already running to Jonathan, having seen the battle sway, when Aaron fell. He knows his courage, but more importantly he knows the disgrace he must feel for failing today.

"Our bodies will fail us, it's what they do. Just ensure your heart continues to stand strong and you will live long past the days of your body's final failure," David says, squeezing Aaron's shoulder tightly. He quickly redirects his sights to the top of the boulders. Using the leverage of Aaron's shoulder, he pushes off, climbing to the top of the large stones. "Stand with pride, Aaron, another victory is about to be claimed."

David's eyes survey the entire battlefield. His measured scan from across the field atop the elevated stone, allows his mind to process the entire layout encircling him. With his division nowhere to be seen, David knows their positioning is perfect for the coming maneuver. He has split his division into two parts, concealing them among the rolling hills to both the east and west. With the enemy sporadically scattered throughout the field and having left their lines in disarray, David unleashes the order.

With a single word, two flanks emerge and rush over the hill. As if the gates restraining the floods have been ordered to open, the two walls of human flesh converge, smashing into the enemy. The swift action and overpowering momentum from the sides is something to behold. The slaughter is unchallenged as the warriors smash inward. The wave of soldiers crashes with swift violence, and by the time the swell of soldiers dissipates it's too late. The enemy has been drowned. Not in the clear liquid of the ocean, but in the thick crimson of death.

There is no chance for David to even dismount the stone before the battle has ended. The men erupt in cheers and turn their attention to David, who remains standing like an iconic statue atop the boulder, surrounded by carnage. The whole battlefield erupts with shouts of victory.

"As they cheer for you, so do they fight," Jonathan says.

"My brother, they fight for what we all fight for, freedom for our people. We are all servants, nothing more."

David's eyes stray, still searching for that unique fighter. He needs to find out who his commander is so that he can learn more of this warrior's skill and attitude, and possibly barter for him. David is in the midst of building a deadly fighting force that of which the nation may never have seen. His style, tactics, and aggression are continually evolving and he needs more pieces to fit his mold.

If the army is going to continue to be victorious, they will need to adapt to more unorthodox methods. David could surely use a warrior with knowledge of concealment and ambush techniques to lead his men on scouting raids and parallel movements. With nothing more than his preference of weapon and the scars on the backs of his hands to identify him, David knows one thing.

I need to find that Hebrew.

69

Saul's feet are sore and swollen in his sandals. He is exhausted and his back is beginning to tighten, but a smile creeps across his face as he crests the long, winding road leading into Gibeah. It is by far his most favorite time of year. The season of war has come to an end and the streets are lined with family, friends, and proud veterans who have long aged beyond their place for war. Everyone present is waiting to show their support of the soldiers that have defended their homeland once again.

As Saul rounds the final bend, the city, his capital, and the crowd swarming the streets materialize over the hill. Cheers erupt, hands wave, and overzealous women jump excitedly, seeking nothing more than eye contact from the king for a brief moment in passing. If they're lucky, maybe he'll reach out and touch them. Saul's grin widens with the thought.

This is why we fight, he thinks.

The hands begin reaching, grabbing at him from the sea of people, as he continues the path toward the palace. His eyes search the crowd, looking for those for whom a mere glance would bring them joy. After all, they have come out and waited, standing a long time, just to lay eyes on royalty, victorious royalty nonetheless.

One after the other, Saul notices that the eyes aren't all focused on him – not on his great stature that leads the entire army. No, they have drifted and are yearning to catch a glimpse of someone else.

Saul's grin fades. *Who could they possibly be looking for?*

David walks with Jonathan and Nathaniel by his side at the front of their men. He feels all the eyes in the crowd gazing down upon them. Or are they? He glances from face to face, catching one gaze after another. No, their eyes are more focused. They are gazing directly upon… him.

The feeling is quite unnatural. He is more accustomed to blending in, but over the years the attention on him, especially after the giant, has grown and his reaction to it has evolved to the point where he no longer displays his discomfort, but this is more than he has become accustomed to.

He understands that many find it easier to celebrate that which they can see, touch, that which they can understand. David slows his step. Looking deep into their eyes, he can see the truth. Their hearts are revealed. They are blinded by status, celebrating the flesh of man rather than the true cause of their victory.

Lest he become arrogant by the blessings provided by Yahweh, he reminds himself, *this is not why we fight.*

"The king has killed his thousands!" a voice shouts from the front.

"And David his tens of thousands!" a woman replies.

The crowd roars with laughter and cheers.

Jonathan laughs, turning toward David. "Just a servant?"

David shoots Jonathan an unpleasant gaze. The remarks toward the king are not to be taken lightly. But before he can respond he is distracted.

A gorgeous woman, slim with a tight athletic build, stands motionless amidst the chaos and locks eyes with him. She grins, as if she knows something that he doesn't. She has David's full attention.

She recognizes me, David realizes.

He can tell by the way she knowingly smiles, waiting for his eyes to focus and recognize her. They do and suddenly it hits him. *Ezsri!*

David fills with excitement. He has no time to stop, they both know it, but the years of separation seem to not have affected their connection in the least. Ezsri flexes her arm and points to David, as if to say that she could still take him. He laughs, missing her playful humor, but not missing the way that she would constantly get the best of him with his limited technique.

He looks to his arms and winks back, letting her know that the old days have passed. Ezsri leans forward and David's eyes follow her as he moves away. The two enjoy one last glimpse of each other and the moment fades as the crowd envelops her behind him. The smile stretching across David's face as he remembers the years of his youth is hard to suppress. They were good days. And, hopefully, there will be many more to come. He knows Ezsri will always have a spot in his heart, but it's the king's daughter, Michal, that has captured his whole heart. He turns back to the front, thankful for the past, but excited for the future.

Saul peers over his shoulder after noticing the attention has been diverted and now he sees to whom. Apparently, the cheers have been turned toward David's favor. Saul's stomach turns with indignation at what he sees. His vision constricts under the crushing weight of his insecurity. Rage rushes through his body like storm winds swirling violently under his skin. His eyes continue to tighten until his pinhole focus locks solely on David's laughter, laughter at the most inconceivable of remarks.

He's enjoying every last bit of this, Saul thinks as his heart swallows any remaining doubt before plummeting into the bellows of his stomach. *Maybe I was wrong about him all along.*

70

David wastes no time stripping out of his hefty bronze battle armor, replacing it with lightweight linens that drape and flow from his muscular frame. His body, still wet with perspiration, is instantly refreshed when he steps out into the open air that blows almost endlessly across the top of Mount Gibeah.

Instead of heading toward the rest of the soldiers that gather with their loved ones near the water wells, David descends toward the valley as he always does, alone. As much as he enjoys the camaraderie, there still remain times when he must pull away and renew, and the still water of the Gibeah spring pool and the tranquil sounds of the wilderness are the balms that his drained soul longs for.

His feet are callused and pain strikes his shins with each step. Each step, however, brings him closer to settling his mind and shocking his body with the cold, refreshing mountain water.

He pushes forward to the bottom of the mount and through the thick brush that circles the pool of water like a crown of privacy. Boulders are a perfect accent, adorning the ring of foliage like rubies strewn in gold.

Without hesitation, David drops the clothes that cover his hardened, perfected body. He wades into the freezing cold water hidden idly in the shade. Every muscle in his body instantly contracts and a chill covers his flesh, like a bed of pine needles sticking his skin in all directions. The ice-cold spring water shocks his lungs as his chest dips below the surface.

After the long season of war, the silence is bliss. With his head back and eyes closed, he listens to the trees rustle in the breeze, sounding like the Great Sea colliding with sandy beaches, sending his imagination back to his youth. The tension wrapping him finally releases, allowing him to relax. The stillness is everything he imagined it would be. He dreamed of this moment often while fighting in the campaigns far from home, and it feels good to be back.

In no hurry and without a care, he eventually wades back through the water toward the shore. Feeling the sandy, stony ground again under his feet, he lets the water line dip just to below his waist. David opens his eyes before leaving the pool and revealing himself in the process.

His heart seizes in his chest at the figure directly in front of him. He stops dead in his tracks, the breath in his lungs holding fast. His fear turns more toward embarrassment as he realizes who it is. Reclining comfortably on a boulder, holding his clothes in her hands, and wearing a playful grin, is King Saul's daughter. No longer does she wear a jasmine blossom in her hair but the same alluring eyes that caught his attention that first day in the palace are once again at work on him now.

Michal bites her lip as she drops his clothes to the ground three paces from the water line. "Come and get them," she says playfully, holding back laughter.

David looks down. He's in no shape to get out of the water.

"I'm waiting," she says, grinning.

The look in her eyes is a look that David has seen a thousand times before. Over the years, they have grown together, and being the king's daughter, Michal has always gotten what she wanted. Now, those exotic eyes beckon him to leave the water, beckon him to expose himself both physically and mentally. David begins to believe that her persistence may eventually wear him down, and there is a good chance that eventually is right now.

They have kept their underlying love for one another a secret, at least from King Saul. Jonathan and a few others know, but David is aware that even though the king promised this daughter for the giant's death, he has yet to offer her. Therefore, she is off limits. As she slides off of the rock, she appears to purposely lift her garment, exposing her bare leg. David's willpower is slipping faster than Michal slipping down the side of the boulder.

Don't move, he tells himself, fighting his lustful emotions harder than any battle that he has ever fought with a sword.

Leisurely, she bends down, picks up his clothes, and lifts her purple dress, holding the bottom of it in her hand, teasing it above the water. She wades out, her eyes exploring David's bare chest. The water deepens with each step, and she reaches him just before the water soaks her fabric.

She offers his clothes and he reaches. Michal slides in close under his arm and David's mental strength evaporates as she tilts her head back, revealing a neck like a gazelle welcoming the lion's final strike. David's body floods with passion. As she guides her lips to his, an internal spark ignites into an uncontrollable fire. He wants to let go and enjoy the moment but a nagging thought continues to cross his mind as her soft lips connect with his.

You're always being watched, not only the eyes of a kingdom, but the eyes of the creator himself, David tells himself.

It's a thought that continually plagues him. Then, with the subtle sound of leaves rustling in the distance, the moment is over. David is rushed back to reality. It's no longer just a fear. Someone *is* watching.

As Michal gasps in panic, David covers himself and charges into the brush to see who is spying, but he's too late. Whoever it was is gone, hidden by the foliage all the way to the hilltop. Still holding his clothes tight to his naked body, and hidden by the brush, David bends down to dress when he notices a snagged piece of fabric hanging from a thorn. It's the common cloth of a royal guard's tunic.

The question now, however, is whose tunic?

71

The town of Ramah sits just north of the capital city of Gibeah, but the two cities couldn't be farther from each other's way of life. The city of Gibeah thrives with activity. Travelers pass through, often staying the night and providing a steady stream of currency and stories, keeping the entertainment endless. Ramah, on the other hand, is quiet, slow, and at night the city vanishes into the dark. The only lights that burn throughout the night are the lamps perched in the windows of the town shrine.

After the city of Shiloh, which held both the nation's altar and the Ark of the Covenant, was destroyed by the Sea People, Samuel settled in Ramah and dedicated a new altar there, replacing nearly three hundred years of annual sacrifice in Shiloh. This time, however, the sacred vessels, including the Ark of the Covenant and the Ten Commandments, would be secretly stored in a distant city, Kirjath-Jearim.

Although Samuel is close to Gibeah, he hasn't journeyed to the capital since the confrontation with Saul. Samuel's harsh words so many years ago have been his last to the king. There is no need to see him. He can feel that something is changing, and soon. He kneels in silence, waiting for the wisdom that whispers to his soul.

Earlier in the day, he felt that something, after all of these years, had begun to shift. Like waking from a deep sleep, his spirit is alive once again. Now, as he kneels here inside the dimly lit shrine, he hears that all too familiar whisper. He knows the time is approaching. The tide of the kingdom is rising and soon all that was once secure will crash down upon the gritty sand of which it was once united.

"Whatever the test," Samuel prays, "may you be with your anointed. May you be with David."

With the pit of Samuel's stomach tightening, he knows one thing is for sure. *The tide is turning and David is going to need every bit of help he can get.*

72

Marching across the border into Israelite territory, the Philistines move with speed. They have come to conduct much-needed raids for supplies. Kilech slows his pace and drifts back toward the rear of the formation. It is not the threat of crossing into one of Israel's twelve tribes that has him on edge, but rather the absence of his protector, King Achish. Without the king's presence, Kilech is at the mercy of his commander, and scribes are better off unnoticed.

Their march is toward the vulnerable city of Eshtaol in the Hebrew territory of Dan. The city sits on the edge of the plains where the hill country begins. It is one of the few Israelite locations that are not completely fortified by the walled, mountainous landscapes.

Eshtaol is far enough from Saul's forces in Gibeah that his army could never muster in time to repel a quick raid. It will be an easy plunder, now that the main force has returned for the end of the campaign season. Kilech inscribes their march with meticulous precision. King Achish has made it clear. He wants to know the details. He wants to ensure the spoils are accounted for prior to them passing through anyone's hands.

Recording such a raid has become second nature, so much so that Kilech could fight and record the battle from experience. After all, he has had more than ten years of traveling with the army, and there is no better place to taste bloodshed for the first time than a raid on a complacent city, a complacent *Hebrew* city.

For most of the night he has kept his distance from the commander, but now he will need to come face-to-face with him if he is ever going to get what he wants, if he is ever going to get his chance. And with the Hebrew city lights of Eshtaol flickering in the distance, his time is here. He feels the army's march slowing to a halt and knows that this is his moment. His opportunity will be narrow during the short period of preparation before the raid takes place. If he is ever going to get his chance, it is now. Now is the time to move.

He steadies himself, preparing to face the commander as he approaches, passing by the soldiers who have stopped for one final check before the attack. He can feel their eyes watching him as he nears the front. He has suddenly become aware of every awkward move his body makes as he nears the seasoned commander.

Kilech recites the question in his head over and over as he contemplates possible reactions and responses that the powerful commander could give. He catches the commander's eye and, without warning, blurts out his question, as if throwing up the absurd request. Kilech's body flushes as his nerves search for an escape.

It sounded terrible. But Kilech is pretty sure that the message was clear enough. "I want a chance to fight."

The commander looks him up and down with disdain radiating from his face. Kilech stands rigid, like a submissive dog letting the pack leader inspect him. He isn't nearly as solid as the others, but he has become much stronger now that he has been training. He is still slender, but he would no longer consider his frame to be pathetic. Weak, possibly, but not pathetic.

The commander does not look as impressed, but after a short pause he obliges. "Fall in the rear of the attack force, you should be safe there. And if you'd like to finish off a few of the women and children to get your fix of bloodshed, be my guest."

His words are filled with sarcasm, but Kilech doesn't care. He has just been given the go-ahead on his first real mission. It is his first real opportunity to become a man, and in the chance encounter with a defending soldier, a possibility of becoming a warrior.

"Grab your gear and load up. We're moving out soon."

For the first time, the command for soldiers to load up and move out is referring to him. The moment has just become real. After ten years of anticipating this moment, he is not as excited as he thought he would be. He's anxious, nervous, and now, wondering if he made the right decision. Up until now he has only pictured his first engagement ending in victory and success, but after considering what he is about to do and where he is about to go, the moment finally hits him.

I could die tonight.

As his body floods with fear, he reminds himself of the night that he watched those three warriors on the top of Michmash cut down his people right in front of him. Although terrified, he will get his retribution and come one step closer to avenging that unforgettable night. He shakes the anxieties and blocks all fear from his mind.

Tonight he will make his own unforgettable night. He will make the Hebrews believe that *he* is a savage.

73

Still gripping the small piece of torn cloth from a royal guard's tunic, David pushes his way through the thick wooden door and enters his room. Inside, the stone wall interior that once felt elaborate and prestigious now feels tight and constricted. The fact that his room is on the inside of the palace does not only mean it is one of the smaller rooms, but also one of the few rooms without any windows.

Knowing that someone was spying on him with the king's daughter at a most vulnerable time, a time when details won't matter but perception will, he feels the already constricted walls squeeze even tighter.

I was standing naked in a pool of water with the king's daughter, alone, intimately kissing her without permission.

David doesn't need to say it out loud. He can hear in his head how terrible it will sound. Surely servants will arrive soon to deliver a message,

"The king requests your presence."

David considers heading to the king's chamber to address the situation and intercept the message before the situation gets out of hand. But what if it wasn't anyone spying, but merely coincidence and the king is never told about it?

It would be a terrible mistake to address the king about a situation that he may never hear about. After all, David has already rejected King Saul's offer to marry his eldest daughter, Merab. For David to confess his love for Michal, much less speak of what took place in the water, would make for more than an awkward dinner with King Saul and Merab at the table.

Besides, King Saul does not need anything else added to his

mind. He has exhibited his own problems, including fits of rage that can spill over into violence for the simplest and sometimes the most ridiculous of reasons. In the last few months the king has thrown his spear at David twice, in hopes of pinning him to the wall and ending this "rise to possess the heart of the people" that he claims David is pursuing. A rise that Saul himself initiated.

David cannot understand it. It was, after all, King Saul who placed him in charge of a thousand troops. It was the king's decisions that lifted him to the national spotlight, that helped mold him into the dangerous warrior that he has become. Now it seems even the lyre can't calm the king's soul. Instead, it infuriates him.

David tells himself it's King Saul's age and the demons that have plagued his mind for so long finally getting the best of him. He has been nothing but gracious up to now, treating David as a son throughout his adolescence. Maybe it's just the aging process. Whatever the reason, David's love for his surrogate father has not wavered, nor will it ever waver.

I'm telling him, David decides.

It is the only choice, the only honorable choice, and if a scout were sent to report David's actions to infuriate the king, David can intervene now, before it gets out of hand. Closing the door behind him, David heads down the hall in search of the king.

It's time he knows the truth.

74

Kilech strides forward, approaching Eshtaol. His hands are trembling. At any moment now, he could be killed. He knows the thought is ridiculous, especially as he marches in the rear of the formation, in the safest position available. The threat may not be real, but the fear is. He doesn't expect much, not real action anyway. If anything he may have a chance to confront a coward or two running for their lives. Dagon knows the Hebrews have plenty of cowards.

Without warning the formation dissolves, vanishing into the city and Kilech is left alone, surrounded by darkness. He is unsure where his unit went or how to find them in the confusion, he halts, terrified, as the violence unleashes, and the silence erupts into chaos.

They left me.

The warriors of Gath raid with aggression. Their movements, their attacks, their orders all happen so fast. Kilech is stuck, immobile, unsure how to slow his mind which spirals wildly out of control.

Finally, his body reacts. Survival instinct overcomes his paralyzing fear and he sprints into a nearby building to seek shelter. Possibly more than death, he sprints to evade the embarrassment his panic would cause him. This is his chance to earn respect. Standing frozen in fear in the open as the battle rages all around him, will bury his reputation more than being a weak scribe could ever do. He would rather chance dying quietly as a pathetic scribe than to live openly as a coward.

Moving through the small building, his every step is measured and calculated. The dimly lit rooms cast shadows that flicker with the firelight dancing along the walls. The house is silent, and then something moves in the next room. His chest pounds against his armor. There is no more hiding. His time to become a man has come, and it waits for him with hushed breath, on the other side of the wall.

Gripping his sword tightly, he creeps across the threshold. His mind is overstimulated. He is taking in more information than he can ever process, but then he lays eyes on the cause of the commotion. A woman curls back into the corner of the room. There are no children, no family, and most importantly no men. Not a soul is nearby.

She is alone.

As the muffled screams and clanging armor outside continues, Kilech switches from war and fighting to personal satisfaction. Not being a respected warrior in Gath means that even the prostitutes are picked over before he gets to them. Now, however, there is a beautiful, defenseless woman lying on the floor with no one to stop him from doing as he pleases. The smell of burning wood, oil, and flesh hanging in the air does not discourage him. Bizarrely, it only excites him more.

He is focused, blind to his surroundings. Tonight will be memorable in more ways than one. Her terrified expression as she recoils more tightly into the corner is not going to deter him.

She will want me by the end of the night, he tells himself as he releases the strap on his armor.

The power he feels in this moment is unmatched by anything he has ever felt. All of the years of submitting to everybody, being afraid of everyone are over, now *she* will submit. *She* will be afraid.

He moves in close. The scent of her body arouses him. He runs his hands through her hair, in an attempt to enjoy the moment, but he can wait no longer. The time has come. His armor and weapon lie on the floor and she hasn't moved. She continues to tremble, with tears running down her face, but she hasn't attempted to escape or fight back.

Maybe she does want me, Kilech tells himself.

Kilech moves in but the woman's breathing turns sharp and her eyes shift to the door behind him. The scuff of a footstep sends Kilech's mind into a spiral.

This can't be.

Reacting, Kilech dives for his sword as the silent intruder charges. Kilech rolls to his back, thrusting his blade up toward the ceiling. He feels the tip plunge into something. He has never felt a sword enter a man's flesh before, and he realizes this is what it feels like.

The full weight of a man, lunging in anger, lands on top of Kilech. Suddenly, the tight muscles relax, and the man slides down the sword, his stomach coming to a rest on Kilech's hand grip.

Now, face-to-face, the man's last breath gargles out of his mouth and blood drips onto Kilech's chin. He attempts to push the man off him but the woman beats him to it. For the first time her emotions release. Her shriek is a sound that Kilech has never heard from a human. She rolls the man away from him, wrapping her arms around his lifeless body.

Kilech stands and collects his armor as he reflects on how far he has come. Once wishing to only feel the touch of his mother's comforting warmth, he now has become one of them, one of the savages that he once feared.

The room quickly fills with soldiers flocking to a woman's scream, like mosquitoes to the Jordan River, and all of them are staring at Kilech in amazement. They seem proud. The moment is not what he thought it would be. His emotions are mixed. He is now one of them, but he is also no longer who he used to be.

Finally, Kilech turns his attention to the woman, whose pain is evident, as she ignores the threat of the soldiers pouring through the door. She clings to her dead. This man obviously means everything to her. It begins to make sense. He was the sole reason she remained motionless. She had hoped he would save her. Her pain hits Kilech like a club to the chest.

I just killed her husband.

The night has just begun and Kilech is more confused than ever.

He has now earned respect from the men, all while losing it for himself in the process.

75

Saul stares out the window, his drapes swaying in the wind, a wind that enters with the sound of a voice whispering in the room. It repeats the words that have plagued his mind for days.

Tens of thousands they cheer. The number continues to repeat, suffocating his focus from anything else, *tens... of... thousands.*

David left only moments ago and Saul was pleased to have just heard David's expression of love for his daughter, but the whisper warns of his intentions, of his growing popularity and power. The words of the shepherd have fallen on deaf ears.

Saul knows that David must be hiding more than what he reveals. His words are nothing more than manipulation. David is cunning, and his eyes are set on the throne. It is a shame that the boy wasn't what Saul had once thought. He loved him like a son. *Had* loved him.

The couriers have departed and soon Saul will see David's devotion. If not devotion, then he will be proven to have been right all along.

David is your greatest threat, the dark silhouette says, before slipping out the window, letting the drapes once again fall.

David hears footsteps approaching his room. He opens the door and meets the couriers in the hall, deciding to face the repercussions head-on instead of hiding in wait. The couriers deliver the message and it is not what he was expecting.

The king is delighted in me?

David can't believe what he's hearing. The fact that King Saul *wants* him to marry Michal, after all this time, is amazing, but he needs to see the spokesperson's eyes. He needs to know the intent more than just the context. He needs to get him off what he has been told to say. So he prods with a question.

"I am nothing more than a poor servant. How could I of all people become the king's son-in-law?"

The uneasy courier takes the bait. He rolls the scroll into a tight tube and responds in his own words. "He wants you to trust him. The king is pleased and requests no dowry…"

The young courier's eyes redirect to the floor as he pauses uncomfortably, swallowing hard. David waits for the catch that he knew had to be attached.

"…no dowry other than one hundred Philistine foreskins for his blessing and for his daughter's hand. He has granted you two days' time for the delivery of his request."

With that, the couriers depart.

And there it is, David thinks, knowing it was too good to be true.

Whether the king is pleased or not is anyone's guess. The reality is, however, with the right group of men, the task is feasible.

David has no time to contemplate the ever-changing emotions of the king. He has an opportunity to fulfill a desire, to join the royal family, and only a short time to do so. He still has to gather intelligence, capable men, and a mission plan before heading off to fulfill the request.

He grabs his gear and heads out into the night, preparing for the first time to assemble his most elite warriors, for a raid unlike any he has ever attempted. And he knows the first warrior that he needs to locate.

I need to find that scout.

76

Henick approaches a group of silhouettes standing under the moonlight at the edge of the palace field. He came directly after being awoken in the middle of the night. When he heard the order delivered to him by David's messenger, he believed that he must still be dreaming. He was made aware that David, the commander of the third division, has requested his presence for an unconventional attack on the Sea People.

He had fallen asleep while making arrangements to return home, but he's glad he stayed the night, that is if he isn't still dreaming. He finds himself in disbelief as he approaches the muster of soldiers, preparing to find out exactly what this mission will entail. The whole situation is unreal.

He sees David casually talking to some of the senior men. It isn't long before Henick notices that *everyone* is senior. Even the youngest warrior among them, Eleazar, is a senior captain.

This is quite a team David has assembled, Henick thinks. *What am I doing here?*

David's wisdom and command is well beyond his years. He stands, talking with men twice his age, as if he were the elder. They look up to him. Part of it, Henick is sure, has to do with killing the giant. They were all there to witness it. It was possibly the single most amazing human feat any of them will ever witness. But the respect seems to go even deeper than that. His words are charming, his mannerisms confident, and his skills, well, they are unmatchable. He has an understanding and a command on the battlefield that no one has ever seen before.

Now, standing here this close to him with only thirty to forty men, Henick feels intimidation setting in. David's eyes lock with his.

Henick tenses, realizing that he just got caught staring at the commander in awe.

Relax, be natural, he tells himself as David makes his way to him.

"I am impressed by the way you fight," David says. "You have a very unique style that most wouldn't understand, especially those that have been trained in the ranks."

"Thank you, sir. I have always been fascinated by the way you fight as well, obviously since the days of your youth and, of course, Goliath. That was an amazing day." Henick feels his face flush as he hears how pathetic his words sound.

"Well, no one would have known that the Philistines were on our doorstep if not for you and your skills. Those skills are the reason you are here with us tonight."

Henick is at a loss for words. The commander just looked him in the eye and complimented him. *David actually knows who I am.*

David steps back and lifts his voice so everyone can hear. "Knowing that the enemy will be raiding one of our western cities as they typically do, the king has asked for me to assemble a raid team of our own. We will hunt down the raiders and give them a welcoming that they won't soon forget. This isn't something we are accustomed to doing, so the enemy should be caught completely off guard. But we must focus and each must perform like the elite professionals that we are."

David pauses, making eye contact with every soldier as if to gauge their reactions in contrast to what he is about to say. "To be honest, the king does not know that we are gathering tonight, much less who I have selected. All he cares about is my delivery of one hundred Philistine foreskins for his daughter's hand in marriage. And I have an allotted time to do so. That, however, is the secondary mission. First is eliminating the enemy's advance on our western front. In other words, with the king's order, I have been given the authority to do something that I have always wanted to do – destroy the enemy with a covert ambush under the cover of night."

Each warrior nods and confirms their allegiance with a fist over the heart. Henick again feels David's gaze on him. His excitement is almost too great to contain.

"Our scout will move ahead of our formation, ensuring that our movement is steady and uncompromised. Advancing one ridgeline ahead at all times, he will signal and direct our movement toward our objective. Are there any questions?"

David looks around but no one says a word. Mostly everyone nods that they understand. "Then we will head west through the valley toward Ekron. It is their closest city, and if they have crossed our borders, you can be assured that wherever they have entered, Ekron will be their fallback. Also, if any runners are coming to warn the capital then we will intercept them and be hours ahead of any element the king could assemble."

David hands Henick a torch. "If you find the enemy's encampment, light this on the back of the ridge and we will rally there. Now go, and may the Lord your God be with you."

Henick feels a rush over his entire body with the final words of David sending him off. He grips the wooden stave tightly and sprints over the hill into complete darkness. Tonight, again, his scouting will help make history.

⊹══╪══⊹

The march back to base camp in the foothills is not far but Kilech is exhausted. With his mind in conflict about the night's events, his body feels it's taking the brunt of it. He has just killed an innocent man, in front of his wife nonetheless, and yet he has finally tasted the carnage of battle for himself.

His conscience tussles with pride and shame as he considers what he has done. Has he grown stronger because of the bloodshed? He still feels inferior. But maybe he will earn respect and finally be looked upon as a warrior, a man, or at very least maybe he is one step closer to earning a spot in the ranks.

As the warriors begin to relish the plunder of the night's raid, the familiar sounds of men pleasuring their fleshly desires fill the air. Kilech turns from the warm, crackling fire and sets his eyes on a lone, quiet tent. He watched as they threw the beautiful, *his* beautiful, widow inside and left her. A sudden thought bubbles to the surface, like air escaping from the blackness of the ocean depths, and again it prods one simple question. What *would* it feel like to lie with a woman?

Slowly, his conscience is blotted out as desire begins to burn in his gut. He moves toward the tent, rationalizing his actions.

I only want to hear her breathe, he tells himself.

With his ear turned toward the tent's side wall, he calmly listens, envisioning her with every exhale.

His fingers crawl toward the tent door. *I only want a glimpse of her lying alone,* he tells himself, *nothing more.*

He slides the tent flap to the side and slips inside. Curled against the back, visibly shaken, the woman doesn't move, she doesn't scream. She just lies there, waiting.

Kilech tries to turn back but it's too late. Any compassion has been seared, swathed by his screaming flesh. His lustful desire will not be quenched until this is over.

The obnoxious laughter of soldiers approaching his tent halts him, but they soon pass, leaving him once again alone and in charge. There will be plenty of time to scribe and count the treasures. Now it's his turn to enjoy the rewards that Dagon has granted. He moves toward her with a flippant thought aimed at quenching any remaining concerns for her safety.

At least this will be quick.

77

David sets his gaze across the ravine to the faint orange flame flickering on the distant ridge. He feels the warm bodies of his men blocking the light breeze to his back as they huddle behind him.

"That's our mark," David says, shifting his attention to the horizon.

The half-moon is not ideal for moving under cover of darkness, but it's not terrible either. It provides enough illumination to see your footing, yet still providing concealment as long as you don't move too fast and remain off the ridgelines.

Because of the moon's current position, only five fingers from the horizon, David knows that they don't have much time. The night is halfway through and the last thing anyone wants is to be anywhere close to the Philistine camp with only thirty-five men in their force. It has been a long season of war and David knows everyone's body is worn and battered, but right now they must bury their misery and press on. The sunrise is coming.

"We need to move."

Having moved across the bottom of the ravine with swift precision, David feels a surge of power flow through his legs, propelling him up the steep climb. Over his shoulder he catches a glimpse of the dark moonlit figures following, charging up the hill behind him. He can't help but grin. It's good having a small force of elite fighters that don't need to be pushed to keep up, unlike the large, often sluggish, army. It's even better to have Benaiah with him once again.

The torch is snubbed as David and the men reach just below the ridge.

"What do we have?" David says, meeting Henick toward the top.

"It looks to be a company of Sea People, roughly two hundred retreating from Eshtaol. I imagine they plan on moving the plunder during the day."

David leans over the crest of the hilltop and considers his options. "When we move, we can't afford to have any runners. As close to Ekron as we are, they would have an entire division on our heels before we ever hit the ravine," David says, turning back to the men. "Nathaniel, direct your team to the western rear and set up security, ensuring that no one escapes toward Ekron. I will lead the main assault team."

David notices Henick drifting toward the rear. "Scout, where do you think you're going? Did you think you were no longer needed?"

<hr/>

Henick squeezes through the solid wall of warriors, each of them with years of combat experience and training. He moves to the front, feeling every eye on him.

What could he possibly want with me?

David smiles. "You think I didn't notice your weapon of choice, your style of fighting, or your tactics that have been sharpened from the hardened years of living in the shadows?"

Henick, unsure what to say says nothing at all.

"You're not made for the ranks. You're made for tonight. You will lead the second assault team to the northern flank."

Henick's breathing stops. His heart, packed with anxiety, flip-flops inside his chest. His dream has arrived with no warning. Only a few years ago he was ridiculed for his weaponry and fighting style, but now he stands at the front of the men who teased him, ready to take charge of them in a raid that he has only dreamt of carrying out.

The men are divided into each of their respected teams and then form a line below the ridge. Each of them checks the warrior's gear in front of them, ensuring that their armor and weapons are silenced for complete stealth. Tonight they will need every advantage they can get.

"Cut the tents and work your way inward toward the fires. We will converge on the flames once every Peleshet in the tents is removed from this earth. Gather the women and children to the rear. Nathaniel, they will be yours to secure once the tents begin to burn."

David turns toward the fires burning in the center of the enemy's camp. "Once they know we are here, there is no reason to be silent. Bring the chaos, let their minds swirl as we cut them down. Let them know that our borders are not to be crossed, nor are our lands to be tread upon."

With an affirming nod, Henick leads his men down the winding path toward his destiny, life in the shadows.

Tonight, every Philistine that has plundered our women and children will taste the bronze of my dagger.

Henick can't help but grin as he sets his eyes toward the tents as he dips into the darkness.

78

Inside the warm tent Kilech feels sweat run down his uncovered chest. He moves closer, telling himself that if he moves slowly toward her then what he is about to do won't be so wrong. As he lowers to his knees beside her legs, she coils tighter, pulling them to her chest. Her sobbing grows louder to the point where Kilech worries that she is going to call attention to them.

Kilech reacts, muzzling her mouth with his hand. "Enough!"

Shifting his hands to her shoulders, he shakes her. She's about to ruin their inconspicuous empty tent, and by the sounds of footsteps now approaching, it seems she already has.

⊰⊱

Henick prowls like a lion, moving on to his third tent as he wipes his last victim's blood on his tunic. He slowly slides his blade in and up the tent wall, slicing an opening large enough to step through.

He has no fear of being heard. The sounds of a struggling woman inside are perfect masking for his entry. He rehearses what is about to happen. He knows that before the Philistine inside can realize what is taking place, he will feel the wrath and the blade penetrating him. An evil breed and a perfect death.

Fixing his blade forward, he steps into the tent unnoticed.

⊰⊱

Kilech hears someone enter the tent. His first thought is to surprise him, killing him when his guard is down so that he can finish what he started, but he knows that he would never escape having killed one of his own. He would be killed before his next breath.

She ruined it, he thinks, having already enjoyed the night in his mind.

A loud burly laugh erupts as more enter. The soldiers grab him by the waist, lifting him to his feet.

"Not so fast, scribe. You can have," the large Philistine warrior counts the soldiers piling in, "fifths, after *we're* done."

Looking into the eyes of the men, he can see that they are not joking. There's no chance he will be allowed to stay. Before he can even finish the thought, he is lifted into the air and shoved out of the tent, toward the fire. He stumbles across the dusty ground, defeated, and slowly slumps against the warm stones. The laughter that once filled the tent quickly turns into grunting and painful cries, and then, oddly, a still silence emerges.

Kilech waits, on edge, his eyes fixed on the woven goat-hair walls. Finally, the tent flap whips open. Expecting to see one less Philistine standing in his way to the woman he desires, he leans forward in anticipation. The man who comes out, however, is no Philistine. Instead, a Hebrew emerges wiping his bloody dagger across his tunic.

Those were the painful cries of men, Kilech realizes to his horror.

The warrior's eyes burn with the reflection of the fire as he homes in on Kilech, who now pulls back against the rocks.

What in Dagon's name is…?

"Leave him," a voice says, stopping the warrior's dagger from drawing more blood. "Spare one… to warn the others of the slaughter that comes from attacking our land."

The warrior with the dagger sheaths it without questioning the man's words, letting out a scoff toward the cowering Kilech as he passes. He apparently believed that a half-naked man, curled against the fire, alone and in fear, couldn't be a real threat.

Kilech, relieved, continues to hug the stones in terror as one by one the Hebrew warriors emerge against the firelight. Their faces materialize from the blackness like spirits, laying waste to the remaining soldiers. He imagines that there must be hundreds of them by the way they move with such speed, wiping out any opposition before word of their arrival has a chance to spread. It becomes clear that there will be no one here to save him, no one but the commander of the Hebrews who withheld the dagger from him with a simple order.

The commander is young, Kilech notices, much younger than most of the Hebrews under his command. He takes charge with authority and with swiftness. He orders the women and children to the middle of the formation and turns back, his eyes focusing on Kilech. The stare feels like it reveals all of Kilech's insecurities while striking fear into him, and for some reason he can't look away. The warrior's eyes are mesmerizing.

They look so familiar, he thinks.

Soon, the Hebrews are gone, like a breeze that sweeps through an open door, snuffing candles in the dark. An eerie silence falls across the camp. Kilech cranes his head over the stones but no one is there. Slowly, he rises, measuring each step as he makes his way toward the tent. Hesitant, he presses inside. The scene is horrific. Blood has been slung in every direction. Bodies lay scattered across the ground, each with their tunics cut open. The woman is gone, and by the looks of it, so are the most sacred parts of each of the men.

Kilech instinctively grabs his crotch out of empathy.

That could have been me.

79

The elevated city of Gibeah, hovers in the distance like a rain cloud, promising relief from the hot desert sun. After trekking all night, pulling off a successful raid, and crossing the hill country back toward the capital, David is feeling the effects of a worn, aching body. Now, with the sun beating down and the adrenaline having worn off hours ago, he can only imagine how his men are faring.

Their grunts that follow each exhausted step toward the summit are a clear indication that they are as relieved as he to finally be home. David's swings the heavy cloth bag to his opposite shoulder, attempting to relieve the throbbing pain caused by carrying the results of the king's request for the entire journey.

As the men arrive at the south city gates, David thanks each of them individually for their loyalty and professionalism before he sends them on their way.

His message is short, accompanied by grunts and head nods. No one wants a speech. They only want rest and to be released to their families and David obliges, but not before first ensuring that each man knows the seriousness of keeping this mission, this unit, a secret. The last thing David wants is to jeopardize any of the men involved if the king did happen to have alternate intentions for ordering the night's mission.

David turns and sets his attention on the palace. He knows that Saul's ear is constantly filled with precautions, his mind plagued with paranoia, every thought fearing an attack on his throne. The time has come to face Saul's true intentions. Whether or not he expected to see the sack filled to the brim or David cut down by the enemy, the king's face always bears his intentions. Either way, David knows that deep down in Saul's heart, he loves him and whatever is blinding him in this moment of anger will soon pass and again his eyes, his arms, will be open.

⋞══⬦══⬦══⟫

Saul's feelings twist in his gut, unsure what to feel at the general's report.

David has returned.

Abner's begrudging words ring in his mind. His immediate thrill is quickly replaced by disappointment when his doubts are backed by Abner's pessimism.

"Do you think it is possible?" Saul asks

"I don't see how. He has most definitely returned having not only failed, but having disobeyed a direct order."

The door to the throne hall swings open, saturating the spacious room with blinding sunlight. David enters as a silhouette wrapped in the day's bright golden hue.

"Surely you haven't gathered all one hundred in this time," Abner says, stepping toward the approaching David, with agitation in his voice.

"No," David says, eyeing him as he passes toward the king.

Saul is torn between relief and disappointment. David is safe and is as vulnerable to failure as any other man, yet it is somehow unsatisfying that he has returned a failure. Part of him wanted David to return victorious and marry his daughter, but he understands the implications of that as well, as he is constantly reminded in his ear and his night visions that the throne is more important than his feelings.

"You have failed to bring all one hundred and yet you enter before the king with such arrogance?" Abner's voice rings with contempt.

"No, I do not have one hundred," David says before turning back and lowering the sack to the floor at Abner's feet, "but *two* hundred. For the king's honor is worth twice my command."

Saul stands, halting Abner before he decides to do something regretful. "Then you shall take her as your own and become my blood as I have promised," Saul says, interrupting as he makes his way toward David. He wraps his arms around him with questions swirling through a black mist, a black mist that has *become* his mind. How did David accomplish such an unconceivable feat? He pulls David in, embracing him tightly.

Keep him close and he will not see your intentions, Saul tells himself.

⁝⊰⧓⊱⁝

David is surprised by King Saul's impulsive hug. Not because of the timing but because it is so rigid. There is not even the slightest amount of emotion behind it. As if two children who hate one another have been forced to hug by a parent, the king's stiff posture is void of true sentiment. A realization even more terrifying is the evident rage pouring from the eyes of the king's most trusted confidant, Abner.

Abner watches, unable to contain his resentment. David has often suspected General Abner of being threatened by his quick rise to the public eye. But his unsupported belief has now manifested right before his eyes. The general's disdain for him is becoming clearer by the moment but it's the small subtlety that Abner has obviously overlooked that confirms David's growing suspicion of the general's devious intentions.

The small tear in his tunic stands out like a blazing wildfire.

So that's how it's going to be.

80

Saul sits on the edge of his bed, staring at the stone wall, enjoying its simplicity. The joints aren't perfect. The colors are different shades and the edges have random textures, but most importantly the stones don't talk back. They don't ask questions that can't be answered. No, they just do what they were created to do. They are a wall. There is nothing hidden about it. No ulterior motives. It's just... a wall.

After the exhausting day filled with a whirlwind of events, it feels like the right thing to do, staring at a wall. The wedding was quick and for all purposes, meaningless. Performed by the priest on short notice to ensure that public knowledge of it would be minimal at worst, oblivious at best, Saul decided to immediately hold a private meeting following the so-called celebration.

He was unsure what the next steps should be regarding David and his seemingly unstoppable rise to power. Kingship was handed to Saul and it has never been easy. There are so many decisions, decisions that will cost valuable lives, territory, even his throne, and... his family, if he were to wrongly make the next decision unwisely. He always knows where to turn and he is thankful for such an experienced cousin, friend, leader, and general.

Abner made a good point. David is much more than once thought. He is more than a shepherd, more than a musician, and more than a just a warrior. He has a gift, and if God is upon him then we must expose it.

"We will lose control. We will lose the throne," Abner had said emphatically.

Now, Saul feels more like a servant following orders, but he knows it must be done. *He,* after all, is *king.*

The knock on the door is right on time. Saul turns from the idle wall to his door that swings open. Saul must now find out if it is true. The words of the prophet Samuel swirl in his mind as David enters.

As you have torn my garment so has God torn the kingdom of Israel from you this day and has given it to a neighbor of yours. One who is greater than you, the strength of all Israel.

"Well, my boy, how was she?" Saul attempts to sound compassionate.

"Father?" David looks uncomfortable.

"How was my daughter, your wife? Was she good? Did you enjoy her?"

Saul moves closer, breathing in deeply, taking in the moment. He wraps his arms around David tightly, reminding himself that if it is true, if David is called to remove him from his throne, sadly he will have to detach himself from his love for him, this son that he has grown to embrace.

"Never mind that… Sit, play me something that will calm a bedeviled mind," Saul says, watching him carefully. He sits in the chair that is conveniently located next to his spear, in case what he believes to be true is true.

Saul enjoys the last few moments in David's presence as he begins to play. The drapes blow in the breeze as the war between peace and destruction wages in his mind. He waits patiently, watching David's every move until curiosity begins to claw at his scalp. Finally, he can wait no longer.

"Why is it that you close your eyes when you play before me?"

⋯⟩⟨⋯

David hasn't been able to enjoy one minute of playing with the king's intense stare bearing down upon him. Now, the words delivered bluntly seem to explain why he was truly called to the bedchamber tonight. His playing slows. He is unsure how to respond.

Do I just ignore him?

He has seen the king enraged many times. After all, that's the reason he was summoned in the first place, to calm the growing temper and paranoia. Few times has he been the target of Saul's rage, but tonight seems to be one of the few. Like the smell of sulfur stinging the air as a volcano boils underneath, David senses a warning of something much bigger preparing to release. The mountain begins to rupture.

"Look at me!" King Saul demands.

David freezes, his fingers plucking the last few strings before silence overwhelms the room. He can feel his eyes burning with the Presence of Yahweh, and if King Saul is looking, David is convinced he will see it too.

He opens his eyes, staring at the floor, too terrified to glance up. Like a child who wants the love of an angry father, David continually gives him the benefit of the doubt, but could never muster the strength to respond in matching anger. He leans, shifting the weight of his body over his heels ever so slightly anticipating the king's next move.

The silent tension in the room is building like stones being stacked one by one in the wooden bucket over a well. David knows that Saul, being the rope, is going to snap at some point, but the question is when. With each dragging moment that passes, another stone is placed in the bucket. And then the strangest of things happens. Laughter erupts.

Saul is not only laughing, he's laughing hysterically. The kind of laughter David remembers enjoying while reliving tales of the old days with a group of friends or listening to a family member speak of an embarrassing story. It's a hearty laugh that comes from the gut and grows with each breath. This whole time David has kept his eye on the tension of the rope, waiting for it to snap, but it seems the final stone has been placed and the bottom of the bucket was first to break. He never saw this coming, but then again, there isn't much that surprises him anymore when it comes to Saul.

The laughter vanishes as quickly as it had come, but the room is only still for a moment. David feels the inevitable approaching and then it happens. Saul lunges, stretching toward his spear. David jumps from his chair, having already prepared for a quick escape. He dives toward the threshold of the door as the spear buries itself between the stones above his head, killing nothing but the idle wall.

81

A rapid, heavy knock at his door springs Aaron from his sleep. For a moment he's unsure if the sound was in his sleep or... the pounding repeats. It is definitely at his door. He unlatches the lock.

"Jonathan?"

He has a seriousness in his eyes that immediately startles Aaron, and his hands hurriedly wave for him to follow.

"We don't have much time."

Aaron doesn't think, he only responds. Together they sprint down the halls and leap multiple stairs at a time in the stairwells. Aaron tries to process what Jonathan is quickly explaining.

David might be in trouble?

The two reach the throne hall when Jonathan abruptly stops, running a finger down the wall. "Have you ever played in the secret passages?" he asks.

Aaron processes the question, his mind overloaded.

What is happening? he wonders.

"No, I haven't."

Jonathan presses his hand flat against the stone. A slow, heavy jolt sounds and the stone wall cracks open. "Now is a good time to start."

Voices and footsteps approaching from the hallways resonate around the high, arched ceilings. Aaron has no choice but to enter the darkness since Jonathan's firm hands shove him into the narrow passageway that has just materialized in front of him.

"Listen to what is said on the other side of this wall. If harm is coming to David, run and get him out. You're going to have to feel your way down the passage. If it comes to it, only you will be able to save him."

The door's shadow eclipses across Jonathan's face, until the stone entry shuts, sealing Aaron in the blackness of the cramped passageway. The thick darkness is stale, but cool, and Aaron can't help but wonder what creatures could be crawling their way toward him right now. The muffled voices on the other side of the wall escalate as the guards muster for what feels like an eternity until finally the room falls silent.

Cringing, Aaron swipes his hand, checking for spider webs before putting his ear to the damp wall. He listens, attempting to make out the king's muffled words, but only a few words out of each sentence are clear enough to understand. So, steadying his breathing, Aaron presses his ear tighter to the stones, forgetting now about any of the creatures accompanying him as King Saul's voice escalates.

What is he saying? All of the echoes of the throne hall, the body movements, the coughs, and the random responses from the men gathered, continue to hinder Aaron from deciphering King Saul's words. He begins to feel the weight of responsibility pressing on him since Jonathan is putting David's life in his hands. Aaron considers leaving and playing it safe.

Just tell David to get out and we can sort it out later, he tells himself.

Aaron prepares to navigate the passageway when again silence fills the room. The muffled voice, which can't be mistaken for anyone but King Saul's, clearly illustrates the meeting's intent. His words penetrate the stones as if he were standing before Aaron directly.

"Kill the shepherd boy."

With a rush of energy flooding Aaron's body, he turns but trips with his first step into the darkness. With the weight of Jonathan's instructions and David's life now depending on him, he knows that if he is to carry out this mission, he must calm himself and just move forward. Standing, moving into the darkness, he realizes that more than calming his body, a much larger problem has arisen. Not only can he not see, but he has no idea where he is going.

82

David slides into the soft silk sheets of Michal's large bed. Being the daughter of the king has its benefits, he assumes as he glances around the spacious room adorned with two windows on its northern wall.

He strokes his beard, flattening it, making sure it is straight and presentable, for the night's coming events. He slings his shirt across the room and considers taking his tunic off as well.

No, he thinks, *I'll let her do that.*

His heart is racing and his mind spins with expectations of the night ahead of him. They have waited for so long and have built up years of desire and tonight it will all release in an explosion of passion and love. Now that they are officially married, there is nothing to worry about. They can enjoy each other's wild desires freely.

Maybe I should take off the tunic?

David continues to overthink every scenario in anticipation of the perfect night. Soon she will enter and he will see the beauty that he has longed to see. Until then, it seems, he will be an anxious wreck.

Aaron moves fast with his hands outstretched at his sides, his fingers guiding his way along the walls. He has made two right turns so far and there is no sign of a way out anywhere. Part of him feels like he will be stuck in here forever. If he doesn't make it to David in time, that may be a reasonable choice.

Then, the floor ends. His foot slams into a hard surface, tumbling his body forward. He expects to hit a wall but continues falling until his body slams into multiple raised surfaces, the edges of which stab into his ribs.

A staircase... Of course.

Bruised, he leaps to his feet and races toward the top. After a short climb he slows. The air has become stagnant. He senses a structure in front of him, as if the cool musty air were the perspiration of the wall itself, wafting into his face. His hands converge, feeling in front of him and just as he thought... a dead end. Or is it?

Pressing his weight forward, he feels the wall jolt open, grinding a stone door forward into an expanding sliver of firelight. He walks out into an upstairs hallway and immediately sees a woman wearing a robe and walking alone. The jasmine tucked into her long black hair is a dead giveaway.

"Michal!" Aaron calls out as he races toward her. "Where's David?"

Michal stops. She looks confused. "He's waiting for me in my room. Why? You look so – "

"They're going to kill him."

"What?" She tightens her robe. "Who?"

"Go, you can buy him time."

Aaron's intensity and breathing escalates as the sound of footsteps climbing the stairwell toward the hall reaches them.

"Who sent you?" she asks, becoming more concerned.

Aaron stops and looks her dead in the eye, knowing this is all she will need to hear. "Jonathan."

She covers her mouth as she gasps. Jonathan's word is as iron amongst the people, especially when it pertains to David. Michal tears off down the hall and reaches her door just before the guards do. Aaron backs into the darkness, away from the flickering wall sconce, but never pulls his eyes from the scene in front of Michal's door.

"Surely you are not intruding on the royal daughter's quarters unannounced?" she asks, blocking the men as she steps in front of her door.

The first soldier offers some pathetic excuse, something about hearing a scream from her chambers. She responds with an ease that only the king's daughter could muster in such a tense situation.

"Well, I am fine. Thank you for your concern," she snaps back.

Aaron pads farther down the hallway as more men now join at her door.

"And David?" the officer prods.

More guards pile into the hallway, converging from every direction. Aaron hears them approaching from behind and moves toward the scene as if he were one of their group. Now at the door, he hears General Abner approach from behind him.

"There is much concern I see," Michal says. "It seems that David is not well. But I assure you I will take good care of him. Now, if you will excuse me?" She cracks the door open and slides inside before slamming it shut.

"Guard the door. I will bring the king," Abner says, turning toward the staircase.

Hearing the voices outside the door, David leans onto his side as Michal enters. She locks the door quickly and David knows that he's in for a wild night. She's out of breath, excited to get the night started. His eyes wander the seductive curves under her robe, waiting for the silk covering her flesh to drop.

Should I get out of bed and meet her? Or should I wait here?

"You have to go," Michal says, her voice powerful.

This wasn't the way I had imagined it starting.

David sits up. "What's wrong?"

"My father is coming to kill you."

David relaxes lying back on the bed. "That's just the natural reaction of a father. We're married. It's –"

"I'm serious," Michal says quickly, cutting him off. She grabs the bedding, quickly knotting the blankets and sheets together.

David can't believe his eyes. She is overreacting on possibly the most important night of his life.

Is this married life? he asks himself.

"Your father is not well. This isn't the first time that he has attacked me, nor will it be the last. That does not mean I can abandon him. He has treated me better than my own father," David says, with no intention of moving. He knows that she could never understand. It's what he is here to do, to help the king. "I will not leave him."

Her eyes say she is not convinced. "This is not one of his fits of anger. As much as you wish it were." She brandishes a blade and pulls the pillow from behind his head, slicing it open, and extracting the horsehair from it. "David, he is not your father, he is the king! And right now you are in his way." She pauses for effect, placing her hands on his cheeks. "David, the kingdom is about to come down upon you."

Sensing her seriousness, David sits up. "How do you know for sure? How do you not know this isn't just another fit?"

"My brother said so."

David's chest tightens. "Jonathan?" He jumps to his feet. "What did he say?"

She tosses the blankets, now tied end to end to end, out the window. "He said go."

"My armor, it's in my room." David hesitates.

"David, trust me, just go. There is no time." Michal grabs his head, turning him into her lips. "I'm sorry… but I love you."

A fist pounds against the door.

"Michal!" King Saul's voice shatters all remaining hope that David had clung to.

"Go."

He glances out the window. The drop is frighteningly far, he hesitates.

"I can't do it."

But he has help.

83

Saul has had enough. He leans forward and lunges, barging through the door. "Show yourself, David." He moves Michal to the side and homes in on David lying motionless under the covers.

"What is wrong, Father?" Michal pleads with him.

His daughter's words are drowned out by the rage bursting inside his skull. It is too late for sorrow, too late for compassion, and far too late to hide his true intent. He is here to protect the throne, the kingdom, and nothing more.

"Stand or I will cut you down like a dog."

"He does not feel well, Father," Michal says, attempting to step in front of Saul, but he presses her to the side with his arm.

"Disobedience to the king is sentenced by death," Saul reminds her before ripping the blanket off David.

Saul, fully anticipating a cowering David, is shocked at the sight before him. The lump that was David's body hiding under the blanket is… a bronze statue wrapped in goat hair? It's hard to digest, but he has just been played like the lyre that has sat upon David's lap.

He's not here.

Saul's vision blurs as his brain swells with a crippling thump that repeats faster as it builds pressure with each painful strike. He can feel his face burning as reality sets in.

He whips his head around to Michal. "How has my own blood deceived me in this way?"

"He fled on his own. What am I to do... kill him?"

Furious, Saul turns toward the door and gives his general the simple order that he has been waiting for.

"Find him… and kill him."

David looks up to the window. He hears the hatred spewing from the king.

They were right, he realizes, hearing for himself that Saul had planned to actually kill him, something that he couldn't bring himself to believe only moments earlier.

If it weren't for Michal's hands pushing him out the window, he would most likely still be in the room, at the very least as a corpse.

What have I done wrong? David wonders.

David searches for an answer but there is none. There is no reason for this injustice. Part of him longs to turn and go back, demanding answers, but he knows the answer. The king has been persuaded, even haunted, to this conclusion that David is after the throne, that for some unfathomable reason David actually wants to become king.

Having heard King Saul's "search to kill" order projected from the window three stories above him, David decides that it's wise to gain as much distance as he can from those ordered to kill him and ask questions later. With the sudden shift in the king's attitude and David's world instantly flipped upside down for no apparent reason, his mind overloads with uncertainty. With voices now clearly outside the palace in search of him, there are no decisions left but to run.

Sprinting shirtless into the dark, the rhythm of his feet and his heavy breathing quickly fill the otherwise calm night air. Blindly, he runs from everything that he has ever known. The past nine years have meant the world to him and now in a blink of an eye it is gone. His thoughts churn with each step. What has he done to deserve this? Why has Yahweh left him so quickly? Was this the life he was called to live, the life of a fugitive? His long gait shortens to a trot as his mind recalls the event that has since fallen dormant in his mind. The memory sends renewed energy through his muscles and turns his attention to the north.

Without hesitation and with only the clothes covering his body and his royal ring on his finger, David charges into the tree line, his mind focused, blocking out the pain from branches smacking his chest, thorns grabbing at his legs. There is only one man on his mind now that could possess the answers he is searching for, and with any luck, the one he seeks will still be in Ramah, the city of the sacrifice.

84

Samuel carries his pot of oil down the dusty streets, heading for the town shrine, as is his custom three days a week. The constant burning of shrine lamps, strategically placed in the windows, is a symbol that Yahweh is available at any hour, but the lamps do not fill themselves.

Samuel does not mind the walk through the fresh air, but the vases filled with oil seem to get heavier with each trip, and he is certain that the sun slips closer with each step. How the days of his youth have come and gone. Never would he have thought that such a short trip would challenge his physical abilities.

Reaching the door to his home, the shrine, he notices footprints leading through the front door. It's not uncommon for men to enter under the weight of their guilt, but no one feels guilty at this hour of the morning, unless they never slept of course.

Guiding the door open with his shoulder, while still gripping the vase with both hands, he considers the thought of an intruder, but at his age he figures if his day has come then his day has come. There is no more time to worry about these things. These are the worries of young men.

Samuel enters the dark room as a blind man into his own home, walking the same path as he has done for years, while his eyes adjust to the room from the brilliant sunlight outside. Just as he suspected. Movement, by what appears to be a man sitting in the corner of the room, catches his eye. Moving closer he can see that the man is young, but being highlighted under a vibrant sunray beaming through the window he cannot see his face.

"Can I help you?" Samuel asks, shuffling toward him, still clutching the vase.

The man turns with a posture that Samuel recognizes instantly. Samuel's worn, trembling hands almost fail him as the vase slips through his fingers. He grips the smooth pottery just before it falls to the floor, which now he notices is lightly speckled with dried blood.

"My… David, it has been so very long." He can hardly contain his joy. He stares for a moment at David, now all grown up, his face highlighted by the sunlight, as tiny glimmering flecks drift through the burning hue all around him. "Are you all right?"

"That's why I'm here," David says.

Samuel notices the small cuts and tears that have ravaged his limbs. He sets down the vase that has since become weightless. The door opens and Samuel's protégés, two young priests both clad in long cloth robes, enter as they do every morning. Their entrance stills as their eyes set on David. They silently question whether they are truly seeing what they think they are seeing until one of them finally speaks.

"This is the boy, the one you speak of?" the priest says, still staring in awe.

David's face twists with concern. "What of me have you spoken, prophet?"

Samuel realizes by the look in David's eyes that it is time. The boy is ready and this is the moment that Samuel has remained here on earth to ensure takes place. "Only of whom, and who, you are."

With the tails of their robes and wet cloths in hand, the priests lower to their knees and begin wiping and blotting the blood from David's body. David shifts more uncomfortably now, his eyes begging for answers.

"Who am I? And why does the king seek my life? What have I done wrong?"

"You, David," Samuel moves toward David with slow, deliberate steps, "are much like an orphan whose father of great riches has passed away. The orphan will live his entire life in poverty unless a messenger delivers the father's will. David, I am the messenger."

David straightens. "And what is my father's will?"

Samuel lowers, grabbing hold of the cloths, now soaked with David's blood, in his hands. He squeezes them, letting the blood trickle to the floor. "That this blood would no longer be the blood of a shepherd boy, but the blood… of a king."

85

Kilech's exhaustion has finally caught up with him. He enters into a slumber that has his imagination running wild. It begins to play with his greatest fears. First, his body becomes paralyzed as he lifts his gaze. Above him, a familiar warrior stands, his legs straddled, his body towering over him. In his hand he grips a long Philistine iron sword. The warrior never lowers the sword. Instead, he just stares, exercising his power, his control.

Soon the warrior turns, having stolen Kilech's soul, and vanishes into the darkness. Suddenly, only the warrior's face returns, hovering, approaching with the wind like a ghost in the night. It is the heir of the Hebrews and with death in his eyes he speaks. "I will haunt you," he says with his last breath, a breath that crackles with fire and scorches Kilech's flesh.

Kilech knows that he's dreaming, but it doesn't help the fear as he watches his flesh decay, revealing his bones, bones that quickly crumble and swirl with a gust, as mere ashes returning to the earth.

The bright rush of flames from the Hebrew's breath consumes what's left of Kilech's spirit, its heat rushing toward even his conscience. Kilech has just been devoured from the inside out by the Hebrew that he so desperately wants to kill.

Kilech jolts forward from the ground, gasping for air as he wakes. His face is hot to the touch from the fire crackling in the cool night. Slowly, Kilech lets his eyes wander. He exhales, now remembering that he is safe, just outside of Ekron as he waits for the next caravan to arrive, returning him to Gath. For the first time he realizes that Gath has become his home. He is no longer fearful of its gates but comforted, welcomed among the warriors. Even if he isn't well respected, at least he isn't a

Hebrew dog.

The dream felt so real, as if it was a message, and yet Kilech doesn't care about its meaning. Even if his bitterness is to kill him, he will gladly die if only he lives long enough to return the favor.

As the lone survivor of the attack on Eshtaol, Kilech realizes that he can make up anything he wants and no one will know the difference. He could potentially gain power and enter the ranks through conforming history the way he wants it to be seen. His mind wonders at the possibilities and the newfound control over his life until his mind once again fades, slipping back into the night, this time with a soft but permanent grin, a new power over his destiny.

After almost two weeks of hiding in the north, gathering his thoughts from what Samuel revealed to him, David has finally departed the security of Ramah. He has spent the entire night traveling south, contemplating his next possible decision, but now, staring up at the dark palace, he questions his final choice. He questions his sanity.

The only movement inside is from the guards patrolling the hallways with oil lamps, the orange flicker followed by their shadows eerily drifting past the windows. If there is anywhere that David shouldn't be its right here and he knows it. But still, there are some questions that need to be answered and some unfinished business left to take care of. There is only one way to sort out this entire thing.

I'm going inside.

Scaling the wall, entering through a window, and moving through the corridors, David is astonished at how easy it is to gain access to such a valuable bedroom. With the guards' complacency working in his favor, as well as his knowledge of their positions, routines, and the hallways they patrol, David strolls right in without so much as a thought of getting caught.

Now comfortably secure inside the bedroom walls, he slowly pads to his target, knowing how quickly the reflexes of a slumbering commander can be, coupled with the fact that every warrior sleeps with a dagger at all times. David minimizes the risk by pouncing, grabbing the right wrist before it can reach for the blade, while simultaneously covering the commander's mouth with his left hand. He waits until the surprised and widened eyes fade and the pupils dilate, before releasing.

"David?" Jonathan whispers.

David grins. "It's good to see you too, brother." David, sensing that he is in the midst of King Saul's hornet's nest, cuts right to the meat. "I need to know how I have wronged your father so badly that he now wants me dead."

"You're not going to die. He has sent men to find you in the north three times but each time –"

"I know. I watched what Yahweh did to them. How he covered them and how they began prophesying with Samuel. As did your father when he came, but –"

"My father does nothing without telling me first. Since he has returned he hasn't mentioned you at all."

"Your father knows very well that we have a covenant. He would keep his intentions from you if only to withhold your grieving. He knows what it means to me, to eat not like a servant... but as a son. I need to know if this is the end."

"Whatever you want me to do, I will do it for you," Jonathan says, sitting up.

"Tomorrow is the New Moon Feast and I will not come tomorrow or the night after. If your father asks, tell him that I requested to return to my father's home for a sacrifice. If he responds with anger, then I will know my fate. If I am guilty then why hand me over to your father? Promise me that you will kill me yourself."

Jonathan looks repulsed. "Never. Just the opposite. I pray that the Lord would deal with me ever so severely if I did not send you away in peace. It has become evident who you are. A part of me could see it the day I met you. If you go, promise me that when the day comes you will not cut your kindness from my family, not even when the Lord has cut all of your enemies from the face of the earth."

The words of Samuel replay in David's mind. Still, the reality seems unreal, but now Jonathan, the heir of the kingdom stands before him acknowledging the same belief. David is the next in line. "Nothing has changed nor will it ever, you have my word."

"I will bring an archer, and after my time with Father, you shall know for sure."

David lets his eyes rest on the one man who has never left his side, knowing that at the end of the feast everything that he has ever known may vanish, along with the bond that he has created with his mentor, friend, brother.

"I'll be waiting."

86

Sitting silently, surrounded by his royal court on the second floor dining terrace, Saul attempts to let the late afternoon breeze that gusts between the stone pillars ease his mind, but it does no such thing. Seated away from the door in the far eastern corner of the porch, he rests in the most honorable position in the room, and yet his head throbs with pain as if gripped by an invisible spirit, his skull resisting the pressure of being crushed, his emotion resisting rage at the empty seat in his peripheral.

Every seat has been taken except for one, the seat next to Abner. Saul's mind swirls with reasoning. The boy that he raised, that he cared for, that he lifted into royalty has defied him in the midst of the entire royal court. The child that appeared to embrace each holy festival with reverence is now absent for the New Moon Feast.

It seems that his devotion was nothing more than an appearance.

Saul lets that word "appearance" sit and fester in his mind until it begins to spread. He can feel the awkward stillness of the room grow to an unbearable weight. The voices in his head grow louder. Together they reveal the thoughts of each individual seated at the table, and they are all questioning his command, leadership, and authority now that David has revealed yet another weakness of his for all to view.

The empathy that was creeping in, drawing Saul toward guilt, has been shattered, splintering each fragment of remorse into nothing more than a powdery dust. He gave David the benefit of doubt yesterday at the opening Feast of the New Moon. Maybe he was unclean, but today, today is pure rejection.

Jonathan's eyes are fixed on the empty plate in front of him, his body rigid.

It becomes blatantly clear to Saul.

He knows what David is up to.

"Where is he?" Saul says, clenching his jaw. The words, which are laced with anger, cut through the silence, surprising everyone at the table, including him. He exhales, attempting to soften the question. "The son of Jesse has missed both the feast yesterday and now today. Where… is… he?"

Jonathan doesn't move as Saul watches him like a viper eyeing an empty nest. "David pleaded with me to grant him permission to return to Bethlehem. His family is observing a sacrifice and his brother ordered his presence. If he has found favor then to his family he would return. That is why he has not come to the king's table."

Saul feels every mind at the table tearing in, ripping open his kingship, his authority, and inspecting it. The room is full of the most intellectual minds and experienced warriors that he could find and he will not be revealed weak in this moment.

My own son is even playing with me, he thinks.

Even with only the pillars, which straddle the surrounding open skyline, the porch seems to be closing in, tightening the already suffocating grip he feels from every eye now fixated on him. He responds with a monotone voice that creeps on the edge of haunting.

"You are not the son of royalty, but of a perverse and rebellious woman. Do you not think that I, the king, know what is happening behind my back? That you have sided with the son of Jesse to your own shame and to the shame of the mother who bore you?"

The room has faded to black. Jonathan has become Saul's sole focus as his memory of Samuel's prophecy rises to the surface. Saul cannot control himself any longer. His mouth spews the thoughts that he has tried to contain for so long.

"As long as the son of Jesse lives on this earth, neither you nor your kingdom will be established."

Saul notices that he is standing, shaking, with his fists pressed firmly against the table. He turns toward the stunned royal court and continues letting out the built-up years of frustration, the fear of losing his throne, and the pent-up rage that has accompanied it.

"Now, someone bring him to me. David shall not take as much as one more breath on this earth!"

"What has he done to deserve this sentence?" Jonathan shouts, standing.

Saul blindly reaches back, gripping his spear. The blatant disrespect has thrust him back into darkness, a darkness that he can no longer control nor hide from. His entire body erupts in unmanageable anger as he hurls his spear toward his own son. By the time his mind clears, Jonathan is gone, and as the fog of self-preservation lifts, he realizes that so has his appetite.

87

The matted down grass under David's back is comfortable, but as he lies hidden behind the boulders on the far side of the field, his mounting anticipation reaches its peak when the sun dips over the horizon. Each second that passes now, David knows that he could be one moment closer to an array of arrows landing nearby, a signal that his life will be changed forever.

Please just let it be the way it was.

David longs to see nothing more than Jonathan's childish grin hovering over him, letting him know that everything is going to be fine. The darkness is creeping across the sky and David can only imagine that the conversation has taken place.

Dinner should be over by now, he thinks, turning his ear to the soft breeze that sweeps across the open field.

There is a small hope, an odd longing of David's, that if an arrow were to fly tonight that possibly it would find a lodging place in him, ending this suffocating pain. Before David can entertain the idea of a swift death, he hears a projectile tearing through air and then burying itself into the soil only a few paces from his feet. Another follows immediately behind the first, cutting its way through the sky.

David brightens at the sound of Jonathan's voice, but Jonathan's words are carried away with the now-gusting wind. David peers to the side of the boulder where he sees Jonathan's hand motion, waving the archer farther away from the palace, toward oblivion, toward a place of no return.

With the soft tips of the arrows striking nearby and Jonathan's clear signal that his home is no longer safe, David's life has flipped inside out. He no longer has a home, a wife, or even the most simple of things, freedom.

Where do I go from here?

The pain builds and then, like a dam made of rotted wood, it breaks, unleashing the full flow of despair from David's soul. All of the relationships, memories, and bonds that have been formed are instantly severed by one man's madness. He lies back in disbelief. His hands, fingers, and toes slip into a numbness that he knows is only the first side effect of many more to come, for a despair that will never depart.

"I'm sorry, brother," Jonathan says, catching his breath on the other side of the boulders.

The warm voice immediately lifts David's spirit. His thoughts momentarily refocus from his future misery. David is weak, but not so weak that he can't show respect. He lowers to his knee, but Jonathan grabs David's shoulders, holding him at eye level.

"It has been my ambition to become the greatest warrior this land has ever known," Jonathan says. "To become one that is remembered, revered… a legend. I have fallen short and continue to do so, but I know that such a man exists and I will die proud and full of honor to have fought by his side. You have a gift, David. You have earned a seat at the table and one day that gift will bring you home."

Jonathan diverts his eyes to the ground, seemingly unable to bear his next words. "This is goodbye, my brother." Jonathan's quivering chin overcomes his attempt to hold back his rising emotions. He finally breaks and the two of them stand face-to-face, no longer caring how they look, just as a child weeping in a mother's arms. "A farewell between your descendants and my descendants, forever."

David steadies his breath that now squeezes through his throat that is swelled as if a stone were lodged inside.

"Forever," David says, acknowledging.

They embrace, each sending one another off with a kiss on the temple. The bitter taste of Jonathan's sweat sits on the edge of David's lips. He figures that it is a fitting end for a beginning that he never could have imagined.

David turns, breaking eye contact with undoubtedly the best man that he has ever known.

Until paradise, he thinks as he turns and his eyes to the south.

88

Resting just outside Ekron, Kilech finally receives word that there is a caravan heading south toward Gath. Coming from the north, the caravan will not only be large, Kilech figures, but will consist of everything from soldiers to women and children. The journey south will most definitely take longer than expected.

I should have just walked, Kilech realizes.

At least his travels should be safe, being that a majority of the convoy will consist of soldiers. Many of them are still returning to their homes, and a slow but safe journey is better than a speedy death. He reckons that there is no room to complain. It seems that his wavering faith in Dagon is becoming stronger by the day.

Each battle that he survives brings him one step closer to feeling like a real sea warrior. He has never stepped foot on a ship, but the years of living in their midst has begun to wear off on him. And with Gath now as his permanent home, soldiers such as these traveling from the north look at him differently. Even though he may not be a full-fledged warrior, he lives among the hardest of men, and therefore he is one of them.

He packs his stone tablets, those on which he scribed the events of Eshtaol. He has had plenty of time to create his own version of the Eshtaol raid and just hopes that it is authentic enough for Achish to believe. He nestles them in safely and prepares his belongings for the trip south. If the pace is what it usually is for a large force, Kilech places their arrival just before light as long as nothing slows them down.

David mindlessly swipes the branches away from his face as he wills his legs to just keep moving him forward. How could he fall from power, become a fugitive, and have nowhere to run in such a short period. It seems impossible, like a dream. No, a nightmare, a nightmare in which he is fully alert with no chance of waking up. This nightmare is now his reality. It has all happened so fast, so unexpectedly. David does the only thing he can do. He heads for the nearest city, one where the people can be trusted, and one where he can replenish and prepare for the coming days.

The small city of Nob is nestled in the dense forest west of the Way of the Patriarchs between Gibeah and Jebus. David knows once the news of his banishment reaches the four corners of Saul's kingdom he will have nowhere to turn. Nob will be his last stop.

He pushes out of the brush and approaches the shrine as he did in Ramah. This time, however, it will not be Samuel, but a priest that he has not spoken to directly for years, Ahimelek.

Through the windows, David watches shadows moving about inside, each opening glowing with the soft light of the burning oil lamps. He takes a breath, stowing all of his emotions and anxiety inside, turning on the warrior, igniting the flame of the commander persona that always dwells just below the surface – the persona that Ahimelek and whoever else inside would expect to see. Thrusting open the door, he enters as if he is late for an appointment.

Ahimelek stutters, visibly shaken at the sudden arrival. "David, what a pleasant surprise." The priest jumps to his feet, slowly backing toward the corner.

David surveys the room, his training having fully kicked in. It is no longer an act to overcome the day's sorrow, but his true ruggedness and self-preservation rising to the surface after years of training and fighting.

King Saul's captain shepherd, Doeg, back peddles from between the two of them. David eyes him. Doeg is the unaccounted surprise element, a Saul benefactor who will surely report David's random appearance if he can't come up with an excuse as to why he is here, and fast. They're staring at him, confused, but more so concerned.

"Do not be afraid. I am here on secret business of the king. No man is to know I was here. My men are positioned in hiding throughout the surrounding forest. Now, I must be brief. I need five loaves of bread or as much as you can muster so that we may continue our journey."

Ahimelek's hands are still trembling as he reaches under the table. "David, all that I have is this consecrated bread, provided the men have kept themselves clean and from women."

David takes the bread. "The men's bodies are holy even on missions that aren't holy. Now, do you have any weapons here? I am obviously in a hurry to carry out the king's orders."

Again, Ahimelek frantically turns and reaches behind the ephod. "The sword of the Philistine Goliath, who you slain, is here, still wrapped in cloth. Nothing else."

"Give it to me. There is none like it." David glances toward Doeg one last time before turning back to Ahimelek. "Thank you. You have no idea what this means to me."

David departs into the darkness with a loaf of bread and a sword that threatens to pierce his calves due to its length, even while strapped to his back. Right now he just needs to escape the twelve tribes, each of them capable of directing the king toward his position if Saul so decides to continue pursuit. And knowing the king already attempted to take his life three times past Ramah, David doesn't believe it will end soon.

He needs to escape the nation for the moment, and the valley to his east will do just that. It will not lead anywhere promising, just the opposite, but as an easy route away from the grasp of King Saul it seems to be the only choice. The only problem is where the Valley of Elah ends.

Right now he would travel to the gates of Hades to escape the kingdom collapsing around him. Somehow it feels like that is exactly where he is heading – into the mouth of darkness and across the threshold of the underworld. To the city that lies beyond the valley.

Gath.

89

What am I doing? David wonders as he passes the historic bend in the valley where the giant fell at his feet.

He pauses, staring at the exact spot, feeling the weight of the sword slung on his back. The hillsides are silent, everyone has gone home, and apparently all of them have forgotten what Yahweh did that day. There is no more cheering, no more celebrating. It's just David and the star-studded sky above, a sky that will soon be blotted out by the black clouds rolling in.

It's hard to believe the direction that he now walks alone, and the evil that he approaches just to escape one man. He continues passing lights on the hills until there are no more cities. He has crested into enemy territory and now begins to truly question his sanity. Exhausted, and with the city lights of Gath dimmed by the low storm clouds misting the sky in the distance, he collapses to the ground to rest his thoughts even more so than his body.

His family begins to weigh on his mind. He wonders if he will ever see them again. He wonders what they're doing right now, or if they're thinking of him. They could never guess that he would be here. No one could and that is precisely why he is.

He contemplates his options. Maybe he can fight for them, as a mercenary just as many others have done. Or maybe he can just pillage food for the time being. Either way his body is fading, quickly slipping into a fatigued slumber. Before he knows it, before he can control it, he's dead asleep.

✦━━✦━━✦

The city lights of Gath are finally in view, and Kilech never would have thought when he was young that it would be such a welcome sight. He can imagine laying his head under shelter, and maybe now after revealing how heroic he was in Eshtaol, the king himself will give him a woman.

Suddenly, the convoy stops. Kilech can already taste the sweet coconut and watermelon on his lips that will be waiting for him in the king's chamber and now, just before reaching the city, something has stopped the entire caravan? Shouting from ahead escalates until chaos erupts. Kilech, being the scribe that he is, moves toward the front to find out what is happening. What could cause him to wait for his tasty return?

Then, as the word passes along the long line of exhausted travelers, it becomes clear. A sleeping enemy soldier was just discovered by the roving guards – and it seems this soldier is no ordinary scout.

90

David struggles to get free, but his legs, his arms, and his head are being pulled simultaneously in different directions. Voices shout as a crowd forms, tightening the pressure on every part of him. He turns his head away from the nails scraping his eyes and the fingers hooking into his mouth. The taste of filthy, oily sweat is gagging him, but even more so are the few words being shouted that David has come to understand.

"Rajanya," one of them shouts before the crowd passes it along. He looks to his ring still snug on his finger, announcing to the world that he is royalty. "Glyth," another yells as the sword is pulled from his back. The crowd continues to grow. Men endlessly approach from the darkness, each of them adding their piece to the puzzle of who he is.

Before he can protest, his hands are bound and he is yanked upright as the crowd parts and an older man with dark eyes enters, speaking fluent Hebrew, which for the moment is a welcome sound. The soldiers huddle around as he looks over David's body for a moment, appearing more intrigued than anything else, especially noticing the royal ring still snug on David's finger, a damning object that he had been wearing when Michal unceremoniously helped him through that window.

"Why are you here?"

"To meet with King Achish." David pauses, awkwardly. "And to seek asylum among your people," he says, looking to the dirt when he speaks the word for the first time aloud.

The man looks skeptical. "If this is so, then you have come to the right place." He motions for the soldiers to release their tight grip and motions for David to follow him.

The man leads the caravan toward the city, and eventually to the palace of King Achish. David runs the scenarios in his mind as they pass through the defensive walls of the city in which he has killed so many. Shadows sway against the iron gate in unison with the orange reflection of the fires. The eerie black stone path beyond the gate appears to be burning as if it truly were the entrance to Hades. The moist air casts silhouettes that rise into the sky like giants wandering the streets.

Each time a shadow appears, David fears that Goliath has returned from the belly of earth for retribution. He knows that his mind is playing tricks on him, but what isn't a trick is the revealing light that soon will illuminate his face, removing all doubt about who he is.

The ground rhythmically rumbles under his feet in a pattern that could only originate from one source, giants. The crowd is completely surrounding David. There is no turning back.

David now regrets ever leaving his own land. The darkness of this pagan city snuffs out any remaining hope. The evil is tangible. It is all around him, physically haunting him from every direction. He can taste it on his lips and feel it inside his gut. Overwhelmed by the malevolence of even the common residents now pouring into the streets, David digs his heels into the dirt, shouting, flailing more with every push.

The crowd that continues to grow presses on every part of him. It's like an ocean current, and David is at the mercy of its movement. Right now they are all heading to the palace steps. The dark stone building is surrounded by large burning sconces that with each step closer reveal more of David's features to the masses. Quickly, the knowledge of who has entered their walls spreads like a plague as residents and soldiers alike continue to pour into the streets.

This is not how I envisioned my life ending, David thinks.

With the crowd continuing to grow more rowdy with each passing moment, David succumbs to the realization that he can no longer rely on the king's reasoning alone. This will not be a calm dialogue in which David can exploit Achish's greed and persuade him to welcome

David as a mercenary.

Arriving in the midst of the night with an unruly crowd hell-bent on his death, the king will surely move to appease the crowd unless David does something drastic. He knows that he only has one chance at winning over the king's favor, and now it won't be by showing his strength. He doesn't fight the fear. Instead, he embraces it by entertaining the most likely outcome. He envisions being ripped apart by the crowd and his body sent back throughout the twelve tribes.

The building chaos and thoughts of his morbid end begin to affect his hands first. The trembling spreads until his entire being is overcome by fear. Now is not the time to stand in honor, now is the time receive mercy by all means necessary.

⊹≻═╋═≺⊹

Kilech moves along the side of the rushing crowd. Each time they pass under one of the torches he gets a better look at the man they call Hebrew royalty. The man looks as if he is terrified. It's obvious that he is not the one they thought killed the giant, but then the captive glances toward Kilech, and even though this man is swarmed by hundreds, Kilech still feels a wave of insecurity when their eyes meet.

It feels like the man has looked deep into Kilech's soul and judged him inferior, or maybe Kilech did so subconsciously. Either way the remarkable thing is, he instantly recognizes him and the crowd was right all along.

How could this be?

It is the eyes that remind Kilech that only a few nights ago this man was leading a successful raid against his people. He is almost unrecognizable as he no longer stands with authority and power, but cowers and recoils as he is dragged before the steps of the king. Kilech watches skeptically, knowing what he saw in that quick glimpse of the man's eyes.

Moving onto the steps, Kilech waits for King Achish to descend into the chaos. Pulling out a tablet, he intends to appear to record the event. Having a position as scribe to the king, Kilech is planning on fully using his title to secure a front row view in order to quench his curiosity.

The crowd begins to rage as King Achish descends the steps toward the man they call rajanya. King Achish pauses, appearing to have the same confused revelation of not only who has been brought before him, but how terrible he looks.

A voice shouts from the crowd, drawing the eye of King Achish. "Isn't this David, the royal Hebrew warrior? Isn't he the one they sing about? Saul has killed his thousands, but David has killed his tens of thousands?"

Kilech notices drool coming out of David's mouth, and before the king can respond the giant killer collapses to the ground and begins convulsing, quickly covered in his own saliva. His limbs jerk frantically and he moans like a wounded animal.

This is not the man that I saw in Eshtaol, Kilech thinks, growing wearier of David's actions with each passing moment.

King Achish lifts his hand, calming the chaotic swarm of bodies. "Am I short of madmen that you would bring this Hebrew here to carry on in front of me?"

King Achish steps down toward him and lifts David's chin. David's eyes are unfocused, mostly white, and drool, like the rabid dog that he is, foams from the corner of his mouth, dripping onto the king's hand.

King Achish jerks his hand away, letting David's head fall to the ground. "He is insane. Why bring him to me?" The king turns, waving his hands toward the gate. "Turn him loose, back into the darkness. He will not last the night."

The crowd begrudgingly disperses, leaving David curled in the fetal position at the base of the palace steps. Kilech slowly makes his way to the top, but never enters. He can't take his eyes off of David, staring in awe at what this man is compared to what he once was. He remembers watching him defy the gods as he struck the giant. It was a feat that only the divine could have accomplished. Now, however, he has obviously lost whatever gift had been given to him, or has he?

The street has all but completely cleared, deserting the lunatic where he lies. Kilech almost turns to go inside, but David's head slowly turns as if he is looking to see if anyone is left, if anyone is still watching him. Standing perfectly still, Kilech observes as David slowly stands, scanning the surrounding area before grabbing Goliath's sword and sprinting into the darkness toward the city walls.

Kilech can't believe his eyes. The whole thing was a ploy, an act to deceive the king and, remarkably, it worked.

Deceiving Hebrews. I imagine that this will not be the last we've seen from the likes of this Hebrew. The rajanya.

91

Looking up into the bright blue sky overhead, Abinadab thrusts his sickle over his shoulder, airing the painful blisters on his palms. He often stops and remembers David outworking all of them in this very field, even while taking the brunt of all their jokes. He never thought he would miss him as much as he does, but it hasn't been the same since he left. By this time each year, David would have already stopped for a quick visit while moving throughout the tribes, attempting to strengthen the alliance.

This year, however, there has been no sign of him. Abinadab attempts to picture what David could be doing this very moment, but it's hard to imagine. Their lives have become so vastly different on every level. They pass every so often in the ranks during wartime, but David's position keeps the talk to a minimum.

"It's been quite a while since I've had the pleasure," Abinadab's father says, entering the field, his gaze far off.

Abinadab turns, not having heard his father's false voice in years. It's a voice reserved for high-level officers, or those well respected by others. And just as Abinadab suspects, three of Bethlehem's elders have converged on their land. Their bodies are old and slouched, but their pace is quick and hurried, leading Abinadab to believe that something is terribly wrong.

"We do not bear pleasant news, my friend." The youngest of the three is first to reach his father and places a not-so-comforting hand on Jesse's shoulder.

Abinadab wanders closer, tuning his ear to every word. His father's voice has lost the welcoming edge afforded to such guests as town elders.

"David?" Jesse asks, sounding truly concerned.

Abinadab's breath stalls. *It can't be. I saw him return at the head of his men.*

The elder's hand patting his father's shoulder is an uncomforting silent answer. "You may want to gather your belongings. There is not much time."

His calm authoritative father quickly turns rigid. "Is my boy all right?" His father's voice wavers on the verge of trembling.

"For now. We have been told that he is in hiding west of Azekah."

"Gath? There is nothing but Gath west of Azekah. Why in the world would you think he's there? What is going on?" Abinadab's father runs his hands through his already thin hair. "Why would he go anywhere near there? What happened?" Jesse stares at the eldest among them and very plainly asks again. "Is my boy all right?"

The elder takes a breath before responding. His eyes avoid Abinadab's visibly shaken father. "He has been declared a fugitive."

"A what?" Jesse looks as if he's balancing between anger and distress, unsure which emotion to let loose.

The elder's low gaze never wavers, as if he were prepared for the grief. "The king's servants will not be far behind. I warn you, you must leave now."

As Jesse turns for the house, he makes eye contact with Abinadab and then enters the dwelling without a word. Behind the elders, dust plumes into the air on the distant ridge as marching soldiers twist down the long switchback toward the city. Their time is quickly slipping away.

"All of this because of David," Shimea says, sounding more angry than concerned.

Abinadab turns, now realizing that every brother is standing behind him and has listened to the whole discussion.

"What could he have done that the king would seek all of our lives?" Eliab says, watching the same movement of soldiers marching down the hill.

"We are all capable warriors, are we not?" Abinadab says, knowing full well what is happening. "Whatever has happened is no fault of David."

"He's a fugitive," Shimea says pointedly.

"And now so are we," Abinadab responds.

"He is in the enemy's land as an outcast surrounded by lord knows what kind of giants," Eliab says, doubling down on Shimea's hopelessness for the situation.

"And did he not slay the greatest among them before our very eyes? God is with him." Abinadab plunges the sickle into the dirt. "And so am I."

Inside the dwelling, their mother's shriek over the news of David pierces the air. Her sobbing is heart-wrenching and compels Abinadab to act. He turns to his four younger brothers. "Grab every able weapon that you can find. If he can survive Gath then I know exactly where he'll be."

92

David slogs through the hot summer day, with a stolen shirt wrapped around his head, as he travels back down the Elah Valley, having learned that Gath would not welcome him. He will take his chances in his own nation. Many of the twelve tribes have yet to fully submit under the rule of King Saul. Even though word has most likely spread, there will still be those that will side with David, especially in Judah. The question is, who.

David has traveled to many of the tribes hoping to realign the land under one ruler. But it seems many of them had foreseen this day coming well before David. The one thing that he has learned in his travels is that no one is to be trusted.

Having dodged being spotted near Azekah and Socoh earlier in the day, he now approaches familiar territory. If he will be safe anywhere in the nation it will be in the Tribe of Judah. There is nowhere else but the hill country where he can hide and still feel somewhat in control. The outskirts of the next town, Adullam, will keep him far enough from home yet still in the hills that he knows better than anyone. What better place to hide than directly under the king's hand. Plus, there is only one person on earth that knows about this spot and he trusts him with his life.

With a renewed sense of optimism, David shakes off his dangerously rash decision to head toward Gath, which was motivated by his blinding need to escape the constricting reign of Saul. If he's going to survive, it's going to be on his own terms. He will hide right under the king's watchful eye in a land that no one navigates better.

David races into the brush when the city comes into view. With a rush of hope he begins the climb toward the summit that overlooks the city of Adullam.

If I'm going to die, David thinks, *it will be in Judah, and it will be on my own terms.*

93

Abinadab treks across the hills, heading west after veering into the forest from the Way of the Patriarchs road. A night of sleep in the dense forest with only the supplies on his back has his mind swirling with doubt.

What am I doing, he questions with each step deeper into the brush.

The initial rush of brotherly protection is wearing off and he begins to wonder if he'll even find David in the middle of the hill country's thick foliage. It would be virtually impossible if he didn't have a clue as to where he might be. He heads toward the only place that David spoke of as where he actually feels safe from the outside world.

It was the day that Abinadab went searching for him upon request of the prophet Samuel. Abinadab never forgot it. His brother spoke of a cavern so large that he could shelter his entire flock inside if a storm arose.

"I noticed the cave with a bear carcass at the entrance. Was that your work too?" Abinadab had asked David as they made their way to Samuel.

David didn't look too eager to answer. "I didn't have a choice. Apparently, I had taken his home for the night and he went for one of my sheep."

Abinadab was taken aback, not by the fact that his brother killed a bear, but because of the supposed size of the cave. "I know you don't sleep away from your flock, and there is no way that cave could shelter you and two sheep much less the entire flock."

David put his hand on Abinadab's shoulder as if he were the older brother. "There are openings the size of your waist that widen so large you could bury a city inside," he said, laughing.

"No!" Abinadab truly didn't believe him.

Then David paused, as if contemplating whether or not he should continue. "There is a cave in the mount above Adullam where a great oak marks an entrance that is no larger than you or I. Inside you could house an entire army. It's massive, filled with multiple ways out, some to cliffs but others to streams."

Abinadab remembers well the next and last comment David ever spoke to him of the cave of Adullam.

"Someone could disappear in there and no one would ever find them."

Those are the words that Abinadab now rests his future upon.

"Abinadab!"

He whips around, immediately recognizing the voice. Shimea and Eliab have succumbed to following him and they now make their way up the path toward him. Behind them, one after another, men appear around a turn in the path, following his brothers, each carrying a weapon or farm tool. Many are still dressed for the fields. A few are dressed in what Abinadab would consider ragged armor at best. They continue coming, one after the other. The number grows to around one hundred he would guess.

"What is this?" Abinadab asks as the men file behind.

"They came in the night. Men continue to join our cause. Everything is gone, everything." Shimea says.

"The elders said that they have no reason against David," Eliab says, "none whatsoever."

Shimea hugs Abinadab, visibly shaken.

"Mother? Father?" Abinadab looks over Shimea's shoulder, searching for them, but all he can see are the line of men stretched over the hill.

"They are behind us, in the middle of the formation."

Abinadab is in shock. "There are more?"

Shimea nods. "The surrounding towns of Judah have been hearing murmurings, and our home blazing in the night served as a beacon, a call to arms against tyranny."

"They want to fight?" Abinadab still can't believe his eyes.

"David has been good to them. Trust me when I tell you, much of Judah will die for our brother," Eliab says, at last awoken to the reality of the following that David has amassed.

"How do you know where he is?" Shimea asks.

"Trust me, I know where he is," Abinadab says, praying that David hasn't forgotten. "Well, let's keep moving."

They march now in the hundreds, climbing and descending the steep terrain, moving much slower than before. After only a few hours of marching, more men approach from the north.

"We hear that you are heading to fight for David?" a man asks as he walks toward Abinadab.

"He is my brother." Abinadab looks the man over. His armor is directly from the palace. "And what is your cause?"

The man's eyes intensify. "I was there when he slew the giant. I fear your brother far greater than I fear the king. Given the chance, it would be an honor to serve him," the man says, straightening his muscular body upright. From his body posture and armor it is clear that he has deserted the army altogether.

Abinadab looks to one of the others. "And you?"

"We are all in one way or another in trouble, whether in debt, remorse, or mourning." He motions to the men following behind. "Some are thieves, some deserters, some are even cheats. If we are not welcome here then where else is there for men like us? We have nothing left. What else is there to do but fight?"

Abinadab's first reaction is to turn them away, but he knows David. David will corral and build these men into the fiercest fighting force known to man. "You will become fugitives?"

The men smile. "That we already are."

"Then you will fit in just fine."

94

With multiple cave entrances conveniently located nearby, David roams the top of the hill gathering firewood with little fear that he could wander too far from one of the many openings that lead into the labyrinth below. Constant access into the underworld of tunnels will be his only safeguard, and as night falls he will need to prepare for the constant chill underground.

He piles the wood behind a ring of brush that conceals a black hole, an opening that dips into oblivion. The straight drop into the cavern below will serve as a perfect smoke stack, concealing the bright fire thirty paces below the surface and releasing its smoke, filtering it through the tall pines above.

David looks down to the isolated city lights of Adullam. His thoughts are plagued with a fear that slithers down and takes its form as a hand squeezing his heart. His chest tightens as he realizes that he is alive, and yet by all accounts dead, cut off from the world that continues to exist without him. In less than a week he has plummeted from royalty to beneath even his life as a child. He can no longer roam the earth as any other man, but now will live below it, as if an animal banished into darkness.

Sitting alone in the silence of the wilderness, he feels much like he did in the days before his rise to fame. The only difference is that now the walls of this cave will serve as a prison, the trees as his guards, and the sky… he glances up.

"Yahweh, everywhere I turn there a trap is set for me," he says, looking to where he should have turned earlier. "Give me strength and release this soul of mine from this prison."

David can't help but feel abandoned, his soul parched from

comfort. His fingers long to play a melody, but he has nothing more than the cloth that wraps his body and the sword of Goliath. The battle that he has fought for years in the flesh, he now struggles to win in the mind.

Sitting perfectly still with his eyes fixed on the heavens, he takes in the enormous expanse of creation above. He breathes in deeply, letting the cares of this simple life, this fragment, this vapor of his existence against the backdrop of eternity vanish from the weight of his burden. He begins speaking words of encouragement, but with each word his eyes fill with tears of sorrow.

"Deliver me that I may give thanks unto Your Name." David's throat constricts with each word, his voice cracking under the pain that sprouts from his soul. "May the righteous surround me, and may you deliver me from my adversaries, for they are too strong for me alone."

After a short moment contemplating his current situation, realizing that he could never figure out how God could ever rescue him from this, David turns back to finish the fire. He knows he must not ever fall complacent, and everything he touches must be replaced as if he were never there.

I'll be fine, he tells himself.

For now this life will work, up here there is not much threat of an army marching in search of him, but rather the random stroll of a shepherd happening upon him.

How ironic.

95

Abinadab crests the final hill. The city of Adullam sprawls out at the base of the mount.

This is it, he thinks, hoping that this is truly it.

His eyes strain through the dark, searching for the large oak tree that David had referred to so many years ago.

"Keep the men here. I think we're getting close," he says, motioning for Eliab to stop as he and Shimea continue, slowly approaching the rubble of stones.

Together, they maneuver the jagged terrain that becomes more uneven and treacherous with each step. As Abinadab rounds a boulder into a clearing on the far side of the hilltop he lifts his gaze, focusing his eyes on exactly what he has been searching for. A tall, twisted oak stands before him, silhouetted alone against the night sky.

"You see that?" Abinadab asks, moving more quickly now.

He steps toward the base of the tree but Shimea's arm wraps around his waist, stopping him from moving forward. Abinadab's eyes follow Shimea's gaze down to where his foot would have landed had he taken another step. The black cavity below stretches out in a narrow tear, a gash across the stony ground as if the earth were ripped deep into her core.

Abinadab can't believe his eyes. *It's really here.*

He doesn't hesitate. He has everything riding on what's inside this opening.

Please tell me you weren't joking, David.

Using Shimea as his leverage, Abinadab lowers into the tight hollow until his feet press against solid ground. With each step it feels as if he may be lowering himself into his own tomb. Gently combing his hand along the sharp edges, he pads along, descending deeper, until the dot of light behind disappears. The pitch-black is not comforting in more ways than one, but mostly because there is no sign of human life. With only the echoes of his footsteps and the occasional stir of something rustling past his sandals, each step is looking less promising.

Afraid of stepping off a cliff to his death, and with no way of knowing the landscape, Abinadab stops, defeated. It appears they have wasted their time. It's becoming alarmingly evident that it will take forever to search this labyrinth of tunnels without light. "Let's go, br –"

A firm hand covers his mouth while a pointed object digs into his ribs. He yells, but only a murmur comes out.

"Abinadab?" Shimea's voice echoes through the cave.

The hand lets go and the object eases from his skin.

"Shimea?" David's voice bellows in the cavern.

"David?" Abinadab turns and wraps his arms around David, unable to see a thing. His head presses against David's chest, and for the first time in days he actually feels safe.

"You remembered," David says.

"I was just praying that I wouldn't be the only one… and that you weren't just kidding," Abinadab says, finally letting go.

He can picture David's smile in the dark, which calms any remaining doubt that they will be all right.

David's hand pats along his arm until he locates and rests it on his shoulder. "It's good to feel and hear you, brother." David lets out an exhausted laugh. "I was just about to start a fire. Is it just the two of you?"

"No, we brought a few friends." Abinadab turns toward where he believes Shimea may still be standing. "Shimea, go tell the others," he says, making a useless hand motion in the blackness.

Abinadab follows David into a chamber with a massive hole in the ceiling, revealing the night sky. He can hear David stacking the wood, and soon the sounds of shuffling feet arise out of the dark behind him. A flame finally ignites deep within the kindling and builds into a fire. The orange glow first reveals David's strong features contrasted by shadows as firelight crawls up the large domed walls, highlighting the surprise that has since entered.

Abinadab watches as David looks over his shoulder, his eyes settling on the men that only multiply as the flickering light stretches farther into the cave. He rises slowly. David's words desert him for the moment as he watches the growing number of men that continue to file into the space.

Abinadab already knows the number, has already seen the crowd, and yet the support that his brother has already garnered from the Tribe of Judah is emotionally moving. He can only imagine how David must feel, laying eyes on them for the very first time. The men continue funneling into the tunnels that surround the chamber like spokes of a chariot wheel, disheveled and rugged men, but men prepared to stand nonetheless.

"This is more than a few," David finally says, his voice thick.

Abinadab smiles. "It's an army."

96

Saul paces restlessly in the open field, waiting for his top officials to congregate around him. Seeing that they have almost all arrived, he forces himself to sit. With spear in hand, he waits under the shade of a lone tamarisk tree. It has been over a week since Saul's men found the dwelling of Jesse, son of Obed, deserted, and rumors are spreading that David has help.

Which one of you is hiding the truth from the Lord's appointed? Saul wonders while glancing over every man standing before him.

The time for courtesy is over. Having been nothing more than a simple farm hand himself, Saul has always attempted to live humbly and respectfully, but where has that taken him? The only true control he has ever felt is that which Samuel has given him by publicly anointing him as king.

My power was given to me, not earned. Now… I will earn it.

After Commander Nathaniel strolls up, completing the assembly, Saul lets the silence sit, his eyes still roaming his men.

"Men of Benjamin, will the son of Jesse give all of you fields and vineyards? Will he make all of you commanders of hundreds and commanders of thousands? Is that why you stand against me? No one tells me when my son makes a covenant with the son of Jesse? Nor are you concerned about how my own son," Saul makes eye contact with Jonathan, pausing, "has incited *my* servant to lie in wait for me, as he does today?"

He steadies the grip on his spear, unsure if he should lash out, proving his anger and power, or continue to wait in silence, watching for the eyes of the traitor to reveal himself.

"I saw the son of Jesse come to Ahimelek the priest, son of

Ahitub, at Nob," a voice calls out from the back of the men. The crowd of officials parts and Doeg, the captain shepherd, steps forward, his gaze crawling along the ground. "Ahimelek inquired of the Lord for him."

"Is that all?"

"He also supplied him with bread," Doeg pauses, "and the sword of Goliath."

Saul notices Doeg's hand trembling at his side, his face buried in terror.

Finally, the respect I deserve, he thinks.

"You see how easy that was? That's all I wanted, a little honesty." Saul stands and approaches the visibly frightened Doeg. Still gripping his spear with his right hand, he places his left hand on Doeg's shoulder. "You are a good man, Doeg."

His attention turns back to the officials. "Now, go fetch me Ahimelek son of Ahitub, and bring all the men of his family while you're at it."

97

David squeezes through the crowded tunnels, slipping into a deserted passageway for a moment of privacy. After separating himself from the masses, he happens upon a glimmer of light and follows it. The growing beam leads him to the opening of yet another tunnel. As he approaches the source of the light it becomes apparent why he has never found this entrance. It's not an entrance at all, but a treacherous exit.

He sits down in the opening, letting his legs dangle off the edge, making it feel as if his sandals could touch the tops of the pine trees swaying below. Sheltering everyone inside the caves seemed like a great idea only a night ago.

Babies crying and children already complaining about the food is pulling his concerns far from where they should be. Soon they will be out of supplies, and the conditions inside the cave will be unsanitary for the length of time they will need to stay. They are safe for now, but if Saul continues to scour the area in search of them, David will need to find somewhere safe for those who can't fight for themselves.

He sits still, quietly contemplating where they should go and only one place comes to mind. If he wants to survive, and take advantage of the manpower that has been given to him, he will need to escort the families out of Israeli territory.

We have to head to Moab.

⊰━◈━⊱

"We will take charge, just as we have been ordained to do," Saul hears a voice say, unsure if it is in his head or somewhere out in his room, somewhere hidden in the darkness. The voices are beginning to blend together. Real or not, what once was disturbing is now comforting. He can feel power growing in his chest and whatever is causing it he doesn't care. It feels good, good to once again have control.

Saul realizes that he should have been doing this all along. A grin spreads across his face as he lies back down in bed, his drapes closed to obstruct the midday light from pouring in. He lets his mind drift, allowing it to freely wander with no fear of judgment or fear that any single thought is off limits. The grin widens until a faint chuckle escapes as he recalls the horror on the faces of his officials today.

They were truly mesmerized by my calm demeanor, my authority.

Saul can only imagine what they will think in a few days when the house of the high priest arrives. The thought bolts Saul upright in his bed. The slight crack of midday sun between his drapes is gone.

How long have I been in here? Saul wonders.

The feeling that he has lost his mind has fully manifested. He's no longer sure if it has been half a day or half a week that he has been entertained in the dark. He contemplates sprinting into the hall to begin a frantic search for answers, but the soft voice returns, ensuring that he stays where he is.

We are right where we want to be. Let the chaos fuel us and we will reveal to the nation that the king is here to stay at any cost.

Saul imagines his next move, and the grin returns.

98

The past few days have been grueling with an almost nonstop pace, but as badly as David wanted to remain in the safety and comfort of the caverns, he knew that he would never be able to feed and provide for the families accompanying his men. After all, this is not their fight and the survival of everyone diminishes with their presence. It was a hard decision to leave the loved ones behind, but it needed to be made.

David has led his entire force east where the families have been safely left across the Dead Sea in the protection of David's great-grandmother Ruth's homeland, in the town of Mizpah. The king who has been at war against Saul was encouraged to find out that Israel was in discontent.

My first alliance has been formed, David mused.

When they return to Judah after a full week of travel, David halts the men just south of where it all began, near Adullam in the eerie forest of Hereth.

He has always been fascinated with this largely forsaken corner of Judah, but for those who are afraid of the dark it can play with the mind when ghostly shadows emerge at nightfall. The ground is covered in a spongy green moss that has grown up the massive black cedar trees towering in the landscape like giants marching to war, their thick branches have twisted upward and entwined into a dark, mangled canopy above.

It is these haunting features that have spawned the legends, tales of a single man that lurks in the darkness and hunts those that pass through with evil intent in their hearts. David has never seen such a man here in these forests, but then again his heart is pure. At least he likes to think so.

Hundreds of men lower their gear and lie down after a long march from the kingdom of Moab. David's feet are sore, his body is tired, but the prophet Gad from Moab issued him a word of encouragement.

"You are not to stay in the stronghold. Return to Judah," he said.

He didn't need to say anything more, nor did he need to know the details. It was enough to assure David that he has not been called to hide.

Now, resting here in the forest of Hereth, David contemplates his next move.

"David, you have to come see this," Eliab says from the edge of the cliff.

"I've seen the view. Enjoy it while you can. We'll be moving soon."

"David, I'm serious. The Philistines are raiding Keilah!"

David runs over to the edge of the cliff and scans the majestic, sprawling view that reaches out before him to the rolling canyons below. Eliab pulls David in close. Pointing his finger toward the city, he draws David's gaze to the buildings just inside the gate.

"They're looting the threshing floors," Eliab says.

David looks on, his heart burning with the injustice of his people being robbed of their vital rations. He knows the painstaking process of threshing wheat firsthand. Not only is it the right decision morally to attack, but David considers the options of growing more alliances among Judah as a benefit as well.

David closes his eyes and relaxes his mind, focusing on the still, small voice. "If it be your will, Father, I will go."

"What?" Eliab asks.

David ignores him, listening until his answer comes. It doesn't come in the form of a voice but a knowing deep down in his heart that the Lord is with both him and his men to serve justice among his enemies.

David moves through the men that are resting their sore bodies. "We need to go. Get your bodies upright, gentlemen. Keilah is under siege and I know a few hundred men who are ready for a good afternoon's fight."

"It is disheartening, but what are we really to do?" a soldier asks from the crowd.

"We aren't prepared for war against the Philistines. We are untrained, tired, and many of us have only farm tools to bring against their army," another says.

"Then what are we doing here?" David asks, looking over the men. For the first time since being a fugitive he feels power flowing toward his hands. Every ounce of his body wants to return to what he knows best.

"The best way to get experience in war is by war itself," David says. "Each of you has a leader, and that leader, a captain, and that captain, a commander. You are in good, seasoned hands I assure you. And as far as weaponry, you will have the pick of your heart's desire once you lay waste to the enemy at our door."

David makes his way back to the cliff where his officers have assembled.

"David, the men are terrified. They have been the entire trip. If they are fearful in the forest of Judah, how do you think they will fare against the Philistines?" Eliab says, sounding truly concerned.

David, pinned by his officers and brothers, doesn't say a word. He pushes through them, turning his back to their negative thoughts and facing the open expanse. Their voices fade as he lowers to his knees on the edge overlooking the sheer drop with Keilah in the distance between the sweeping canyons. He knows there is only one to turn to when he's beginning to doubt.

He closes his eyes, letting the wind pelt his body and ripple his clothing back like a flag flying in the breeze. The trees begin to rustle as they sway from side to side. He senses the sky darkening with swirling clouds moving in from the east as the ground trembles from thunder rolling across the hills. It is the power of Yahweh beckoning David into action. Opening his eyes, David expects the army to be standing in awe, but nothing has changed. Inside, however, the storm is brewing.

David stands, without a care how the others are looking at him. He knows what needs to be done. "Let the men rest. Tonight we will move into Keilah," David says, making his way back to his gear.

99

Saul studies the high priest Ahimelek as he hesitantly steps forward. Disgusted by the height of his treason, Saul would have already cut him to the dirt, but with Ahimelek being the high priest that he is, he gives him the respect that he deserves.

"Listen now, son of Ahitub," Saul says, as he adjusts the royal ring of gold on his finger.

"Yes, my lord."

Saul calmly strolls in circles with his hands interlocked behind his back. "Why have you plotted against me, you and the son of Jesse, giving him bread and a sword?" Saul asks, now walking more slowly around the priest, his gaze fixed to the ground as if he were looking for something. "You inquired of God for him, did you not? And now, because of you, he lies in wait for me."

Ahimelek looks confused. "Who is more loyal than David? He is of your own, your son-in-law, captain of your royal guards, and the most respected in your entire household." Ahimelek's confusion turns more toward insult as his voice lifts, his face turning stern. "Was this the first time that I inquired of God for him? Of course not! Let your wrath pass from all within my house. I want nothing to do with this matter of yours."

Saul is beside himself with anger as the priest spews his words, each more blasphemous than the last. And all of it directed toward him, the king.

He has lost his concept of exactly who I am and the power that I possess, Saul thinks.

"Cut him down and his family with him. They sided with David, and now they will join in his fate."

Speaking the order out loud feels much more empowering than he could have imagined. As if a second personality is emerging with each word, Saul now senses more control than ever before. But no one moves. No one raises the sword against the priest, nor his family. Instead, they stand in shock at the command.

Saul smirks inside, thinking of how this disobedience would have affected him before. Either anxiety would have crumbled him, causing him to seek counsel, or anger would have propelled him to rage. Now, however, it is his servants that are feeling the pressure and Saul plans to ensure it never swings back toward him again.

He eyes Doeg, who appears horrified. He *is* the reason the priests are here, after all. Doeg's gaze veers from contact, and his skin almost visibly crawls backward, as if knowing his future and wishing to be no part of it. Seeing firsthand that fear controls one's actions quicker than a mere God-given position, Saul knows how and who will crumble under pressure and it will no longer be him.

"Doeg," Saul says with force, lifting his chin as he notices the visible dread that washes across Doeg's face, "turn now and slay each priest. May every ear hear the sound of betrayal."

Doeg doesn't move. It's obvious that he is fighting an inner battle, and by the looks of it, his desire to live is winning. He just needs a little push. Doeg flinches as General Abner unsheathes his sword. Gently, he wraps Doeg's fingers around the hand grip and steps back. Saul has removed himself from the attention of the officials and has successfully positioned all eyes on Doeg whose strength is disintegrating under the pressure, his tremulous hands preparing to strike.

Saul stands watching, enjoying every bit of it.

The bloodcurdling shrieks of the helpless souls in Keilah echo across the canyon floor, raising the hair on the back of David's neck. For the moment, twilight speeds their march toward the gated city, but soon nightfall will dip the low, twisting canyon into a blanket of darkness. He will need to issue strict and precise orders to ensure that the disheveled army of bandits will not collapse into chaos at the first sign of trouble.

"How do you plan to pull this off?" Abinadab whispers.

David barely acknowledges his question. "*We* will pull this off."

"I will follow you to the end of my life, but I am not so sure about our possibility of success. I don't think that any of the men see whatever it is that you see." Abinadab looks over his shoulder.

David follows his gaze. The men are battered, undisciplined, and ill-equipped as they stagger along the rocky terrain. David senses that without his intervention chaos may ensue well before any hardship presents itself. It is quite a change from the Eshtaol raid.

"Bring the men and follow me," David says, climbing to a vantage point on a boulder at the edge of the canyon.

As the men huddle around, David points to the city wrapped in high stone walls. "I understand that there is concern regarding our numbers. You may see four hundred men with us, but in our favor I see a city wall that holds nearly one thousand men. I see the cover of darkness which used correctly is worth the surprise of five hundred men in the light. Add it up and we have more than enough."

David jumps down, takes a stick, and outlines the city ahead of them in the dirt. Using it as a pointer, he draws the approach lines for each section. "I will lead the main force of two hundred over the rear wall and we will push toward the front gates. Abinadab, your force will enter and lie in wait near the gate. When their main force has bottlenecked at the entrance, you will unleash the chaos which, by the looks of our men, they are well equipped to apply." David grins as the ragtag army still falling in line proves his point.

He turns toward Shimea, his stern tone returning. "With the

remaining forces you will cut down any that escape. And Eliab, I will need you with me for control on our sweep. Each division has been fractionalized into teams. Each man, follow your leader, and each leader, your captain, and movement will be swift. Any who cannot follow this simple plan," David pauses, letting the reality sink in, "will be taken care of for us."

The men part and take charge of their responsibilities. As David separates from the main force and leads his men toward the rear of the city walls, he again feels alive. In charge of his men he is no longer consumed with despair, but focused on the task at hand. He just hopes that the others are as confident.

Two hundred men scaling the rear wall of the city takes longer than expected, but with the Philistines focused on gathering the plunder, the outposts have been abandoned, a mistake often made by complacent raiding forces.

Always watch your back, David thinks.

He marks the enemy's first mistake as he and his men slowly stalk toward the unsuspecting Sea People. David holds up his hand, stopping the forward progress as men pour into the city streets, unloading their bounty into a pile.

At the drop of his hand, the wave of silent destruction begins.

100

Henick stands perfectly still, tucked into a dark recess of the rock face, at the sound of footsteps approaching. A figure appears, sprinting through the valley. Henick waits patiently, watching, ensuring that whoever coming is alone before he steps out into the open.

As the threat draws near it becomes clear that he is not a soldier, nor a scout, but in fact a boy, a young one at that. His lack of training is evident by the amount of noise he creates as he fumbles his way through the open expanse of the ravine, taking no account of his surroundings.

He looks like me years ago delivering news of Jonathan's victory to the king, Henick thinks, *only much less aware.*

Confident that the boy is harmless, Henick moves into the open, placing himself in the boy's direct path. If a message is being delivered then it will go through Henick first. He knows how terrified the boy will be. After all, he was in the same position not so long ago. Knowing that his first reaction will be fear, Henick prepares to settle the boy before he has a chance to run.

The boy is only a few paces away when he finally realizes that someone is there and his reaction is exactly what Henick expected. He stops dead in his tracks, eyes bulging and mouth gaping. Henick reaches out, showing his open palms.

"Hebrew, do not fear," Henick says, now recognizing the boy's face. He has been one of Saul's messenger's for only a few months now. "I once was you… and if you keep moving like that in the open you won't last a week in the war season."

Breathing heavily and completely caught off guard, the boy takes a second to adjust. It appears that he recognizes Henick and is able to settle down a little. He bends over, resting his hands on his knees.

"David is south, in Keilah. He just attacked Keilah," he says, still panicked, as if running for his life.

That doesn't make sense, Henick thinks. *David would never attack one of our own.*

"David attacked Keilah?"

"No, the Philistines did. Sorry. David wiped them out, but he's still there."

David wiped them out?

Henick can't believe what he's hearing. "How?"

"With his army," the boy says, still breathing heavily. "I have to warn Saul."

"What? What is there to warn? David is eliminating our enemy. Why not just let him be?"

"He's an enemy of our nation and I am under orders from the king himself."

Henick glides his fingers along the grip of his dagger, but his conscience wins the battle between preservation and honor.

I should, but I can't kill a naïve child.

"Do what you must, but David is not our enemy and neither will he be in Keilah when Saul arrives. I'll see to that myself."

Henick moves aside in a silent gesture of grace, a hint to the boy to move along before he changes his mind about letting a runner live to report such news to the king. The boy glances to Henick's hand hovering over his dagger and suddenly understands. He darts off as carelessly as he arrived.

Now aware that Saul has dispatched any number of young scouts, devotees, to hunt for David, it becomes evident that this journey has become as important as any of his others. Henick watches as the boy rounds a turn and disappears into the hills.

But Henrick is still not alone. There is movement coming from the far ridge, movement coming from the direction of the capital. A long, dark shadow snakes down into the ravine behind him and the leader looks oddly familiar.

It's a busy night.

Henick waits and his suspicion is confirmed. There are more defectors than he thought.

"What are you waiting for, we need someone to scout our path," a rough, distinct voice calls out.

Henick grins. "It's good to see you too, Nathaniel," he mumbles under his breath.

Surprisingly, he is happier to see him than he has ever been, probably more so than *anyone* has ever been. Over the broad shoulders of Nathaniel the dark, trailing shadow that just crested the ridge materializes before him. Two hundred fully armored men march, ready for battle. Henick suddenly senses that becoming a deserter was the safest choice.

"You're heading south, I take it?" he asks

"Well, we aren't heading north," Nathaniel says. "I've never witnessed anything so vile in my life."

Henick nods in agreement. "Word is already reaching the palace. We should get moving."

Nathaniel's face twists into a scowl. "I know a thin young messenger carrying light armor isn't telling *me* to get moving."

Henick grins. "As you command." He turns and sprints south, leaving the safety of numbers behind. Once again, he is on the run. Once again, he carries the nation's message on his lips.

⊹⊱⊰⊹

This better be good, Saul thinks.

Having been woken in the night, Saul shuffles down the steps, half asleep, in his robe. As he reaches the throne hall he sees a young boy, catching his breath, as General Abner watches.

"What is it?" Saul's raspy voice echoes off the sterile walls.

"He has news of your servant," Abner says.

Saul's eyes focus, the cobwebs in his mind clear, and he is wide awake. "Go ahead."

The boy lowers to his knees and faces the ground, but Saul is in no mood for royal antics.

"Carry on with it." He pinches the skin under the boy's chin and lifts his gaze to meet his own. "Where is the shepherd?"

"My king, I was scouting south of Adullam and witnessed a city being defended by a foreign army."

Saul attempts to be calm, but his arm seems to have a mind of its own, and reacts as if controlled by a demon. Whatever its plan, it has already been set in motion.

Saul's vision narrows as he switches his grip to the boy's throat. He yanks him up, choking him in the process. "Get to the point. What foreign army would stand against our enemies?"

The boy gags as he tries to answer while Saul's fingers are wrapped around his throat. Saul suddenly realizes what he's doing and relaxes his grip, surprised by his own reaction.

"They say it was the army of David, my king."

Saul sucks in a breath. Abner's eyes find him struggling to unearth the word. "Army?"

He's gaining alliances.

Saul realizes that he is going to need more men. "What city?"

The boy stretches his neck forward and swallows hard. "Keilah, my lord."

101

Inside the walls of Keilah, a dark and silent liberation has begun. The residents of the fortified city have slowly entered the streets. Some of them, mostly the women, spit on the corpses of the dead, men, who only hours ago used their soft, innocent bodies as nothing more than objects for the release of their own short pleasures.

The women who have lost husbands, children, or both, scream wildly with no care left for the world, their cries rising from the canyon floor to the pit of David's stomach. There is never joy when Peleshet are involved. They plunder not only for supplies, but torture and genocide.

David can feel the eyes of the city observing him as he counts his own dead, respectfully lining up their bodies outside the front gate. Some of them he had just met, others he doesn't even recall their faces, yet all of them mean something to him. The death lining the stone wall is no longer a result of the sacrifice for the nation, but now something much more sobering.

They died for me, David thinks.

He looks over each body, some of whom were brothers or sons, leaving behind parents and siblings. Others were fathers, leaving behind wives and children. The so-called successful battle to defend Keilah has come at a cost in which some men have given everything and all for his cause, whatever that may be.

David lowers to his knees and outstretches his hands, placing them gently on the cooling flesh of the fallen. Over the years his prayers have changed as his life experiences have turned. Tonight will be no different.

A sudden patter of approaching footsteps diverts his attention. Oddly, alarmingly, they are not coming from the city. They are coming from behind, from the canyon, from the north.

"David!"

David looks off, hearing the familiar voice of Henick, but sees something more, farther off in the distance. A dark shadow, like a low-hanging cloud made of soldiers serpentines through the valley behind him. For a moment David is unsure if he should prepare the gates in defense, or welcome the strangers as allies. At the sight of Henick's face it seems the latter.

But who is he bringing?

"It is so good to see you commander," Henick says, exhausted. "I come with warning."

"Is that so?" David turns rigid, diverting his eyes toward the unit approaching in the distance.

"Not them. I'm with them."

David shoots his gaze back to Henick, dumbfounded. "Breathe then tell me what is going on."

"Sorry," he says leaning over to catch his breath. "Saul has slaughtered the entire house of..."

Henick's heavy breathing, his hurried words, his emotional tone, all fade into a blur, swirling together inside David's head. As David hears the rest of the message, numbness spreads across his flesh like frostbite crawling inward from his limbs, enveloping everything, until resting deep inside his heart. The king who was once anointed by God, once a valiant leader, commander, friend, and father now lays the sword to not just any family, but the family of the high priest.

All because of me. David can't help but blame himself.

Henick continues to speak, but David hears nothing other than, "Ahimelek is dead."

David's men file out of the city to greet the arriving force, but David can't get the image of Saul's atrocity out of his mind. It plays over and over again, as if he were there watching. He hears the screams, sees the grim aftermath so vividly that for a moment it feels more like a recent memory. Then the armed men that were following Henick stagger in. David recognizes many of the faces, but he ignores all of them, including Commander Nathaniel. Instead, his full attention is set on only one.

"I'm sorry," David says, cutting his way through the men on his way toward him, his chin quivering. "I'm so sorry."

David is unable to hold back the tears that now stream into his beard as he reaches him. He lowers before the young man who stands with his father's ephod draped around his neck.

"He killed them all," Abiathar says, still wide-eyed with shock.

David looks him in the eye. "It is because of me that your family is dead. I knew that day when your father helped me that Doeg would speak. I am responsible. I am responsible for your whole family."

Abiathar places his hands on David's shoulders and returns the gaze. "Saul is responsible for my family."

David places his hands on Abiathar's as his demeanor sharpens. "Stay with me, and do not be afraid. The same man that wants to kill you also wants me dead. You will be safe with me."

"We have not come for safety," Commander Nathaniel says before coughing into his cloth. "Quite the opposite, actually."

David wipes his wet eyes. "We can accommodate your request as well," he says, drawing an uncommonly friendly smile from the commander. For the first time, David lifts his gaze, actually taking in the reality of what stands before him. Two hundred men, armed, trained, and prepared to do what they do best, fight.

"I hate to interrupt, but as we speak Saul is receiving news that we are here," Henick says, stepping forward.

David pauses, quickly analyzing the situation, but there is only one option. "Grab all the Peleshet weaponry, anything you wish. Take hold of a portion of their livestock as well and meet at the gates by the end of the third watch. We will push east before first light."

David will no longer rest and wait out Saul. The only option left is to distance his men as much as possible, train them, and prepare them for what now seems inevitable.

102

As morning's first light pierces the horizon, washing the nation with its blinding golden hue, Samuel walks alone. He gazes at the radiant glow that slowly pushes the darkness across the ground as it rises, stretching its reach into Ramah, but his mind is anywhere but in the present.

It has been a good life, Samuel thinks, knowing that the end is near.

It is hard to believe how fast it has gone. From being born to a barren mother whose prayer had been answered, to when she dedicated his life before Yahweh as an offering, taking him to be raised in the tabernacle of Shiloh.

The place of peace, as Samuel remembers vividly, was anything but peaceful.

It was there where he would first hear the voice of God, but like everything in this life, nothing lasts forever. The Philistines would soon destroy it, and Samuel's teacher, his mentor, and father figure Eli, would die.

With memories pouring in, Samuel senses that his last breath is upon him. He takes his remaining steps across the field adjacent to the shrine. As one of Israel's last remaining judges, he recalls the moment that God anointed him as a youth to not only call the nation back to repentance, but to gather an army and lead it into victory against their enemies. He sees much of himself in the young boy that stood amongst his brothers, anointed for a purpose that only Yahweh Himself could foresee. That young boy, Samuel knows, having seen David only weeks ago, will take the helm of this nation and do for it what he could only have dreamed.

Now, with his aged body giving out before his very eyes, he gently lowers to his aching knees. With a soft, wrinkled hand, he pulls the dry cloth, soaked with David's blood, from his robe and drapes his arms over a low hanging branch. It is the single elm tree amidst the field of green, his last sign of surrender, obedience to a God that has been nothing but good to him.

The elm, a tree with magnificent branches that spread wide and far, has become a symbol of dignity and faithfulness.

A fitting end, Samuel thinks, having prepared for this day to come.

Hearing the voice of Yahweh calling once again, he knows that indeed it is now time to travel toward the true Shiloh. With a long draw of his final breath, he slips away and this world dips to black.

He watches now from above as his kneeling body remains still, his arms hanging over the branch with his hands clasped together. Just as he pictured it, a perfect image of his life, a final symbol of kneeling in prayer with his face toward the ground. The cloth in his hand falls to the earth, the blood of David coming to rest at the foot of the tree.

Samuel turns his attention to the sky, leaving his aged body behind.

There is no better ending, for now life truly begins.

103

The land of Ziph is a landscape from that of nightmares. The desert, which is located in the southern reaches of Judah, is a wasteland of harsh terrain and even less desirable climate.

With razor-sharp rock formations that shoot into the air like stone barbs protecting the earth from the tormenting sun, the desert looks more like a graveyard of mountain skeletons, their rib cages scattered wildly across the desolate ground.

It is a perfect barrier, Henick thinks as they move through the relentless environment on their escape from Keilah. Now, with the harshest location to their backs, the men settle in not far from Carmel to the far south. The deep, rolling sandy hills provide adequate cover and an escape route where they can train freely yet remain protected. David's genius is becoming more apparent with each calculated decision.

Henick is amazed at the attention to detail that David administers, even in the middle of Hades itself. He knows when to pull the reins, when to ease them, and when to snap them down on backs, with force. It is obvious that he is preparing every man for intense combat. It doesn't appear to matter what their titles are, David has made it painstakingly clear that everyone will train for precision and for brutality – .and at that, David is the master.

The first one awake, the last to eat, and by far the hardest on himself, David has quickly become forged as more than their leader, but as a mentor and friend. Henick's captains finish their training and return to the main unit to prepare for David's nightly gathering, a meeting in which every detail of the day is scrutinized and prepared for correcting in the day to come.

"Henick, we're meeting in the tent," Eliab says, passing briskly.

Henick runs to the tent, knowing that no one wants to be the last one in. He slides in just before the last few officers enter. The last one, Eleazar, closes the flaps and stands as the guardian of the gate.

"To those of you who stand in this meeting for the first time, understand me. You are not here by accident," David says, pacing through the tent, inspecting each warrior's attire. "Your names have been submitted by your commanders because of your ability to not only fight, but to lead. I will be separating you into your new commands tomorrow. If we are going to ever stop running, we must become as hard as iron and fight as one body. We have armor and battle experience from Keilah and, most importantly, an understanding of our weaknesses."

David turns now, looking directly at Henick. David has become a good friend, and yet when he is in his leadership mode, he is still intimidating enough to make a grown man pass out with his gaze.

"You... I don't like your name," he says with a dead stare.

The tent fills with awkward chuckles. Henick feels like a three-legged elephant sprinting in the open. He senses every eye on him. His heart races and he can feel his skin turn red.

"I think you need a new one." The officers laugh and cheer, seeming to know where David is heading. "Nathaniel told me that years ago he remembers you mentioning that you wanted nothing more than to become a true Hebrew. Well, if you want to be a true Hebrew you're going to need a true Hebrew name."

Again the officers erupt in cheers. Henick can't believe what he's hearing. As the tent fills with excitement, hands pat his back and rub his head, congratulating him. Nathaniel stands in the corner with a tight-lipped grin, watching it all unfold. Henick smiles back.

"To the man that carried the torch in the darkness, showing the way for Yahweh's people..." David puts his arm around him. "I present to you, gentlemen, 'Yahweh is light.' Uriah."

Uriah does everything he can to hold back the tear forming in his eye. This moment is too good not to enjoy it, but he would never live it down if anyone saw so much as a single drop.

David continues about tactics, training, supplies, and so on, but Uriah doesn't hear another word. The meeting ends and the men leave as the first watch of the night begins.

"Congratulations, brother," Abinadab says. "I've taken Joab already, so you're going to be taking Abishai under your wing. He'll need to be taught how we do things."

"Abishai?"

Abinadab grins. "You didn't hear him say anything past Uriah, did you?"

Uriah nods. "Not a thing."

Laughing, Abinadab continues. "He's one of the new leaders under you. He's also my nephew, so…"

"Got it. We'll take care of him," Uriah says, noticing Abinadab's concerned look. "But don't worry because I won't be easy on him."

Abinadab laughs, but then suddenly it cuts short.

Uriah freezes, having heard the same sound that startled Abinadab. The two men stand motionless, their heads tilted, listening.

A faint echo in the distance that somehow sounds more human than the others has caught their attention. The sound of a stone falling or a sandal scuffing across the hills carries through the wind like a shofar blaring after battle. Uriah's eyes meet Abinadab's and simultaneously they swing their gaze behind them, to the rolling hills.

A black speck, standing upright on two legs, sprints up a distant hill. Someone is running and it's not one of the shepherds that they have been watching over.

Uriah feels a sinking dread overwhelm him. "Where do you think he's going?"

"I was afraid you were thinking that."

Abinadab heads toward the tent. "David, we need to talk!"

104

Staging the armor by the boulder where he always places it, Aaron notices that Jonathan is nowhere to be found.

He's always here by now, Aaron thinks.

After waiting long enough, he heads back in to search for him. The army will be gathering soon, and for the first time Jonathan won't be waiting for them when they file into formation. Aaron heads for the steps, but King Saul has already claimed them. He descends alongside his most trusted general, oblivious to Aaron's presence. Aaron would rather keep it that way so he dips right and circles around the side of the palace avoiding contact with the duo at all costs. Since the rift between King Saul and Jonathan, Aaron has attempted to remain completely out of the king's attention.

After checking the first floor and finding no sign of him, Aaron sprints up the stairs and approaches Jonathan's room.

Nothing.

Aaron heads to the only person who may hold the answer.

Arriving at Michal's door he notices that it's open a crack. "Michal, are you in there?" he asks, knocking.

The light tap on the door swings it open even more and Aaron notices movement inside. Through the opening, he sees Jonathan's sister half-wrapped in her bed sheets roll off of a man lying in a pool of sweat.

Aaron diverts his gaze to the hallway, trying to erase the image and yet remembering it at the same time.

"Aaron?"

Aaron painfully lifts his gaze to hers and attempts to not appear awkward, but he fears that's not working in the least.

Not only is this Jonathan's sister and David's wife, but she's also

Saul's daughter, Aaron reminds himself, feeling even guiltier now.

He can't help but divert his eyes to the floor, away from her beauty, as she bundles her sheets under her arms to cover her chest.

"I'm sorry. I'm just looking for your brother," he says.

"Why do you need him?"

"For the march south? I haven't been able –"

"If Jonathan isn't out there already, it's for a reason," she says assuredly.

Her eyes tell him more than her words ever could. Those emerald eyes always talk more than her voice, more than anyone's voice for that matter, ever could. Her disappointment washes across her face, and Aaron can sense her thoughts.

Saul.

"He's going for David again, isn't he?" Aaron asks.

She nods that he is.

"Hasn't he learned? How many times does your father need to fail before he gives up? Haven't his trips to Ramah or to Keilah taught him anything? Even when he cornered David on the side of the mountain in Maon he couldn't capture him. Maybe it's for a reason. You'd think he'd learn." Aaron glances around the hall, dumbfounded. "Even in the room in which you now stand David has eluded him. If it were to be, David would have been delivered into his hands already."

"I know," Michal says, lowering her head.

Behind her a man approaches and wraps his arms around her, looking over her shoulder to Aaron, who finally confirms that it is, in fact, Phalti, Michal's new husband, issued to her by her father in an attempt to secure a border alliance and, no doubt, remove David's memory.

"Well, my love, if your father is headed for David maybe I could help. What do you think?" Phalti says, grinning before kissing her neck. Michal looks as if she may possibly stab him.

The awkwardness that Aaron felt just a minute ago quickly falls to the floor. His eyes dilate and his breathing escalates. His narrowing gaze studies the pathetically soft human from head to toe.

"You don't know David, do you?" Aaron blurts out, his body on the verge of shaking, his hands on the verge of striking.

Phalti's grin fades as Aaron imagines stabbing his sword straight through his shiny brown eyes. Aaron's thought of what David could do to Phalti is cause enough for at least a devilish grin.

"One day, I pray you get to meet him."

105

The scouts of Ziph have sold out David and once again he has been flushed from his location, never being able to fully trust anyone.

It only takes one, David thinks, realizing that this is his new life, picking up at a moment's notice and traveling across wastelands with dwindling resources.

It may be the most challenging fight, this war of attrition, the constant battle, settling only to move again. They are becoming more drained with each journey, and with each upheaval, more frustrated. Saul is wearing them out, whether he intends to or not, solely by keeping them on edge. They need a break, and soon.

As the mountainous desert landscape finally levels out, a seamless horizon emerges. With it, a familiar salty breeze gusts a reinvigorating coolness against David's face. The sluggish pace of the men instantly quickens as fresh air that beckons of sea water sweeps across them.

With each step the blue expanse before them widens, stretching as far as the eye can see. The dry, monotonous, unforgiving desert is already gone from David's mind. He lets the thoughts of starry nights and floating in the water under the blue sky replaces everything else.

"We should build a boat and just live on the sea," Shimea says. "Saul would never look there."

The grunts and moans that have played like a melody for the last few days turn to light laughter. Some can only offer a heavy breath accompanied by a dry-mouthed smile.

"That is absolutely the dumbest thing I've ever heard," Eliab says from the back of the officer's formation.

"Why, like he's going to bring a boat through the desert to come get us?"

The comment sparks more laughter.

"What would we eat?" Eliab challenges.

"Fish, you idiot."

"Yeah, because the Dead Sea is loaded with fish, right?"

David contains himself, but he always did love when Eliab shut up Shimea.

"Not to mention the size of a boat needed to hold six hundred men," another voice says from farther back.

David turns, amazed at what he just heard. Abishai, his silent young nephew who always keeps to himself, has just opened his mouth, and toward Shimea nonetheless. David grins and turns back, holding his laughter inside. The most amusing part is that Abishai's face remains stern as if not intending it to be confrontational. But David caught his eye.

A dry sense of humor, David thinks. *I never knew.*

"Wait. What?" Shimea looks amazed. "Did Abishai just speak? What would you know? You were just weaned from your mother's –"

"Enough," Nathaniel shouts, clearly agitated.

"Just stating facts," Abishai whispers, loud enough to draw Shimea's eye.

David takes a long exhale. The men have been constantly on guard and have been trained into numbness. It's good to hear a little edge back on their tongues. Something about it feels a little like the old days.

"Permission to break rank?" Uriah says, conforming to the new rules about ranked movements.

"What is it?" David responds.

Uriah breaks from his position just behind the top commanders and matches David's pace at the head of the men. "If we head a little farther south we can rest in a place that the locals call En Gedi. The men will love you for it."

"Place of the spring goat?"

"Trust me."

David nods and turns the march slightly to the right, now heading south. As he draws near, the oddest of things happens. The water lowers with each step he takes until he realizes what he is standing on.

David walks to the edge of the plateau. The sea sprawls in every direction before him, but at his feet is a sheer cliff the span of three hundred paces. The palm groves along the coast look like mere weeds from this height.

The last few months have been brutal. They have taken each long journey to evade the king and his three thousand-man army, from Moab to Keilah and now Ziph, even coming as close as sharing the same mountain. It was only a Philistine raid in the north that forced Saul to abandon his quest.

Now, sensing the grip of Saul tightening around their location, David needs a break, and this dead end isn't what he was hoping for.

"Uriah?"

Uriah steps to David's side. "We're almost there."

He's smiling?

David finds it odd. "Why are you smiling?"

"You'll see, my lord." Uriah darts along the edge of the cliff and across the flat sandy ground. He cuts back toward the open desert and then suddenly the earth swallows him whole.

David can't believe his eyes. He races toward where Uriah had been. The army follows David's lead and every man breaks rank, all heading for the same spot. One warrior from the middle of the formation passes everyone else as if they were standing still. If David wasn't so worried about Uriah he would stop and watch the amazing stride. Then, the thin soldier with the blazing speed slows and he too disappears into the ground.

With each step the impossible becomes more understood as a

dark shadow emerges in the ground ahead. As if the aftermath of an earthquake, a split in the plateau materializes as they near its edge. David stares in amazement at the deep cut in the earth that steps down and widens like a natural staircase. Inside, a flowing spring cascades down the path with lush green vegetation to its side. The magnificent view is capped by the waterfall that spills over the edge toward the palm groves and eventually drains into the sea at the bottom.

Uriah, already having made his way to the waterfall's edge, stares up from a boulder, the water flowing over the edge at his feet. Vibrant flowers and grasses surround him as he lays down his weapons and takes off his shirt.

"Did I tell you, or what?" he says, turning and jumping.

A few seconds pass and then a splash sends the men running in waves to join him.

David is blown away by the beauty and vital resources that couldn't have come at a better time, but his mind snaps back to his number one focus, and it's not having fun. He grabs Shimea and Eliab, one with his right hand and one with his left, stopping them as they race toward the waterfall.

"We do not get the luxury of pleasure until we know it is secure. If you want to be officers, you will do more than act like it. You will eat, breathe, and sleep like it." He lets go. "Set up a perimeter and start a rotating watch."

David sends them off and hears Nathaniel already cussing the shirtless men. David scans the men who are now standing in terror as they receive Nathaniel's ear beating. He notices the thin warrior who runs like a gazelle standing toward the back, still fully dressed and armored.

"Hey, you."

The warrior turns, laying surprised eyes on David, swallowing hard. David can't believe his eyes. The warrior with such blazing speed is his own nephew, the youngest of his sister Zeruiah's three boys. David could never have imagined that he had such a stride, but he's glad that he does.

"Asahel, go get Uriah," David says.

Asahel nods and is already in midstride toward the boulders.

Uriah ascends to the top of the waterfall, looking for David.

"Are you having fun?" David asks.

Uriah hesitates, unsure how to answer the loaded question "Yes," he stutters, "Yes, lord."

"Good, because *that* will get men killed someday," David says, pointing to Uriah's weapons left behind on the rock. "We don't leave our weapons behind unless they have been ripped from our corpse or handed off to another that watches our back. And we are never the first at anything, except combat. If you want to lead men then you must always think of them first. Not what they want, but what they do not know they need."

David places his hand on Uriah's shoulder. "Do you understand?" Uriah nods as David takes a breath. "You can never forget a dying man's face, knowing that you are the reason. That you didn't train him hard enough, you didn't equip him well enough, or you didn't take the time to exploit the potential that he has until it is too late. That man will haunt you every night when you lay down your head. I see them all."

He shoots Uriah a glance as he turns. "Trust me."

106

Saul walks alone through the desert, approaching the sheer rock formations which rise into the air like the teeth of a wood saw. Moments ago he noticed a group of shepherds resting near this very location, and he now approaches them. His men are halted far behind, concealed by the dunes as he finally makes eye contact with one of the elders.

He lifts his hand and plants a welcoming grin on his face. "Good day, my friend," Saul says.

The shepherd's eyes widen at the sight of Saul's attire. The man bows his head and holds out his hands, showing respect and that he brings no threat. "Good day, my king," the shepherd says as he uncomfortably shifts in his robe.

"I am looking for my son-in-law. He has a large detachment of my army and I need to ensure that he receives adequate supplies to continue his mission. Last I knew, he was here, but I haven't been able to locate him. You haven't by chance seen the direction in which he may have headed, have you?" Saul says, offering three silver coins in appreciation.

The shepherd stands, but he seems to question the moral decision as he stares at the silver.

A young shepherd steps forward and answers. "Yes, my lord, they headed east toward the sea a few days ago. Your son-in-law spoke highly of you and was gracious to us while they were here."

Saul hands the silver to the elder and smiles. "Gracious my kingdom shall be to you and your family."

Turning back toward his three thousand men concealed behind the dunes Saul lets the fake smile fall from his face. After months of hunting and coming so close, it appears that David's fortune is finally running out.

Pinned with their backs against the sea, Saul thinks. *It's over.*

With plans to now spread each division wide across the desert floor, Saul can ensure that David will not double back. In only a matter of time he will have nowhere to run, and this will all be over.

I'm tired of fearing for my life.

With scouts and guards deployed, including Asahel, who David has affectionately nicknamed Gazelle, David's men can finally begin to relax. David can finally relax. After training the entire morning, each warrior knows their defensive positions, their role in the battle scheme, and the superior to whom they should report, ensuring an accurate head count during the chaos that is sure to find them.

David strolls along the spring's crystal-clear water that flows effortlessly between the rocks. Safely concealed twenty paces below the brutal dry desert, the high stone walls rise increasingly upward with each descending step along the paths cascading stairway. As the ravine grows wider and deeper toward the waterfall, the cool stone walls that shelter the twisting stream provide a perfect temperature and an escape from the blazing sun, allowing the lush green landscape to prevail. It is as if God has split the plateau and revealed this hidden oasis for this very moment.

They needed this, David thinks, hearing the constant splashes as men leap from the waterfall.

Cupping his hands, he lifts water to his mouth. The ice-cold spring water stings his dry throat when he swallows, but he doesn't care. He can't seem to get enough. He pours it over his head, letting it drip down his hardened body, his flesh now extra taut from the wet chill, his skin rising into little bumps. For the first time in weeks he stares at his own reflection. His face is worn, his skin filthy, and his eyes tell the story of life on the run.

Feeling alive and restored from his time in the heat, David nears the edge and crosses at the top of the waterfall, finding a perfect spot to rest along the rushing water. The sheer cliff that towers sixty paces above the base of the plunge pool has somehow eroded a smooth arched entry into its otherwise impenetrable outer shell.

Stepping inside, David can't believe his eyes. Smooth and dense, the interior cavity is hollowed into a dome which is dimly lit by three natural arched windows, each worn smooth, giving it the air of a majestic palace spire. Each window reveals a different view from one distinct vista to the next. David looks to the left and can't help but grin, watching the men leap over the stone edge, drawing his eye to the second archway where they plunge into the blue lagoon below.

He stills in amazement, feeling as if he's weightlessly floating over the palm groves sprawling to the right. They stretch all the way to the sea where the sun reflects in rhythmic patterns as waves roll to the shore.

"How long do you think he's going to continue hunting us?" Eliab asks from behind.

David turns, having missed Eliab and the priest Abiathar sitting in the dark at the entrance of the caves. He stares, but his eyes have yet to adjust from the bright sunlight. He moves toward them, splashing through still water puddled on the stone floor. Taken off guard, his mind searches for a pleasant answer, but it finds none.

"Until death, I would imagine."

David can now see Eliab, his stoic older brother. The one he has always looked up to, now stares uncertainly at the ground, his tone revealing his longing for answers and his need of comfort from his youngest brother.

"Then what is *our* future? Are we to run for the rest of our lives?"

David hears his brother's pain that reverberate off the solid stone

342 | D A N I E L   J .   G E I S E L

walls. The chamber of dense rock seems to close tighter with each unanswerable question. The truth is, David is taking one step at a time just like any of them. The reality, David realizes, is that he could stay here forever if Yahweh would so allow.

Realizing that David truly has no answer, Eliab breaks the silence. "When you were young and the prophet sought you...What did he anoint you to be all those years ago?"

David turns his gaze back to the sea. "You wouldn't believe it if I told you," he says, remembering all the times he was mocked, ridiculed, and belittled by his brothers.

"I think you'd be surprised," Eliab says.

David ponders how to say it, but his thoughts are interrupted.

"You have been anointed to be set apart from the common man," Abiathar says, now making his way toward David. "That's what an anointing is for and yet you have not entered into the role of a prophet or a priest as far as I can see. It appears that your anointing was kept secret for a reason." Abiathar eases into David's peripheral vision, forcing his eyes to turn to him. "I have lost my entire family due to whatever it is you are called to become. I will follow you to the end of the earth, but I just need to hear it for myself."

It feels like everything, including the rushing stream, has gone silent as David now prepares to speak the words out loud for the first time.

"King Saul does not seek my life because I have been anointed a prophet, a priest, or even a vessel of his message. He seeks my life because I have been anointed..." David shifts his gaze to his brother then back to Abiathar, meeting the eyes of both.

With a slow, steady breath he finally says, "...king."

107

Asahel squints, craning his neck, unsure if his mind is playing tricks on him. After being noticed for his unique speed, even nicknamed Gazelle by David himself, he has been sent to the edge of the dunes about an hour's walk across the flat surface of the plateau. After staring into the bright desert sand for what feels like an eternity, he fears the movement on the horizon inland to the west is nothing more than an exhausted mind. In the far distance, something is appearing, the individual dots growing into one large black spot on the side of a sandy hill.

That's no mind trick, he realizes.

Asahel's stomach drops. Terrified to report a false alarm he questions his decision. But as the number of black specks grow, now darkening the entire hillside in its shade, it becomes clear that it is more than a shepherd with his flock.

It's an army and they are heading right for us.

Asahel, alone, far from any security, and with an entire army bearing down upon him, jumps to his feet and darts back toward En Gedi. Driving his legs harder with each stride as fear and, oddly enough, excitement propel him across the smooth landscape.

He has been chosen for one reason and he will do everything in his power to clear the long desert flats before anyone can spot him or his direction of travel. With everyone enjoying themselves in the oasis, they will need all the preparation time they can get. As Asahel's legs pump faster than ever before he is confident about one thing…

David chose the right man for the job.

The long run passes by with lightning speed and as he nears En Gedi his lungs squeeze tight. He begins sucking air, his breath on fire, as the edge of the land comes into view. As one of the youngest warriors in David's army, Asahel would rather keep a low profile and blend in, but as the entrance to the ravine becomes visible he braces for just the opposite.

Leaping down into the descending oasis, Asahel prepares to call complete attention to himself in his role of the bearer of bad news. Right now his fears and self-confidence will have to wait. David and the army will be prepared. Asahel is going to make sure of it.

With one shout, he turns the relaxing army into a fury of commotion, preparing and arming themselves for the fight of their lives.

⊹⊱⋅⋅⋅⋅⊰⊹

Saul follows his men down a dangerously narrow goat path. He carefully places his feet with each descending step, and still it seems that each step is more precarious than the last. His footing feels loose, his balance unstable, and yet he can't help but stop periodically to stare over the edge as if testing his fate, or maybe estimating his chance for survival.

The cliff face to his side continually bumps his shoulder, nudging him toward a gut-wrenching fall and horrifying death. But as the steep grade finally levels out, eventually dropping him gently onto the shoreline, he stops for a moment to feel the warm sand squeezing between his toes. He releases a breath that he's sure he's been holding the entire descent.

His legs are sore, his body fatigued, and his head is pounding under the heat of the blistering sun. Locating David's men has become a secondary objective now, falling quickly behind the need to find some adequate shade.

I can't have anyone see me like this.

Feeling as though he might collapse at any moment, Saul orders his men into the palm groves to recoup. He figures David must have either continued farther south or is hiding his army deeper in the palms along the water's edge. Either way, Saul knows that he is tightening the grip on David's position.

It won't be much longer and this will all be over.

As the men dip into the palms, Saul takes notice of a boulder jutting from the cliff, providing what looks to be the perfect location for much needed privacy and shade. As he nears the beckoning shade, he hears water trickling somewhere high in the cliff. It grows louder as he nears until it becomes almost a gushing, satisfying flow from above that relaxes his tension. For the first time today he feels the need to relieve himself.

Slipping into the darkness, Saul enjoys the chilled air drafting from somewhere deep within the cliff and lets it draw him forward. Finally, there are no eyes on him, no one watching his every move or judging his decisions. It's just him and the blackness that surrounds. Feeling free and unable to see anything anyway, he closes his eyes, exhales a long breath of relief, and enjoys the solitude.

David and his most trusted men, his reliable few, his battle-hardened officers, have silently waited here in the depth of this darkness with six hundred men at their back since receiving news earlier in the day that a possible detachment of the king is approaching. Now, everything converges into one dark, musty cave.

"This is your moment," Nathaniel whispers. "God said that he would give your enemy into your hands for you to deal with as you wish. Well, now is your chance." His hand grips David's shoulder, saying more than words ever could.

I have to do this, David tells himself, willing his body forward.

The silhouette of Saul highlighted by the sunlight pouring in is unmistakable. As David edges forward, ensuring to keep his sandals from scuffing in this chamber that echoes the faintest of noise, he notices that Saul is completely lost in his own world. It is a side that David realizes he has never seen, no one ever sees. Believing that all eyes are off of him for the moment, Saul relaxes, discarding his powerful facade. His shoulders slouch and his head drops forward. Finally, he looks like he is at peace.

David has the full advantage, his eyes, which have already adjusted to the darkness, scan the ground before each measured step. His hand grips the dagger's soft leather handle as he halts within arm's reach of Saul. He can hear Saul breathing. He can still smell the fragrance of Michal on his clothes. It's amazing how sensitive you become when sand and male body odor is all that you have left. He inhales, thinking of her soft touch and what could have been.

He examines Saul's body with his gaze, unable to remove himself from the memories that pour in from the past. Those are the legs that carried him when he could walk no farther. Those are the arms that lifted him when he could not lift himself. David knows the real Saul, the kindhearted man that resides deep inside the image that many fear. If only it could be the same as it had been. If only the king could see that it's all in his head.

No matter the consequence, David knows that if Yahweh established Saul's reign then it will be Yahweh that topples it. He cannot strike down the Lord's appointed, nor can he raise his hand against Jonathan's household. The fact is… he loves Saul.

But his men are relying on him.

Condensation drips from the ceiling, like the base of a grinding wheel clicking in perfect rhythm, a simple reminder that time is slipping away. David extends the blade outward, his hand trembling, his heart rattling against his chest. He strikes and feels only a hint of resistance as the blade passes through with ease. But only a slice of fabric from the fringe of Saul's robe falls to the ground. David, against all expectation, has withheld his wrath from the king.

Not realizing that he has been holding his breath, David lets out a steady exhale as Saul strolls into the sunlight, oblivious that his fate has been teetering on the edge of David's blade.

David drops to a knee, overwhelmed, his mind swirling with questions.

"What are you doing?" Abinadab asks as the men emerge behind him from their positions.

What am I doing? David wonders, questioning his own decision. But he knows the truth. *"It wasn't time."*

"Not time? When will it be time?" Shimea says while grumbling whispers stir behind him.

David whips his head around. "How long would a king with six hundred men last?" David snaps, livid at his brother's public challenge. "If I am to gain an allegiance and lead the nation then I must remain blameless. I will not have the blood of the anointed king on my hands."

David noticed the cavern went silent when he alluded to becoming king.

Apparently everyone was waiting for me to settle the rumors, David thinks.

With renewed vigor in his step, David marches toward the light.

"David, what are you doing?" Abinadab asks, the concern in his voice lifting it to a high-pitched whisper.

David responds without missing a stride. "Growing our alliances."

108

"My king!" David announces, boldly stopping Saul in his tracks. "Where are the words that proclaim that it is I who seeks the king's life? For what cause has this been placed upon my shoulders? If this were true would I not have taken your life?" David lowers to a knee. "Father!" he shouts, pulling the attention of the entire army toward him.

The king's chin jolts upward as if the term has pierced his back. Then, hesitantly, he turns toward David.

David lowers his head and stretches out his hand holding the piece of Saul's robe. "See that there is nothing in my hand of wrongdoing or rebellion. I have not wronged you, and yet you are hunting me down to snuff out my life. May the Lord judge between you and me. And may Yahweh avenge the wrongs that you have done to me, but *my* hand will not touch you."

David stands. His fingers, which clutch the torn cloth, now point directly at General Abner, and his next words are delivered for him alone. "As the saying goes, 'from evildoers come evil deeds.'"

Saul feels every single eye of his three thousand-man army bearing down upon him. David has just pulled the most daring move that Saul has ever seen and now Saul feels as if he is standing naked, completely vulnerable for everyone to freely inspect. Thankfully, David has just turned some of the attention elsewhere.

Saul glances to Abner, having noticed David's pointed indictment. Abner's eyes burn toward David, who Saul now realizes has no cause for it.

"David, is that your voice…?" Saul pauses, unable to finish his thought.

Without warning his throat constricts and the muscles in his face contort as the memories of David's younger years spring an unforeseen emotion upon him. He never expected to react like this, but then again he never expected to be confronted in such a bold manner either. He struggles to collect himself, realizing just how closely he had eluded a certain death. Realizing that David had spared him.

"My son." The words escape quickly as Saul struggles to catch his quivering breath.

What have I done?

Saul focuses on the dirt at his feet, his body slouching in surrender. "You are more righteous than I," Saul says. "You have treated me well, but I have returned to you nothing but evil. The Lord *has* delivered me into your hands and yet here I stand. When a man finds his enemy, does he let him get away unharmed?"

Saul acknowledges that there is no hiding his shame. His face, the once impenetrable dam, begins to crack. His lips pinch and his cheeks crinkle, folding under the pressure building behind his mask, and he realizes that he has lost the battle of his emotions. The mask that he has worn for all of these years is beginning to shatter. He feels the touch of that long-desired Presence, the one that only David could muster. And with it, his suspicions are confirmed. David is the one.

"May the Lord reward you for your treatment of me today. I know that you will be king and that the kingdom of Israel will be established in your hands." Saul takes a step forward, his mind all but forgetting his three thousand soldiers.

His quivering voice settles as a trail of tears clear a path through the dirt and grime above his beard. He no longer cares what anyone thinks. He has done what others believed to be right and has acted out of fear for long enough.

There is one true fear that has consumed him, driven him, even to this very point. Now that he stands before the one prophesied to take his place he must know the answer to the question that has been haunting him for years. He needs reassurance now more than ever.

"Now swear to me by the Lord that you will not kill off my descendants or wipe out my name from my father's family."

Saul stares up to David who stands elevated near the cave entrance, his chiseled physique planted firm like the statue of a pagan god.

"I give you my word."

109

Abinadab gathers his belongings and looks off to the lush green terrain that surrounds them, his stomach twisting in knots. The last thing anyone wants to do is leave this place. They have begun making this oasis their home and again, just like that, they are uprooted. He hears the growing murmurs amongst the men and can't help but side with them.

Just before he chimes in with his own displeasures, Shimea beats him to it.

"He could have killed him. He *should* have killed him. This would all be over," Shimea says, throwing his belongings to the ground in disgust."

"David knows what he's doing," a deep voice grumbles from within the cave.

Shimea scoffs. "Yeah, and what's that? Exhausting an army of rejects, training them for no reason, marching them back and forth across the wastelands? Because that's all I see happening here."

"That's because you're too wrapped up in your own misery to see straight. You're a worthless mind and a useless body created for the front lines to spare the others more time," the voice responds from the darkness.

Shimea's chin lifts and his chest puffs out as he stares into the cave. "Yeah, like no one else is in misery right now. If you have something to say why don't you come right out and say it?"

Abinadab steps back, separating himself from Shimea as the man steps from the shadows. Shimea doesn't move, but Abinadab isn't fooled. He has seen his brother's displays when he feels threatened. He strokes his beard as if that proves he's comfortable, sure of himself. Right now, Abinadab fears that Shimea may rub his beard clean off.

"You have been running your mouth nonstop. I'm just wondering if you're going to shut it on your own or if you would like some help."

Shimea recoils. "You do realize –"

The man, now standing directly in front of Shimea, is gazing down to ensure eye contact. His thick chest is almost pressing against Shimea's chin. "You think because your brother is the warlord that somehow you're privileged? That somehow it's acceptable to disrespect him?"

Shimea lowers his eyes, either from fear or to admire the man's stature. Either way his gaze drops from the man's black beard to his thighs that anchor like pillars supporting a stone palace wrapped in flesh. Abinadab is nervous just watching as the encounter unfolds before him. He's never seen his brother cower so quickly.

"You wouldn't know a tactical move if it reached out and grabbed you by the throat. Your brother just showed three thousand of Saul's most elite soldiers that their king is a liar. And he did it alone, allowing you to cower back here in the darkness." The man nods to the thrown gear. "Now pick your mess up and get ready to move."

Abinadab watches as Shimea opens his mouth to speak, but wisely decides against it. The silence that had swept the cave evaporates with a unified exhale from everyone present, relieved that whatever just happened is over. As the man leaves the cave everyone returns to their business. Uriah, having been standing next to Abinadab the whole time, looks over with a lopsided grin.

"Who was that?" Abinadab asks.

"There are a few men that you don't want to agitate, and that was one of them."

Abinadab nods, finding the comment obviously apparent. "What's his name?

"Eleazar," Uriah says. "And trust me, when he truly begins to fight, everyone will be asking that very question."

110

Departing from the oasis of En Gedi is one of the more difficult things David has had to endure. As much as it helps having the camaraderie of the men around him, it makes it that much harder leading them when there is no end in sight. These are the moments when he wishes that he was alone and didn't have to worry about everyone relying on him as he drags them aimlessly through the wilderness.

With En Gedi now far behind them, David searches for the next answer. The men, as he can already hear, are growing hungry, thirsty, and weary. The supplies are all but gone and there is nowhere for them to turn.

I know that you have the answer, but with each passing day it becomes increasingly harder for me to see it, David thinks as desperation sets in.

He is in the midst of the wilderness with dwindling supplies and the threat of an army lying in ambush at every turn and yet David senses that Yahweh is still in charge. Still, the loneliness and lack of clarity concerning his future is disheartening.

How much longer will this continue?

"David," Nathaniel's voice calls out.

David doesn't hesitate nor does he slow his step. "I know... the men are growing weary."

Nathaniel clears his throat. "I don't mean to push the issue but –"

David crests the hilltop hoping for a miracle. Nothing but wilderness lies ahead. Nathaniel's voice fades to a mumble. David's thoughts are elsewhere. He needs answers and he needs them fast. Movement in the distance catches his eye. It's nothing more than a shepherd wandering the hills, but it gives him an idea.

"When we were near Carmel last, we stayed just south of Ziph and watched over the shepherds there that were shearing their master's sheep."

"Yes, we did," Nathaniel says, confused.

"We fed them, took care of them, and protected both shepherds and their flock." David's gaze is steady, focused in the distance. "What was their master's name? Nabal?"

Nathaniel grunts, seeming to now understand David's thought process.

"I think it's time we receive our payment," David says, turning to meet Nathaniel's eyes.

"How many would you like to send, my lord?"

"Only ten, but with a clear message." David tells Nathaniel everything that he wants said and sends him off to gather the men. It doesn't take long before Nathaniel's voice explodes, sending the rear of the formation into chaos. David shakes his head, smiling.

I guess every leader has their own style.

Watching Uriah depart and nine others fanning out behind him, David hopes that it won't be long until his men are again fed and restored.

"David?" Shimea approaches hesitantly. "Do you have a moment?"

David stares, amazed at his brother's sudden manners. He nods.

"I know I have been rough on you over the years. And often I open my mouth when I shouldn't."

"It's all right –"

"No, it's really not," Shimea interrupts. "I've teased you your whole life, and I'm beginning to realize that it's me who is the joke. I don't know how you dealt with it all these years, but I've never seen anyone so focused, so disciplined, and so honorable as you. I thought the prophet had made a mistake when he chose you, but I want you to know, for what it's worth, that truly knowing you as I do, I would have chosen you too. I have been here and on your side, but only as a brother. Now, I want you to know that I am here and will serve you as not only my brother, but as my commander."

David wraps his arm around Shimea's head, pulling him into his body. "When you get a taste of your purpose and a glimpse of the One who designed it for you, a teasing older brother no longer carries much weight."

"But how do you not doubt? I mean, as we march through desolate lands scouring for food, I have a hard time finding that purpose."

David releases him. "Who says that I don't doubt? Every man doubts, but to remain faithful you must remind yourself that just because you can't see clearly doesn't mean it's not unfolding perfectly." David glances up toward the clouds drifting across the blue sky.

"The sun never sets on the earth. It is the earth that turns its back on the light. Even on a cloudy day the sun still shines as bright as ever. Just because we can't see it or feel it doesn't mean it's not there. If it weren't for the clouds, we would lose the comfort of the shade. Without the rains our plants would die, and without the night there would be no rest. You see, brother, sometimes our darkest hour can be our greatest gift."

David looks over the six hundred-man army that has formed since his expulsion. "When you are in the darkest hour, remember to stay faithful for the light is just around the corner." David cracks a smile. "Now get back to your section before Eleazar catches a glimpse of you at the head of the men."

Shimea's lips purse tight. He's obviously surprised and possibly a bit embarrassed that David already heard of the ear beating that he had taken earlier. "As you wish, my lord," Shimea says, dipping his head to show that he truly is changing.

111

Restless, Saul stares out the window of his sleeping quarters. He has yet to have a good night's sleep since David left the palace. Since that day it seems there is a massive void in his heart. The image of David, holding a piece of his robe, flashes across his memory.

He could have killed me. He should have killed me.

The reality of what David did is hard to believe. Saul knows without a shadow of doubt that David will be the next king and yet he withheld his wrath? Was Saul to remain a mentor to David, training him for his future office? Did he banish the boy out of his insecurity alone? With more thoughts swirling around his mind than ever before Saul decides to make his way through the palace, a relaxing walk, in hopes of clearing the chaos in his head.

It feels like the direction that he once had, the purpose that he had carried with him day-to-day, has vanished. Now, life has no reason. It has become stale, monotonous, each day blending with the last. The only thing that draws attention from the mundane is David.

Going into the stairwell, Saul stops, surprised that General Abner is already occupying a stair.

"Can't sleep?" Saul asks.

"No, I can't turn off this mind from wandering off into the abyss." Abner looks over his shoulder to Saul in the darkness. "He's playing a dangerous game and attempting to use your most valuable forces against you."

Saul is surprised at the outburst. Apparently this has been on the general's mind all night as well. "I fear that I may have put him in this position myself," Saul says.

Abner stands and turns, now directly in front of Saul. "That is exactly what he wants you to think. Thinking like that will make you forget him until it is too late and he is storming our gates with more intelligence on our defenses than any enemy before him."

Saul shakes his head, disagreeing. "He could have killed me and he didn't. If he was so hungry for power then why wouldn't he just have ended it? He doesn't just see me as a king, but as a father."

"No! You're playing into his hands!" Abner snaps. "He's turning the people against you. If he kills you then he is instantly the enemy. But if he shows his loyalty then you become the tyrant, and just like his pathetic army, your kingdom will begin to defect."

Saul knows that David, now with his own loyalists, could never return to Gibeah as if nothing ever happened. If Abner is correct and there is no one else in the land with more battle knowledge than David, then there is only one thing that must be done. But it won't be Saul that decides.

"What do you recommend we do?"

"What we have already set out to do. This time, however, we finish it," Abner says.

Something just doesn't sit right with Saul as he considers what Abner is again proposing. However, he has yet to sleep and going back on the hunt will again focus his mind, his purpose. It is clear that Abner fully believes that if David isn't killed, then the kingdom of Israel that is already so divided will most likely fall completely from Saul's grasp.

The general's words ring ever true as Saul reminds himself of Samuel's message, "one that will possess the heart of the people as well as the throne." Saul realizes that this is precisely what Abner is speaking of.

David must first win the heart of the people before taking my throne.

What needs to be done becomes clearer than ever. Not what he wants to do, but what *must* be done.

"Rally the troops, general. We'll head south at first word of his whereabouts."

And maybe I will finally get a good night's sleep.

112

David moves past the men toward the returning ten. This time Uriah marches at the head of the formation.

"Well?" David says, already reading Uriah's body language.

"It's not good. I told him what we had done, that we had watched over his men and his livestock and took care of everything in our sight. His response was to ask insolently, 'Who is this David? Who is the son of Jesse? Many servants are breaking away from their masters these days. Why should I take my bread and water and the meat I have slaughtered for my shearers, and give it to men coming from who knows where?'"

By Uriah's tone, David can imagine the mocking response from Nabal as if it had been spoken directly to him.

This rich, filthy, and arrogant master believes that no one can stand against him, David thinks. *Today, he will find out who the son of Jesse is.*

He turns toward the men, some asleep, some casually listening to his dialogue with Uriah.

"Everyone up!" David yells as he storms toward his armor. He straps his sword to his side and notices that every eye has been awakened and is now watching his every move. "Prepare yourselves for war. We are heading off to secure our own supplies."

The men, seeing that David's entire tone has changed, scurry to prepare for battle. Not a single word is spoken, from the commanders to the common man.

David walks up and down the ranks, his eyes burning with sudden rage. "Nathaniel, Uriah, and Eleazar bring me four hundred hungry souls. The rest will stay with the gear."

In an instant his commanders have four hundred of their warriors in formation and David takes charge, leading them swiftly over the ridgelines toward Nabal's compound.

Seeing the compound off in the distance, David slows his men to a halt. Having his leaders quickly ensure that all preparations have been made and that all the men are indeed ready, David moves through the ranks to make everyone is aware of what is about to take place.

"We have safeguarded the property of a man who does not value or respect our good favor upon his household. We protected his livestock and this fat, rich little piece of filth has decided to repay me evil for good."

David turns toward the compound in the distance. "May God have my head, if by morning I leave one male alive of all who belong to Nabal."

David moves through the ranks toward the front, preparing to order the charge, but something far off catches his attention. He emerges from the sea of men into the open and looks upon a beautiful woman approaching. David orders his men to follow him down into the ravine to meet her. When he reaches her, she quickly dismounts and falls at his feet.

"Pardon your servant, my lord. Please forget the words of my wicked husband. He is just as his name is, Nabal the fool. I did not see your men come, but please accept this gift and know that the Lord has kept your hand from bloodshed and has kept you from avenging yourself with your own hands."

She glances up, meeting David's eyes. "The Lord your God will certainly make a lasting dynasty for you, because you fight the Lord's battles, and no wrongdoing will be found in you as long as you live. Even though someone is pursuing you to take your life, you will be protected in the bundle of the living by God, but the lives of your enemies he will hurl away as from the pocket of a sling."

David is stunned. This woman speaks as though she is a prophet, as if God were filling her mouth with the words that only he needed to hear. He remains standing in silence, letting her continue.

"When the Lord has fulfilled for you every good thing he promised concerning you and has appointed you ruler of all of Israel, you will not have on your conscience the burden of needless bloodshed or of having avenged yourself. And when the Lord has brought you success, remember your servant, lord."

David can't believe his ears. In an instant this woman's heartfelt words, words that could not have come from anywhere but Yahweh himself, has turned his heart of stone-cold vengeance into a bowl of honey, pouring out forgiveness.

"Praise to the Lord, the God of Israel, who has sent you to meet me. May you be blessed for your good judgment and for keeping me from bloodshed this day and from avenging myself with my own hands. Otherwise, as surely as the God of Israel lives, not one male belonging to Nabal would have been left alive by daybreak."

David looks over the supplies that she has brought. Two hundred loaves, two skins of wine, five dressed sheep, cakes of raisins, grain, and pressed figs. The supplies are endless. He motions for his men to collect all that she has brought. "You may return in peace. I have heard your words and accept your request."

David watches her depart as his men divide the supplies amongst themselves to carry back. She is beautiful, young, and obviously has a heart after Yahweh.

She's intelligent, David thinks.

He can't let her go without knowing her name. "What is your name so that I won't forget you?"

She turns and lowers back to the ground, her dimples revealing her pleasure at answering. "Abigail, my lord."

David nods. "Abigail, I will not forget what you have done, nor will I forget you."

David returns with the supplies presented by Abigail and expects to see some excited warriors ready to satisfy their hunger. Instead, he is received by more concern. It seems the land of Ziph is filled with more than just sand cats and leopards. It also appears to be crawling with rats.

113

Kilech rushes to king Achish's sleeping chamber. The dimly lit stone hallway always makes the trip toward the king a little more terrifying, especially when he has no idea why he has been summoned. He stops, gathering his breath and checking over his attire, before knocking and entering the room.

The king sits waiting on the edge of his bed and, fortunately, his demeanor appears pleasant.

"Kilech, my son. Come, sit with me." He pats the bed next to him."

Kilech pads across the room and joins the king at his side.

"You have served me most honorably for a very long time. I would hate to lose you and your skills, but I have watched you, and have noticed for quite some time now that you want something more. Is this true?"

Kilech swallows hard, unsure if there is an underlying question, or if the king is truly asking what he seems to be asking. He decides his fear will not lead him to a lie, especially a lie to the king.

"Yes, my king, it's true."

King Achish turns with a grin. "And what is this *more* that you desire?"

"Only by your grace, my lord, that I would serve with the men on the lines."

Achish nods. He gazes over Kilech's thin frame seeming to take pity. "Well, a man's heart is a powerful thing, isn't it? I read your story of how the battle of Eshtaol played out. It was quite impressive how you managed to kill so many and yet still survive." The king's head lowers as he looks through his brows, letting Kilech know that he wasn't fooled. "I cannot lose you as the trusted scribe that you have become. However, I will grant this desire, because nothing in life is worse than a passion unfulfilled."

Kilech exhales a long breath. "Thank you, my lord."

"Now, I will order you to the rear of the coming battles to ensure your safety, but in the lines, nevertheless, you shall be. You will begin training as soon as first light."

Kilech feels a rush of emotions, from thrill, to fear, and back to exhilaration. His cheeks rise from ear to ear with his grin as he makes his way to the door, spurred by a final fatherly pat on the back. He dips his head one more time in respectful excitement.

"And Kilech,"

"Yes, my lord."

"May you find the revenge, you so longfully seek."

Kilech raises a devilish smile. "I fully intend to, my lord."

⊹⟨═╪═⟩⊹

"Where exactly did they say he was?" Saul asks.

Abner steps to his side as they both overlook the rolling hills in the desert of Ziph. "He was last seen on the hill of Hakilah facing Jeshimon, which is not far to the east."

"Then we shall move to the base of Hakilah and set up for the night. If he does not come out then we will push into the wilderness first thing in the morning."

Saul and his three thousand personal guards move into an opening and settle in for the night. Once again the Ziphites have proven themselves loyal, having announced David's whereabouts. Saul had ordered them to keep an eye out and record David's precise movements, and now he believes to know exactly where David and his outlaw army reside. In the morning it will all be over. And, hopefully, so will his life of living with paranoia.

⟨═══◆═══⟩

As Saul's army dips into the valley Asahel stands from the grass which has perfectly concealed his position. With his face, first covered in mud and then dipped in leaves, he might as well have been a ghost watching Saul and his men marching past as he lay on the edge of the tree line.

With Saul's men long gone and the coast finally clear, Asahel motions that it's safe and men as far as the eye can see stand from their prone positions like buried corpses rising from the earth. Asahel sprints back through the woods with another warning of eminent danger, but first he needs to find Uriah.

114

Uriah hurries toward a waiting David with the message from Asahel. "The scouts have confirmed Saul is among them."

Having seen movement across the hills, David dispatched a section of scouts to confirm that it was, in fact, Saul. It seems the king's word has truly become worthless. David turns his attention to his army that is continuing its training regimen as it does from dawn to dusk daily.

"Eleazar, enough," David yells, halting the training for the night. "Line everyone into a full ring of security. I want roving guards protecting the perimeter."

"Yes, my lord," Eleazar says, quickly turning and unleashing orders to the men.

David turns to Uriah. "Bring me your section. We're heading out."

Uriah moves with speed, gathering his men, as David sprints to the top of the hill overlooking Saul's army, which is now sprawled out across an open field, having already settled in for the night. David scans the three thousand soldiers until he spots the two most important men in the entire army. King Saul and General Abner lie side by side in the center of the camp.

"Who wants to go down into the camp with me as I find my way to Saul?" David whispers over his shoulder.

"I'll go!" a voice he recognizes eagerly responds.

Behind David sits Ahimelek. With his body folded in on itself, the whites of his eyes showing, and his head moving from side to side in denial, it's clear that he has no intention of joining.

"Uncle David, I'll go," Abishai says again.

"I heard you the first time," David says. "You can go, but you better not do anything stupid. I'm not going to survive a bloodthirsty king only to have your mother murder me," David says, eyeing his nephew.

"I promise."

David exhales. "All right, come on."

The two sneak down the hill toward the sleeping army. *What has happened to their discipline?*

He notices that everyone is comfortably asleep. Only a few guards on the edges continue to fight the heaviness of their eyelids, but their heads bob up and down as they succumb time after time.

David and Abishai slide past the outer edge, creeping toward the inner circle of the invading camp. The ground in between each soldier becomes less abundant with each carefully placed step toward the center. Men roll, arms flail, and legs kick into the open spaces, causing David and Abishai to adjust their footing at almost every stride. As they pad ever so lightly into the center of the three thousand men it becomes clear. If one man awakens it will all be over.

A loud grunt stops David and Abishai dead in their tracks. David's attention snaps left to where the loud, disrupting noise originated. The soldier adjusts his body and smacks his lips together as if chewing the air in an unsuccessful attempt to rehydrate his dry mouth. His eyes open, but only for an instant and he's back to sleep.

David makes eye contact with Abishai on his right who parallels his movements. David holds up his hand as if to say relax and keep it slow. Together they converge on the king who lies in a sleep so deep that David might as well have been playing the strings for him. He has a peace about him that David only saw when he played all night. The sight, he knows is not by chance. He glances to the stars above.

Thank you for providing this peace amongst the camp of my enemy.

Standing this close to Saul while he sleeps, David becomes

transfixed by the king's features. As if looking at his father, David can't help but feel hurt, rejected, and abandoned. As much as he would love to reach down and wrap his arms around Saul, he knows the man to his side would never let the king entertain his return. Still, standing here surrounded by a sea of soldiers, all of whom are under orders to destroy his life, David realizes once again that with the blessing of Yahweh there is nothing to fear.

"Yahweh has delivered your enemy into your hands. Let me pin him to the ground with one thrust of the spear. I won't strike him twice," Abishai whispers.

David holds out his hand, still gazing down at the slumbering king. "Grab the spear and water jug next to his head and let's go," David says kneeling down, the words of Abigail flooding his mind.

Who can lay a hand on the Lord's anointed and be guiltless?

"The Lord will strike you, or your time will come with age, or you will go into battle and perish. But the Lord forbids that I lay a single hand on his anointed," David says softly, as if Saul were listening.

He can't pull his gaze from the king. Something deep inside whispers to him that this will be the last time he will ever lay eyes on him in such a way.

A great paradox, David thinks. *My greatest victory will come from my greatest loss. My life will be secured by death.*

His eyes drift, settling on Abner who sleeps within arm's reach by Saul's side. David stares at his neck, the thin flesh that protects the main artery that when severed causes the enemy to abandon all tactics. He imagines Abner doing what so many have done before him in battle, focusing only on clenching the unrepairable injury until succumbing to the gruesome death.

"David," Abishai whispers while waving his hand in a frantic motion. David realizes that Abishai is soon to be out of the army's ranks and he himself has yet to move. Having let his mind wander in all facets, he knows it's time to let go. With one last glance back, one last sight of Saul's resting body, David knows its time.

With the spear and water jug in hand, David sprints to the top of the hill overlooking the army. Comfortable that he is a safe enough distance away and that his army is within earshot behind him, he steps forward onto a small ledge high above the field and makes his move.

"Abner! Son of Ner!" David waits as his voice echoes across the hills. He can see movement, waking soldiers now rolling about. Abner leans on his side, staring up into the darkness.

He hears me.

David presses again, knowing that Abner is now fully awake. "Aren't you going to answer me, Abner?"

Finally, a voice calls back. "Who are you, calling to the king?" Abner responds.

I'm not one of your fools, general.

David knows Abner's ability to manipulate and today he will have no part in it. Finally, he calls him out directly. This should have been done some time ago.

"You are a man, are you not? Who is like you and wields such power in all of Israel? Do you not have enough power to guard the king?" David lets the question sit even though most of the army, which is now awake, won't understand what he is referring to.

Abner has been tasked with protecting the king physically, but David's pointed question refers to the mental protection. Abner has not only failed the task of keeping Saul from evil, but he has guided his hand to it.

"Someone came to destroy your king and what you have done is shameful. You have not guarded your master, the Lord's anointed."

David can hear the grumbling of the soldiers now as they attempt to figure out what he had discovered years ago. He holds up the spear and the water jug. "Neither have you protected him tonight. Look around and tell me where the king's spear and water jug that were placed by his head have gone."

"Is that your voice, David my son?"

The word "son" hits David with unexpected force. But this time anger prevails. He has had his moment and he understands that no matter what, it will never be the same. It will never be as he wishes it could be.

"Yes, it is, my lord the king." Turning his attention now fully to Saul. "Why are you hunting me? Tell me what have I done? What am I guilty of?" David pauses, letting the silence answer for him. "If God has incited you against me, then may he have me as an offering. If, however, this is the manipulation of people..." David pauses hoping his point hits home to Abner. "Then may they be cursed before Yahweh himself, for they have driven me from my share in the Lord's inheritance and have said, 'go, serve other gods.' Now do not let my blood fall to the ground far from the Presence of God. You, the king of Israel, have come to look for a flea as one hunts a partridge in the mountains."

"I have sinned. Come back, David my son. Because you considered my life precious, I will not try to harm you again. I have acted foolishly and have been made terribly wrong." Saul's voice fades into a tremble.

David hears his passion, but he knows better. The outcome will always be the same for a man that cannot stand strong on his own much less against adversity. He has been lifted higher than his foundation can support. David pauses, reminding himself to never let that happen to him.

"Yahweh rewards everyone for their righteousness and faithfulness. As I have valued your life that God has delivered to me, so may he value my life and deliver me from all trouble." David throws the spear over the cliff. "Here is the king's spear. Let one of your young men come and get it."

Having said what he needed to say, David turns and heads up the hill. Then, he hears Saul's voice.

"May you be blessed, David my son. You will do great things and surely you will triumph."

Abishai stops, hearing Saul's voice, but David's hand gently pulls him back around.

"Keep moving," David says, knowing that Saul's words were genuine. "He knows that he's drowning, but there is nothing left for us to say or do." David puts his arm around his nephew and departs from Saul's voice, determined to make it the last time.

"We're going where Saul will never dare to tread."

115

Aaron watches Jonathan from a distance. His usual vibrant manner has deteriorated so much that he now borders on depression. He doesn't train the way he used to, nor does he laugh the way he used to. He hasn't been the same since David left. Nothing has been the same since David left.

"He always had something to teach me," Jonathan says, seeming to have sensed Aaron's presence. "And surprisingly it hardly ever involved warfare." Jonathan turns, patting the step next to him for Aaron to come join him.

Aaron descends the steps under the cool night sky. His hope of finally conversing with Jonathan without interruptions is coming true.

Jonathan looks off as if wondering where David might be this very moment. "We had more in-depth conversations about why we're on this earth than anything else."

Jonathan glances to Aaron with a smile. "You know he used to talk about Yahweh like he was his father?" Jonathan laughs. "I used to say to him all the time, 'David, he's your God and you are to fear him.' And he would show me somewhere in the scroll of Moses where it says 'is He not your father that has bought you?' Which would open up a whole new slew of questions regarding when did God *buy* us?" Jonathan's laugh fades with the wind.

"And what would he say? …About God having bought us?" Aaron asks.

"He spoke regularly about a Presence that would be with him, often in times of solitude or extreme warfare. He would recite the first scroll of how Yahweh promised to send his seed into the earth and how Abraham cut a covenant with his son as a sacrifice. This same Presence that stopped Abraham, David felt very confident, walked with him into battle with the giant, as well as sat with him in the silence of the wilderness. He believes that this human form of Yahweh that Moses spoke of will one day come, just as Isaac was prepared to, as a sacrifice, a savior."

Noticing that Jonathan is no longer humored, Aaron holds his laughter in.

That sounds crazy, he thinks.

"Do you believe him?"

Jonathan turns back to the moonlit view. "I do." He pauses, seeming to become emotional. "I felt that very Presence on the hill of Michmash. I just didn't know it at the time."

Aaron looks off in the direction of the pass. Off into the direction of that legendary cliff. So many years ago and yet it feels like yesterday they were standing side by side, striking down an imposing army.

Looking back at it, it was almost too swift. A memory flashes across his mind. The fear in the eyes of the men was not focused on either of them, but above them, and next to them as they slew the enemy that night. Aaron stuffs it back into the recesses of his mind where all the memories of bloodshed are hidden.

Aaron wants to keep this communication with Jonathan open, but he's unsure how he'll respond. Figuring that he needs to know either way, Aaron plunges headlong into it.

"I hear that... he has moved into occupied land."

"So I hear," Jonathan says, his tone dry, his gaze as sharp as before.

"He has had your father twice and has let him live, but now he moves into Philistia?"

"He's a man of his word. What else can I say?"

"What do you think he plans to do?"

"From what I hear, he has gone and retrieved the families from Moab and marched right into Gath." Jonathan bursts out with laughter at the sheer craziness. Suddenly though, his thoughts seem to drown out the humor. "He has requested deserted land south of Gath. He will be a gatekeeper for Achish, all the while living where my father would never set foot." Jonathan turns to Aaron. "He's a genius, a genius with incredible courage, one the likes of which I have never seen. Nor may we ever see again."

Aaron elbows Jonathan's arm. "You have also pulled off some incredible feats. Don't be so quick to overlook what you have done. I was there for every bit of it."

Jonathan pats Aaron's knee then uses it to press off into a stroll. "Well, I'm nearing the end of my life as a warrior. David, however, is just beginning his."

116

The last few weeks for Abinadab have been a blur. After retrieving the families from Moab and racing them west across Judah, fearing another collision with Saul with every step, David has done the unthinkable. Abinadab's youngest brother not only returned to confront the king of Gath, but also convinced him to loan their entire band, families and all, land in the south. It seems David's unique ability in war was a strong negotiating factor for both sides. Now, they are not only living in enemy territory, but are mercenaries for a foreign king …and everyone is beginning to question the direction of their future.

The wasteland would grow on him, Abinadab had told himself after settling just outside the small village of Ziklag. But it hasn't happened yet. Located to the far southwest of what once belonged to the Tribe of Judah, the small village in the Negev desert has since become a Philistine province under the kingdom of Gath.

Abinadab grows restless and moves outside into the recently built city of tents now housing not only the army, but the families as well. Abinadab can't help but see the tents as eerily similar to his ancestors' crossing over from Egypt and their forty years of wandering. The only difference is he sees no Promised Land at the end of this wilderness.

Wanderers, he thinks, *what are we doing here?*

Shimea is grumbling again, quietly this time, and Abinadab can't blame him. The last few months they have watched as David slowly transitioned his commanders. Abinadab, Shimea, and Eliab have had to relinquish much of their responsibility to the likes of Eleazar, Shammah, and Uriah, much less to even their own younger nephews Asahel, Abishai, and the rising success of their oldest brother, Joab.

A recent addition that Abinadab is still unsure of is the warrior that followed their army from Hereth. Shammah is the newest officer, but he hardly says a word. His hair is wild and his gaze is even wilder, but his calm demeanor, almost eerily calm demeanor, may be his most frightening characteristic. He could slay one hundred men and casually sit down afterward for a bite to eat. No smile, no frown, just another day.

Each day more men join, many of them having commanded thousands, but are now defecting solely to aid in David's cause. Abinadab hates to admit it, but he is no longer sure what the cause actually is.

David's officers are strict when it comes to the chain of command, which makes it hard for Abinadab to get much time with him. His brother is always strategizing, planning, and running reconnaissance missions for future campaigns. Abinadab has witnessed countless men getting ear beatings, or as the officers call it, "corrected."

Men used to casually speaking to David are now berated by his closest guards for disregarding the chain of command. David has remained the same, but it seems that everything around him has changed. It's a change that Abinadab knows must take place to keep all the new commanders and old friends in order, but it's still hard.

In the distance, officers laugh as David makes gestures with his hands and it seems the meeting is coming to an end. Abinadab strolls toward him, keeping his eyes anywhere but in the path of the oncoming officers that have broken away like lions in the hunt, spreading out through the tents and shouting for their respective soldiers to gather for a briefing.

He keeps his eyes on the wild one in particular. This new officer fascinates him. He is not like the others. He's quiet, always watching, scanning for something. Even Eleazar appears to acknowledge his commanding demeanor.

With his long hair hanging over his wild eyes and a thick body that lacks the definition of an elite warrior, he is a man of his own breed, a man that David quickly took a liking to.

Shammah had tracked them from Hereth, observing their movements for months while deciding if David was a leader that could handle his gift. The rumors surrounding Shammah's legendary feats have already spread throughout the ranks. And there are those who say his name when declaring that the forest of Hereth is haunted, where the enemy enters but somehow never returns.

Abinadab doesn't take his eyes off Shammah as he watches the new officer continue to observe silently through his dipped heavy brows and long, straggly hair, like a monster peering from the bushes. Abinadab is beginning to believe that the legends are true. Shammah *is* the ghost that haunts the hills of Hereth.

"Hey, you looking for me?" David asks.

Abinadab jerks back, startled.

The voice is a welcome relief, a comforting tone of safety from the chaos just created by the officers, and a distraction from the haunting thoughts that Shammah's gaze has spawned in his mind.

David waves Abinadab over. "Walk with me," David says. "What's on your mind?"

Abinadab feels the likes of Eleazar watching him, but having David at his side is like an invisible wall of protection. They might look, but no one will say a word.

He decides to ask what everyone has been thinking. "I know that you have a plan –"

"But why aren't we hiding in Ziph, the caves, En Gedi? I think you know the answer to your own question," David says with a smirk.

Abinadab smiles, mainly because he is happy to be walking with David again. He knows the reason they're here, but it doesn't mean anyone is going to like it. "What about –"

"Gath?" David says, interrupting.

Abinadab genuinely laughs. This time he was caught off guard by David's mind reading. "Yeah. It is at least developed, and with our numbers..."

"It *is* developed, but *also* littered with prostitutes and idols." David stops and places his arm around Abinadab, turning with him to face the small village of tents. "A warrior culture must never take their eye off what they fight for. Should the darkness of the pagan lifestyle enter our camp then we might as well count ourselves already defeated. You would be surprised how quickly a single woman can divide men among the ranks when their focus turns from their purpose. I am not here to enjoy life. I am only here to protect it. Never forget why our people were taken into captivity in Egypt. We are sharpening our blades as we speak."

Abinadab exhales. "But at least to the north we were somewhat protected. It seems down here on the fringes of nowhere we are exposed to the raiding forces coming up from Egypt, much less the always roaming Amalekites."

"If we are to build our force, we cannot do so under the eye of Achish. We are free to run this tent city as our own, and as for protection..." David shoots Abinadab a look as if to say, you should know better.

"Living secure among the protection of a stone Dagon or exposed under the protection of Yahweh? I think you know my choice, brother."

David lowers to his stomach after noticing a young toddler crawling from his family's tent. Abinadab cracks a smile at how quickly his brother can go from a battle-hardened military strategist to a loving brother, to a playful boy rolling on his back to make a child smile.

"David," Eleazar's voice shouts from the front of the tents.

Abinadab notices soldiers loitering, all of whom have their full attention focused to the north. David holds the child's hand, guiding her back into the tent. The family laughs as they take her into their arms. David then calmly proceeds toward Eleazar.

Abinadab's stomach tightens at the sight that has stirred the soldiers and officers from their tents. From the dust cloud drawing near, a band of men approach, Saul's men, all of whom are his most elite.

Then, Abinadab's attention is diverted to those following behind them, men he has never seen before. These men carry shields and spears, their faces are battle-worn, scarred like lions, and with eyes that stare with the emptiness of death.

Abinadab doesn't know if he should grab his sword or run and hide when David meets them face-to-face. His officers stand boldly behind him. Abinadab creeps forward, listening to the exchange, unsure if they should be preparing to be attacked.

"And to what pleasure do I owe to this greeting?" David says, standing unfazed, looking their leader directly in the eyes.

"I am Ahiezer, the captain –"

"I know who you are," David interrupts. "What I don't know, however, are what Saul's kinsmen, his most elite bowmen, are doing in my city."

The man, Ahiezer, bows his head and lowers to his knee. "My apologies, my lord." The twenty or so men accompanying him follow to their knees. "We have come to serve you and your cause."

"And what is my cause?"

"To fulfill the prophecy, to become king over all of Israel and unite her under the hand of Yahweh once again."

David glances to the men bearing shields and spears. "And you?"

"I bring only eleven, my lord." The man's head lowers slightly, his eyes never dipping from David's gaze. "The least of which, a match for one hundred men."

Abinadab notices that no one laughs. From the looks of it, the man is telling the truth.

David looks each of the men over, inspecting them, his feet remaining planted firm where he stands. Finally, he speaks with an authority that even surprises Abinadab.

"If you have come to me in friendship to help my cause, then my heart will be joined with yours. But if you betray me, even though there is no guilt on my hands…" David lets the moment sit, each moment weighing heavier than the last. "Then may God find you before I do."

One of the captains, a fierce-looking man, begins to shudder. Tears fall from his eyes and he lowers before David. He cries out blessings before the Lord's anointed, seeming to have just confirmed what so many are seeking to know. Many of the men are confused, but Abinadab watches in awe, having seen such a meltdown before.

The spirit of Yahweh can crumble even the hardest of men.

117

Kilech, sore and dehydrated, is beading with sweat as he rolls to his back. The training over the last year has been brutal, but he has grown to love it. He may not be a purebred warrior, but the lifestyle is second to none.

Having been released by Achish to take part in three raids so far, Kilech has finally tasted the lust of combat. More importantly, the women that line the streets upon his return are more than willing to show him respect, albeit with a small token of his appreciation in the form of silver. He still maintains his focus on why he began this quest, this desire for killing, and it is never far from his mind.

Revenge.

"Kilech."

Suddenly, his body isn't nearly as sore. He leaps to his feet, responding to the voice of King Achish.

"Yes, my lord."

Achish, meandering toward the gate, begins to speak expecting Kilech to join stride as he typically does. "There is a battle preparing to take place and it will involve all of Philistia."

Kilech's eyes grow as Achish details the coming war.

"We will head north and gather with each city's army heading toward the Jezreel Valley." Achish stops, taking a moment to look at Kilech. "You have permission to speak openly to me."

382 | DANIEL J. GEISEL

Kilech feels a wave of anxiety rush over his body. He has never had such permission with the king. He nods, understanding.

"I have decided that the warlord to our south has been faithful and could provide a valuable asset to swinging the tide in our favor."

Kilech is speechless. He digs for something to say, but the statement didn't seem open for a response. He pauses awkwardly before putting words to his thoughts, but only one comes out.

"David?"

"You seem surprised?"

Is he just looking for me to agree? Kilech hopes not.

"I am, my lord."

"Good, you're being honest," Achish says, advancing once again toward the iron gates. "I did not take in the Hebrew to keep him safe nor did I bring him in to make use of him, but to separate him from what he is destined to become, to dry out his rise to power and to remove Saul's most valuable asset. But he has proven to be a thorn in the side of Judah, continually raiding their cities, filling our streets with their plunder. And now I have the undeniable power to provide David with the strength to eliminate Israel's king, while making David a national traitor."

Kilech remains hesitant to trust a Hebrew. "What if he defects?" Kilech asks with caution.

"And where would he run? He has severed his ties everywhere but here. If he defects then *we* kill him. I believe we can trust him." Achish stops just as he reaches the gate to the steps. "Speaking of trust, I would like to have an insider's view of the war and I know only one man, one warrior capable of both script and warfare. I trust you will be the man for the job?" Achish says with a grin as he pushes the gates open and descends the steps into the city.

Kilech can't believe his ears. The time has come. His hard work, his entire adult life has finally converged on this very moment and only one thing remains left to accomplish and it continues to rest in the forefront of his thoughts.

Avenge my father.

The sound of cattle thunders across the hilltops as David's men return the spoils of yet another raid, continuing his war effort on the enemies of Judah. This time it was the Geshurites to the south, the last time the Amalekites to the southeast, and the time before that the Girzites just east of the coastline that stretches along the water's edge to Egypt.

Unlike the typical warlord, David's military decisions are not formed from a deep yearning of power and riches, but instead from concern and the well-being of his homeland. And his presence has shifted the power, acting as a shield for Israel from the onslaught of attacks from the south. The provoking enemies have finally been placed on their heels.

With each victory David leaves no evidence of his presence. Everything that breathes is snuffed. By the time his men depart, there is no one left to warn or describe what took place. As if an army of ghosts swept through, sucking the spirits from the bodies that now lie motionless in a heap of death, with only their rotting tongues holding the truth. The blood trail evaporates with the last gasp of life and suddenly it is only David's word that Achish will ever hear.

He usually mutters the details of a city in Judah or Simeon, claiming that he only wars against his own kin. The truth is, he has not only lightened the attacks on his homeland, but has also spread the spoils amongst their cities. David's military prowess has begun to establish a political stance within the tight-knit communities, especially in Judah. At the very least he hopes his people will not believe that he has defected into a Philistine warmonger.

384 | D A N I E L   J .   G E I S E L

"Where do you plan to tell Achish that this plunder came from?" Eleazar asks with a laugh, as the newly acquired cattle herds pass.

"I'm not sure. Maybe I'll tell him… Bethlehem," David says, provoking them both to laughter. David admires the stamping herd, which sprawls as far as the eye can see, through the tree line, and over the crest of the hill. "After Achish receives his fair share from wherever he wants to believe we've raided, send the remaining stock to Hebron."

Eleazar nods. "Count it done."

It has been a long season, the victories have been hard-fought, men have died, but new warriors have been born. The army, although not large in size, is now comprised of seasoned warriors. Leaders that hold the capability to take charge of hundreds are the least experienced in this army. David once believed that his force he hand-picked to raid Eshtaol was the most elite group of men he could ever hope for. Now he has an army of such men.

The march back is long and slow and David is relieved to finally arrive. He can now sit and rest his legs, but not for long. After marrying and taking in women who would have otherwise become widows, David now has a family of his own to return to. Abigail and the others will be waiting when he's ready, but first he needs to relax and rid the battle scars from his mind as best he can.

Fires begin to ignite one by one until the camp becomes as the sparkling sky above, dotted with bright flames scattered amongst the darkness. David enjoys his fire positioned away from the noise that so often drowns out the thoughts that he so desperately needs in order to relax.

Sitting fireside, alone in Ziklag, David stares into the blazing glow that transfixes his eyes as much as his thoughts. It has been so long, this journey, not the physical march to camp, but the mental journey since Gibeah. There seems to be no end in sight, just a long, drawn-out death where his body continues to age, his spirit remains locked inside his flesh, but there is no life left.

His joy is dwindling like a fire that has burned through all of its wood. The river that once ran inside has become stagnant. For a man who remains the leader of the direction of so many, David would never speak of his true feelings. With the force of a rolling boulder, he moves toward a goal that he could never define. The frightening fact of the matter is… David feels lost.

How long must we wander? he asks. *How long will men smear my reputation and plot my death without cause?*

His deepest fears creep to the surface. Did he make the right choice? Will he live here in this wasteland forever? Maybe the families, the soldiers, and the friends have all been misled into this mistake, his mistake.

It will be on my head, if so, David thinks.

David places his lyre on his lap and plucks a few chords, unable to muster the energy for much more. With an unexpected crash, his will has been broken. He closes his eyes, lifting his chin and letting his mind whisper prayers, or maybe they're complaints, to Yahweh.

"Have you forgotten?" a raspy voice asks, barely lifting over the crackle of the fire.

David opens his eyes, surprised that anyone would interrupt him. An older man, well past his days of fighting, sits across from him.

David almost cracks a smile at the sight of Jokim, mostly humored by his timing. It figures he would be here right now. Jokim can read a warrior like no one else and he always knows what to say and when to say it. Men of such wisdom are a more valuable asset in the ranks than most leaders will ever know. Today, David is the focus of his insight.

"Have you forgotten the darkest hour on the border of blood, Ephes Dammim? It was your hand that was used to show Yahweh's greatness against the giant. Have you forgotten the foundation of your plea to Saul, the lion and the bear?" Jokim stokes the fire, sending small glimmering flakes into the sky.

David feels guilt seeping from his pores. The embarrassment of leaning on his own knowledge and strength has weighed him down, and now Jokim is calling him out on every bit of it.

"Or that Saul removed you from comfort in En Gedi, Abigail fed you in Carmel, and Achish offered refuge where Yahweh now strengthens your influence from here in Philistia of all godforsaken places?"

Jokim stands and turns, staring off to the fading horizon. "What I once saw in the king's eyes…" he pauses for a moment before turning toward David. "I now see in yours… You are anointed, David. Just never forget from where that anointing comes." Jokim takes a step toward the edge of the darkness surrounding the small fire, but he pauses as if sensing David's struggle.

"What if I'm not ready to be king?" David whispers.

Jokim, his lips pursed tight, gazes upon David as a loving grandfather would. "Well, that's good because they don't need a king… they need a shepherd." With that Jokim crosses the threshold of darkness and fades back into the camp.

118

David enters his tent, seeking refuge from any more human interaction, with Jokim's words still bobbing above the flooding thoughts filling his head. Inside the goat hair walls of his tent, a much-needed sight redirects his mind.

"Welcome home," Abigail says, her bottom lip playfully beckoning and full, as if filled with sweet honey. It plays heavily in her provocative grin as she lies reclined on her side, waiting.

David cracks a smile and moves toward her. She stops him with a hand on his chest, tilting her head.

"Did you wash?"

"Last, just to make you wait," he says, moving past her arm.

"As usual. Let me check just to keep you honest." Her words are laced with laughter.

David strips down to his naked chest as Abigail glides her hand along his stomach, her fingertips rising over the eight rippled stonelike muscles hidden under his flesh. David grabs her arms, pulling her up to meet his lips.

It was this woman, Abigail, who intervened on her husband's behalf, saving David from the guilt of slaughtering all the males in her entire household. Nabal would have been cut down before the dew evaporated from the ground that same day but, instead, death came to him only ten days later by way of a sudden sickness. David took it upon himself to not only marry Abigail and Ahimoam of Jezreel, saving them from the sense of worthlessness that often follows becoming a widow, but also to care for Abigail's five female servants as well.

Looking at Abigail he can hardly plead nobility as his case. The curve of her features has been fashioned by the springs of En Gedi, the sculpture of her bosom rounded by the wind that shapes the Judean foothills.

She spoke as a prophet that day and still always knows what David needs. With her arms wrapped around the back of his neck the two of them stand motionless, their thoughts exchanged only through their breaths. Outside, a faint drizzle patters against the tent building louder with each breath.

"David!" A man's voice pierces the tent walls.

David's jaw clenches at his name, sending a wave of frustration through his body.

"It's all right, I understand," Abigail says, drifting back to the blankets. "I'll be here when you get back."

David tilts his head to say that he's sorry and leaves the tent, shirtless into the rain. The fires that once burned bright now smolder black smoke into the air, darkening the already black sky. Before David can explode with anger Abishai's gaze draws his attention to the Philistine soldiers mounted upon black horses now trotting among the tents. The charging lead horse raises its head as the reins are pulled back, stopping the massive beast just short of trampling David.

Calm yourself, David.

Aggravated, David lifts his hot gaze up to the rider. "The plunder is currently heading north. You will receive –"

"The king requests your presence at once," the lead horseman says, cutting him off.

The disrespect displayed by this Philistine in front of David's people is like a burning blade twisting in his gut. David holds his stare and lets the stillness sit. His hand twitches as if to beg for approval to unleash the wrath he is so capable of dealing, but David holds steady. His blazing stare for now will be enough, a silent message that the horseman's perceived strength in this moment could vanish in an instant if David so willed it. "I will be there shortly."

The mounted soldier raises his chin. "Not just you, all of you. Gather your men and bring them to the city."

David's soldiers now converge outside their tents, looking to each other in disbelief as they watch the encounter unfold. He feels the pressure mounting, everyone looking to him for their voice, their defense. David moves toward the rider, preparing his case against the preposterous order. "They are exhaust –"

"This is not a request, it's an order," the rider demands, his voice deepening to ensure his authority is understood. He then heels the horse and pulls the reins, encouraging the black beast to rise into the air. The horse lets out an ear-piercing neigh, ending the discussion.

Together, the detachment of horses converge in the field and gallop into the dark, leaving David alone, soaked, and with no option other than to gather the grumbling men and for no other reason other than to appease Achish, the king of Gath.

David feels defeated, more so than ever before, but its Shimea's face, smeared with disappointment, that puts the final stone on the grave. He says something, but David can't hear it over the rain. But he doesn't need to hear it. He can't mistake his brother's lips.

Sadly, David is asking himself the same question.

What have I become?

119

The voice was quivering, stuttering, as the scout reported what he had seen.

"They're gathering, all of them, the fields… everywhere. They're coming." The scout's eyes bulged white, his skin flushed as if he was sick, but he wasn't.

General Abner didn't even need to clarify, nor relay the information. Everyone heard, and everyone knew what was taking place. Saul had seen that same look before, many of them had, but something was eerily different than when thirty thousand had gathered against them in Michmash.

This time the scout had plenty of time, a day at least, to collect his emotions, and still he was agitated. No one in the hall uttered a word. Somehow everyone knew what needed to be done, and by the look on everyone's faces they all knew that this time something wasn't quite right.

Now, five days later as Saul witnesses the armies of each of the five major Philistine cities assembling before him, he understands the scout's terror. Far to the north of the capital in Gibeah, Saul watches an ocean of soldiers marching through Aphek heading north toward Shunem.

All of Philistia has gathered to finally put an end to my reign, he realizes.

The once lush, green mountainside has been turned into a flowing river of iron and bronze. On the outside he remains calm, but on the inside a seed of panic is growing deep in his gut. It grows and grows until nestling tightly in his throat like a thorn bush choking the wildflowers from the brush.

"My God," Saul says, surprised at how steady his voice sounds.

For the first time the loss of Samuel actually matters. Not that he would have been standing here, but at least Saul could have sent someone to inquire of the prophet regarding the outcome, victory or defeat.

Standing in the open field, Saul knows his mind is running loose with fear, but it feels like the entire enemy stronghold is watching his every move. It's absurd, given the distance, to even consider that they are. An entire valley separates the two mountains, but for some strange reason Saul feels their presence closing in, their exhales drying out the air that he now breathes. He can feel their hands reaching, their foreign grip taking hold of him. His breathing escalates and the pulse in his temple pounds.

I need an answer, he tells himself.

He sifts through his options. Every one of them is bleak. It seems that visions, the stones of Urim and Thummim, and the foretelling of dreams no longer work on his behalf. And prophets, those old but often necessary wisdom-seekers, failed him long ago. Now, they have become nothing more than decaying bones to Saul. Every option has dried up with no hint of explanation. He has wasted time on all of them with no glimpse into the future. It is as if Samuel snuffed out the last remaining flame carrying any light that could reveal the answers unknown to men.

As Saul's men file into camp, it becomes clear that they do not stand a chance against the massive number preparing to descend upon them. He knows that this is a moment for extreme measures.

"I need a medium," Saul says, never peeling his eyes from the opposing hill. He can hear men moving around him, unloading tent walls, striking spikes into the ground, but no one responds.

"I need a medium," he says, now raising his voice. Still, no one responds, all of them act as if they aren't paying attention or are too far away to hear the king's voice.

He slows his words, making it clear that he is talking to every one of them. "Find me a woman who practices as a medium, so I may go and inquire of her."

The pounding ceases. The tent spikes no longer slam into the ground. He can hear their minds working, their eyes searching each other. Finally, two voices speak almost simultaneously.

"There is one in –"

"Endor," the other soldier says, completing the sentence.

"Take me to her," Saul says, partly wishing he hadn't.

120

Kilech finally sits down to rest with his new company of soldiers just outside of Aphek. The march has been steady, but for the most part the army has remained well-nourished and rested, allowing Kilech to settle into a rhythm. The soldiers have slowly welcomed him and even appear impressed that he has served alongside the king of Gath for so long.

Now, with the joining armies of Gaza, Ashkelon, Ashdod, and Ekron, the soldiers of Gath seem brutally seasoned in comparison. Only the soldiers of Ekron come close to the battle experience forged by a city that lies on the edge of their enemy's territory. Gath has been and will always be the tip of the spear, and the soldiers that are bred there have the scars and attitude to prove it.

Kilech listens to the soldiers that have already sparked conversation in the group.

"We just got rid of those dogs that were following us," one of the soldiers says, stirring laughter.

"Only a day's march left toward Shunem and they get new orders. Released to the walk of shame," another joins in.

Many of the soldiers are younger, more experienced than Kilech, but younger nonetheless, making him feel a little more at home in the ranks than he thought he ever would.

"The Hebrews?" Kilech asks, knowing for whom the term dog is typically used. He captures the attention of a few soldiers that shift their backs against the ground in an attempt to get comfortable.

"Yeah, that gangly band of deserters just got sent home," a tall, thin soldier says.

David's men? Kilech wonders.

He knows how King Achish respects David and his men. He wouldn't have marched them up here unless he was planning to use them. And from the looks of David's continual plunder, his men were far more experienced than even that of Gath.

"Why did they get sent back?"

"Because they're Hebrews," a soldier says, joining them, his body marked with black ink that tells of his days on ships.

"Yeah, do you need any other reason? You aren't some kind of Hebrew dog lover, are you?" The soldier laughs.

"No, I've just seen them fight and figured the king had a plan. Just wondering, that's all."

"Well, they're dirty, and even if they fight like the gods they will probably make us all sick."

The soldiers bounce their opinions back and forth, each comment more prejudiced than the last.

A soldier covers his arms in dirt and stands, holding a stick like a shepherd's staff. "Please, let me explain how the world is round and how it hangs in a space of nothingness," the soldier says, lifting his voice to mock David. "Oh, and my God also can appear in the figure of a man and one day he will come as a Messiah. Now, wash yourself in running water so you don't get sick and make sure you cut your privates," he says, bursting into laughter with the others.

Kilech admits it is pretty absurd to believe many things of the Hebrew culture. The earth being round is crazy, but to think that traveling east could be continuous might just be the most ridiculous of them all.

The Hebrews do look different and their way of living is, now that he looks at it that way, beneath him. His people, the Peleshet, have developed a high standard of not only iron and tools of war, but also a civilization that is becoming far more advanced than that of the Hebrews, who seem to be stuck in the past.

"They are a joke of a civilization," Kilech says, attempting to join in, but also believing it more now that he has said it out loud.

He feels a hand grip his shoulder. "That's right, we'll just be doing them a favor by putting them out of their pathetic misery when we run them through tomorrow," the tattooed soldier says.

Kilech grins, not imagining all of the Hebrews dead, only imagining *one* Hebrew dead.

121

Abinadab feels the pace of the march steadying itself into the night, but the attitude, the morale of the army has disintegrated right in front of him. After marching all the way to Aphek, already low on energy and rest, they were rejected, told to return home by every king of Philistia except Achish. Now, David's men are exhausted and on the edge of mutiny as they slog back to the ragged tent city, their home in Ziklag. Abinadab is digging for words to defend their current situation, but he is finding none. Even he can't see himself living this way much longer.

Grumbles turn into whispers. Whispers grow into rising voices which tread terrifyingly close to the ears of the commanders, commanders such as Eleazar and Nathaniel.

"What would have happened if they didn't send us back home against Achish's wishes?" a soldier asks. "We would have been forced to slaughter our own brothers because David was too afraid to lift the sword against Saul."

Abinadab knows that it wasn't fear that made David's choice, but he may be the only one who understands it, and right now he stands alone encircled by a growing frenzy of anger. The most vocal soldier of them all is a stout warrior with a thick jaw and strong neck that Abinadab has come to know by the name of Hezro. Hezro is not holding back the fact that he is livid, and by the sounds of the men surrounding him he is clearly not alone.

Abinadab notices familiar sights now marking their path and takes a thankful breath of relief that the men are almost home. The frustrated army will have plenty of time to cool down with Achish off to war and their families once again by their sides.

"I'm not in favor of raising my children as the slaves of Sea People. Am I supposed to be happy that Achish thinks we've been reliable to him? Am I supposed to be excited for David that the Philistine king has found no fault in him and favors us?" Hezro no longer attempts to conceal his voice. "David hasn't been reliable to *us*! I can find some fault. We've been rejected by absolutely everyone. Not to mention… how am I ever going to find a wife to continue my name in this godforsaken land?"

"I don't believe your location should be as much a concern as your looks."

Hezro snaps his head toward Shimea. "What's that supposed to mean?" he says, clenching his jaw.

"It means I doubt that we will soon be heading into any cities full of blind prostitutes."

Shimea's bold humor causes some of the tension to release, allowing the escape of laughter for the first time in hours, maybe days.

"You know what Shimea…" Hezro's voice tails off.

The declining banter comes to a sudden halt as Hezro lifts his face toward the sky scenting something. Abinadab smells it too. The sting of sulfur hangs in the air. Strong odors now blend together and waft through the ranks, all having one thing in common – they're all the smell of something burning, notably the scent of charred wood, dirt, and… goat hair.

He looks ahead, but the soldiers all around him block his line of sight. Men push, others rise on the balls of their feet while craning their necks to see what lies ahead. Frenzy spreads through the ranks. Abinadab glances up, his eyes crawling north into the twilight.

Black smoke coils in evil plumes, rising like towers above Ziklag. It takes only an instant to gather the information.

Our village is burning.

398 | D A N I E L   J .   G E I S E L

Abinadab is almost shoved to the ground by the soldiers who are all breaking free like a dam shattering, releasing a flow of human flesh that pours over the hill in one unstoppable flood. Every husband, father, and child, realizes at one simultaneous moment that everything is gone.

Abinadab ignores the escalating heat that burns stronger with each step forward as he sprints through the blazing flames. Chunks of ash fall from the sky as the horrified shouts of seasoned warriors rise above the crackling, blazing fire.

He stares at what was once his dwelling, now a pile of collapsing ashes engulfed in flames. From the sounds of men crying out, to the eerie silence, to the absence of women and children, it seems the rest have found the same fate.

His legs lock at the thought of his young family being… he ends the thought before any terrible images can materialize in his mind. What he sees is hard enough. He doesn't need to imagine it also. The air is too dry, too hot for tears. He doesn't know if he could produce any even if it weren't. There is no hope, no future, and no life left for any of them to desire.

"No, no, no," Shimea shouts, rushing past Abinadab toward the field.

Abinadab peels his eyes away from the flames to follow Shimea who sprints toward a furious mob. A growing number of men, apparently finding the same outcome, have now turned their anger toward David.

Abinadab also takes off in a sprint as the mob now converges on his brother.

"You! You killed them. We follow you and this is our –"

"What are we going to do now? Tell me, David, what is your –"

"My children are dead, they're dead because of you!"

The pain and hate in their voices blends as each of the men curse David. Some of them reach for stones. Others begin to hurl them toward

his brother. The chaos is mounting faster than Abinadab can process
what to do.

The enraged soldiers have pushed so tight together in their swarm
around David that Abinadab can't get to him. Then, the unmistakable
roar of David's commander erupts and immediately men begin knocking
each other over as they are pressed backward faster than they can gain a
footing. Slack-jawed, Abinadab watches as Eleazar emerges from the
scattering crowd. Veins tunneling blood swell against his flesh. The
cords of his neck protrude like leather straps and his fists are balled like
clubs of iron as he crashes through the mob with more force than a tree
clearing the brush as it falls.

Abinadab doesn't need to say a word. Eleazar has said everything
that needed saying without actually speaking. With Eleazar leading the
charge, other officers and David's brothers following suit. The crowd
eventually disperses back into the fluttering ashes, leaving David
standing alone in the darkness.

He is oblivious to Abinadab staring from only a few paces away
as the last few men vanish toward the embers. Abinadab notices David's
hollow eyes first. He appears lost, the way someone looks when they
have nothing left. The way someone looks when they have followed a
trail for so long that they have forgotten where they are. The way
someone looks when they realize everything they have built has turned to
ash.

After what feels like an eternity, Abinadab is unable to watch his
brother stare off any longer, and having no words to utter of his own he
turns and leaves David behind, alone. To move away is painful, but
rightfully so.

After all, this *is* because of him.

122

After slipping past the massive army of Philistia in the night, Saul now approaches the steepest part of his climb in the day.

The switchbacks leading toward the small, isolated town of Endor are steep, but without their back and forth zigzag cutting through the hillside, the incline would be impossible to ascend. The narrow dirt path feels tighter with each step, and when he nears the halfway point he is enveloped by darkness. Trees and brush have overgrown, creating an ominous archway of foliage blocking the sunlight, broken only by small gaps between the leaves. The penetrating pinholes of light flicker across the path as the wind rustles the tree branches, closing and opening new miniature portals to the bright sun above.

Saul tells his mind to relax, that his thoughts are running free, playing evil games as he nears the sorcerer, but he can't shake the feeling that something is just ahead of him, beckoning him to keep climbing. The higher he climbs the darker it gets and this being, this presence that now guides his way, reels him in more tightly to this terrible idea.

Saul's senses heighten, and with every step he not only hears but feels a crunch under his feet. He can picture the crumbling dirt and stones and he wills his stride to quicken as an uneasy tingling in his ankles now crawls up his shins, like long nails clawing at his legs. This hill and everything around him feels awake. Like a living, breathing creature that has been waiting for him to arrive.

His skin is covered in miniature bumps because the trees are communicating with him, the faint gusts of the wind whispers in his ear. "Wherever you're going, you're going the wrong way." The breeze tails off into the rustling tree branches and sounds like snickering children.

He knows that he should turn back, but back to what?

Running his hands through his hair as if cleaning it of cobwebs, Saul now crests the top of the hill into the village nestled there. The soldiers stop as if they will go no farther. Their bodies turn rigid and their feet have set into the ground, not daring to tread another step. They point and his gaze follows their direction. Saul needs no other explanation. It has been a full day since his decision to come and only now is he beginning to regret it.

He slowly approaches the small dwelling in the deserted village. It seems abandoned yet alive all at the same time. Reaching his hand to open the door, Saul senses the presence calling out to him one last time. He doesn't hear it or see it. He just feels it telling him that this is the last time, the last warning, the last wall, the last… door.

He turns the knob and enters, his breath pinched, trapped inside his chest.

Inside, a woman mindlessly moves about the tiny room as if her door never opened. She reaches for a pot of boiling water and moves it to the floor. She then flourishes a sharp blade and plunges it into the side of a fish, slicing it forward along the bone to remove the meaty flesh.

"You shouldn't have come," the woman says.

Saul's head tips forward as if digging for reality. He is startled by the woman's intuition.

"I said… can I help you?" she repeats without ever looking up.

Saul now questions if his mind has conjured up this whole imaginary fear. He could have sworn he heard her say something different.

It's just me, he tells himself.

He now wonders if he's even in the right location. By the looks of it, it's possible that the medium that once lived here has moved. Nothing in this house screams sorcery. Even the woman doesn't look the way he would have imagined. A band of fabric wraps around the top of her forehead and is tied in the back below her hair which is bound together like the hind end of a horse. Saul lets his eyes wander. The room is gently decorated, rich in color and appealing to the eye.

She glances up, intrigued that this man stands in her doorway with his head covered by the hood of a cloak and has yet to say a word.

Her face is pleasant, almost shockingly so, but then Saul notices her eyes. They are a familiar amber color, but slowly the color fades to reveal a black film that covers them, as if windows suddenly revealing her soul, windows that reveal a storm raging inside this beautiful shell of a woman. He no longer questions which house the medium occupies.

"I told you, you shouldn't have come," she says with a grin that makes him feel more than just uncomfortable. He now feels cornered.

He can feel her eyes clawing at him from across the room, burrowing into his bones to extract his fear. He squeezes out his words that he has come so far to mutter, reminding himself that he has nowhere else to turn.

"Consult a spirit for me. And bring up for me the one I name."

"I'm sure you've heard what Saul has done? Mediums and spiritists have been cut from the land by his order." Her eyes begin searching him. "What are you trying to do to me? Are you trying to trap me? I have done nothing wrong."

"I swear by the name of the Lord for as long as he lives, you will receive no harm for this."

The woman slouches. She regrets entering back into her past or maybe it's only this stranger who has her stalling. Finally, she cracks.

"Whom shall I bring up for you?" she asks in a dry, irritated voice.

"Bring up Samuel."

123

Abinadab joins the others, sifting through the ashes in search of life, in search of an answer as to what happened to their loved ones. As he glances around to the others it becomes clear. Everyone has the same outcome. Not a single bone has been discovered. The site was cleared before the fires began. Abinadab realizes that their loved ones may still be alive. If there is any hope in this situation, anything positive to cling to... this is it. What they are going to do about it, however, is another question altogether.

Looking over his shoulder, Abinadab notes that his brother is still in the same location, still in the same position as he was last night. If it weren't for David's chest slightly rising with each breath, Abinadab would be convinced that his brother had been turned to stone. He continues watching, feeling sorry for more than just a brother, but a man who has been crushed and has lost all hope. He considers consoling David, but then notices something more than his chest moving. As his eyes focus he realizes that David hasn't been sulking this whole time, actually quite the opposite. David's lips are moving. Subtly, but... moving.

"What do you think?" Eliab's deep voice asks from behind.

Abinadab almost jumps, startled by his brother's unexpected presence, but he's too exhausted, too transfixed to move. He responds without pulling his eyes from David, not as much as even a blink. "I think he's praying."

He's been praying this whole time.

Abinadab senses a tinge of hope that only a moment ago he had not realized was there.

"He's not sulking," Abinadab says, finally turning to Eliab. "He's preparing."

⊰══╬══⊱

The doubts and fears that riddled his mind only a night ago are still present, but David has now ascended above his emotions as if climbing through the clouds, finally reaching the vast view atop the apex of the mountain. He is seeing clearly. The horrific images and possibilities of what could be happening to their families no longer play like a scroll unrolling over and over in his mind.

David has no other option but to place his entire belief, trust, and even his life, in the hands of the One who has brought him this far, the One who has kept him alive through the impossible. The One who can see what lies ahead.

He has lost track of time, but it has been at least a night, and now an entire day of seeking not direction but repentance.

The direction will come, he tells himself.

Right now all he cares about is reconnecting with his Father, becoming still enough to again hear his soft, whispering voice. Who better to seek, who better to turn to in disaster than the creator of all existence, the One who holds the design of everything, including the intricate workings of his own life?

"Forgive my sins and create a pure heart in me. Do not banish me from your Presence. Instead, grant me the peace, the joy that only comes from your salvation. Save me from this place, from myself. Though you have broken me and crushed me, I will again be filled with joy."

David feels the sensation of a soft wind cooling him. He knows the air around him is stagnant; this feeling, this breeze that now washes over him is internal. It is the very Spirit that moved across the waters of the deep and formed the heavens above. Now, as if rainfall wetting the parched mouth of a beggar, David's soul feels its first drop of refreshment.

An assurance sprouting in his gut confirms that the tide is about to turn, the swells are rising, and this desolate land dripping with fear and despair is preparing to be washed by the hands of wrath, hands that he has been training his whole life for this moment. He needs a solid confirmation to act upon the thoughts brewing in his mind, and he knows just where to turn.

"I need Abiathar."

124

The warmth that now glazes Samuel's eyes beckons them to open. Muffled voices from somewhere far beyond grow louder inside his head until he can distinguish that it is two people, a woman and a man speaking back and forth. As if waking from a deep sleep, oblivion, Samuel struggles against the urge to remain in this state of slumber.

The shriek of a woman's voice echoing beyond a barrier of stone, or maybe wood, pries open Samuel's eyes, thrusting him back into existence. He feels a weightless tug as if pulled upward by a spirit ushering him from the core of the earth. The aching old body that once accompanied his life has been peeled away like the shed skin of a reptile, leaving him feeling young, but still half asleep.

As darkness fades and light appears he can see a figure looking down at him.

It's the woman.

He ascends toward her as if rising from the ocean floor, her face above the surface becoming more horrified as he nears. Her scream intensifies until he is just shy of breaching whatever substance separates them.

Samuel understood few words during his weightless climb to the surface, but one was clear and repeatedly uttered by the hysterical woman, a name that Samuel would rather not hear again.

Saul.

Samuel, having finally reached the room, stares at a man lying prostrate on the floor. The man who disregarded his every word in life now lies in submission before him in death, begging to hear Yahweh's voice once more.

"Why have you disturbed me?" Samuel asks.

Saul's outstretched fingers begin to tremble. He reaches forward as though attempting to draw help from the afterlife "My enemy stands against me and God has departed from me." Saul's voice quivers, matching his now shuddering hands. "He no longer answers me, neither by prophets nor dreams. So I have called upon you to tell me what to do."

Samuel pauses, staring at the king in disbelief. "Why do you consult me now that the Lord has departed from you and has become your enemy? He has done exactly what he predicted through me. He has torn the kingdom out of your hands and given it to one of your neighbors, David."

Samuel feels the weightlessness subsiding. A cloud of darkness coils around him, warning of his dwindling time. He cuts to the point.

"Because you did not obey the Lord or carry out his fierce wrath against the Amalekites, he has let this come upon you. Both you and Israel will be delivered into the hands of the Philistines." Samuel pauses, preparing to deliver the final blow. "And tomorrow you and your sons will be with me."

Samuel delivers the message and Saul's eyes have been less than comforted.

With that, darkness closes in, wrapping him in its chill, and once again his life fades to black, his mind at peace.

Saul feels the presence evaporate, leaving him alone outstretched along the cool stone floor of a spiritist.

How far have I fallen?

There is nothing left, no one else to turn to, nowhere else to go. Tomorrow, Saul now realizes, he will die, his sons will die, and everything he knew would one day come now has a time. It will come tomorrow. The thought is morbid, yet the strangest thing happens. Saul's face crinkles and he begins to laugh.

It is the last reaction he would have expected, but he can't stop it. The laughter pours from deep within and now builds on the verge of hysteria. Saul thinks he has finally gone mad. Tomorrow he will die and today he laughs uncontrollably. He grabs his stomach, grinning from ear to ear, releasing years of tension, stress, and worry.

Finally, the emotion subsides. His laughter disappears to wherever it arose. He pushes out a few short chuckles, but there is nothing left. Painfully, the room falls silent.

I tried to win the heart of the people just as you said, Saul thinks.

Anger replaces laughter when he remembers Samuel's words. Then, a faint whisper enters his mind as if Samuel heard his thoughts from the grave.

I only said he would capture the heart. It was you who added the people. It was never about capturing the heart of the people, but rather the heart of Yahweh.

Saul feels the last bit of energy leave his body. This whole time he has been hanging on to his own power with every last bit of strength. Now, however, it becomes evident that his strength will not be enough. His life as king was served for this life alone. And now it seems that this life is over. What now will remain, if anything, for the life to come?

125

As the glowing stars fade under the rising bronze sky, David reaches his boiling point. The peace that came and was so prevalent throughout the night has departed, leaving him no longer fearful, no longer full of joy and peace, but filled with a desire he has not felt in ages. He has taken the ephod from the priest, Abiathar, and now waits for the answer to his question. Should he wage war?

His gaze drifts to the sleeping army. Many of them are the fiercest fighters he has ever witnessed yet once again David is forced to stand alone, unwavering as even the strongest of men lie broken. The men, all of them lying in the field with no shelter left to cover them, begin to take the form of something David is all too familiar with. An image flashes before his eyes, one that he hasn't seen for far too long.

The men lying in the field appear not as defeated warriors, but as a flock needing a shepherd, a protector.

David's eyes dilate like a cornered beast's and his breath draws steady. He is fully aware of what he has become. His hands, callused and hard, have been sculpted in battle for this very moment. They have been trained for war, his fingers for battle, but nothing has ever been made in all of creation that has a more prepared mind. David doesn't care if a thousand men fall at his side or ten thousand at his right hand, he knows, right now… nothing can touch him.

He is overwhelmed with a silent knowing, a solid confidence, and an unbridled determination, but so far it has yet to be unleashed. Finally, David receives his answer.

Pursue them and trust me, he hears. *They will be yours.*

With one gentle word his teetering mind has been pushed from the ledge. The world has crashed upon his shoulders, but there will be no more soaking in the pain. No more fearing the worst. His future has been confirmed and now there is only one thing on his mind.

Retribution.

His armor feels light as he smacks his greaves against his shins, tying the leather straps tight. The chest plate slams over his shoulders, and as he thrusts his sword into its sheath he can hear bodies stirring in the field behind him.

With his sword strapped to his hip and his mind wrapped in vengeance, David sets off, hell-bent to annihilate anyone in his wake. Pressing his way up the hill he can hear the sound of soldiers rustling and moving around, but he doesn't bother looking. He has one goal and no one is going to stand in his way.

"David," a voice calls out from behind.

David pauses. Hearing the voice of Abinadab has always done that to him.

He's not going to stop me, no one is, he reminds himself before turning around.

It takes a moment to process what he sees. Every soldier is gearing up, fully arming themselves with their battle gear. One wave after another, the hardened warriors file into their ranks. The army glistens like the Dead Sea under the bright morning sun.

Eleazar places his hand over his heart. His hand tightens into a fist and he slams his chest twice – and the entire army follows suit. He then releases a war cry so loud the sleeping residents of Gath, a day's march to the north, may awaken in fear they're being sieged.

The double pound on the chest reverberates louder than a band of war drums, and followed by a deep roar that bellows like thunder, the display is enough to chill the desert sand. But all David knows is that they had better be ready when the time comes, because he is not holding back.

"Leave the weak behind," David says with lifeless emotion. "Bring only those who are prepared for a slaughter."

126

Saul can't stop thinking about his experience with the spiritist of Endor when he sets his gaze on the opposing hill. The hill is blotted out with Philistine flesh wrapped in the iron of war. Now, with the light of day shining upon the enemy, it is clear that every Peleshet city in the coastal region has amassed here to his front. And as Samuel said they would, they are preparing to descend upon him. With his entire force assembled, Saul realizes that he is still outnumbered five to one.

At first light this morning he tried to warn Jonathan, but as usual his son wouldn't listen. Jonathan's men were too valuable for him to leave them behind, even if it meant certain death.

"I won't die," Jonathan said. "Not of old age anyway." He smiled and unsheathed his sword, pushing Saul's protective hand away. "Not even death can hold me back from this fight." Those were Jonathan's final words this morning. And that was it. He was swallowed into the ranks like a grain of sand washed by the breaking tide.

Now, as both sides make their final adjustments the reality sinks in. He cannot stop time. The orders are shouted and the armies charge. Saul stands paralyzed. The ear-piercing collision that usually rattles the brain is… silent. The wave of iron clashes into the ripple of brass and Saul's mind hears nothing but Samuel's voice. "Tomorrow you will be with me."

Treading backward up the hill, he searches for three of his sons, Malchi-shua, Abinadab, and Jonathan, who are now most certainly engaged in the chaos below. Saul's mind begins to wonder how it will all play out. Is there a way to avoid it?

No, it's inevitable, he tells himself. *You can't escape the eyes of death.*

While images scroll through his mind, preparing him for this final hour, and with his empty stare focused on nothing and yet everything all at once, he catches a glimpse of a familiar form. A warrior amidst a sea of carnage is attracting the attention of the entire Philistine army. Like a whirlpool they churn around him, but one by one he makes each of them pay. He is a warrior fighting like a hundred men. And it is clear that this warrior has no fear of death.

Jonathan!

Only moments into the battle and already Saul's greatest fear is unfolding. The overwhelming numbers of the enemy are doing more to the minds of his men than enemy swords ever could. The ranks break, running in all directions as the waves of Philistines rush through them. The chaos of retreat has begun.

Aaron strikes and counters the onslaught of attacks, but he can hardly keep up with Jonathan who is now fighting with more passion than he has ever seen. The speed, the ferocity, and the fearlessness of his movements are staggering to witness. Aaron quickly becomes concerned that Jonathan is saving nothing in reserve.

He's fighting like this is the end.

A slight break in the rush of the Philistine lines and Aaron catches a glimpse of what waits beyond, nothing but bodies, endless bodies. A flood of warriors rush down the hillside, each of them eager to be next, but all of them waiting, holding their ranks just like they have been trained to do, except one.

Aaron watches this *one* in between the swinging blades and jabbing spears plunging through the air. This *one*, he notices, is reckless, driven by terror, but driven nonetheless and it seems that his target is Aaron's greatest fear.

Up until today Kilech has only seen widespread combat from a distance. Now, sprinting through the ranks and descending the hillside amidst the twisted mangle of human flesh, he can actually feel it and smell it. The difference between watching from afar and actually being embraced by it, he notices, is how tuned his senses have become. As if he is a wild animal, his instincts come alive, his brain stimulated, sending signals to his body warning it of every possible danger. The daily aches and pains have become numb and now only one thought drives his every movement... survival.

With each stride toward his destiny a new sight appears before him, each one a sight his mother would have certainly shielded his eyes from. Flaps of flesh dangling from men as they continue to fight, others strike with one hand while holding their intestines from spilling with the other. Some have already succumbed to their injuries, their bodies sprawled open revealing their insides that Kilech never imagined could look the way they do.

Wounds gush, bones pop, and the sharp stench of human entrails is so strong it can almost be tasted. His fingers, now gripping his sword, continually stick together from the warm, tacky sludge that covers the ground. He knows it's warm because he has fallen in it, not once, but twice, and it now covers most of his legs, flinging off with each step.

If his father had not taken him into this culture of war, where would he be? He knows that he wouldn't be here sprinting toward his final moments, his courageous end as a warrior. Nor would he soon escape into the hands of the god of his people, the god of the sky that brings forth the rains. For years he thought that it was a mistake that he had been whisked from his mother and brought to this land. But here he is today preparing to bring death upon the enemy's heir, something that even the strongest have failed to do.

Something my father failed to do.

With no fear of repercussion, Kilech ignores all shouts to fall back in line. He will finish what so many have started. Even if it's the last thing he does.

127

David hasn't slowed his pace and already it has taken a toll. Two hundred men have remained in the Besor Valley unable to cross, their bodies wrecked by the constant pace kept over the last two weeks. David didn't hesitate to leave them behind. They weren't hard enough for the slaughter ahead.

How could anyone stay behind when their wives and children are…? David stops the thought. Nothing else matters, not the pain shooting up his shins, not the ache in his shoulders, not even the fact that he doesn't know who or where the enemy is.

He will provide, he tells himself. *Keep moving and He will direct my steps.*

"David."

His attention diverts toward the far edge of the field. Asahel sprints to a matted pad of grass. Motioning David over, it seems that he has found something, or better yet, someone.

David moves swiftly and as he reaches Asahel he lays eyes on the discovery.

"Bring him some water and something to eat," David says without even blinking. His eyes are locked on the boy who lies before him. "Who do you belong to, boy? Where do you come from?"

The split in the boy's chapped lips makes his words hard to understand and his accent makes it even harder, but he pushes the words out. "Egyptian, slave of an …" The boy licks his lips and prepares to continue with a deep breath. "Amalekite."

Abishai tilts a jug of water above the boy and pours a slow steady stream into his mouth. After a few nibbles and sips of their offerings he seems better, but like a stray dog he is grossly thin, malnourished, and shivering even under the blistering sun.

"I became ill and my master abandoned me three days ago," the boy says before catching his breath to continue. "They left me here to die… not even willing to bring me home after forcing me to partake in the raids of many of the Negev cities."

"And Ziklag?" David asks.

"Yes," the boy says, swallowing the dry air. "We burned Ziklag to the ground."

David feels the rush of what the boy just said.

Trust me and go, he hears again, replaying in his mind. "Can you lead me down to this raiding party?" David asks gently, containing the rage within.

The boy nods weakly. "Promise… you won't kill me or hand me to my master."

If David weren't so enraged he would grin at the thought of what he will do to this boy's master. "You have my word."

128

Body parts smack into Aaron and metal clangs off his armor as if he were sprinting through the forest and being struck by branches at every angle. But these aren't branches, they're weapons wielded by an enemy determined on his destruction. Like fighting out of a den of poisonous snakes, he knows it's nothing more than a matter of time before one of these vipers sinks their deadly iron fangs into his neck.

The close calls are mounting and the confidence that his training affords him has vanished. There is no comfort in this moment. This… moment… this is a moment that has haunted him since becoming the armor-bearer to the most amazing man he has ever known.

Jonathan to his side is still holding his ground somehow. Some inhuman power has possessed him, freeing his swordsmanship into a beautiful display of violence. His blade glimmers like a chiseled gemstone hurled through the air.

Aaron turns his attention to a running soldier, a reckless warrior who has continued down the hill, passing all but one rank on his descent toward Jonathan. With the soldier's arms and legs barely keeping up with his growing speed, he's now moving faster than Aaron ever could have anticipated. He's closing distance at a rate that Aaron had not expected.

There is only one decision and it's not much of a decision at all. It's a requirement. A requirement that he agreed to when he took the job of armor-bearer, but it is the love of his leader that thrusts him into this plan that will cost him a significant loss of ground and protection. He grimaces, preparing for the pain that leaving his security behind will bring.

Still, he lunges forward to intercept. His body now becomes fully vulnerable, all for the safety of his leader, his friend, and his brother in arms. The words of Commander Nathaniel reverberate in his mind.

"Many of these men are as capable as you. But when you fear death you hesitate. They all will, and when they do they will all die. Jonathan knows that. His years of knowledge far surpass his age. He did not pick you to live for him, but to die for him."

It seems that moment on the hill was only yesterday, but Aaron has now fought for years without a single hesitation. Today will be no different.

But to die for him.

The sprinting warrior's pace slows as he maneuvers between his fellow soldiers. He is now close enough for Aaron to strike, but something isn't right. Aaron needs one more stride but his leg isn't moving. With a quick check of the ground, his injury becomes horrifically apparent. An arrow has lodged between the tiny bones just above his toes, plunging all the way through the arch of his foot and pinning it to the ground.

Not again.

The running warrior is now coiling for a strike and Jonathan... is out of time. With a roar that tears through his lungs, Aaron musters the courage to yank his thigh upward with his free hand, ripping his foot through the arrow, snapping the wooden shaft in the process.

With his foot no longer spiked to the ground, Aaron is free to lunge, completely exposed. He braces for the impact, but nothing can prepare him for the pain he is about to endure. The first blade penetrates, then the second, followed by the third as he moves with one goal toward his final target, willing his riddled body forward.

The movement of war, the sequence of arms and legs reacting to one another has always appealed to Aaron as more of a fluid dance than a barbaric clash of violence. Today, however, it seems his final dance has arrived, he just hopes he is ready for the music to stop.

The blade of the running warrior stretches forth toward Jonathan as Aaron's arm is simultaneously struck from behind, knocking his sword to the ground. The running warrior has now covered the entire slope from the back of the formation to the front as he thrusts his blade forward. The weapon that just struck Aaron's sword from his grip is now returning toward his ribs for the death blow.

It all happens so fast. Then, in the midst of this final decision between protecting himself or Jonathan every movement slows and Aaron for the moment lives in the peace of knowing he has never hesitated, not once. Although those that hesitate die, it seems today even those who don't eventually will.

But to die for him.

As the speed of combat returns, Aaron has already lunged, making his final decision. Stretching his arms toward the warrior, that he strangely notices has the softest skin he has ever seen in war, Aaron grabs the blade of the sword with both hands, the pain sears through his palms like gripping a rope pulled from a sprinting horse. The tighter he holds the more pain he endures. Aaron wraps his fingers tight, clenching his teeth, begging for more pain.

He has left his torso completely exposed and now he bears the result of his decision as a blade from his side finally buries deep into his ribs. Pain he never thought could exist emerges as pops and snaps fill his ears. A warm liquid rises into his throat and he knows… he made the right choice. Jonathan *was* wise beyond his years.

He made the right choice by choosing me, Aaron thinks as a grin spreads across his now shuddering teeth.

While he still holds the blade, the ground comes up to meet his side, then gently meets his head as the liquid now rises into his mouth. As he gazes sideways at the dancing legs covered in armor continuing to fight, he can't help but find humor in the fact that Jonathan's last image of him will be something spewing from his mouth, yet again, in yet the end of another battle… his final… battle. The legs moving about in perfect harmony drift to a blur as the music finally fades.

129

Kilech stands still, breathing heavily from his long sprint down the hillside. His emotions are bundled in a confusing mixture of awe and horror. He has finally received the honor of standing side by side with the soldiers in the ranks, in not just in any battle but the largest formation of battle lines since his youth. He has moved through tens of thousands with disregard to any and all commands for one purpose, to kill the man from Michmash.

His plan had unfolded perfectly.

"One must not be more hardened than the man he opposes. Only be presented with an opportunity, an opportunity to strike a vulnerable point," Achish had told him years ago.

Kilech had decided to create his own opportunity and it had worked with precision until… until that devil warrior by his side did the unthinkable.

It was the same warrior that fought alongside the heir on the hill of Michmash all those years ago. Kilech could never have imagined that a man would reach up with his bare hands to grab the blade of his sword. But there it lies wrapped by the warrior's white knuckles and severed fingers, fingers that continue to clutch it even as the rest of his body remains limp on the ground.

Kilech and Jonathan lock eyes, both apparently in shock at what just happened. Before Kilech can realize that Jonathan has moved it's too late. He can feel the dark spirit moving in, preparing to snuff the last bit of light from his eyes. Looking down, he sees an image of grimacing proportions, one that he will have nightmares about, but this time it's his own body.

Completely horrified, he gasps, but sharpness in his gut replaces where only moments before breath used to be. He tries again, but there is nothing, nothing but a shot of pain stretching toward his throat like a bolt of lightning striking from inside his chest.

Before Kilech can react, he notices Jonathan struggling to pull the sword from somewhere deep within his body. Kilech can feel it lodged against his spine and although the pain is unbearable he can see the end forming in the eyes of this evil dog. He bears down planting his feet firm as the Hebrew struggles one last time for his blade and then… it's too late.

The Hebrew heir, Jonathan, is stuck by three separate strikes, each delivering a fatal blow. The soldiers pull their weapons from his teetering body and move on as if this demon warrior were as any other. Kilech knows better.

He grips the Hebrew's hands, which continue to clutch the lodged sword, and pulls him in close, sliding the blade into his own gut even deeper. The pain sears as the iron scrapes against his spine but he fights the pain, pulling him close enough to hear his voice. Close enough to hear his final breath.

"You killed my father on that hill." Kilech's pain is now washed away by the hate pouring from his last breath. "Now, I've killed you… and will go to Dagon… as a warri –"

Kilech reaches deep for one last breath, but it has already escaped somewhere in the air above the bloody chaos.

He never has quite figured out why his father meant so much too him. After all it was his hands that continually pushed him into the fighting ring. And it was his hands that dragged him toward the cliff which, oddly enough, saved his life. It was there on top of that hill, the hill of Michmash where he would ultimately find his life's goal while watching his father get cut down right in front of him, as the young Kilech hid in a tree line, terrified.

Well, he's not hiding today, and he's no longer terrified. He has become a warrior. And now it's time to be carried off to Dagon. To be reunited with the warriors that paved the way, warriors such as... his father.

Standing erect, unable to bend his legs with the blade still nestled deep in his spine and the Hebrew prince now coddled against his knees, Kilech watches an expression wash over this Hebrew's face that surprises him. It's the same expression that the armor-bearer, now lying eyes open staring at the sky, has displayed across *his* face.

A grin.

Like a river of blood flooding his eyes, the world turns red. The moment has come... he fights it, but destiny finally wins. He feels the cool fingers of death pulling him from his warm body and suddenly he realizes that whatever these two warriors just witnessed that caused their faces to express joy, he is not sharing the same experience. As he claws to stay in the pain searing his flesh, it now becomes evident that wherever he is headed is filled with more torment than his body could ever receive in this life.

The two men responsible for that bloody night are now dead, but Kilech is reminded of the third, the third figure that appeared then vanished into thin air. Could he have truly been a man, or the God from a world that Kilech now prepares to enter?

His clawing grip is no match for whatever this being, this presence, possesses: an unfathomable strength that now pulls him. With one last glimpse of his mangled body, the look on his face distorts into a horrific grimace. Most certainly it is not a grin, but a bulging-eyed glimpse of the horror to come.

130

David has followed the abandoned slave's direction and it has led him directly to the Amalekites. He lies prone on the edge of a crag that hangs high above the camp, allowing him to view their movements as if he were an eagle soaring just below the clouds. The enemy that he has been craving to locate spreads wide and deep across the rocky expanse below. The boy did exactly what he said he would do and now David will take care of the rest.

The unpleasant voices of the Amalekites reverberate surprisingly loud against the distant ridge, and their clear excitement is eating at David's patience. The high outlying walls encircling the camp have apparently given the army a false sense of security.

Every cheer and every spurt of laughter is like a dagger twisting in David's gut. While they recklessly enjoy themselves, David is mapping out every detail of his plan to exploit it.

At nightfall the wine press will be applied until there is nowhere to turn and their camp runs wild with the liquid squeezed from their veins.

They will shout all right, David thinks.

The layout of their camp is simple. Huddled down on the wide valley floor they are encircled. Only a small bottleneck leads in and an even smaller path leads out. The rage building in David almost blinds him, but he steadies himself, knowing the time will come to unleash the hand of God upon the valley. For now he must keep a clear mind.

"Eleazar, left flank. Nathaniel and Shammah, right flank. Uriah, Asahel, and Abishai, take Joab and close in from the exit path. I will take the front and plunge directly through their heart."

David continues to make each of their responsibilities extremely clear, ensuring that each leader knows his roles.

He covers the schemes of maneuver and avenues of approach, but not the same way that a general of a massive army would. His tactics have been adapted from both the large-force strategies of armies and the wild animals that rely on their instincts of stealth and precision. He knows there is nothing better than the feeling down in his gut, the intuition begging him to listen.

David understands the power a lion must feel while patiently waiting, watching its prey. A lion is not the biggest animal, nor is it the fastest or the strongest, but when the lion enters the field every other animal is aware of its presence. Every animal, no matter its size or power, knows that it has just become the prey.

It is the attitude, the mentality of the beast, the absence of fear that causes the larger elephant to run and the stronger crocodile to hide. The plotting and preparing, mixed with the savagery of its attack, has given the lion a reputation that breeds fear around even the threat of its presence. It is the instinct of the predator and right now that innate understanding is coiling tightly every fiber in David's frame, preparing him to pounce.

David scans the tents that surround the three stone buildings anchoring the center of the camp. Tonight, he will earn his reputation as a lion. From this night forward when his enemies look into the darkness, wherever they are, they will wonder. They will fear that somewhere out there David is lurking, plotting the savage kill. Tonight he will give them an image of violence that no man will ever forget.

As night falls and his leaders have all taken their positions, David begins the descent with one hundred men following his every step. Abinadab taps him on the shoulder after every silent count to one hundred, letting David keep track of their timing.

As David's men reach the bottom of the valley, the other divisions already have disappeared behind the tents. They now rely solely on their timing. Quietly encircling the larger prey, they have begun with stealth and are preparing to roar into an all-out massacre. David's commanders, his wild beasts, have converged for their meal.

"Thirty," Abinadab whispers into his ear.

David glances back. Each man is focused, staring into the glowing firelight, determined to seize what is theirs. The barbarians that now stand between them, their wives, and their children, have no idea what is about to unfold. David doesn't have children, not yet, but he can see the pain, the anger, forming into tears as the men behind him listen to cries and screams of innocents in terror.

Most would men lose control and need to be held back at this moment, but not these men. After leaving the two hundred behind, he is left with the most disciplined group of men in all of combat. They understand the moment and what needs to be done. He is confident that through his callused hands Yahweh's entire wrath is about to pour out over these pagan devils. It has been four hundred years of brutality from their people. Ever since the exodus out of Egypt, when they slaughtered the women and the children, they have been an enemy of God, and tonight David intends to finish what Samuel had instructed Saul to complete.

The night continues to erupt in laughter shadowed by the shrieks of young voices filled with fear.

"Fifteen," Abinadab says.

The moment floods their bodies with an incredible sensation that makes the brain no longer experience pain. Like the drug of a wild plant, this numbness covers David from head to toe as it has before, but tonight he notices every eye is just as fierce as the next.

"Four hundred years ends tonight. Take what is ours and burn everything else to the ground. Tonight, we will remove their names from the generations."

David turns back.

"Three, two, one."

David grips his sword and everything goes black. The sounds that begin filling the thick night air are those of nightmares. The sky fills with the bustling activity of the afterlife as the full wrath of David's gift, the gift of war, is unleashed in a way that only those in the valley have or will ever witness again.

But the night is still young. David has only begun to warm up.

131

King Saul stares in awe as he tries to breathe, but the air in his lungs has evaporated. He reacts out of terror, needing, wanting to find his son. He sprints forward into the battle that has since turned into a bloodbath. His mind has been shattered and his legs can barely hold his body upright as his quivering heart rattles like a caged animal inside his ribs. He has heard it said that there is nothing worse than witnessing the death of your own child, and as he sweeps his gaze across the battlefield he now understands this statement threefold.

It feels wrong to even think it, but it's true. Jonathan's death hurts the most. How could he have been so caught up with retaining the throne that he actually thought of murdering him just to keep it?

What have I done? Saul asks himself, directing the question to the still, small voice that has remained silent for so long.

Hysterical, he runs as if drunk, staggering through the battered ranks of dying men. He needs to see him one last time. He watched as the crowd of warriors collapsed in Jonathan's area of battle, but he needs to be sure.

I need to touch his face one last time.

As he nears the location where he last saw Jonathan alive, he suddenly feels a hand on his shoulder and hears a voice, the young voice of Saul's armor-bearer. He has remained at the king's side, but Saul is staring through a tunnel, a pinhole of stress and focus. The young voice echoes through a chamber in Saul's head that suppresses the words. He hears of something being *overrun* and the need to *turn back* but Saul can't. He won't.

Then in an instant… he knows he should've listened. He finds what he is looking for.

The dirt drags him down to its world as he collapses to his knees. He pushes a scream from his gut, but nothing comes out, he's silent, as if his voice were blotted out by the dark horror before him. He breaks. The regret of the last ten years pours out, soaking the dirt beneath him. The reality of what he has done to himself, his family, and his nation finally becomes clear to him. It is all wrapped up in one disturbing image.

My son.

He tries to reach out, but nothing will move. He's paralyzed.

Jonathan's body has been mangled by the… Saul can't even call them by their names.

They're not even human for what they've done to my son.

Nothing matters anymore. His kingdom, his family, his… A loud pop cracks against his back, jolting his face into the dirt. A sharp pain materializes and immediately he knows that an arrow has buried itself deep into his flesh.

He's surprised to find that he actually welcomes the pain in contrast to the view of his eldest son, the heir that was never meant to be.

"Give me another!" Saul cries out and two more jolts strike his body.

I don't care anymore.

"Get up, get up. They're going to kill you," his armor-bearer's muffled scream drifts past him.

Saul feels a hand under his arm, pulling him to his feet. "He's gone. Don't let them do the same to you."

He realizes that the young boy is right. He needs to move back up the hill and out of the enemy's reach. He can't help but turn for one last glimpse of his son, of Jonathan. His heart can take no more and he knows what needs to be done.

They reach to just below the top of Mt. Gilboa when Saul turns back and for the first time faces the darkness that has haunted him. It still looms like a spirit calling to him from the bottom of the mount. This time he will no longer run from it, but embrace it.

"Take it," he says, offering his sword to the young soldier. "Take it and kill me before they get to me, before they get the satisfaction."

The boy is horrified, unsure what to do. His job is to die for the king, not to murder him.

Seeing the boy's mouth gape and no words coming out, Saul knows he won't have the courage to do what needs to be done.

Saul firmly stabs the grip into the ground and relaxes his stomach on the blade, letting the tip rest just below his sternum. Now he can hear the soldiers breathing heavily as they climb, their steps treading closer, torches now burning, illuminating the hill. The point presses harder as he leans more weight forward.

"My king," the boy finally mutters, horrified.

King... what do I know about being a king?

He once asked himself the question of what he had become. He finally has his answer. Staring at the ground with a sword prepared to plunge into his chest, he realizes that this is the embodiment, the single image that will define his existence. This is what he has become. As if living someone else's life, speaking someone else's words, following someone else's direction, he now drifts back through the memories of a wasted life. A life paralyzed by fear. A moment paralyzed by regret.

He remembers himself young on his father's farm, enjoying life. Where did that boy go? When did he become someone else? As if the veil is stripped away for this final moment, he can see clearly. He is finally ready to bury these thoughts that have haunted his mind, feeding his insecurity. He now sees the fear that drove him to clutch everything so tightly and yet now he has lost it all. If only he could see David one more time. If only he could hold each of his boys one last time.

I will, he tells himself, letting go of his strength, the last bit of energy holding him up.

The tip presses firm then without warning bursts through his flesh, sending him forward as it plunges freely, the iron gliding along bone like fingernails scraping along a smooth stone until bursting out the back, securing him to his final resting place. His gaze suspended just above the ground watches the crown that tumbles from his head and settles just below his grasp, no longer within reach. His arms go limp and a single bead of blood drips from his fingers which curl open, finally releasing whatever it was that he had clutched for so long.

132

Colors and images are nothing but a blur. Slowly they begin to clear through the fog that covers David. Halfway toward the center of the camp, David finally gets a glimpse into the wake of his destruction as he hears the ripping, the tearing, and the splitting of human skin. He moves with ease as he collides into more bodies, smashing into them like a crazed bull in a crowd of children. He strikes another blow and feels warm refreshing liquid splash across his legs, his face, and his chest, sending him back into red, back into a subconscious state of brutality.

Crushing impacts, grunting, and screaming are at a distance, as if David is listening to them from the far end of a dark tunnel. Then, they begin to grow again. Louder and louder, they claw deeper into his head until he hears the rhythmic thumping of his blood pumping past his ears, and with each thump his eyes open. His conscience clears, giving him another taste of tonight's passion for vengeance.

He has no recollection of how much time has passed, but when he opens his eyes, he is deeper into the camp than he thought was possible. He is moving with a rapid pace as bodies scatter all around him. Whatever it is they see before they die, it fills their eyes with terror. An urge rises in David to turn around, but he knows it is not behind him.

He is the terror.

He has become the nightmare, shifting through the shadows of his enemy. He looks down and sees his hand clenching his sword, filthy with human remnants. His arm rises and the splashing begins all over again. Bodies twist, curl, and contort as they collapse into heaps of mangled flesh at his feet. They quickly pile up around him as his body count continues to climb. He moves faster now, his strength rising.

Before he knows what has happened, he is closing in on the epicenter of the camp with not a clue as to how he made it this far. Only fragments of the night are recalled in his memory. The only thing that remains the same is Shammah to his right and Eleazar to his left. He strains to focus but again the Amalekite soldiers darken, dissolving back to blurry silhouettes, silhouettes that are slowly losing their shape. David is once again dipping into blackness. His vision fades once more as waves of red wash over him. Severing, screaming, and snapping…

Silence.

Abinadab stands in awe, his body rendered useless as he witnesses his brother storm through human flesh with more aggression than he knew was capable of being unearthed. The sight of David, once merely his younger brother and now acting as the eldest in such a form has caused Abinadab to fall slack-jawed, watching in amazement.

He never knew that a sword could shatter a man's upper leg bone, but he just watched David do exactly that. As if the souls of an entire army have banded together into David's hands, he fights his way from the safety of the group. He is unyielding in his speed and his wake of destruction leaves all the men transfixed on his new nature.

Breathing heavily and with blood-drunk eyes, David whips his attention to Abinadab and shouts. "Get the women and children out!"

Abinadab's body jolts with terror at those eyes. David is filled with an intensity that convinces Abinadab that tonight his brother is a vessel tasked with delivering the outpouring of the whole wrath of God.

As Abinadab pulls the women and children from the clasps of the rotting Amalekite fingers, he attempts to cover the eyes of the purehearted. A war, a battle, is one thing. But this is neither. This is the retribution that Abinadab can hardly believe is a result of his brother's single path of destruction. This is a night that even the hardest among them will never forget.

Abinadab hands the families off to Nathaniel who is guarding the women and children that flood from the fires, all of which appear, to his amazement, not to have been violated or harmed in any way.

He turns and sprints back into the city of tents toward the center where the screams of grown men now replace that of the once terrified children. As he moves deeper, thick black smoke fills his lungs. Warm liquid covers his forearms. He realizes that he is no longer in his element. He is not bred for this level of warfare. The men that now surround his brother make Abinadab feel like a child among men, but none of them as much as David.

He thought he had seen it all, but then he reaches the epicenter of tents where his brother now climbs up on the edge of one of the stone buildings, a few cubits into the air. Abinadab can't believe his eyes. There he is, the young little shepherd, the one they used to mock, surrounded by a pile of Amalekite bodies. The whites of his eyes flash that icy shimmer that Abinadab had only seen revealed when the oil was poured over his head… a moment of anointing, a moment of peace. This time, however, those eyes are piercing, like a burning oil lamp behind a face bathed in the blood of the enemy.

David's sculpted body drips crimson while a burning intensity pours from his voice. It booms over the roaring fires that now surround him on all sides.

"Tonight may the soil be cursed by their blood and the air cursed by their breath. And by morning may they be forgotten, for tonight even their bones shall burn!" David shouts into the night. His officers release their war cries and suddenly the chaos and heat of the fires surrounding Abinadab feels more like a coffin that even the architect of Hades himself would fear.

Abinadab considers what happened here. David has just done in a single night what their people had failed to do for hundreds of years. Saul surely will lose his kingdom one day for this very mistake, the Amalekites, a mistake that David has now obliterated with a vengeance that will be heard for generations.

The day Samuel poured the oil over David's head plays slowly in Abinadab's mind as he watches his brother, covered in the remains of the enemy. He is taking full charge of the direction of his people. For the first time Abinadab sees it, the king that was prophesied all those years ago, the one of Judah that will hold the scepter and pave the way for the Messiah to come, the one that will defend the promised land. It's him. It's always been him.

They didn't know it at the time because Samuel was so secretive, but now it's as clear as the waters of En Gedi. His brother has separated himself tonight.

He is both the shepherd and the lion.

David leaps from the stones to the ground. Covered in soot and blood he turns his attention to those who cannot fight for themselves.

His flock.

With every last one of the wives, parents, and children safely accounted for, the night sky erupts with flames. The image reminds Abinadab of Ziklag, only this time the smell of human flesh accompanies David's departure.

And this time, David is in control.

133

Two lifeless bodies silhouetted, suspended and slumped over their fixed swords, is as solid an image as Benaiah has ever seen.

Israel has fallen.

He feels the hope, the direction, and the security of everything he has ever known vanish with one image. He stares at the hill, which is swarmed by enemy warriors climbing toward the top. Their torches blaze a glowing path of gold as the hundreds that now follow behind have become mere shadows walking against the clear night sky beyond the ridge. Finally, an echo of cheers erupts like circling hyenas have reached their kill.

Benaiah stands alone in the field, surrounded by corpses and the violent evidence on his hands, and yet with one death the war has been lost. With only one son remaining in Saul's line and Ish-Bosheth being anything but a kingly prospect, Benaiah knows that General Abner will almost certainly take full command. The thought sparks a question.

Where has he been?

He's not angry that the often overzealous general isn't around. It's actually been kind of pleasant, but where has he been during this whole battle? It's almost as if he knew the end before it began.

He's a coward if that's the case, Benaiah thinks.

Benaiah draws a long breath, knowing his next decision will alter the rest of his life. He has wanted nothing more than to follow in his father's footsteps, to become a valiant warrior and lead the nation to prosperity and security. But now it seems that only one man, an old friend, can make that happen.

Knowing that his next decision will risk leaving his reputation in the dirt, all to join a group of outlaws banished by a now-deceased king,

Benaiah turns his back on the hill and sets his gaze south. Finally, feeling returns to his otherwise broken spirit. He always knew there was something different about that young shepherd. He felt a connection every time he heard David play music.

The lyre called him to David that night, luring him toward the boy as if called by God to train by his side. Tonight he hears the soft tones playing once again, this time not to train by his side, but to fight. With a renewed hope and an understanding of Abner's coming wrath, Benaiah once again moves in the only direction he knows, forward toward the music.

134

Just as the sun's golden petals disperse the darkness, so David's violence has been returned from whence it came. The long march back to the waiting two hundred, the men who refrained from entering the battle for one reason or another, has served as a much-needed time to unwind.

Over the course of the night, as David walked in silence, his vision of the world slowed. The war drums pounding in his ears softened to a patter. And the echoes of war cries screaming for retribution faded to faint whispers. Their hushed tones remind him that this animal within, this wild beast of vengeance, is always lying dormant, awaiting the next victim in need of protection to awaken it. David's instinct to protect has become a doorway, allowing the wrath of God to pour though him like a sealed iron vessel of war.

"Everything is accounted for," Eleazar says, approaching David with a plate of sizzling lamb meat in his hands. "Nothing is missing." He pauses, as if contemplating what he is about to say next. "And not one of them was touched," he says, sounding surprised.

David looks off to the families now reuniting with the two hundred men, to his wife Abigail playing outside the tent with neighboring children, to his brothers embracing their wives and their sons and daughters.

"Though I may not understand, though I may grieve, I will follow your word," he mumbles, not talking to Eleazar, and blindly staring in awe.

"What?"

David finally notices Eleazar still staring at him and holding a plate of food.

"Just make sure everyone has eaten, and well. Today will be a feast, a remembrance of what was done here."

Eleazar holds out the plate toward David. "Everyone has eaten and they have eaten well, as they always do. Please."

David begrudgingly takes the food. The warm juicy meat quickly takes him back to when he was young, and the days with Benaiah, and his mother's cooking. As his mouth salivates with every bite, he notices his nephew off in the distance just finishing his own food. He apparently waited until most of the others had eaten as well.

"Joab was one of the few that didn't fall behind in the midst of chaos," David says, continuing to watch him from a distance.

"He can fight with the best of us," Eleazar says. "And he has an understanding of the battlefield that can't be taught."

And, it appears, the character to lead as well, David thinks, always noticing the little things.

Nathaniel had joined them. "He commands well, but," Nathaniel says, stopping to clear his throat, "he's young."

The three men stare off, watching the unexpected rise of Joab together. David can't help but look at Nathaniel and be concerned for his health. The rag that he pulls from his mouth, David notices, is once again covered in blood.

"I'll be fine," Nathaniel whispers, motioning for David not to worry about it.

"That's why he's going to be dangerous," Eleazar counters, turning attention back to the youth of Joab.

"You say that like it's a good thing," Nathaniel says. "He's like a boulder teetering on the top of the cliff. At some point it will break free, but when? I don't want to be under it when it does."

David turns to Shammah, who passes behind them. "What do you think?"

"I like him. He's wild, but I like wild," he says in his low, grumbling voice.

"Excuse me, gentlemen," Abishai says, hesitantly approaching. "David, we have a few men disagreeing with the decision to distribute the spoils to all six hundred men and their families."

"Who?"

"Mainly Hezro, lord"

"Bring him here."

The officers huddled around David fall silent as the scruffy warrior nears. Abishai trails at a distance behind Hezro, appearing terrified of the reaction that David may give. David recognizes the man as one of the few that can truly hold his own as a warrior of bloodshed. Now that David puts a face to the name, he remembers thinking that some of the men look intimidated around Hezro. The strong-jawed soldier carries a presence that projects that he is not to be agitated. David can only imagine how he must act when not in the presence of officers.

"Your name is Hezro?" David asks.

"Yes, lord."

"What seems to be your complaint, Hezro?"

"No complaint, lord." Hezro swallows hard. "I just didn't think that the two hundred men that didn't fight should receive the same as all of us that did."

"And do you know who gave the order to take care of the two hundred no differently than the four hundred?"

"Yes, lord."

"Who?" David asks calmly.

"You did… lord."

"And you thought it wise to question my order?" David lets the question sit. "Your sword does not make you a warrior. That comes from your mind and your soul. As long as I am the head, those that are for us will be treated as if they were our own. A shepherd does not segregate his flock to enable the strong, but keeps his flock together so that as a single unit they find strength much greater than the few ever could."

David stands and places his arm around Hezro, turning him toward the families that are reuniting with those that were left behind. "We will fight for those that cannot fight. We will speak for those that cannot speak. And the sick and the weary will be treated the greatest among us." David senses that Hezro's rough persona isn't a facade. He is a true warrior, but something deep inside isn't quite settled. "Do you have a family, Hezro?"

"I do not, my lord."

David senses that he's expecting to be cut out. His reaction says it all, the dip in the shoulders, the loss of eye contact, and the discomfort that shows on his face. After all, that's why many of these men are here. They are castaways.

"I don't care if you are the most violent of warriors or fight like a girl with two left hands. If you are in our army, our family, our community, you will be treated fairly." He waits for Hezro's eyes to lock with his. "I will not abandon you," David says, pausing. "I will not cast you away, but if I hear that you are murmuring against another one of my orders, or knowingly spreading division amongst the ranks… I cannot promise that these men around me won't see to it that you never murmur again."

"Yes, my lord." He pauses, returning a solid stare into David's eyes. "Thank you," Hezro says, before dipping his head in respect and returning from where he had come.

"He's going to be one of our greatest gifts, mark my words," David says.

David looks over his men, reflecting on their growth. His inner circle is taking shape and the leadership that has formed out of the small group of men over the last two years is undoubtedly more experienced and advanced than anything he ever witnessed in Gibeah.

With men like Hezro, men that possess such an enormous amount of potential both on the battlefield and in building the warrior community, David realizes that his task delves much deeper than warfare. He is responsible for the lives lived as much as he is responsible for the lives taken.

Sensing that his men would stay by his side through the entire night, David knows he must order them to leave. Their devotion is such that he must remind them to enjoy life, to smile, to separate themselves from the tasks of their roles and embrace the little things.

"Tend to the weak and lie with your wives. Enjoy them tonight, you deserve it, but never forget whose hand delivered them back to you, Yahweh and Yahweh alone."

The men hesitate, as if unsure how to release from their devotion to duty.

Shammah's deep voice breaks the silence. "Emunah," he says, as if nudging the men to follow his lead with a simple word they all repeat in unison before departing toward their families.

David can't help but grin. Shammah's words are few, but when he speaks it's always worth it. Emunah is not just a declaration of faith, but faithfulness and firm action according to Yahweh's will. He prodded them into action while at the same time acknowledging Yahweh as David had just instructed them to do, and all with a single word.

Shammah may be as wise as he is violent, David thinks, never having believed that he would ever equate anything to the level of Shammah's ability on the battlefield.

It seems the hardest of times have done nothing but prepare the men for whatever lies ahead. The last few years they have been as barley on the threshing floor: each of them reaped from their fields, brought here to be threshed, beaten down, and ripped open. To some, it breaks them. They cannot see past the hardships, and their husks are burned.

Their nutrient, their abilities, their purpose is stifled by their fear – and often just before the grain is released.

David again turns his gaze on his men. They have been reaped, threshed, and now, it seems, the winnowing is upon them. Their true potential, it appears, is preparing to be unearthed.

I fear not for my men, David thinks. *But for the men that would dare stand against us.*

135

With the discord of the army made fully clear by their unharmonious marching rhythm, Abner knows he must bring unison back to his men, and he must do it quickly. They have lost their king, he has lost his cousin and friend, and yet the emotion is not as painful as he expected. His mind is focused on the task at hand. And right now, Israel must birth a new king, a new leader, a new hope of victory. After all, the mission, no matter who is in charge, must remain the same.

The rebel David must be stopped.

Abner turns to the brothers Rekab and Baanah. "Find me Ish-Bosheth and prepare him immediately to receive the crown," he says.

It's obvious by their long pause that they are not in agreement with the order, but they do not say a single negative word. Instead, they respond in unison.

"As you command."

Abner can hear the disparity in their voices and he couldn't agree more, but there is no other choice to make. Ish-Bosheth is possibly the least example of what a warrior is, and his leadership is pathetic at best, but he is, after all, the remaining son of the king. He is the one that the nation will perceive to be the rightful heir of the throne, and right now perception is all that matters.

"Israel is without a king. By morning she will have one, and we will be back to what we do best." Abner grips their shoulders. "We are all that stands between Israel and her enemies now. A king is nothing more than a symbol to comfort the people, a mouthpiece of security and direction. We are what drives that security and direction, so do not worry about who wears the crown. I am still in control."

With that, they seem to be at ease, and with their confidence restored in Abner as their general and ultimate decision-maker, they depart on their mission.

The mission is still on task. However, now there will be no distractions.

David's time has finally run out.

⊱⊰

Watching the men reconnect with their families the last few days makes every last step, every last bursting callus, and every last kill worth it. Ziklag is gone and everything about it has been burned to the ground. The men have no shelter, but the laughs and even the cries of the children are comforting. It means it is once again their dwelling place. David sits in peace and yet something inside is stirring. He senses a storm brewing in the distance; the weather is about to break.

David knows that he has the best men a leader could ever ask for. As he watches them care for others and check on the injured in their commands, he catches movement out of the corner of his eye.

Uriah and Asahel have a man in their grasp and they are running David's way. Without saying a word, they release their captive, letting him fall. His body thumps to the ground at David's feet. David glances to both Uriah and Asahel, but they look too fearful to speak. Their avoidance of eye contact and fidgeting is worrying to David.

What could be so terrible to say to me?

It seems that neither of them is willing to pass whatever message this foreigner has brought. David immediately thinks of the war in the north, the battle of Gilboa, that he almost took part in. The possibility of this message begins to take form in his imagination.

David snaps his attention to the man. "Where have you come from?"

"I escaped from the Israeli camp," he responds, out of breath.

David feels his body fading as numbness crawls across his flesh. "What happened? Tell me." David leans in.

"The men fled. Many of them died." The man's demeanor brightens as his eyes climb slowly to meet David's. "Saul and Jonathan are among the dead."

David stands, but his legs are weak. "How do you know? How do you know that Saul and Jonathan are dead?"

"I was on Mt. Gilboa and saw Saul slumped over his sword. He leaned against his spear and called out to me when he heard the chariots approaching. He asked me to put him out of his misery. So I did."

The man reaches into his satchel and David's heart sets pace with a new rhythm. It feels like a fish flopping somewhere inside his chest. He falls back into his seat. In an instant the man brandishes the objects from his bag and every word uttered from his mouth becomes truth.

The crown that David had seen on Saul's head since he was a child is now lying at his feet, a single trail of blood dried along its edge. The man continues to talk, but David doesn't hear a word. The symbols at his feet speak more truth than words ever could. It takes only a moment, but when it finally registers, he shatters.

His father for so many years is dead. His brother, his mentor, is dead. Just like that. No warning, just gone. They are both dead. A void that David never saw coming opens like the caves of Adullam, splintering throughout his entire being. His eyes are dry, but like the clear skies before the deluge, looks can be deceiving.

Only three days ago he was ravaging a city with no remorse, and today his emotions are as brittle as clay. With one simple word, the man David once was, the man he has become, and everything that he has ever known, shatters like an oil vase tossed from the cliff. Although the years have been filled with running and eluding death, he now fully understands his greatest fear has come true. It is not only the loss of his *royal* family, but the loss of his childhood.

His throat swells as he attempts to hold back the emotions, emotions that without warning burst though the weakest points in his body. They flow in a river that can't, won't, be held back. The liquid pouring from his eyes blurs his vision as his mind drifts to all the memories that now flood his mind. He can hear the entire population of Ziklag gathering around, spreading the news.

With one outburst of pain manifested in the form of anger, his tunic shreds with a violent tug of his fist. The sound of tearing leather and cloth spreads across the gathering crowd in a unified show of remorse. David collects himself enough to refocus his attention to the messenger.

"Where are you from?"

The man doesn't hesitate. "I am the son of a foreigner, an Amalekite," he proudly admits. He has no idea where they just returned from and it is obvious by his tone.

David's voice deepens. "Why weren't you afraid to lift your hand against the Lord's anointed?"

The man's face contorts awkwardly. It's obvious that he's confused as David's disgust and anger now become apparent.

"May your blood be on your own head, forever."

David nods, granting permission, and one more Amalekite falls to the ground, lifeless.

The sorrow is crippling and the weight is tangible as it presses his body lower. Only his knee stops him from falling to the ground on his face. The dried blood, it was Saul's blood. David can hear something happening around him, a rustling in the crowd, but the grief is overwhelming. There has been so much death. The cries, the sniffling, the whispers, it all fades and suddenly, all of Ziklag is silent, eerily silent.

He can feel the staring eyes of the people upon him. He forces himself to glance up, and when he does he is stunned. The entire camp is standing before him in complete stillness, as if speaking the same message in perfect unison. Hundreds of men, women, and children have shifted their focus directly toward the bloodied crown at his feet. The sound of the breeze is the only disturbance as everyone seems to be thinking the same collective silent thought.

Eleazar breaks the tension. "What are we to do now… our king?"

He lowers to his knee, bowing his head. Behind him, one after another, everyone lowers like a collapsing hillside until every man, woman, and child is bowing before him.

His moment has come.

With a slow steady breath, David attempts to regain his composure and shift back to the leader that he has become.

"We are to rest."

He glances across the faces that are eagerly anticipating his next words. They are all prepared to follow his every move. He knows that he cannot disappoint. They have hidden here for long enough. The time to take his rightful place has finally arrived. It is time for an uprising.

"…For tomorrow we march to the mountains. Tomorrow, we begin our journey home."

136

The gold crown glistens as the morning rays saturate the throne hall. The golden symbol of authority is lifted and placed upon Ish-Bosheth's head. He leans back, his eyes gazing to the ceiling as if embracing the weight of the new power that this single ornament has brought him. Perhaps he's remembering his father, and all of the hardships that this symbol upon his head had brought him.

Abner watches his odd mannerisms. Maybe he's thinking about how inhumane of a death his father had to endure in a battle in which Abner wasn't even present to witness. Either way, Abner really doesn't care what Ish-Bosheth is thinking. Precious time is slipping away.

Ish-Bosheth stands, holding his hands up as if this crown has actually empowered him. He prepares to address everyone in attendance. "I would like to address a few things."

But Abner steps in front of the newly crowned king and faces the crowded chamber. "The king would like for everyone who is not in the military council to please make their way to the door. He will be making an official statement for the nation tonight." With a nod, General Abner's men begin rushing the attendees out the door.

The chamber seals tight and Abner turns to Ish-Bosheth. "We have much that needs attended to, and right now is not the time for speeches. We have an enemy that is knocking on our door and we must bring the nation together and use your father's death as our rallying cry."

Ish-Bosheth leans forward. "You think now is really the ideal time to respond to the Philistines? They have assembled a force greater than we –"

Abner steps toward Ish-Bosheth with a speed and menace that drops the king back into his seat. "Was it the Philistines that your father was so adamantly hunting in the last years of his life? Was it the Philistines that challenged the throne that you now sit upon? Has it been the Philistines that have been systematically sending the spoils of war throughout the tribes of our nation? No, the Philistines are not our greatest threat. They are a major concern, but only from the outside. I am speaking of a threat that will spread like the boils of a leper throughout all of Israel if it is not contained. And that threat is what I am committed to ending at your father's wishes. The pagans will be the least of our concerns if Judah rises from underneath our grip."

Abner slaps a piece of papyrus down on the king's lap. "Sign the army under my command, and I will fulfill your father's wishes. I will ensure your throne remains."

Without questioning another word, Ish-Bosheth presses the seal, making General Abner's wishes his command. The entire army is at his disposal once again, and this time he will make sure the mission is completed.

David is as good as dead.

137

The fresh aromas of cedar, mixed with the sound of trickling spring water, are welcoming signs that not only is David in Judah, but he is nearing his destination. While he lived in Ziklag, only one city continued to sit on the edge of David's tongue. His mind constantly filled with her importance and welfare. His victories led to numerous war spoils that over the years have been sent into the nation and her tribes, but no tribe more than Judah and no city more than Hebron.

The smells, the sweet taste on his lips, and even the warm breeze that draws sweat from his already depleted pores are refreshing. It is the welcoming of new beginnings, a renewed sense of freedom to move about without being hunted around every corner. But still, concerns nestle in the back of his mind that his reputation, hopefully, hasn't been wrecked over the years. David knows deep down that his steps have been directed here. What he has yet to find out, however, is if he and his men will actually be accepted.

After being on the run for over eight years and living in enemy territory for almost two of them only to arrive after the king's death, the reactions could be less than favorable. Nevertheless, this city is where David is convinced he is being called. The first sign of human activity draws his attention up the hillside. It seems that it's time to know the truth. It's time to find out who is on his side and who is not. One thing is sure. David is done with running.

<hr>

Nervously he waits, his eyes focused on the tree line at the bottom of the hill. He has been told that David's men are approaching and it doesn't take long before the army materializes amidst the large cedar trees that shelter the landscape. Like ghosts they emerge from under the darkness of the canopy. Benaiah sees a familiar gait of the man at the head of the army. The fast-paced, strong warrior that marches with no sign of hesitation can only be one man, the outlaw himself.

Benaiah stands firm, understanding that it has been quite a while since the two have spoken. Unsure how David will receive him and his loyalty, Benaiah prepares for the worst. Power often breeds corruption, and by the look of David's men, their disciplined march, their hardened bodies, and their confident eyes, David is in no lack of power.

Benaiah's chest tightens as David's gaze lands upon him. David halts. His men freeze instantly. The tension builds in the silence as David's entire army surveys whether he and the few that stand behind him pose a threat. Benaiah stays perfectly still, letting David make that decision. Without his conviction that David is still the man he once knew, Benaiah realizes that he would never be standing here in the open, defenseless, nor would he have gathered the people of Judah to rally inside the city walls. He has put his own name on the line for David and now it is time to find out if it is rumor or his gut that is true about David.

David's head tilts to the left, as if he doesn't believe his eyes. The warm air seems to become overwhelmingly hot, flushing Benaiah's skin as he waits for David's reaction. Then, without a moment's warning, David pushes off in a full charge toward Benaiah.

This is what it all comes down to, he realizes.

Benaiah fights the urge to step back, but then he relaxes, noticing David's hands are empty and his face is covered with the contagious smile he has seen so many times before. Benaiah prepares for the impact, but David's forward momentum lifts him from his feet. The squeeze is the tightest embrace that he has ever felt. Benaiah can't move as David's strength pins his arms to his sides, relegating him to just accept David's joy. David pushes him back as laughter escapes in his elated voice.

Benaiah reaches but David grabs the back of his neck like a father would his son and pulls him in tight.

"I've missed you, brother, it's so good to see you," David says, now holding Benaiah's shoulders as he stares face-to-face. "I can't tell you how good it is to see you"

"I was hoping you would say that," Benaiah says, releasing his tension.

"Why wouldn't I?" David asks, throwing an arm around Benaiah's back. "What are you doing here anyway?"

"I realized that it was you. You are the one who has been called to lead this nation. When word got out that you were headed for Hebron, I did my best to rally support for your return."

David stops midstride, staring at Benaiah. "You did?" David swivels to the left and right, noticing only a handful of men with Benaiah. "Well, it's a good start."

Benaiah smiles, his eyes shining. "Yeah, I've only gathered a few." With a hand motion welcoming David to enter into the city, David enters the gates.

The entire city erupts with applause and cheers from crowds that line the streets. In front of him, the masses have created a single path that leads directly to the shrine. David stands still, appearing to be in shock. Benaiah knows that it must be overwhelming after all he has endured, but there is still one more reveal. Benaiah lets his sister have the honor.

"Welcome home," Ezsri says, placing her arm around David's shoulders. "I believe they want you to walk this way. There is something that all of Judah would like to present to you."

Benaiah feels the hopeful rush of Israel's future surge through his body as David makes his way through the crowd toward his long-awaited destiny and the single ornament of gold awaiting its rightful resting place.

138

General Abner looks out over the rolling hills of Benjamin that surround the palace atop the mount of Gibeah. His personal guard has been trained, equipped, and prepared for the very moment that now presents itself. The civil war between the north and the south, between Judah and Israel, has begun.

Abner knows that in time David will be too strong, will have garnered too much support to suppress what seems to be inevitable. The window of opportunity is closing fast, and he knows there may not be a better time to seize what is rightfully his...

Control.

Realizing that he has wasted enough time preparing, Abner heads for the door. The weather has begun to turn, the clouds now ushering in a chill over the fields as winter approaches. The long quiet season will only provide more time for David's force to grow and prepare for yet another spring. The time is now.

"Where are you heading in such a rush?" Ish-Bosheth asks as Abner brushes past him in the hall.

"I will leave enough forces for the defense of our walls and enough leadership for you to continue your daily responsibilities. Just keep your exposure to a minimum for a little while," Abner says without slowing down.

"But where are you going, general?" Ish-Bosheth says with the weight of concern hanging on his words.

Abner doesn't miss a stride. "I'm going to war."

David sits in the repurposed stone building which now serves as his palace, surrounded by the fortified walls of Hebron, dwelling on the words of a young spy that just filled his ears.

"General Abner is preparing to move south toward Hebron."

David understands the move without much thought. It's obvious that Abner knows his time is limited and his power is fleeting. If he has decided to move in the month of Shebat, then he must be desperate or he is being led right into their hands. Either way, David will not remain in the city to once again endanger the lives of those that are innocent.

"I know that we are prepared, but what is your plan?" Shammah asks, surrounded by Eleazar, Abishai, and the newly appointed Joab.

David takes a long breath, letting his lungs fill with the thick Judean air. "I plan to take care of a threat that should've been taken care of a long time ago," David says, stripping himself down to his tunic and sword. "Gather the men, we're heading north."

139

David crests the peak adjacent to the mountain controlled by the Jebusites. The peak of Mt. Moriah floats above the fog to his side like a passing ship. To his front lies a slow-grading dip in the field that splits the two forming battle lines a distance apart. The tall pines sway, rustling with an eerie calm that highlights the silent battlefield that awaits chaos.

The two commanders of their respective armies have finally come head-to-head, and David couldn't be more prepared yet conflicted. A kingdom divided, a civil war, and a showdown of military wits is preparing to unleash, and David sees it as a losing proposition. Either way, Hebrews will die today.

"Have each man grab for himself a solid stone," David says as he makes his way to the front of his men, his eyes never wavering from the army aligning to the north. "Place them at your feet." David hears the thump of stones as they sink into the soil. No one says a word as they respond with immediate discipline.

The wind turns crisp as it whips up over the western edge. The grass no longer remains still but blows in waves, and the trees sway as if restless. Drifting clouds overhead cast a shadow, a perfect setting for what is about to take place. The movement behind David comes to a halt. Gear has been tightened, shields prepared, and swords gripped. A subtle peace enwraps David, warming his skin as he feels the moist touch of a flake from the heavens.

One by one, flakes fall from the sky, each one sizzling on David's warm flesh. Steam rises from his body like a hot spring in the dead of winter.

He turns, marching back through his men. "You do not need a speech to tell you what we are against today. Only remember what we have been brought through, brought from. You are no longer an army of outcasts and rebels. You are the army of Judah and this is *your* home."

He turns back, making his way to the front of the men. "Remember the days of the giant, remember the wilderness, remember… Ziklag. Do not look at the number that stands against us. Look at the One who stands with us. Victory is already yours, gentlemen." David's voice rolls from his tongue with a confidence, a steady tone that is more powerful than any war cry a soldier could muster. The time has come.

General Abner shivers in the cold as the thin mountain air whips against his flesh. The rare appearance of snow materializes above as it falls gracefully from the sky. A single pure white flake catches his attention as it dances with gravity, slipping alongside the tall swaying pines. For now the horror preparing to unleash before him is forgotten. His mind embraces a moment of peace as he follows the flake until it lands and is immediately embraced by the mounting snow on a soldier's fur vest, a sliver of warmth that outlines his otherwise frigid bronze armor.

Nervous rustling, clanging armor, and stamping horses fill the silence, drawing him back to reality, back into the imminent death that stands before him.

All around him, his army aligns, preparing swords and shields. The snow crunches beneath their heavy feet, weighed down by iron and bronze. Muffled orders are shouted from afar. His commanders have taken charge, their eyes uncertain, scanning the landscape.

In the distance, a few hundred men stand ready for battle. Their numbers are small, but Abner knows their men are among the most experienced on the field of battle. They are violent yet calculated. They have nothing to lose and yet they fight with experienced precision.

Abner watches as one man moves to the front of their ranks. All eyes are on him. Even across the vast expanse of the valley he is unmistakable. He is the sole reason they have marched thousands here today. One man, this man, has become the focus of an entire kingdom.

What man fights at the front of his army? Abner thinks, looking at David as nothing more than an arrogant warlord.

"If he wants to die, then ensure you kill him first," Abner says to his officers. "When he withdraws, his men will collapse. Kill him and the rest will fall."

The order spreads like a wild blazing fire across the ranks. Everyone is aware that there is only one man that needs to die.

David.

140

David steps out to the front of his men and studies the army before him, their order, leadership, and body language. Abner's men are trained, but only because they have to be. They are dressed for warmth, not bloodshed. They are fidgeting, because they know their fate. David stands at the front of his men, knowing that the eyes of a few thousand soldiers are watching his every move. An entire army has assembled for one reason, to kill him.

His shoulders are bare, but his chest is sheltered by armor. He doesn't shiver, not even a blink from his iced eyes that appear more vibrant with each steam-filled breath. His frame is lean and chiseled. He stands tall, like a statue, unaware of the thought of fear.

Glancing back over his shoulder, an army a fraction of the size he opposes stands behind him. Disciplined, his men stand firm. There is no rustling or nervousness. Their eyes are focused, but in their number they do not stand a chance. For some reason they are not concerned.

He takes three more steps forward, away from his men, separating himself in the open.

"David, that is far enough," Abinadab's voice calls out.

David grins, thinking of how quickly his brother has forgotten. "Abinadab."

"Yes, brother."

David remembers the image like it was yesterday. "Do you remember the eyes of the lion?"

"How could I forget?"

"Look across the valley to the eyes of the general and tell me what you see." David can hear saliva separating from Abinadab's cheeks as he imagines a grin rising on his face.

"I see a predator stalking its prey."

You can become the predator as opposed to the prey simply by the bait you choose, David remembers.

"An old friend taught me this," David says, glancing back to Benaiah.

David plants his feet firm as his attention refocuses. The time has come. His hand grips the sword, veins pumping, iced eyes staring as the Presence arrives by his side. The stillness doesn't last long. With a loud shout from behind the opposing ranks, the war begins.

A rumble crawls from the bottom of his feet to his chest as Abner's men charge. The massive wave roars toward him, enveloping the field, approaching closer, closer. There is no turning back and in this moment he realizes that his men have yet to question a single order. All of them have placed their lives at his every word, not out of fear, but respect, trust.

As the charging soldiers near, David lowers his body weight preparing for the collision.

"As I withdraw, flanks hold firm until we reach our footing," David shouts as the deafening wave of bronze and flesh bears down upon him. Just before impact, he charges, his skin taut, every fiber of his muscles rippling just beneath his flesh. His teeth clench as he lowers his shoulder into the crushing blow.

The first soldier collapses, his bones shattering like the bark of a tree struck by lightning, but the sheer force of the army lifts David from his feet, launching him backward, back into his men. Now, fighting from the inside of his own formation, David withdraws one step at a time letting his men slowly lose ground.

Abner's men roar with excitement as David and his men are pushed back, their center slowly caving with David at the core. Even with Shammah to his left and Eleazar to his right, David is driven backward. The flanks, however, have continued to hold strong with little to no attention remaining on them.

Hold strong.

Suddenly, he feels the solid stone, the stone that had been driven into the soil only minutes ago, pressing against his foot as he steps back. They have reached their fallback point and now the real work begins.

"Dig!" his voice strains as he shouts. "Dig!" The desperate cry shoots a pain through his throat as if he were swallowing a sword whole. "Dig!" His weight shifts and suddenly he feels the advancing army's momentum come to a crawling halt.

If you choose correctly, the predator will be so focused on what is in front of him he will neglect what is to the side of him.

The battle has become a deadlock as each one of David's men find their footing against the large stones placed strategically in this very location. The advance is stifled as David's men now hold firm. It has become a perfect "withdraw and hold," as the wind rushes across the eerily still battle. Only heavy breathing and shifting metal interrupt the silence.

David can sense every one of his men holding their strength, waiting for the order.

It's time.

"Push!" David shouts. He can feel the soldiers, who have been leaning on his shield flinch at the intensity of his bellow.

Chaos erupts again, but this time David's men don't hold back. The trap was set and now David fully intends to finish what was started years ago. He presses off, letting his sword run wild through the surprised Israelites. With every kill, he grimaces, knowing this is not the enemy. It is his own kin, his own people that have been swayed against him, but right now it is kill or be killed and David has found himself to be terrible at the latter.

Eleazar and Shammah unleash a barrage, taking the opposing force by shock. Abner's force had no idea what had been lying idle, waiting for this very moment. The tide of battle shifts with a violence of action that turns the widened eyes of the Israelites bright white.

David has seized control of the battle and not just by strength, but intellect.

Abner watched his men smash into the outlaw army while perched safely atop his war horse. The battle that had seemed far too easy for the reputation that David and his men had amassed, now reveals exactly what the general had feared.

His men have followed his command to perfection. They have focused all of their attention on David and now his men have collapsed, funneled into the formation of a horseshoe. With each of David's flanks now free to move and Abner's army trapped in the center, continuing to be compressed tighter, David's men close the flanks around the rear of the army, completing a perfect circle of combat, a circle that immediately eliminates the ability to move much less fight at full strength, deeming their training and numbers useless.

The temperature seems to have dipped to an unbearable chill as Abner realizes that David has just outmaneuvered him with a fraction of the men. Death would be a welcome sensation over this internal decay that is ravaging his insides.

It now becomes visibly apparent that Abner had every right to fear David. But the general has one last arsenal to unleash. And this time he won't hold back.

"Release the archers." The command is brash and dangerous. Abner knows this, but he doesn't care

"Sir, our men are too close to the enemy. We will be killing our own forces."

"That's an order," Abner says, surprised by the coldness of his voice.

After a long, awkward pause, the commander finally obliges. "As you command."

141

David's men squeeze tighter and tighter as thousands of Abner's most trained are crushed with no room to maneuver or apply their abilities. The spears and swords of David's men stab in clean and return dripping of crimson with little to no resistance. The battle seems to be easy, seems to be over, and then the first arrow sticks in the skull of an Israelite directly in front of David.

Before he can shout an order, Nathaniel has taken off in a full sprint toward the small archery detachment across the field. One by one arrows rain down upon both forces. Only David's men are positioned to block with shields. The general's men before him are trapped and at the mercy of their own archers.

The sounds of war fade as David stares off to the general, who sits comfortably atop his now back-trotting horse. Just like the lion, he's prodding, waiting for the easy kill.

Before David can turn his attention back to the battle before him, Nathaniel catches his eye. With three arrows stuck in his chest, he falls to his knees. The men behind Nathaniel continue the rush as he shouts orders from the ground. A slow rise back to his feet and another arrow lodges deep into his shoulder. The seasoned commander doesn't fall, but seems to be enjoying the slow death. David swears Nathaniel is grinning from ear to ear as he once again charges, plunging his sword into the first terrified archer he reaches.

The arrows have stopped raining down, but Shammah has been gashed on the shoulder. Benaiah lunges forward in a rampage against what David knows to be many of his closest friends. Eleazar and Joab have teamed up and are taking on an entire flank together. The men have proven they will fight to the death without a moment's notice. And David is honored that such men would fight by his side.

He dives back into the chaos and swears that somewhere deep in the sounds of clanging armor Samuel's voice is speaking to him. He hears it as clear as the morning sun shines.

"It is not that any man is made above another..."

David bites down and slams his sword against the bronze of an enemy soldier attacking Eliab.

"It is that every man faces decisions that will define who he will become..."

He breaks through to the opposing force's epicenter, hoping soon the men opposing him will give up and he can save them, but they show no signs of quitting. David has had enough killing.

He grabs one Israelite by the helmet, pulling his face into the upswing of his knee, dropping the soldier to the ground. Abner's men are out of options. The fighting eventually slows as David goes into his war trance, sensing that the general's fighting beast has been injured. He prepares to finalize the blow.

"It is only the few who will decide to be remembered..."

Abner gallops his horse into the trees from which he descended. David has won this encounter, but he remains confident that this will not be the last.

As the blue haze of clouded moonlight covers the field, all has fallen quiet. David returns to a steady breathing pattern, realizing that the bloodshed has finally ceased, for now.

Walking through the field of the dead, the two opposing forces lie side by side, each from the same blood, and each drawing a wrenching compassion from David. He moves up the hill toward Nathaniel, who proves him to be right. He *was* grinning. David looks to the cloth that is full of blood, blood from his lungs. He was going to die. Now he has died with honor, a fitting end for an old friend. David kneels beside him, and with a gentle hand closes the commander's eyes.

Again, Samuel's voice comes. *"For everyone will die... but only a few will leave a legacy."*

With his men more experienced than ever and no one standing a chance against his growing numbers, David, the crowned king of Judah, looks off through the trees to the opposing Mt. Moriah, shining like a beacon in the midst of the storm, Yireh Shalom. He knows in this moment that his future is inevitable.

"She... will one day be yours."

The voice fades as the silhouette of Samuel disappears, crossing the vast expanse toward the mountain that is calling David's name, calling David's legacy.

A single pure white flake glides back and forth, tumbling as it descends within the swirl of a frigid breeze, like an innocent shepherd boy. It lowers gently into the carnage, settling on the bloodstained snow. And like a warrior king, each pure white flake is taken over one by one by the crimson stain of war until finally it blends in and is indistinguishable... no longer pure, but now completely covered in blood.

KEY HISTORICAL POINTS:

1. David was on the run for approximately eight to ten years during Saul's quest for his life. So it was most likely years in between each encounter.
2. The sling was one of the most lethal weapons in ancient warfare. It was easily concealed and inexpensive to build, which is why shepherds so readily carried them. An expert with the "shepherd sling" causes an impact with far more power than what is required to deliver a fatal blow.
3. Archaeological evidence has revealed that Bronze Age armies used single combat to determine the outcome of battles. The detailed description of Goliath's armor also fits the discoveries of this time period. These details suggest that the battle was recorded much closer to the event than once believed.
4. Saul's "palace" wouldn't have been elaborate. In fact, David was living in a separate house when Saul came to kill him.
5. Saul became king while Israel was not only divided, but constantly harassed on all sides by invading forces, including the Philistines who had moved to within miles of Gibeah. The added stress certainly wouldn't have helped an already insecure leader.
6. Jonathan was at minimum ten years older than David and at most twenty five years older.
7. Buildings with walls four meters thick made of massive stone boulders have been located in the ancient city of Gath. There aren't any buildings in all of the Levant that compare to the enormous structures found in Gath. Additionally, inscribed on the walls was the name Glyth, (Alwt). The ancient name of the notorious giant that we know today as Goliath.

A SPECIAL THANKS

Thank you for taking the time out of what I'm sure is a busy schedule to read this novel. I hope you've enjoyed it, but more importantly I hope that it inspires you to never back down from a challenge, to stand when others sit, and to never lose faith even when darkness surrounds you. I pray that you slay the giants that are standing in your way and that you not only persevere, but discover the reason you're here.

Dwelling on this story for as long as I have has changed the way I look at life and I hope that in some way it has done the same for you.

I would love to hear your thoughts & see your Reviews!

God Bless,

Dan